NUECES TRUTH

ALSO BY MARK GREATHOUSE

The Frontier Chronicles

Perilous Trails

Wyoming Calls

Longhorns North

Warpath

The Tumbleweed Sagas

Nueces Justice

Nueces Reprise

Nueces Deceit

Nueces Blood

Nueces Grit

NUECES TRUTH

TEXANS FACE WAR'S REALITIES

THE TUMBLEWEED SAGAS
BOOK 6

MARK GREATHOUSE

WOLFPACK
PUBLISHING
— EST 2013 —

Nueces Truth: Texans Face War's Realities
Paperback Edition
Copyright © 2025 (As Revised) by Mark Greathouse

Wolfpack Publishing
1707 E. Diana Street
Tampa, Florida 33610

www.wolfpackpublishing.com

Paperback ISBN 979-8-89567-097-2
Ebook ISBN 979-8-89567-096-5

*Dedicated with love to my wife, Carolyn,
and to our two sons, Mike and Matt.*

THE NUECES STRIP

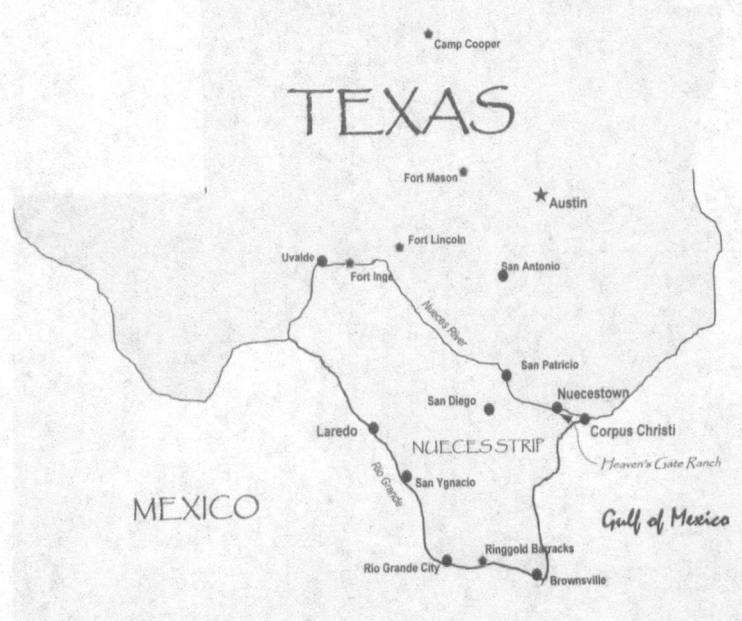

The vast Nueces Strip serves as the primary setting for the
Tumbleweed Sagas. The Strip was also called Wild Horse Desert,
owing to the millions of Mustangs that roamed its prairies. *(Sketch by
Mark Greathouse)*

NUECESTOWN

Nuecestown, Texas, established in 1852 by English and German settlers, was developed by Corpus Christi founder Colonel Henry Kinney along the Nueces River as a ferry crossing. Mostly thanks to the railroad passing it by, it's now a "ghost town" marked only by historical markers. All that remains is a preserved schoolhouse and the old Nuecestown Cemetery. *(Sketch by Mark Greathouse)*

THE CAST

Lucas "Long Luke" Dunn – *Gains notoriety as one of the greatest Texas Ranger Captains ever. Escaped Great Famine in Ireland to seek his fortune on Texas' Nueces Strip. Gained repute as Indian fighter and respected lawman. Conflicted between being lawman and rancher. Comanche called him Ghost-Who-Rides. He and Elisa are raising a large family.*

Elisa Corrigan Dunn – *Married Luke Dunn after losing her family, including fighting off Comanche. She and Luke build the Heaven's Gate Ranch and a life on the frontier.*

Scarlett Rose – *Red-headed prostitute from Laredo who seeks to overcome her past, including*
bad choices of men. Has married Walker Carson, as she begins a new life.

Doc Andrews – *The formerly alcoholic Nuecestown doctor is the conscience of the town.*

Bernice & Agatha – *Nuecestown gossips with hearts of gold. Run the local boarding house.*

Horace Rucker – *Retired Army Colonel turned preacher. Fights off old ghosts to gain self-*
respect and support family.

Rex & Stephen Rucker – *Horace Rucker's sons. Attended Military Academy at West Point. Hold opposing views on slavery issue and consequent loyalties.*

Major Gordon Belknap – *West Point graduate who fights for the Union in Texas. Before war,*
gained battle experience with Luke and the now-deceased Comanche Chief Three Toes.

William Meaney – *Sheriff of Corpus Christi gives a bit of respect to the lawman role by dressing well. But it belies his toughness.*

Jaime Sanchez – *Works as vaquero at Luke Dunn's Heaven's Gate Ranch. Becomes valuable*
asset to Luke. His wife, Julia, helps Elisa with ranch chores.

Walker Carson – *Cowboy and bungling bank robber. Becomes Texas Ranger and then deputy
sheriff. Gets hitched with Scarlett Rose.*

Edward Thorpe – *Wealthy Horatio Thorpe's heir to Magnolia Plantation. Frees his slaves.
Commits to preserving the Union.*

Jubal Strong – *Widower brother to the outlaw "Bad Bart" Strong whom Luke had brought to
justice back in 1856 near Laredo.*

Jake Barber – *Deemed too big and dumb by Confederate recruiters. Earns keep helping Luke
keep the peace on the Nueces Strip.*

JD Smith – *A volunteer for Luke's Texas Ranger posse trying to protect the vast reaches of the
Nueces Strip from marauding Indians and bandits. She's married to Jubal Strong.*

One Arrow – *Young Penateka Comanche warrior adopted by the now-deceased Comanche Chief Three Toes. One Arrow earned his name killing a buffalo with a single arrow.*

Clay Ashley Bell – *Confederate soldier friend of Walker Carson. Served as a sharpshooter
supporting Colonel Yager's Mounted Rifles of the 1st Texas Cavalry.*

Samuel – *Former slave to Horatio Thorpe. As a sort of household slave and then an employee,
Samuel watched over the family's business interests.*

Angus Moncrieff – *Scottish immigrant who bought and sold maverick cattle. Noted for wearing
a kilt, he was purveyor of his own brand of lawbreaking.*

Joseph Cogburn – *Wanted murderer and former slave who runs afoul of Luke Dunn.*

Bent Evans – *Homesteader faced with unjust consequences of fighting for the Confederacy.*

Judge Louis Crockett – *Eastern judge brought in by post-war Texas reconstruction government.*

HISTORICAL CHARACTERS

John Salmon "Rip" Ford - *Soldier, politician, newspaper editor, and Texas Ranger. A renowned Indian fighter, he fought Mexican rebel Juan Cortina. Supported secession, fights in War of Northern Aggression, and helps with post-war recovery.*

Benito Juarez – *Became president of Mexico by Constitutional mandate when liberal President Comonfort resigned. Overthrew Emperor Maximillian in 1865. Served until his death 1872.*

Juan Nepomuceno "Cheno" Cortina – *Mexican rancher, military leader, politician, outlaw, and folk hero. Opposed the Treaty of Guadalupe Hidalgo that ceded Texas to United States and fought against Texas Rangers.*

Captain Ware – *Under Colonel William Yager's command. Active pursuing Mexican cattle thieves on Nueces Strip.*

Costalites – *Lipan Apache Chief. Caused General mayhem among troops and settlers in Mexico and on the Nueces Strip.*

Colonel Theodore H. Barrett – *Union Colonel commanding a newly-raised "colored" regiment and posted to Brazos Santiago near Brownsville, TX in early 1865.*

Coleman Younger – *Cole Younger rode with William Quantrill's Raiders wreaking havoc in Missouri and Kansas. After War of Northern Aggression, formed gang with his brothers and Frank and Jesse James.*

General George A. Custer – *Egocentric Union General who in 1865 was assigned as Chief of Cavalry for the Department of Texas.*

General Andrew Hamilton – *General appointed by President Johnson as provisional Governor of Texas at the end of the war.*

General Philip Sheridan – *Union General assigned to keep law and order in South Texas at end of War of Northern Aggression. Became renowned as an Indian fighter.*

Matthew Nolan – *Sheriff of Nueces County, Texas. Began as Texas Ranger under Rip Ford. Served as a major in the Confederate 2nd Texas Cavalry. Gunned down in revenge killing in 1864.*

THEME

TRUTH

The body of real things, events, or facts; a transcendent
fundamental or spiritual reality.

INTRODUCTION

Nueces Truth: Texans Face War's Realities is the sixth of the Tumbleweed Sagas and brings us to the end of the War of Northern Aggression or War Between the States, if you like. Of course, the Yankees called it the Civil War, though no self-respecting Rebel saw it as anything near civil. The exploits of reluctant hero Texas Ranger Captain Luke Dunn have been at the core of these stories of the taming of the Nueces Strip in the 1850s and 1860s. Hopefully, you'll find this contribution to the Sagas an adventure worthy of your time and emotional involvement. This Saga takes readers through more troubling and uncertain times for Texans, as it became ever more obvious that the rebellion was a losing cause. Climb into your saddle and enjoy the ride.

Texas. Historians have varied opinions as to the origins of the word, but many believe it was derived from the Caddo tribe's word "teyshas" meaning friends or allies. "Texans" caught on to describe the inhabitants of the land that eventually became a republic and then a state.

The Texas Nueces Strip was still mostly a vast prairie of tall grasses and loamy-sands that stretched far as the eye could see and then some. Mind you that "nueces" is a

Spanish word for nuts and refers to the many pecan trees found along the Nueces River. The grasses on the Strip often grew high enough to reach a horse's withers. The Nueces Strip, called "Wild Horse Desert" by some, reached south from the lazily flowing Nueces River all the way to the meandering Rio Grande along Texas' southern border. Its eastern extremity enjoyed the sea breezes wafting in off the Gulf of Mexico from Corpus Christi all the way to Brownsville. Nestled in hills at its northern extreme was the little town of Uvalde near Fort Inge. The semi-arid rolling terrain of Laredo with its nearby Fort McIntosh was generally regarded as the main outpost of the western Nueces Strip. It afforded an easy crossing of the Rio Grande. Corpus Christi founder Colonel Henry Kinney had the foresight to build a road from Corpus to Laredo and another to San Antonio. They were rough but serviceable except when soaked by rain.

The Nueces Strip could be inhospitable six-ways to Sunday. The similarities between natural and human dangers were often striking. Wild beasts competed with humans for territory, yet often could be said to have similar habits. Imagine the intense yellow eyes and coiled muscles of a mountain lion stalking a fawn. Patience. A light breeze stirs the thick fur along his back. The moment of attack must be exactly right. Only an infinitesimal twitch of the tip of his tail reveals the sinewy muscular tension in the beast. He dares not indulge a blink of eyes or lick of tongue. The fawn looks about innocently unaware. Now imagine a bushwhacker, as his eyes sight down the long blue-gray steel barrel of his Sharps buffalo gun. The bead at the muzzle is on the target and cradles in the notch of the rear sight. His finger gently curls around the trigger. Only a slow bead of sweat down the side of his face reveals his intensity. Patience. The moment must be precise. His measured breathing; his slow squeeze of the trigger. The bounty hunter tracking him looks about cautiously, but his soon-to-be tragic fate lies in his being totally unaware. Hunter has become prey.

A leap, a snarl, and the mountain lion is fed. Breath held, trigger squeezed, and a man lies dead.

In its vast silence, The Nueces Strip spills the guts of reality and then sucks it all in.

Inhospitable and uninviting in many ways, but the Nueces Strip drew settlers like moths to a light bulb. Mottes or small clusters of live oak or mesquite offered occasional shade relief on the sunbaked prairies. The often-dry creek beds and arroyos eventually filled with rain water or snow melt and emptied into Nueces Bay and...farther to the east...Corpus Christi Bay. Flash flooding was an ongoing fear. Summers? Well, they tended to be hot and humid. Weather was pretty much whatever you wanted, if you waited long enough.

The Nueces Strip up until 1861 had been exploding with growth, as ranches and farms spread ever westward and communities sprung up seemingly overnight. This was despite a creeping drought that had seriously impacted large swaths of south Texas and left it vulnerable economically during the War of Northern Aggression. The economic impact on those areas had become serious, as livestock perished and settlers were often forced by economics to abandon their spreads. Yet, the telegraph and railroads were expanding their reach, as they'd become an ever-greater contributor to regional commerce. Family, community, faith, and dogged determination were the primary factors contributing to settlement on the Texas frontier, though romantics might be tempted to attribute the winning of the west to a gun or simply a spirit of adventure. Along with settlement came the darker side of human nature, lawbreakers necessitated lawmen to bring justice to the Strip and hostile gangs and Indians demanded larger organizations like the Texas Rangers to keep the peace. However, the Rangers were no longer officially authorized, and lawlessness would get worse.

Slavery figured quite significantly into Texas life, though less so on the vast prairies and brushlands of the Nueces Strip. Texas was not immune to the potential social, political, and economic upheaval of slavery. It was estimated that by 1860 the number of slaves in Texas had reached roughly 180,000, or close to a third of the population. Most of the slave population could be found on the cotton and tobacco plantations of eastern Texas where the soil was especially rich and weather conducive to farming. There was a lingering fear of a slave revolt, especially as tempers began to flare concerning slave versus free states. The very institution of slavery had come to near boiling over as an issue and had exploded into a full-fledged war in 1861 that tore the nation apart. The Nueces Strip was certainly not immune to its fallout.

With the breakout of the War of Northern Aggression in 1861, life on the Nueces Strip would be changed forever. Such was the dynamic of war. It's notable that Texans preferred not to refer to the conflict as the Civil War. There was nothing civil about it. In any case, the frontier of Texas became ever more vulnerable to predators of the human variety. With precious resources poured into the conflict and manpower in short supply, infrastructure such as roads and railways decayed rapidly. This Texas that Spanish conquistador Cabeza de Vaca had explored back from 1527 to 1536 was just beginning to manifest the economic giant that it would become, when the War of Northern Aggression hit hard. With war raging and despite few significant battles in Texas other than Galveston and up on the Sabine River, the Union blockade was effective in causing shortages of many commodities, including coffee, salt, clothing, shoes, medicine, and farm implements. Cotton was a critically important contributor to the Texas economy, and growers were able to skirt the Union blockade by routing it to Matamoros or Bagdad, Mexico. In fact, the cotton trade with Mexico supplied much-needed iron goods, food, dry goods, liquor, and tobacco to Texans and the Confederacy.

Coffee is a Texas staple, and Texans in desperation over its scarcity brewed poor substitutes like barley, okra, and peanuts. Transportation was seriously disrupted, as railroads deteriorated, stagecoach lines became overcrowded, and the few existing roads suffered from disrepair.

The War slowed commerce in general, as exacerbated by ducking bullets and cannonballs. Beyond places like Corpus Christi, Laredo, and Brownsville, South Texas remained an endless prairie of tall grasses and rough brush that stretched to an observer's vanishing point.

There was abundant flora and fauna on the Nueces Strip. If you were on foot, it was advisable to keep an eye and ear peeled for rattlesnakes. They tended to blend in fairly well with their surroundings, so their rattle was often folks first and only warning of an impending attack. The rattlesnake spawned many a "Texas-ism" like "he's so mean he'd fight a rattler and spot it the first bite."

The plentiful and accessible longhorn could be called the "low-hanging-fruit" of the regional economy. They were a hardy breed that could withstand the south Texas heat, fend off disease-carrying pests, and carry just enough meat on their bones to make them reasonably profitable to raise. Originally imported from the Iberian Peninsula by early Spanish priests, the longhorns eventually escaped the mostly failing missionaries, proliferated, and roamed wild and free across the prairies. Millions of the beasts soon covered Texas and especially the excellent grazing lands of the Nueces Strip. They competed with the wild mustangs that had descended from horses also introduced by the Spaniards. Of course, there were the indigenous buffalo, millions of those beasts as well. They were a staple of the Indian way of life. If you liked meat, and any self-respecting folk did, the Texas prairies provided plenty of feed for all.

Despite the roughness of the frontier, the predations of savages and bandits, and a deeply divisive war, the factor that would ultimately win Texas would be the family; the larger the better as children struggled to grow up in the face of all manner of lurking dangers. Families established the ranches and farms popping up not only throughout the eastern portions of the Nueces Strip but across Texas as a whole. The territory east of the 98th meridian that sliced through the very heart of Texas was fast becoming an economic juggernaut, and the Strip was no exception. Its economy was based on growing cotton and raising longhorns and horses. Cotton was bundled and hauled to port for transport to markets in Louisiana and points east. Cattle were still mostly driven to Kansas and Missouri railheads to be shipped to the packing houses of the Midwest, though Corpus Christi would eventually become a hub for the beef industry.

To the west of the aforementioned 98th meridian was the Comancheria. Tribes were pushed ever westward, as they were overcome by a deadly cocktail of socioeconomic forces and disease. Indigenous tribes of Comanche, Kiowa, Apache, and Ute rode free across this vast region that extended into New Mexico and north into the Texas Panhandle.

The far reaches of the mostly untamed prairies of the Strip beckoned to principled men like our protagonist Texas Ranger Captain Luke Dunn. While frontier settlement grew ever westward, there was ongoing worry about the threats posed by Comanche, Kiowa, and Lipan Apache, as well as the rogue marauding bandits from south of the Rio Grande. The tall grasses and brush of the Nueces Strip were surely high enough to hide a growing population of lawbreakers. This all served to keep early Texans on this wild and often lawless frontier ever vigilant. It was easy to make the case for calling up companies of Texas Rangers to patrol the Nueces Strip, as lawbreakers took it upon themselves to go where the military found it politically undesirable. On the other hand, the legislators in the state capital in Austin often were unable to pull together the financial means to fund the necessary companies of

Rangers. This was especially so during the War of Northern Aggression. After the War, they had to rely on the US Army, which could be chancy at best, as it was subject to the politics of whomever was in power and perceiving real or imagined threats.

With the War of Northern Aggression at hand, Texans could no longer rely on the US Army, and the Confederate army hadn't the resources to supply meaningful protection. Texas was a battle-hardened country. Most significant fighting of the Texas War for Independence had been fought on and just north of the Nueces Strip back in 1835 and 1836, and the Strip was scene to the first fighting of the Mexican American War of 1846. The region had been officially ceded to the United States by the Treaty of Guadalupe Hidalgo in 1848, though Texas had already laid claim essentially by squatter rights and having kicked Mexican General Santa Anna's sorry posterior back in 1836. Battle-hardened soil indeed. A key Texas contribution to the war was in providing highly effective cavalry to support the Confederate cause. If there was further blessing to be found, it was that Texas was spared the sort of scorched-earth policies wreaked by Union General Philip Sheridan on the Shenandoah Valley of Virginia.

Law enforcement ranks were seriously depleted during the War of Northern Aggression, and savages and desperados were quick to take advantage. Luke Dunn remained ever-conflicted over his roles of rancher and Texas Ranger, and now war served to complicate his world. Danger lurked whichever choice Luke might make. Prairie fires, blizzards, floods, stampedes, desperate killers, rustlers, and savages were part and parcel whether lawman or rancher. Just about anywhere he rode, death could be reaching for his reins. Luke had built considerable notoriety and created enemies by virtue of his success in bringing lawbreakers to justice. He had also established reliable allies. Yet the War of Northern Aggression pitted friend against friend, brother against brother, and enabled the dredges of society to gain advantage by fair means or foul. When called to continue his role as a Texas Ranger, Luke would be hard-pressed to deliver justice while raising his family. The truth would have to be faced.

In the previous Tumbleweed Saga, *Nueces Grit*, Texas Ranger Captain Luke Dunn had been making significant headway in bringing justice to the Nueces Strip despite Texas' lack of political will and its resources having been stripped bare by the war. Events beyond Luke's control had required a renewed resolve and a major dose of grit. Thus, *Nueces Truth* takes us to the events and accompanying dynamics in southern Texas as the War of Northern Aggression grinds to its inexorable end and endures its aftermath. Despite the war, Luke and Elisa had managed to grow Heaven's Gate Ranch both in terms of land holdings and livestock. How would Texans react to the evidence that the war had become a losing cause? How would the early activities of reconstruction butt up against the innate freedom-loving spirit of Texans? What might be the physical and psychological aftermath on the men who fought and the innocents among those who defended to the last gasps of hope?

While the "Cast of Historical Characters" provides some helpful true-to-life framework to the life and times on the Texas Nueces Strip, woven into the Tumbleweed Sagas are actual settlers of the frontier as drawn from the author's own family ancestry. Peter Dunn immigrated from Ireland in 1850 and established a blacksmith shop in Corpus Christi, John Dunn ranched and grew thousands of acres of cotton that he did in fact haul to Matamoros during the War, Lawrence Dunn fought and died with Captain Ware's Confederate cavalry, and Nicholas Dunn was a rancher, drover, livestock speculator, and Comanche fighter of legendary repute. Such real-life characters coupled with actual events have served to reinforce the historical setting for the Tumbleweed Sagas.

The incredible durability of the western novel seems owed

large to the mystique that's wired into our DNA. It's at least partly because westerns dish up thrills, action, and adventure in a way that entertains while tapping directly into America's pioneer myths. Westerns have also been quite good at reflecting the times in which they were made. There's truly no other genre that reflects their era as well as the determination, courage, morality, and adventure in which they are set. Westerns are effectively a magnifying glass on America's heritage. They trace our nation's shifting self-image from economic booms to crashes, morality to depravity, faith to hopelessness, but invariably rooted in rugged individualism.

My poet/novelist cousin, Mary Maude Dunn Wright (pseud. Lilith Lorraine), in writing the preface to her father "Red John" Dunn's biography back in 1932, posed the question, "Not in the spirit of judging their actions by artificial standards which in their day had no existence, but by asking ourselves if we were in their places, should we have acquitted ourselves as well, and by putting to ourselves the still more potent question: how well have we kept the birthright that thy have given us, how well have we safeguarded the liberties that they purchased through untold privations, how courageously are we meeting the problems that confront us today; in short when we stand before the tribunal of remote posterity, to whom shall the laurel be awarded...?" Y'all might think on that.

The old west represents the brave pioneering spirit of settlers that met the challenges and transcended mere survival to enable America to achieve exceptional growth. The settling of the American west is replete with tales of leveraging freedom for individual achievement. I hope you'll agree that reliving our past—even through history-based fiction—often has the effect of pointing the way to an ever-brighter future. Might we be up to it?

NUECES TRUTH

PROLOGUE

LUKE DUNN HAD GOTTEN hold of a weather-beaten but readable copy of the newspaper from Corpus Christi. The date didn't matter none. Nor did it matter that he'd already been through it front to back. He spread it before him as he sat out on the gallery across the front of their home and sipped slowly from the cup of coffee he'd forced himself to brew. The news about Gettysburg was distressing to many but not nearly so much as the list of local residents who'd passed from the dreaded yellow fever. Many folks were going through what he was dealing with or worse. The yellow fever had ravaged the region once again with a vengeance, and its effect laid a pall across an already war-torn countryside. Try as he might to climb inside the protection of his cool and collected Texas Ranger persona, there was simply too much heartache throughout the community. Heartache...and fear, as the war and now disease continued to ravage minds and livelihoods.

His beloved Elisa still languished with the fever. Every time it looked as though it would break, she'd relapse.

Luke gazed out at the depressingly gray rain-laden sky. Off in the distance, a bolt of lightning rippled across the darkened heavens followed by an earth-shattering clap of thunder. Only yesterday, the arroyos around the ranch were dry as a bone. Rain now fell in heavy sheets on the rock-hard earth. The few longhorns he could see off in the distance grazed uneasily. The beeves were at best confused. They'd stick their snouts upward now and again as though relishing the unfamiliar raindrops glancing off their noses. Luke longed to be out among the beeves. They'd be needing settling down. With such a deluge there'd likely be swollen creeks, and it wouldn't do to lose newborns to drowning in any flash floods. Anxiety clawed at him.

He savored a final sip of coffee grown cold, then stood slowly, folded the newspaper, and sighed resignedly as he entered the house. Tough as he was, there was a sadness about him. He felt tears well up in the corners of his eyes, but he was determined not to shed a single one. Elisa wouldn't hear of it. Nevertheless, it was time to tend to her. He'd keep the cold compresses coming and try to get her to consume at least some of the broth that Bernice and Agatha were good enough to bring. He shed his spurs and boots before tiptoeing up the stairs. It was too early to be waking the children. Luke paused, took a deep breath, and forced a smile before gently swinging open the door at the head of the stairs. He looked around the now musty, stale bedroom. It was more than a tad depressing. In any case, he'd need to change the bed linens. He made a mental note to install one of those windows with a sash, so it could be opened to allow fresh air. He hovered over the bed at this now helpless woman, the love of his life, lying askew under crumpled sheets. She seemed so much smaller, vulnerable, more diminutive than her increasingly frail five foot two.

ONE
YELLOW DEATH

ELISA STIRRED and forced a weak smile, as her eyes opened and strained to look up at him. "I'm sorry to be such a bother, Lucas." Elisa cared more about him than herself. Despite all the sweat-spawning fever and the throwing up of what food she tried to eat, she was ever selfless. Elisa had lost weight she could ill afford to lose, and Luke feared she just might waste away before she recovered…if she was to recover.

"You're never any bother for me, Lisa. Never ever. We must get you strong again." Luke strove to remain positive. She simply had to battle this lingering malaise. He yearned for the feisty, energetic, hard-working wife and mother that he'd grown accustomed to. He was naturally concerned about the beeves that needed to be rounded up, but Jaime and a couple of other *vaqueros* had that under control. Pulling Elisa through? Well, he just hoped his prayers would be answered.

"Did I hear a storm, Lucas?"

"It's just passing through, Lisa. God's teasing us again." Before Elisa caught the yellow fever, their biggest concern had been the lingering drought sweeping southern Texas. The cistern has gone nearly dry several times. The drought was arguably of greater concern than the war.

Lisa slowly rolled to one side to allow Luke to change the bed linens. She watched him. That he was a trail hardened lawman, rancher, dedicated father, and passionate lover mattered not at this moment. She whispered, "I love you, Lucas Dunn."

He smiled as he lifted her onto the fresh linens. "I love you, too, Lisa." He knew that if he didn't get out of the room, he'd be unable to hold back the tears. "I think I hear the children stirring." He smiled gentle-like and tiptoed from the room.

The explosion ripped through the Carson home, sending fragments of cannon shell, shards of glass, and shattered wood seemingly everywhere. Up to now, the despised Yankees had given warnings to the townfolk before randomly lobbing shells. This was unprecedented.

Scarlett's protective instincts had instantly kicked in. After an initial scream of surprise and fright, she had thrown herself on top of her young daughter, Margaret. Other than a few bruises, scrapes, and cuts, they were lucky to have missed the full brunt of the cannonball's path of destruction.

"Stay down, Margaret!" Scarlett raised her head to better listen for the telltale sound of cannon fire. Nothing. "Martha, stay low!"

"Momma, I'm scared." Margaret cowered tearfully beneath Scarlett's protective cover.

Martha, the teen Scarlett had saved from a life of prostitution, peeked from behind the cupboard. "I'm scared, Miss Scarlett."

"I think it's over, Maggie, dear. Martha, you can come out." She surveyed the damage as best she could. The sitting room was a disaster. Wood splinters, glass shards, and dust made the room appear even more devastated than it was.

"Scarlett! Scarlett!" Sheriff Meaney's voice urgently called from outside. "Scarlett, are you all right?"

Scarlett stood, dusted herself as best she could, hugged Margaret, and walked over to the shattered window. She carefully avoided the broken glass lest she cut her bare feet. She peered out and looked down at the sheriff. "Bill...thank God... we're all right. Margaret and Martha are frightened. The sitting room's a mess."

"I think the Yankees' aim must have been off. They never fired directly at civilians without a warning before. I expect they'll send some sort of apology."

"Where are our soldiers when we need them, Bill? When are they going to put a whipping on those damned Yankees? Folks here in Corpus don't know what to think. Some even side with the enemy. I'm sure you were there the other day when they hung a couple of turncoats."

"I expect our men are off fighting for us somewhere, Scarlett." Meaney tried to be optimistic. "Let me fetch my deputy, and we'll help you get your place cleaned up as best we can. I think I have a board to cover your window."

"Thank you kindly, Sheriff. That'd be much appreciated." She put her arm comfortingly around Margaret who'd come to the window beside her.

Young Martha was eager to help. "I'll get the broom." She'd already become quite a helping hand looking after Margaret and had learned enough about sewing to be a true asset to Scarlett's business. The young nanny and now apprentice seamstress was ever grateful for having been given a new beginning. She was as yet unaware of the debauched life that Scarlett had led, the life that sensitized her to the young girl's travails and led her to reach out and offer a lifeline.

"Please do, Martha." Scarlett was still comforting little Margaret.

Meaney shifted uncomfortably as he surveyed the mess

around them and took in the aura of fear that had settled on the room. "Did you hear about Elisa Dunn?"

"She's got the fever, doesn't she?"

"I heard from Luke's *vaquero* that the fever broke. She's going to be fine."

"Thank God. I don't know what Luke would do without her." Scarlett was relieved to hear good news in the wake of a war that had just become all too personal.

"Pete and I will be back right quick, and we'll help you clean up your house." Meaney ran off to fetch his deputy.

"Come on Margaret. You can help, too. Careful with the glass and wood splinters." She looked over at the mahogany side-boy that she and Carson had recently purchased. It was now officially a victim of the War of Northern Aggression. At least, the bottom portion appeared salvageable. Martha was already cleaning up the shards of glass and shattered crystal.

Margaret looked up at her mother. "When will it be over, Momma?" She reluctantly released her grip on Scarlett's dress.

"I hope it'll be soon. Pray it'll be soon." Like other citizens of Corpus Christi and similar towns and cities, the war was taking its toll on mind and soul. The early confidence was waning. Scarlett had seen the newspapers and learned of the terrible loss at Gettysburg. Nearly 4,000 Rebel soldiers had been killed and nearly as many Yankees. Later, there was the taking and burning of the vital commerce hub of Atlanta. General Sherman's march to Savannah had quite literally left a scar burned into both southern soil and soul. The Yankee general had set plantations and towns ablaze as part of a devastating strategy to choke off sources of Confederate resupply. Tens of thousands had already given their lives for the Confederate cause. Yet, in Scarlett's own mind, she saw the conflict as more a Texas cause. She had heard folks talking about Texas once again becoming an independent republic. Being part of the United States wasn't seeming so beneficial. On her occasional walks about Corpus Christi, she couldn't avoid seeing occasional war veterans that had paid a dear price by losing limbs or worse. Those were sights she couldn't shield from Martha and Margaret. If Texas had it to do all over again, would it have become a state back in 1845? She stared to the northeast from the broken-out window and could make out the distant campfires of Yankee troops stationed on Mustang Island. She'd heard that it served as a base for occasional skirmishes and for delivering general mayhem to the region. Indeed, Margaret's question lingered. When would it end?

"Is Momma goin' to be all right, Daddy?" Peter gazed up at Luke.

"Looks like she's going to be just fine, son. Your momma's a strong woman, and God loves her far too much to have her leaving us." He hoped and prayed he was right.

Peter got right to the point. "Does that mean she'll be making breakfast again?" He was speaking for his siblings who'd gotten tired of the fare cooked up by the *vaquero's* wife, Julia, and occasionally by Luke himself.

Luke couldn't help but smile. He'd also appreciate a return to Elisa's fine cooking. "Soon, Peter. Soon."

Peter ran off to share the news with his brothers and sisters.

Luke sauntered out onto the gallery and looked off thoughtfully at the vast prairie stretching off into the distance. But for the nearby road and the Nueces River, they had been pretty much isolated from most of the war's fighting. He thoughtfully caressed his mustache. News about Comanche horse thieves had reached him, and he was resigned to having to pursue them. He missed his friendship with Three Toes and mourned the chief's death. He wished he could connect better with Three Toes's apparent successor, the young Penateka Comanche warrior, One Arrow. He knew that the young chief had observed Three Toes and yearned to learn more of the White man's ways. These thoughts rolled through his mind, as a stiff breeze wafted in from the grasses reaching far off to the horizon. He thought on the Comanche dilemma. The savages were fast losing their land and could too easily lose their cultural identity. They strove to follow the customs of their forebearers in the face of forces that were demanding that they change. The old stories were dying, and with the death of stories came the death of cultures. Raiding their enemies had long been a natural way of life akin to eating and breathing. A game? Perhaps. But a deadly one.

Luke was about to go back inside when he heard a horse approaching. He listened for the telltale clatter of saber. There was none. He was relieved to find that it was a lone rider and Sheriff Meaney at that.

"Luke! Howdy, friend. How's Elisa?"

"She's past the worst of it. Come on in, Bill. Got some coffee brewing."

Luke ushered the sheriff in and poured him a cup of coffee. "What brings you out from Corpus this fine afternoon? Or did you lather up that fine cayuse just for a ride?"

"First off, did you hear the news about that sonofab—" Meaney caught himself and looked at the children. "That Union General Sheridan burned and pillaged the length of the Shenandoah Valley back in Virginia. Farms, towns...all torched by that scoundrel. Wasn't enough to leave it at General Sherman's march through Georgia. Folks are gonna starve for sure."

Luke shook his head. "Sounds like the beginning of the end, Bill. Hard to believe the devastation being wreaked on innocent folks. We all thought nothing could be worse than Sherman's march through Atlanta. Guess Sheridan outdid him." Luke leaned forward. "Bad news, but I can't imagine you came out here just to share news about the war."

Meaney smiled. "You're right as usual, Luke. the Carson

place got hit with a poorly aimed cannonball this morning. Did a bit of damage. Scarlett, Margaret, and Martha are okay but for having been frightened near to death. Walker doesn't know about it yet. He'll be none too happy. Also hear tell some homesteads west of here are being hit by thieving Comanche."

Elisa emerged into the sitting room with a weak but welcoming smile.

"Lisa, sweetheart. You strong enough to be up and about?"

"Good to see you recovering from your ordeal, Miss Elisa." Meaney doffed his hat out of gentlemanly respect.

She smiled weakly. "I expect the children will be over-joyed." Sure enough, she was quickly surrounded. "What did I hear about Scarlett?"

"Bill says her home was hit by a stray cannonball." Luke looked from Elisa to Bill and back. It was clear that an idea was fermenting in his mind. "Lisa, do you think we might have Scarlett come stay with us for a while? She's really close to having that baby, and it would be far safer for she and Margaret."

Bill joined Luke in staring with anticipation to Elisa.

"Why, I should be good as new in a day or so. Scarlett is always good company. We've got room since the addition was finished." Despite her lingering weakness from the fever, she managed to give Luke that penetrating look that a lawman's wife learns to give. "You've got something else on your mind, Mr. Texas Ranger." She could sense a mission brewing.

Luke was ever amazed at how she always knew when there was something of significance to share. This would be no exception. "Been some Comanche stealing horses out past San Diego. I've got to go see what I can do. I figure I'll get Jake Barber to join me."

"Does Jaime have enough help rounding up the yearlings?"

Bill Meaney looked at the two of them and smiled. He knew they'd work it out, always did. "Luke, Elisa, I'll be heading back to Corpus after I check into Nuecestown long as

I'm out this way. That goldarned jail building is getting right decrepit thanks to lack of the funds to fix it." He lamentedly shook his head. "I'll let Scarlett know she's welcome to come on out here. Thanks right kindly for the coffee."

"Good to see you, Bill. When you get to Nuecestown, please give Jake a heads-up as to my plans." Luke escorted Meaney to the front door and saw him on his way. He turned back to Elisa, who was by now already cooking up a meal. He couldn't help but admire her strength after laboring through the energy-sapping yellow fever attack.

"You do what you must do, Lucas," she said resignedly. She managed a smile and broke away from her cooking to give him the sort of embrace he'd missed for the past couple of weeks.

"I won't leave for another couple of days, Lisa, sweetheart." He gave her the sort of look she'd grown accustomed to and had five children to show for it.

"Later Lucas Dunn. Much later."

TWO
THIEVIN' INJUNS

A FULL MOON crossed by the elongated razor-thin silhouettes of stratus clouds hung low on the horizon. Ten Comanche on horseback silently navigated the thick prairie grasses. They paused, as they'd managed to inadvertently stir up a squadron of javelinas. The Comanche waited patiently and worked at settling their ponies, while the wild peccaries scurried off in a squealing cacophony. As if by chain reaction, they could hear a barn owl and then the mournful howl of a coyote. There was too much noise. They'd have to wait for the peaceful silence of the night to return. It would seem interminable, but they knew the value of patience.

The Comanche were finally able to resume their journey. At the crest of a slight rise on the mostly flat prairie, Crouching Lion brought them to a halt. He pointed to a house off in the distance. The cabin windows glowed with light from candles and a kerosene lantern. A thin column of smoke spiraled from the chimney.

By now, he figured One Arrow would have noticed his absence. The chief wasn't likely to be happy at the warrior leaving in defiance of his wishes.

The Comanche war party could make out a dozen or so horses in the corral beside the cabin. The horses were the prizes they sought. Horses were a measure of Comanche wealth. The Anglos and Mexicans were a collateral inconvenience. Crouching Lion hoped they might steal the horses with no interference from the cowboys who were likely distractedly enjoying post-dinner pursuits. He gazed out toward the bounty before them. The whites of his dark eyes contrasted to the broad black bands painted across his face. A stirring in the grasses to his left grabbed the attention of Crouching Lion. "Hawk Nose, what you find?"

"Gate opposite cabin. White men play cards, sing, smoke paper sticks, drink fire water." Hawk Nose then smiled broadly. "No sentries."

It looked likely that Crouching Lion could pilfer the horses with little risk to the lives of his band of warriors. This would please his young chief, One Arrow. Crouching Lion scanned the moonlit landscape before him and motioned his warriors to follow. At about a hundred yards, he pulled up with three of his warriors. They positioned several yards apart and nocked arrows to their bows. They would be ready in case the others of his band stirred up a fight, as they released the horses from the corral.

The Comanche froze as a cowboy emerged from the cabin. He looked around but apparently saw nothing, so he walked around to the side of the cabin to answer nature's call. He soon enough reentered the cabin. The Comanche warriors breathed a sigh of relief and resumed their movement toward the corral.

A few moments later, the corral gate swung open, and the Comanche chased the horses out toward where Crouching Lion waited. A cowboy emerged from the cabin and fired his rifle aimlessly toward the sound of the horses. Crouching Lion stood his ground and took careful aim. There was a sickening thud as an arrow penetrated deeply into the man's chest. The cowboy dropped to his knees and fired again, this time into the sky. Three more cowboys poured from the cabin but were far too late. The Comanche and the horses were long gone.

The Comanche rode at an easy pace back toward their small village. Crouching Lion rightly figured there'd be no pursuit, especially given the combination of dim light, fear of ambush, and the not-so-sober White men having to find horses to saddle up.

Luke and Barber were nearing San Diego. They had been making excellent time, despite Luke having decided it wouldn't do to unnecessarily push the horses. "Jake, when we reach San Diego, let's see what we can learn about this recent Comanche problem. Word travels pretty quick despite the sparsity of human settlement."

Barber nodded, but then slowed and pointed ahead. "Take a gander up yonder, Captain."

Luke pulled out his spyglass and pointed it in the direction Barber has signaled. "Dang! Looks like a Yankee patrol."

Soon enough, a half dozen mounted bluecoats led by a sergeant were approaching. They were about fifty feet away, when the sergeant signaled the patrol to halt. "Who goes there?"

Luke shook his head at what he considered a stupid question. It initially appeared that this was some wet-behind-the-ears non-commissioned officer with visions of battle glory ruminating in his war-ravaged brain. The sergeant couldn't have been much older than eighteen or thereabouts. Luke raised his hand as a sign of peace. "I'm Texas Ranger Captain Luke Dunn, and this is Texas Ranger Jake Barber. We're on the hunt for some Comanche horse thieves."

The sergeant processed Luke's response. "I'm Sergeant

Evans." He paused as he considered whether he wanted to be confrontational with a pair of Texas Rangers who were armed to the teeth. He had numbers but was outgunned. He decided confrontation was not a great idea. "You seen any Rebel patrols in your travels, Captain Dunn?"

Luke shook his head as much to answer the sergeant's question as to wonder at why the man would even ask it. "I'd surely let you know, if I did, Sergeant."

The sergeant thought further, looked over his shoulder at his men, and shrugged slightly. "We'll be up the road apiece, if you do see any rebels, Captain." At this point, he was trying to save face. Following one dumb question with another wasn't exactly adding to his stature with his patrol.

Luke was smiling inside. Part of him wanted to tell the sergeant that he'd reached the bottom of the hole and he should stop digging and leave. He strove to be respectful. "I'll keep an eye out, Sergeant." Luke chucked his horse's reins and headed on past the Yankee patrol.

Within a couple of miles, Luke and Barber entered the town boundaries of San Diego. An ironic smile crossed his face, as he saw a troop of a dozen or so Confederate cavalry. They wore shop-worn butternut gray uniforms, but their sabers were still polished brightly and rifles looked to be in good working order. Luke rode up to the lieutenant who was standing with the troop in front of the dry goods store. "Howdy, Lieutenant. I'm Texas Ran—"

"Yes sir, Captain Dunn. I know who you are."

"Do you also know there's a small Yankee patrol east of here maybe three or four miles away?" Luke dismounted.

"Sorry, Captain. I meant no disrespect. I'm Lieutenant Wicks." The lieutenant offered a salute of sorts as an attempt at showing respect. "My men are tired, sir. We were aiming to take a short rest, but your information sure sounds too tempting not to follow up on. We've heard about patrols in the area, but yours is the first real lead we've had. My men are itching for a fight."

"Well, don't let me hold you back, Lieutenant Wicks."

"Would you care to join us, Captain Dunn?"

Luke might have considered it, but felt that dealing with horse thieves was his first priority. "Thanks, Lieutenant, but I'm on the hunt for some horse-thieving Comanche."

The lieutenant's eyes grew wide, as he realized he had information to reciprocate with. "A bunch of savages attacked a ranch owned by a fella named Colt Riley a couple of days ago. They killed one cowboy and got away with nearly a dozen good horse stock."

"Were they Comanche?"

"We just heard about it a couple hours back from one of Riley's ranch hands who was getting supplies in town. He was pretty certain they were Comanche."

"Much obliged, Lieutenant. We'll see if we can catch up with the man." Luke shook the lieutenant's hand. "Happy hunting, Lieutenant." He stepped back as the Rebel lieutenant mounted up and headed his men eastward.

Jake Barber turned from watching them ride off. "You 'bout ready to find this ranch hand, Captain?"

"San Diego's right small. Shouldn't be a problem, Jake." They spurred their horses and cantered through San Diego. A few locals tipped hats and waved friendly-like. They pulled up in the middle of the main street. To their left sat the general store, to their right the local cantina. Luke nodded toward the cantina. "My guess is we'll find our man over yonder." Riley's cowboy had come for supplies, but was most likely drinking away memories of the Comanche attack. He was about to turn toward the cantina, when the cowboy emerged from the general store carrying an armful of supplies.

"Crouching Lion. You found horses." One Arrow stated the obvious as he stood with arms folded before his teepee appraising the dozen ponies Crouching Lion's band was bringing in.

Crouching Lion stuck his chest out pridefully.

One Arrow nodded. "Where you find horses?"

"Camp White men live in near place they call San Diego."

The chief noted that no warriors had been lost. "Did you count coup? Take scalps"

"We kill one White man. Too many shooting. Much firewater!"

On the one hand, One Arrow appreciated that Crouching Lion had not risked lives to do battle. The horses were valuable and another White man's scalp was simply not worth the possible losses. As it was, the Penateka Comanche encampment was small and vulnerable. They needed every warrior they had.

One Arrow played this game that occasionally flirted with disaster, as he had to keep his young warriors happy with hunts and raids while keeping them alive toward ever-increasing the size of his band. As it was, a regular-sized blue-coat patrol would likely have a fair chance to defeat them. Few of his warriors had the level of battle experience to once again make them the most feared force on the prairie.

"There are more horses, my chief." Crouching Lion had dismounted and stood before One Arrow in a not-quite-challenging pose.

"Soon, my brother. Soon." One Arrow was calculating the likelihood that the Anglos would chase after their horses. He knew that most of the White men were off fighting some great war. This somewhat lowered the chances that soldiers or lawmen seeking justice might come after his band. He respectfully waved off Crouching Lion. "Time near, my brother. Two…maybe three moons."

★★

Luke figured this was the ranch hand that the Rebel lieutenant had mentioned. He turned Big Horse toward the general store.

The cowboy didn't notice Luke, as he was busy loading the supplies into a buckboard. From rumpled hat to well-worn boots to heavy leather leggings, he was every inch the prototypical cowboy, if there ever really was one.

Luke was impressed that the man wasn't drowning his sorrows at the cantina. "Pardon, I'm Texas Ranger Captain Dunn. You got a minute, sir?"

"Ranger, heh? Coulda used you the other night." The cowboy shook his head and then realized his bad manners. He reached out a hand to Luke. "Name's Cort, Tyler Cort."

"Hear tell it was a band of Comanche."

"Seemed like. They killed one of our hands. Run off with a dozen of our finest horseflesh."

"How'd they manage that?"

"Snuck up at night real quiet like." The cowboy began to seem impatient to load up and get back to the ranch. He glanced at the cantina across the street.

"Where's your ranch and what direction did they head?"

"Sonsofbitchin' savages headed north, Captain. Sure as hell wish we had soldiers or lawmen 'round these parts to keep the peace. If we're not losin' horses to Indians, we're losin' beeves to rustlers and hiders." He gave Luke a hard look, as he climbed up into the seat of the buckboard. He sighed. He'd said his piece. "Our place is a half day west of here, Captain. If you're fixin' to handle them redskins yerself, you might want a few more guns. There was maybe five or six of them Comanche that we could see in the dark, but I expect there was more."

Luke saw the cowboy's longing look at the cantina. "You fixin' for a drink?"

"Nope. Mr. Riley will have our hides if we're ever drunk on

his ranch again. Might've whipped them injuns, if we'd been sober."

Luke doubted it would have made a difference. "Sounds like your Mr. Riley learned a hard lesson."

The cowboy laid a sullen glare at Luke. "Lost a good friend, Mr. Texas Ranger." He chucked the reins, and the buckboard lurched forward. "Like I said, them savages headed north so far as we could tell."

Luke wasn't surprised to learn that a bunch of hard-drinking ranch hands actually hadn't a clue as to where the Comanche were headed or even how big the war party was.

"Much obliged, Mr. Cort. I expect we'd best be heading north and see what we can find."

The cowboy halted the buckboard and shot an amazed expression at Luke and Barber. "Just the two of you?"

Luke nodded and smiled humbly. "Pretty much all it should take." Luke already had a suspicion that the Comanche were One Arrow's warriors. He was counting on his relationship with the chief and Three Toes before him to have some sort of reasonable parlay. He also had the buffalo spirit bone that One Arrow had gifted him as a protection.

Luke and Barber watched as the cowboy shook his head as though the two Rangers were crazy and headed the buckboard out of town.

Barber looked over at Luke. "Whatcha have in mind, Captain?"

Luke mounted up and turned Big Horse toward the west. He'd figured the Comanche has run off to the north as a ruse to fool any pursuers. "You ever chase mustangs, Jake?"

Barber gave Luke a you've-got-to-be-kidding look. "You looking to trade, Captain."

"Just thinking, Jake. Just thinking. What do we have that the Comanche might want?"

"Ain't horses the most valuable possession they have, Captain?"

"Let's head out. Maybe we'll find a longhorn or mustang or two along the way. We might trade for horseflesh."

Barber shook his head. Nothing about Luke Dunn surprised him. "I've seen you work, Captain. I don't doubt we'll pull this off. You sure it's One Arrow?"

"If it's not, you darn well better be sure you're carrying full loads in those guns, Jake." Luke smiled. "And hang onto your scalp."

Barber found it just a tad amusing that Luke avoided cuss words. He admired Luke's confidence not to mention his track record of success. He gently poked his spurs into the sides of his horse and fell in behind Luke.

"Where do you go, Crouching Lion?" One Arrow cast an appraising eye on the older warrior's accoutrements.

The warrior pointed to his stomach and puffed out his chest. "Need meat for bellies." Crouching Lion's response bordered on being patronizing and surely disrespectful, as though the chief had no concern for feeding his people. The four warriors with him stood patiently and strove to remain emotionless despite Crouching Lion's obvious disrespect.

One Arrow gave the warrior a hard look. He likely should have anticipated the need for a hunt, but the warrior's attitude was unacceptable, his surliness resented. "Do you need five warriors for a couple of deer?" As much as anything, the chief was concerned that Crouching Lion would put Comanche warriors at risk on some ill-conceived horse-stealing adventure or worse yet lead an attack on a homestead. One Arrow could easily see that his warriors were becoming ever more restless.

Crouching Lion deeply resented being challenged as to his intentions. He knew he was next in line to be chief of this little band of Penatekas, and he was consciously building a resume of achievements such that there'd be no question when it came time for his ascendancy. His sigh was imperceptible to the warriors that awaited him but all too obvious to One Arrow. "I hunt buffalo, my chief," he responded emphatically. "Only buffalo." The tension was quite palpable.

Crouching Lion's sarcasm wasn't appreciated by One Arrow. "Perhaps I join you." It was a hollow offer.

By now, the encampment had grown to village proportions. Crouching Lion rightly figured that the chief would choose to remain with the dozen warriors in the camp. "You welcome to come, my chief."

"Go, and good hunting." One Arrow waved the warriors away and turned to follow Moon Woman into the teepee. As he entered, he longingly glanced back at the warriors riding off with their bows and arrows, ornately decorated shields, and war lances replete with scalps.

"You're amazing, Captain. That homesteader didn't really want to trade for horses, but he gave them up willingly." Barber gave a gee-whiz shake to his head.

Luke had drawn upon the wrangling skills he'd gained in running his Heaven's Gate Ranch and buying and selling cattle. By some fortune, they'd managed to find a few stray beeves. "Those five longhorns were a bit unruly, especially that dang bull. The homesteader knew they'd be more valuable to him, Jake. He'll breed the beeves and sell a couple for horses and supplies. He saw the value…after all, that's what a good trade is about. Just need to point out the value." Luke smiled at his trading prowess. He'd been talking about ranching and cattle trading with his cousin Nick Dunn who was rapidly building a reputation for successfully speculating in livestock despite the ongoing war.

Luke and Barber found themselves tracking below an escarpment up toward Uvalde. The two horses they'd traded

for followed on long leads. For Luke, it brought recollections
of his dealings with the outlaw Roy Biggs. The stands of trees
discouraged a straight ride, as limbs and fallen trees often
required a wide berth. There was a dampness in the air that
tended to amplify the musty aromas wafting off the trees.
Luke necessarily rode past a rather large oak with some of its
roots exposed by erosion. Big Horse had to swerve suddenly to
avoid tripping. The arrow barely missed Luke's leg, making a
telltale thwump as it embedded in Luke's saddlebag. Had it
not been for the saddlebag, Big Horse might easily have
received a disabling and thereby mortal wound.

Barber grabbed his rifle and dove from his horse.

Luke pulled one of his Colts and in what seemed as an
instant had fired several times in the direction from which the
arrow had come. A loud grunt of pain meant at least one
attacker had been hit. "Let those horses go, Jake!"

Crouching Lion saw his warrior fall, and he saw Luke's
trading horses run off. He had to have those horses, and these
two Anglos stood in his path. It was like a signal to he and his
warriors to attack in earnest. War whoops, the sound of
Comanche ponies, and the whoosh of arrows quickly
followed.

"Damn, Jake. Mount up! Follow me!" Luke found himself
charging solo into a hail of arrows. He continued firing as he
spurred Big Horse toward the attackers. His trusty Colt 1860
Army fired a 44-caliber slug that cut through flesh like a small
cannonball. Another warrior felt the wallop of a slug from
Luke's Colt and was unhorsed.

Jake had by now swung into the saddle, quickly charged
after Luke, and began pouring lead at the Comanche.

Crouching Lion gave the signal to retreat. He was stunned
at the bravado of the charging White men. He hadn't expected
the two travelers to quickly respond and with such devastating firepower. As the air filled with the sounds of horses
and guns and the clouds of gun smoke with their pungent

aroma, he instantly regretted his misjudgment of his target. Worse, One Arrow would be angry. It made the Crouching Lion even more determined and even desperate to kill the men and take their horses, especially the handsome big gray stallion. He pulled up among the trees perhaps fifty yards from Luke and Barber, wheeled his pony, and took a closer look at the big man firing what seemed like a virtual cannon at him and his braves.

Luke fired a couple of more shots before reloading. He finally had a chance to make out the attackers nestled in the trees and thought he recognized Crouching Lion from his past visit with One Arrow. He reached around and plunged his hand deeply into his saddlebag past the still protruding arrow, pulled out the decorated spirit bone that One Arrow had given him for protection, and held it high.

Crouching Lion suddenly found himself conflicted. He knew what that spirit bone meant, and he dared not ignore it. The adrenaline rush from the ambush still coursed through his body. He had to think. He waved at his three remaining warriors to stop shooting. They were hunkered down behind trees and at least one was defending from behind his fallen pony. Two warriors were shot and probably dead. One Arrow would be angry, but even angrier, if more brave warriors were killed. The horses weren't worth their chief's wrath.

Crouching Lion grimaced with resignation. He had no choice. To dishonor the tribal protection given Ghost-Who-Rides would result in his being exiled from the Penateka Comanche. He'd never ever be chief. Yet, he was embarrassed at the prospect of confronting Luke. He gave Luke the most evil grin he could muster, delivered a final yell at the two pursuers, and motioned his warriors to retreat. The medicine in this place was clearly bad for him and his warriors.

Barber pulled up alongside Luke as the Comanche rode out. "That was too close, Captain. What made them stop?"

Luke showed Barber the intricately carved and beautifully-decorated spirit bone. "One Arrow gave this to me. It's supposed to protect me. Guess it works." Luke let out a sigh of relief. "You okay?"

Barber nodded affirmatively.

Luke scanned the scene, taken at the irony of his intent to make peace with the Comanche but having had to endure their attacking him. Two savages lay in the damp leaves among the live oaks. One was dead and the other seriously wounded. "I feel that we must be near One Arrow's camp. Let's tend to the wounded warrior and sit him on a horse. We can tie the other over the packhorse. I'm pretty sure the leader was Crouching Lion. One Arrow will be none too pleased with him." He stared at the spot where the last of the band of savages had disappeared from sight. "We'll let them get a bit of a lead on us. I expect they'll take us directly to One Arrow's camp."

"You think they'll try to ambush us, Captain?"

Luke smiled broadly. "Can't imagine Crouching Lion being so foolish. He might be full of wild spirits, but he knows better than to fight a losing cause twice."

"We gonna corral those horses?" Barber paused and stared wide-eyed at Luke's saddlebag. "Dang, look what you've got stuck in your saddlebag."

Luke twisted in his saddle to better see the protruding arrow from Crouching Lion's bow. He dismounted to deal with extracting it. He pulled, but the arrow wouldn't come free. He lifted the flap and peered into the bag. The arrowpoint was deeply embedded in the Bible Luke carried with him. He broke the shaft and pulled the Good Book out. Working the tip of the arrow back and forth finally freed it with minimal damage to the Bible.

"What did it hit, Luke?"

Luke waved the Bible over his head, then out of curiosity opened it to the place where the arrow had penetrated deepest. "Lookie here, Jake. The Comanche arrow points to Hosea 4:6. The verse says, 'My people are destroyed for lack of knowledge.' How about that?" He looked off to where Crouching Lion had disappeared into the trees.

Jake shook his head. "Shame he wasn't trying to learn our ways like Three Toes and One Arrow."

Luke was ever impressed with Jake's ability to often capture the profound essence of a question.

THREE
YANKEE FORAGERS

"WALKER, WHAT BRINGS YOU OUT HERE?" Elisa stood on the gallery staring at the mounted Rebel officer.

"Is Luke around?"

"He headed toward San Diego to investigate some marauding Comanche that have been attacking homesteaders."

Carson shook his head resignedly. "Wish he was around, ma'am."

At barely twenty-one years old, Elisa wasn't used to being called ma'am, especially by the husband of a friend. "Set a spell, Walker. I've got some coffee brewed."

Carson reluctantly dismounted and looked up at Elisa. "I expect a cup of coffee might be just fine, ma'am. Thank you." He sat himself on the edge of the gallery.

She pointed to the bench. "Sit. I'll be right back." She went inside and emerged quickly with a steaming cup of coffee. "What's happening in Corpus?"

"The Yankees blasted us again. This time they did some serious damage to our house. Fortunately, no one was hurt." Carson looked thoughtfully into the cup. "The dang war ain't goin' so well, Elisa. We ain't seen the worst of it around these parts, but I hear the Yankees are doing some right nasty things to folks in Virginia down through to Georgia."

"I had a sense this would be how it would turn out, Walker." Elisa suspected there was something more on Carson's mind. "So...what brought you all the way out here to Heaven's Gate?"

Carson shuffled his feet a bit. "Kinda wish Luke was here about, so I could tell him directly." He offered up a sad look to Elisa. "Luke's cousin Lawrence just got killed by some Mexican bandits. They were Cortina men and had rustled several head of cattle. Lawrence was home recovering from a wound but volunteered to accompany a patrol under a Captain Ware from the Texas First Mounted to negotiate for the cattle. Ware needed someone who spoke Spanish. As I heard it, Lawrence tied a white rag to the muzzle of his rifle and went out to parlay. Negotiations didn't work out. As he began his return ride to the patrol, the cowards opened fire. They shot him in the back. Murdered him. Ware's men attacked and recovered the cattle, but Lawrence was lost."

Elisa drew a handkerchief from her dress and handed it to Carson. This was something that had clearly affected the young man. "I'm so sorry, Walker. War simply doesn't seem fair, does it?"

"No ma'am. I'd become friends with Lawrence Dunn. He had his whole life ahead of him, and it was snatched by a bunch of no-good rustlers taking advantage of this gol-danged war."

"I'll be sure to tell Luke what happened, when he returns. I'm sorry for your loss." Elisa looked off into the distance to gather her thoughts while grasping to change the subject. "How's Scarlett, Margaret, and the nanny?"

Carson quaffed the last of his coffee. "Pretty much gotten over being shook up by the Yankee cannon. We've got a bit of repair to get done on the house. That nanny Martha has been a big help." Carson managed a slight smile. "Lookin' forward to getting our haberdashery business going. The sooner the war ends the better so far as that goes. We stopped selling clothes to the Confederate army. Their paper money wasn't worth much of anything."

"It's great to see you and Scarlett building a life together, Walker." Elisa could see that Carson still held to hope, despite the loss of his friend.

"Well, Miz Elisa, I'd best be moseying on back to Corpus. I promised Scarlett I wouldn't be long. We're grateful for your offer to let Scarlett and the girls stay here for a bit with y'all, but they decided to stay put. It's like she's of a mind to stubborn her way to a normal life. Expect the baby to arrive most any day now." Carson smiled. "I have to make those repairs and get on back to my unit. Thanks kindly for the coffee. Please do tell Luke to come visit. All of you are sure welcome." Carson handed the cup to Elisa, walked over to his horse, and mounted up.

"Be sure to give my best to Scarlett." Elisa waved as he rode off.

No sooner had the dust cleared from Carson's departure and Elisa entered the house to tend to the children, when the sound of horses broke the stillness. A mounted Yankee patrol had been heading west from Mustang Island looking for supplies and—if it happened—trouble.

Jaime Sanchez had just returned with a couple of *vaqueros* from their early morning checking on livestock on the southern boundary of Heaven's Gate Ranch. They had pulled up at the barn and just dismounted, as the patrol rode in.

Jaime caught the attention of the sergeant leading the patrol. The sergeant pulled up. "Hey you! Mexican swine! You helping Rebels?"

Jaime gave serious thought to pulling his rifle from its scabbard beside the saddle, but he'd as soon avoid any shooting. He swallowed his pride in the face of the sergeant's insulting language. He smiled and responded with an even voice in perfect English. "I'm Jaime Sanchez. I'm foreman here at Heaven's Gate Ranch. Can I help you?"

The sergeant turned to his men. "Damn, don't that figure. A Mexican that can speak English. Must be ed-u-ca-ted." He drew out the last word for effect. He turned back to Jaime with a sinister grin. "You got grub for a bunch of hungry soldiers of the United States government? Might do for a few supplies, too."

Jaime looked past the sergeant to see Elisa standing on the gallery with a Henry aimed at the Yankee soldiers. They'd handled Yankee and Rebel foragers before. "Don't want trouble, sergeant. I'm sure you and your men are hungry from your long ride. I'm sure we can feed six hungry soldiers."

The soldiers began to dismount. The sergeant was a little slower than his men. It was a costly delay. A booming shot rang out, and half the sergeant's head disappeared. For a moment, he remained half dismounted, his body suspended as though trying to figure what had happened. He slowly slid to the turf. His men dove for cover behind whatever fencepost was handy and the water trough.

Jaime and his *vaqueros* grabbed their rifles and ran into the barn.

Elisa stood on the porch looking around and trying to determine from where the shot had come.

There was no question that the sergeant had been on the receiving end of a slug from a Sharps rifle. The 50-caliber slug that could stop a buffalo, wreaked serious damage on human bodies.

A Rebel troop soon emerged and demanded surrender of the Union troops. The Yankees were still stunned by what had happened to their sergeant.

Two dozen Confederate soldiers dismounted and formed a

battle line facing the Dunn's barn. Their rifles bore witness to seriously outnumbering the Yankee patrol. "Greetings. I'm Captain Stephen Rucker, and I'm pleased to accept your immediate surrender."

The air was ripped with another shot from the Sharps, and a corral post inches from a Yankee soldier's head was shattered. The Union soldiers, outnumbered and with far less firepower, dropped their weapons and raised their hands high.

Jaime and his *vaqueros* cautiously emerged from the barn.

The Rebel soldiers moved forward, relieved the federal troops of their weapons, and soon had them rounded up and ready for transport as prisoners of war.

Elisa leaned her Henry against a gallery post and recognized Captain Rucker as he rode in. She turned toward him as he rode past the gallery within hailing distance. "Welcome, Captain. You're Horace Rucker's son, aren't you?"

Rucker stopped mid-stride. "Why, yes ma'am. You know my father?"

"We know him quite well. I expect you'll be visiting him in Nuecestown. He's doing God's work as a pastor."

"Yes, ma'am. I recall now—you're Mrs. Dunn. I admire your husband, ma'am. Sure could have used him in the good fight."

Elisa smiled. "He's got plenty of fighting to do, Captain. Would y'all care for some coffee and cornbread before you head out with your prisoners?"

Rucker smiled courteously. "That would be right kind of you, Mrs. Dunn, but there's quite a few of us."

"No problem, Captain. Cornbread's baked, and there's plenty of coffee."

Just then a lone figure clad in butternut gray emerged from a nearby stand of trees carrying a Sharps rifle with its telltale scope. He was handsome but had the look of someone emotionally spent and pretty much going through the motions of his job.

Elisa turned to look at the emerging soldier. "Who's this, Captain?"

"Our sharpshooter." Rucker looked over at the soldier. "He takes lives to save lives." He saw that Elisa didn't understand. "Let's say that his job is to encourage soldiers to surrender rather than fight."

"Seems to work, Captain. Please have him join us."

"Sergeant Bell. Please join us here at the house."

Clay Bell sighed, looked at the Yankee sergeant's lifeless— and brainless—body lying in the dust near the barn, and slowly, almost reluctantly walked over to Rucker and saluted. "Yes, sir."

Rucker turned to Elisa. "Mrs. Dunn, this is Sergeant Clay Bell. Sergeant Bell, this is Mrs. Elisa Dunn. Her husband is Texas Ranger Captain Luke Dunn of some considerable repute."

"Pleased to meet you, ma'am. I've heard of your husband. He's feared by just about every lawbreaker and savage on the Nueces Strip. I hope to meet him one day."

"That's a fine rifle you've got there, Sergeant. I've had the dubious pleasure of shooting with one of those cannons myself." Elisa's comment and accompanying smile broke the ice so to speak.

Bell and Rucker both looked incredulously at the diminutive woman before them. Bell shook his head. "You've handled the Sharps?

"Had the bruises to prove it." Elisa laughed just a tad. "It's a tad heavy, but not much recoil." She figured to impress her guests.

Rucker suddenly realized there was more to be concerned with and looked over at his men near the barn. "Lieutenant, have the men secure the prisoners and stand down. We're going to rest here for an hour. Join us here at the gallery, when you're done. Oh, ask those *vaqueros* to join us as well." Rucker had begun to feel quite sociable. "And Lieutenant, set a couple of pickets. We can't be too careful this close to Corpus Christi."

By this time, Elisa had gone inside and reemerged with cornbread and coffee. Julia Sanchez walked over from their cabin to help.

With cornbread and coffee distributed, Elisa turned to Bell as he sat on the edge of the gallery. "What got you into sharpshooting, Sergeant?" She had a feeling that Bell wouldn't have normally chosen this job he was performing for the Confederate army.

"Word got out that I could shoot the wings off a mosquito, ma'am." Bell grinned bashfully and glanced at Rucker. "The rest is history."

Bell's response grabbed Rucker's attention. He tried to gauge Elisa's reaction and then awkwardly sought to reduce the intensity of the moment. "Guess you did a bit of hunting, Sergeant."

Bell continued, nonplussed. "I much prefer squirrels and deer to humans, ma'am. Lookin' forward to this war ending. Lookin' to get back to ranchin'."

"I appreciate your candidness, Sergeant Bell. When all the hostilities are ended, perhaps you could visit with me and my husband. I expect you and Luke would get along quite well." Elisa turned to Captain Rucker. "Any word on your brother Rex, Captain Rucker?"

Rucker was relieved at the shift in conversation. "He'd received a bad wound up toward Matagorda Bay, but as fate would have it, he fell into the hands of my unit and I was able to tend to him and get him home. Last I heard, he healed up and headed to Washington to serve in the Federal War Department." He took a final bite of cornbread, quaffed his remaining coffee, and offered a wry smile. "I expect I'm grateful we're not shooting at each other...again."

The painful regret in Stephen's words weren't lost on Elisa. "It's been hard on us all, Captain."

As Bell finished his cornbread, stood up, and prepared to go, he glanced back at the last remaining piece of cornbread.

Elisa observed his longing look at the piece of baked delight. "Please, Sergeant, finish that last piece."

Bell looked at Rucker who nodded to go for it. "Have to admit, ma'am, this is even better than my momma's cornbread." The last piece of cornbread became history.

Bell literally licked his lips and turned to Rucker. "I'll see to the men, sir. We'd best be getting these prisoners headed out." Bell gave a nod of thanks to Elisa. "I look forward to meeting Captain Dunn, ma'am. Thanks for your hospitality." Bell strode over to the corral to help assemble the men.

"You're lucky to have fine men like Sergeant Bell, Captain Rucker. I do hope and pray this terrible war goes well for you and your men such that you all come home safely to your families."

"Thank you, Mrs. Dunn. Please do give my best to Captain Dunn. Again, we are grateful for your hospitality. The men truly appreciated the brief respite." Rucker gave a half salute and rejoined his men. "Let's move out, men."

Elisa for her part stood on the gallery with a heavy heart and watched them disappear up the trail. She became aware that Jaime, Julia, and the two *vaqueros* were watching her. "No matter, Jaime. It was a blessing they came along when they did. Those Yankee foragers were up to no good."

Jaime well knew what she meant. He looked at Julia, now standing beside him with their son. "I wonder *Señora* Dunn, when the soldiers will finally stop this *locura*...this craziness."

"I hope and pray Captain Dunn returns sooner than later, Jaime." Elisa smiled gratefully and went into the house.

"We need to be alert, Jake. This trail is almost too easy to follow." Luke was having his suspicions that Crouching Lion might set an ambush. He much preferred being hunter rather than prey. "The closer we get to One Arrow's camp, the more places an ambush-minded Comanche can hide."

Barber pulled up. "First time I've noticed blood, Captain." He pointed to a few droplets on a leaf.

"From the color, I'd say one of them is dealing with a mortal wound. He's likely doing his best not to bleed out." Luke looked around. The trail broadened, as brush gave way to grassier albeit ever more hilly terrain. "Let's split up...ride maybe fifty or sixty feet apart in parallel."

They rode for perhaps another hour, when they spotted a pair of buzzards circling. Luke halted and whispered. "Whatever's got their attention is on the other side of the hill ahead of us. I'll circle round to the right, you go left."

They slowly rode forward with the gift horses and packhorse in tow. They unholstered their Colts, as whatever might be likely to happen would be at close quarters.

"Hey, Captain. Come see." Barber motioned Luke to join him. "The Comanche's been laid out real careful like...like a funeral or something."

Luke had seen how the Comanche cared for their dead. He respectfully doffed his hat and dismounted.

"Whatcha doin', Captain?"

"Just respecting the dead, Jake. This is sacred ground." Luke said a brief prayer to himself, and then scanned the area. "I'm sort of surprised. They've got to be close to One Arrow's camp. I'd have thought they'd bring the dead warrior back to the camp."

"Whatcha think that means, Captain?"

Luke stroked his mustache thoughtfully. "Maybe, Crouching Lion isn't returning to face One Arrow. He'll be too embarrassed to admit to attacking us and losing warriors."

"You think the Comanche camp is very far?"

"Not far, Jake. We'll visit with the chief and make peace, but Crouching Lion has gone rogue. We're going to eventually have to hunt him down unless he finds us first. By my count there's only three warriors, but you know how nasty the Comanche can be." Luke stooped down and lifted a feather from the ceremonial grave.

"What's that for, Captain?"

Luke mounted Big Horse. "Might come in handy, when we find One Arrow." He thought for a moment on the irony of having effectively counted coup after the fact.

Barber nodded. "Sorta proof?"

"Exactly, Jake. It'll confirm Crouching Lion's intent to desert One Arrow's band." He looked up. "With any luck, we'll have enough light to reach the Comanche camp. I expect Crouching Lion is long gone, but we can't be too sure."

Just as the sun was about to nestle below the crests of the hills to their west, Luke and Barber spotted wisps of smoke off in the distant hills. By the time they reached the encampment it was nearly dusk. An unusual mist had enveloped the landscape. As they broke into a clearing and found One Arrow's camp spread before them, it took on an ethereal almost unworldly appearance. It was as though they had arisen from the surrounding vapor.

Pastor Horace Rucker had just emerged from the carriage house, having finished caring for his horses. He took a deep breath, trying to more fully take in the fresh stillness of the starlit sky. The singing of the crickets was broken by the sound of struggling footfalls.

"Father?"

Startled, Pastor Rucker turned to see what at first appeared as some ghostlike apparition in the soft light. "Stephen?"

Stephen's uniform was torn to shreds, his countenance gaunt, his breathing heavy and labored. "H...h...help..." His words trailed off as he collapsed. Somehow, by some superhuman will, he'd managed to crawl, limp, and stagger his way home.

"My God, son…what's happened?" The pastor kneeled beside his son and cradled his head.

"Yankee raiders…caught us unawares…all dead…all dead."

The pastor lifted his son and carried him into the house.

Mrs. Rucker heard them enter, stood to greet her husband, and swooned at the sight. She had seen what her pastor husband hadn't yet been able to see due to the darkness. It was an understatement to say Stephen Rucker's wounds were mortally serious. His tunic was soaked dark crimson with blood. The young Rebel captain was on death's doorstep, his face ashen, breathing shallow.

Pastor Rucker gently laid Stephen on the bed. He could now see the extent of his wounds, and his own long military experience told him that the end was near. That his son had managed to make it home was testament to the human will. "Who did this, son?"

Stephen gasped for breath. "They…the Youngers…they said they'd ridden with…ridden with Quantrill's Raiders." It was all he could do to get the words out. "Saw our Yankee… prisoners. Tried to fight…too many of them."

Pastor Rucker kneeled beside the bed and began to pray. "Dear God in heaven…"

Stephen struggled for words. "Father…give my love to Rex. Tell him he was right."

Stephen's mother appeared at the bedside and stood by tearfully. This was a moment she'd long feared but hoped and prayed to never have to face.

"Mama…" Stephen struggled to keep his eyes open, as he looked up at her. "Love you…ma…" Blood frothed from his lips. A final breath, and he was gone.

She fell into her husband's arms. There was nothing human

that could possibly comfort a mother's loss of her son. Grief was overwhelming.

Pastor Rucker laid his head against his son's shoulder. Great sobs racked his body. There was no comfort, no solace, to be had in this terribly tragic moment.

The heat was stifling. Sweat mixed with blood. Bell gripped the Sharps as though it were his lifeline to survival. And it likely was.

The marauders had moved on, leaving dead bodies strewn along the banks of the Nueces River. Yankee blue mixed with Confederate butternut gray. Blood and guts seemed to be everywhere Bell looked. He felt numb.

The sharpshooter had gotten off a single shot during the attack before being hit by a ricochet with enough wallop to cause a tree branch to knock him down, put a gash across his forehead, and take the wind from his lungs. It was his good fortune to fall among tree roots that hid his position. He watched the melee through a veil of blood, powerless to do more. He thought he saw Captain Rucker staggering off seemingly more dead than alive. It was hard to tell friend from foe in the dim early evening light, much less identify anyone in particular.

Feeling confident that the attackers were indeed gone, he stood cautiously and surveyed the scene before him as best he could. The moans of the dying sent chills up his spine. Bell threw up what little there was in his stomach. He found his way to the river and washed himself off as best he could.

If the survivor he saw was indeed Captain Rucker, he hoped the young officer succeeded in reaching wherever he was headed. As for himself, he was resolved to escape this godforsaken war. He laid himself down beside a pecan tree and was soon asleep. Any travel would necessarily wait until morning.

FOUR
COMANCHE WAY

ONE ARROW'S encampment was more like a village now, as nearly a dozen Penateka Comanche warriors had newly arrived with their families. Crouching Lion might not be missed.

Luke and Barber approached from the west with the sinking sun behind them. A light mist had settled into the air reducing visibility. He could smell the wisps of smoke spiraling skyward from the embers of dying fires. It meant they were downwind, but he knew that with the cover of the mist it would be several moments before they'd be discovered. That they'd been able to actually nearly ride into One Arrow's camp without being noticed was unusual to say the least. In fact, it was eerie enough to raise the hair on the back of Luke's neck. As his silhouetted form astride Big Horse emerged, he looked very much the Ghost-Who-Rides appellation given him by Three Toes.

Finally, one of the squaws emerged from a teepee. Upon seeing Luke and Barber emerging from the fog like mysterious apparitions, an expression of fear spread across her face. She immediately called out to sound the alarm.

In a heartbeat, armed warriors emerged from the teepees.

Luke waved high the ceremonial spirit bone.

Two Comanche warriors saw it and alerted the others to hold their arrows. With seemingly perfect timing, One Arrow emerged not from his teepee but from the nearby woods.

"Ghost-Who-Rides, I saw you on trail."

Luke wondered that the chief hadn't tried to reach the camp ahead of them. "I could have been killed, my brother."

One Arrow smiled, pointed to his crotch, and nodded in the direction of Cactus Flower who was taking advantage of the dim late afternoon light to sneak back into the chief's teepee. He whispered, "Keep woman happy."

Luke offered a wry smile. "Thank God this bone worked."

Luke dismounted, and the two grasped hands as greeting.

"I bring these two horses as gifts to you, brother."

One Arrow looked admiringly at the horses. "Thank you Ghost-Who-Rides." The chief's vision was drawn beyond the gift horses to the two trailing horses, the one with a dead Comanche across its back and the other seating the wounded Comanche warrior. One Arrow gave Luke an inquiring gaze.

Onlookers were already gawking at the procession that had entered their encampment. They surely wondered at what had this White man done?

"Had a bit of a meeting, chief."

It was as they stood beside Big Horse, that One Arrow then noticed the feather partially visible from Luke's saddlebag. "What you have there, Ghost-Who-Rides?"

"Perhaps, we should talk privately. You have a traitor among your band."

The chief raised his eyebrows. "Come." He began to lead Luke and Barber to his teepee, then stopped and spoke to his warriors. "My friends have traveled long. Need rest. We have council later." He was about to dismiss but paused again. He considered the mournful pained expression on the face of the captured Comanche. He motioned to two warriors standing nearby. "Take Leaning Bear to teepee." He ruefully shook his head and hand-signaled for them to take care of their dead brother warrior.

Luke grabbed the feather from the saddlebag and followed the chief. He glanced over his shoulder at Leaning Bear being unceremoniously pulled down from his mount and dragged off. He suspected that the Comanche would have some special way of dealing with warriors disobeying their chief. He didn't envy Leaning Bear's fate.

Luke, Barber, and One Arrow were soon seated around a small fire in the chief's teepee. His wives served refreshments, assuring their guests that a meal would follow.

"I see you have a,"—the chief searched for the words—"a Texas Ranger brother, Ghost-Who-Rides."

Luke realized Barber had never met One Arrow. "Yes. He is a great fighter. His name is Jake Barber."

The chief looked Barber over and smiled. "He bigger than you, Ghost-Who-Rides." One Arrow extended his hand per the White man's custom.

Barber smiled and shook the chief's hand.

One Arrow turned to Luke. "What of traitor, Ghost-Who-Rides?"

"I took this feather from the burial place of one of the warriors with Crouching Lion. Mr. Barber and I killed the warrior in an attack on us led by Crouching Lion. He was trying to steal the two horses I brought as gifts for you. Last we saw, he was headed north away from your village with three warriors."

Cactus Flower gave One Arrow a pipe. The chief drew deeply and thoughtfully. "He was foolish. It is good that he is gone. He will not be welcome here."

"Crouching Lion had attacked and killed several unarmed White farmers. He stole cattle. He attacked a ranch, killed a man, and stole horses. I was sent to find him, but I fear he's already too far ahead of us. I would like to hunt him, but I must return to my woman."

The chief mulled over Luke's lament, then smiled thoughtfully. "He did not go far, Ghost-Who-Rides. He will try to come back for his women, horses, and teepee. We may have busy night."

The thought of laying an ambush for the wayward Comanche held considerable appeal to Luke. "I'm happy to help."

"Comanche must do this. You have justice. Comanche have justice."

"I have one more question, Chief."

One Arrow nodded and passed the pipe to Luke.

Luke drew on the pipe and handed it to Barber. "Many moons ago, a warrior named War Cloud kidnapped a White woman from a ranch that Three Toes and he had attacked. Do you recall what became of her?"

One Arrow pondered Luke's question. The death of Three Toes at the hands of the traitorous War Cloud still haunted him. He nodded sadly. "She was slave to War Cloud. He beat her. She became weak. She ran away in winter." The chief shook his head remorsefully. "She die of cold." One Arrow wrapped his arms around his chest as though trying to warm from the cold. She had frozen to death, but at least her suffering had been ended. "One Arrow sorry for loss."

Barber passed the pipe back to One Arrow.

"At least, the family will know." Luke would send a message to bring closure to the woman's family back east. His attention came back to the present situation with Crouching Lion. "May we stay, Chief?"

The barkeep had opened the front and back doors to the Longhorn Saloon in vain hope that at least some of the overwhelming odors of booze, sweat, piss, wet sawdust, and livestock might dissipate with the morning breeze. It was wishful thinking at best. He swept sawdust over the floor as best he could and disposed of a shattered chair that had been destroyed in a squabble the night before.

Three patrons had braved the atmosphere such as it was and sat at one of the tables that afforded just a touch of that morning breeze.

Two of the men were cowboys, in the loosest use of the word. They hadn't gotten much sleep and looked like it. Disheveled was an understatement. Sweat, cow chips, and trail dust permeated their very beings, likely indelibly impregnated into their pores.

The third man? He was quite different. For one thing, he wore a Scottish kilt. In fact, he wore the entire regalia that one would expect a self-respecting Scotsman to wear. He was a well-muscled man of slightly taller than average height and had a close-cropped but full beard and broad mustache that came to a point at each side. This was Angus Moncrieff. He was supposed to have been some sort of baron in the old country, and his bearing gave off the sense that he was used to being around wealth. Unlike the two cowboys he was engaged in conversation with, he was clean and gave off the distinct aroma of some mildly inoffensive perfume. Were it not for his bulk, serious countenance, and pistol in his belt, he might be taken for a bit of a dandy.

Moncrieff was new to Corpus Christi. He'd dropped a few gold pieces around town at the livery, smithy, haberdashery, bank, and the like, anyplace potentially important to his business. He'd already met Sheriff Bill Meaney and sweet-talked the poor lawman's ears off. He had his eye on Scarlett, but dared not run afoul of her husband Walker Carson who was off fighting Yankees. Moncrieff had heard about the famous Texas Ranger Captain who lurked about the region, but hadn't yet found his way out toward Nuecestown. Oh, and his business was buying up cattle...not always legally.

The war and his sheriff duties were enough distraction that

Meaney had paid little attention to the Scotsman. The sheriff had plenty on his plate what with Yankee naval vessels still hanging offshore, a growing city with associated crimes of opportunity, and a pregnant wife. He had a vague idea of what Moncrieff was up to, but no one had as yet filed a complaint.

"So, lads, you say you've got some valuable merchandise for me?" Moncrieff kept his voice low and snuck a peek at the barkeep to see whether he might be eavesdropping as saloon keepers were wont to do.

The cowboys were not so wily as Moncrieff. Colton, the larger of the two, not-so-artfully blurted, "Yessir, Mistuh Moncrieff. Got 'bout seventy-five head of prime beef settin' a few miles south of here."

Moncrieff gave a glare made all-the-more-menacing by his bushy eyebrows. "Keep it down, boys? Is the merchandise mixed?" He meant to determine whether there might be legitimately owned cattle mixed with stolen stock.

"You got money fer the cattle?" The second cowboy was even less wily.

Again, Moncrieff glared. "If you gentlemen care to do business, you'll keep your voices down and stop naming the merchandise." His voice dropped to a whisper. "The walls have ears."

The two cowboys glanced wonderingly at the walls. "Don't see no ears."

Moncrieff shook his head.

The barkeep was doing his best to listen while busying himself with his cleanup duties in preparation for another raucous night. Despite the ongoing conflict, folks had a mind to let loose now and again to relieve the stresses of the Yankee siege.

Moncrieff shook his head ruefully. "I'm afraid there's a problem right now, boys."

The two cowboys exchanged looks as scruffy as their appearance.

"With those damned Yankees still lurking offshore, there's no way to get so much merchandise out of Corpus Christi to fetch top dollar. I'm going to have to work a deal with the federal troops. They think paying for anything is an inconvenience, so it'll be all I can do to get much of a price."

Colton leaned forward aggressively. "You aiming to cheat us, Mr. Moncrieff?"

"Just telling you like it is." Moncrieff sat back in his chair revealing the ivory-colored bone handle of the beautiful new Colt revolver in his waistband.

The second cowboy pushed back. "You lie! You girlie-skirted sonofabitch." His hand moved toward the gun in his holster. He was far too slow.

About the time the cowboy had barely cleared leather, there was a flash and Moncrieff's gun echoed in the saloon, putting a well-aimed bullet through the man's forearm and sending the man's pistol flying.

The barkeep ducked behind the bar.

Colton pushed back, caught Moncrieff's gaze, and lifted his hand away from his gun. The second cowboy writhed in pain, as he applied his bandanna to the gaping wound in his forearm.

"Don't be foolish. I don't want to kill either of you. I'm telling you how the market is right now. You can drive your merchandise down to Brownsville, but it won't go any better for you there. If you go north, I hear tell there's a Texas Ranger of some repute that might not like your game." Moncrieff looked around. The barkeep had left, likely to fetch Sheriff Meaney. "I'll give you two dollars a head. That's my offer."

The two cowboys looked at each other in frustration. The one was in obvious pain and still trying to stop the bleeding from his arm. Colton sighed resignedly. "Sonofabitch. We'll take yer damned money. Is it Yankee money?"

Moncrieff smiled. "Better." He handed over a bag of gold coins. "I think you'll find that half of it's here. I'll send my people to count the merchandise later today. Then, you'll get the other half. Good day, gentlemen."

Just as the cowboys exited, Sheriff Meaney strode into the saloon. "What's going on Mr. Moncrieff?"

"That's Baron Moncrieff, Sheriff." He gave a respectful look with just a hint of contempt. "Just a slight disagreement. No real harm. Nobody pressing charges."

Meaney couldn't help but look with suspicion at the Scotsman. "You be careful, Mr. Moncrieff." He wouldn't yet tell the man that the barkeep had shared with Meaney the conversation between Moncrieff and the two cowboys. To arrest Moncrieff, he'd have to catch him in the act.

Moncrieff laid on a thick Scottish accent. "Oh, I'll be careful for certain, Sheriff Meaney. You can be sure of that. I'm just a businessman doing my business."

Gunshots from the direction of the docks caught the sheriff's attention. "I'd better see to that, Mr. Moncrieff." He purposely avoided calling him Baron. "You be careful, you hear?"

Moncrieff ignored the slight.

Luke was on his knees in a dark area opposite the entrance to Crouching Lion's teepee. One Arrow sat between he and the entrance. A rain had started, just enough to make the soil muddy and muffle footsteps. The dying embers of a fire glowed, giving off an eerie light.

Luke and the chief looked to their right. They'd both sensed it rather than heard it.

A knife blade ripped a long vertical gash in the side of the teepee, and Crouching Lion stepped through. He was about to call out to his squaws, when he realized that One Arrow was facing him. He heard noises behind him. There was no escape.

"You dishonor your people, weak one." One Arrow's knife struck first.

A gash appeared across Crouching Lion's chest. He'd lost his grip on his own knife so dove for the fire, grabbed a hot rock, came to his feet, and bashed it against the side of the chief's head.

Momentarily dazed, One Arrow dropped to his knees. Crouching Lion found his knife and lifted it to strike the chief.

Luke sprang into action, throwing the full weight of his body behind the shoulder he planted into the warrior's side. Ribs cracked. The momentum of Luke's attack carried them through the teepee entrance and into the muddy clearing in front.

A dozen Comanche watched as Crouching Lion and Luke wrestled in the mud. Luke had the edge in size, but the Comanche savage was a cunning opponent and the slippery footing was treacherous in this sort of fight. The Comanche's hand had been burned by the hot rock used against One Arrow and blood oozed from his chest, but he seemed oblivious to any pain.

Crouching Lion lay stunned beneath Luke for the moment. Each breath brought a paroxysm of pain in the warrior's side. But this was life or death, and he knew he had to fight. He found the strength to roll and managed to get on top of Luke, but the Texas Ranger got a firm grip on the warrior's throat. The Comanche's eyes were bulging and his tongue stuck out, as he sought to catch air.

One Arrow staggered from the tent and began looking for a way to wrestle the warrior free of Luke. He grabbed a lance—a favored Comanche weapon.

Crouching Lion in his desperation felt for and found Luke's knife. With as mighty an effort as he could muster, the savage pushed away from Luke's grasp while simultaneously taking the Texas Ranger's Bowie knife. He'd just raised it high to strike a death blow, when One Arrow's lance struck his wrist with a sharp blow and sent the knife flying.

Luke took advantage of Crouching Lion's momentary distraction and twisted away. He leaped to his feet, set himself, and threw his fist with bone-crushing force square into the Comanche's face. Everyone could hear the ugly cracking sound of Crouching Lion's jaw shattering. A second punch low to the privates folded the savage like an old bedroll.

One Arrow stepped forward and held his arm out across Luke's chest to stop his attack. A barely conscious Crouching Lion writhed in pain. The chief stood firm. "This Comanche justice." With that, One Arrow signaled, and all of the Comanche warriors charged forward.

The Comanche began pummeling Crouching Lion with fists, clubs, rocks, and any other weapons at hand. In but minutes, he'd been beaten to a bloody, barely breathing heap of quivering flesh. Only then did the warriors pull back.

An unconscious Crouching Lion was dragged away from the encampment to the edge of the forest. He was spit upon and left to die. His possessions would be divided up among the warriors, including his two squaws.

What the Comanche had not finished, the coyotes and other scavengers would. Crouching Lion would never see another morning sun.

Barber had been watching the proceedings and found his way over to Luke. "Dang good fight, Captain." His unspoken thought was that he never wanted to be on the receiving end of one of Luke's punches.

One Arrow saw that his warriors were settled. Blood lust had been running high, and calm was in order. He walked over to Luke. "You good fighter, Ghost-Who-Rides." He smiled appreciatively at his own understatement.

"Glad to help, my brother. And you are right handy with that lance." Luke gave a little laugh as he was dusting himself off. He seemed none the worse for wear. He easily found his

Bowie knife, wiped some dirt from it, and nonchalantly slipped it back into its scabbard.

The chief pondered a moment. "Crouching Lion strong body, weak head."

"I must say I'm impressed with your Comanche justice."

One Arrow smiled at the compliment. "It our way." He looked at Luke with mud caked all over his body and then down at his own sweaty frame. "We eat and rest. First, jump in river. Get clean."

Luke followed the chief to the shore of the Pedernales River, discarded his boots, hat, and gun belt—and jumped in. The chief was right behind.

Luke shifted the conversation away from the incident with Crouching Lion. "Three Toes helped me hunt lawbreakers. He was a great tracker."

One Arrow shook the water from his hair. "Three Toes great Comanche chief."

Luke crawled from the water and grabbed his boot, hat, and gun belt. He'd be drip-drying.

One Arrow was beside him, as they walked back to the encampment. "You want hunt with me, Ghost-Who-Rides?"

Luke smiled. "Man hunt? Lawbreakers?"

One Arrow nodded. "We good together. You teach me more about necklace power." He caressed the cross at his neck that he'd taken from Three Toes's grave. He looked over at the youngest of Crouching Lion's two wives. "You want woman?" As the words spilled out, he thought better of them. He shook his head side to side. He knew intuitively that Luke wouldn't be tempted. "No...maybe Mr. Jake?"

Barber smiled mischievously, but turned serious as Luke leveled "the look" on him. "Thank you, Chief. I have woman at home." It was a lie, but it wouldn't do to insult One Arrow.

Soon, they were all laughing, consuming venison steaks, and drinking some concoction laced with peyote. They would all sleep well. Crouching Lion was already a distant memory, and Luke was forging a friendship with the Comanche chief.

Clay Bell slowly made his way westward. The Sharps was a heavy piece to carry, especially with the telescopic sight, but he wasn't about to abandon it. The wound across his forehead had stopped bleeding. He was mostly hungry. As he'd left that morning from the scene of the attack, he took a cursory inventory of the bodies lying about in the eerie vapors of death. Yankees...Rebels...lay about in their bloody repose. But for the blood and the awkward positions, they might have been sleeping. Bell had no idea what a musket ball hitting a body felt like, and he had no desire to find out. It was obvious that several of the dead soldiers had not died instantly, but rather had endured pain and suffering. Now, they were all dead.

He confirmed that Captain Rucker was missing. He made a mental note to one day find out what happened to his captain. He had no intention for now to track where the possibly seriously wounded captain might have gone. Bell's mission, and he was focused on it, was to get home. He was done with sharpshooting.

Luke and Barber had bid their farewells to One Arrow. At least for the present, they were confident there'd be no more homesteads attacked in the region by Penateka Comanche.

One Arrow had given Luke gifts to take home for Elisa and the children. The chief didn't overlook Barber. He gave him an ornately beaded deerskin pouch filled with dried peyote. One Arrow carefully explained its medicinal value. Barber was impressed simply to have received a gift, as he'd been mostly an observer as concerned the fighting action with Crouching

Lion. Perhaps the most important gifts were eight horses that had been captured from one of the ranches that Crouching Lion had attacked. One Arrow had even retrieved some of the tack, as Comanche preferred blankets or bareback.

Luke hoped that this show of gift-giving and brotherhood might rekindle the progress he'd made with Comanches through his friendship with Three Toes. Three Toes's death at the hands of a treacherous rival now seemed to have drifted into the past, as One Arrow was becoming a worthy successor.

Luke and Barber took a trail headed southeastward from the encampment. It took them past what little remained of Crouching Lion's body. The coyotes and other scavengers had already pretty much done their work. A couple of Crested Caracaras were perched in a nearby tree waiting for the travelers to pass on so they could finish their macabre feast. There was a faint odor, so the Rangers put their bandannas to good use. The air freshened soon enough, as they put a bit of distance from the scene. Their plan was to camp under the stars, swinging wide to the west of San Antonio and resting a little at San Diego before riding the final leg homeward. They stopped by the ranch that had suffered from Crouching Lion's thievery and gave them six of the horses. The ranchers were grateful to say the least and didn't begrudge Luke keeping two of the cayuses for all his trouble.

On the second day out, Luke spotted something moving on the horizon. From his lofty perch astride Big Horse, he soon made out the figure of a man on foot. "Jake…take a gander out yonder. Looks to be a White man on foot." Luke pulled out his spyglass and sighted on the figure. "Dang, he's carrying a Sharps." He handed the spyglass to Barber.

Barber looked in the direction to which Luke had pointed. "I'd be careful, Captain. That Sharps is a serious weapon." He knew he was stating the obvious. Pretty much everyone around the Nueces Strip knew of Luke's having been nearly killed by a ricocheted slug from a Sharps. "Looks like it's got one of those telescope sights far as I can tell."

Luke took the spyglass back from Barber. "Dang, Jake, you're right. The man does indeed carry a Sharps with a telescopic sight." It didn't take much to quickly figure that the man was likely a sharpshooter. "He's wearing a gray jacket... maybe a Reb. Maybe a deserter? He's walking right slow, like he's tired or hurt or both."

By this time, they'd drawn close enough for Bell to have spotted Luke and Barber. The lawmen were making no effort to hide their presence. The Rebel sergeant was tired but found the energy to lift the Sharps and peer through the sight. He saw the glint of morning sun reflected off Luke's Texas Ranger badge. He resignedly shook his head. He had no choice at hand as to what he should do. There was no option to flee. The men were mounted and could easily run him down. He could fight or await his fate. He might shoot one but was unlikely to get both. As resignation as to his fate coursed through him, Bell felt as though he'd been walking forever. He was pretty much done. There simply was no fight left in his body. Hungry? He'd subsisted on wild onions and some freshly killed rabbit for which he'd chased off a none-too-happy owl.

Luke drew the Henry from its scabbard and placed it across his lap and against the saddle horn. He and Barber were soon within hailing distance. "I'm Texas Ranger Captain Luke Dunn. Who goes?"

The name resonated with Bell. Could this be the man he'd heard about at that Heaven's Gate Ranch just a few days back? His throat was dreadfully dry, but he mustered enough voice to respond. "I...I'm a friend." He laid down the Sharps and raised his hands.

Luke approached cautiously with the ever-wary Jake Barber riding about twenty-five feet away to his left. "What's your name?"

"Clay...Clay Ashley Bell, sir." It pained him to get the

words out. "I recently made the acquaintance of your family back in Nuecestown."

Luke took an appraising look at Bell. The man was a soldier, apparently a sergeant. He was clearly tired, obviously disheveled, and quite distraught but otherwise appeared unthreatening. Luke was inclined to rely on his own judgment. "You leave your unit, soldier?"

Bell spoke with the slow cadence appropriate to his physical condition. "I was with Captain Stephen Rucker of the First Mounted Texas Cavalry, sir." He saw a hint of recognition in Luke's eyes at mention of Rucker's name. "We were ambushed up west of Victoria by maybe two dozen outliers from Quantrill's Raiders. We'd heard that Quantrill had been marauding through Kansas and Missouri, so these men were ranging pretty far south."

"What were you doing in Victoria?"

"We were escorting prisoners we'd captured at your Heaven's Gate Ranch. The Yankees had been foraging and making trouble for your family."

"Where's Captain Rucker?"

"Lost track of him, sir. Far as I could tell, everyone was killed. The captain might have escaped, as I couldn't find his body among the dead."

"That's quite a rifle you're carrying. By the telescopic sight, I think I know what your job was."

"Yes, sir. I was good at it...but I'm done...finished, sir," he said remorsefully.

Luke dismounted, though Barber kept an ever-watchful eye. "I appreciate your outfit protecting my family. Where are you headed?"

"My family has some ranch land a couple of days west of here."

"You a rancher?" Luke grabbed his canteen and offered it to Bell who took it gratefully.

"Rancher by trade, marksman by reputation, sir."

Luke took in the information. "You know livestock?"

"Ranched since I was knee high to a horny toad. Why do you ask, Captain Dunn?"

"You have family?"

"Yes…if the Comanche or bandits have spared them. My ma and pa, a couple of brothers, and a few hundred beeves."

Luke nodded. "I'm of a mind after the war to acquire more land. I could use some help, if you decide to venture out. My *vaqueros* are great, but I could always use a man that can shoot varmints and make himself useful with the livestock."

"I'll give that serious consideration, Captain." He handed the now half-empty canteen back to Luke.

Luke looked at Barber questioningly. Barber nodded, but Luke had already decided what he was going to do. "Tell you what, Mr. Bell, I'm of a generous mind this morning. I expect you'd get back to your family sooner, if you had a horse. We were gifted these mounts by a Comanche friend, and I'd be pleased to loan one to you. Bring him to Heaven's Gate at your convenience."

Bell was overwhelmed nearly to tears by Luke's generosity. "Sir, I'm grateful. I promise to get the horse back to you as soon as I can."

Luke pretty much knew he wouldn't be seeing Bell until the war was ended. He walked over to one of the horses, threw a few victuals in a pouch, and led it over to Bell. "You'll have to ride bareback, but I'm sure you won't mind. As our Mexican friends are fond of saying, *vaya con Dios*."

Bell paused and handed the Sharps to Luke as he climbed into the saddle. "Thanks, Captain. Thanks very much."

"My pleasure, Mr. Bell." Luke handed the rifle back to the Rebel sharpshooter, mounted Big Horse, and motioned to Barber to continue their ride homeward.

After they'd ridden a few minutes, Barber finally spoke up. "That was mighty generous of you, Captain. You think you'll ever see that cayuse again?"

"I'm sure of it, Jake."

"How can you be so sure?"

"I just rekindled the man's soul. I gave him hope in his fellow man. He'll never forget that."

Barber nodded. "I think I get it, Captain. I do think I get it."

Luke watched a couple of tumbleweeds blow across the trail such as it was. It was still mostly brush country, but they'd soon be riding on the grass-covered prairie.

"Lookie there, Jake. See those red and yellow flowers? They're called Indian Blankets. Elisa loves them nearly as much as bluebonnets." Luke made a mental note to gather a handful after they left San Diego.

Barber smiled and shook his head. One of these days, he'd have Luke Dunn figured out.

FIVE
CATTLE SCAM

MAJOR GORDON BELKNAP longed for the days when he was simply trying to hunt down Comanche. Here he was languishing at Fort Brown with those damnable Rebels taunting him from afar. He'd developed some great friendships before the war and hoped that those would survive the turmoil. He especially thought on his old friend Luke Dunn. He wondered how the Texas Ranger was getting on. From what he remembered, Luke was likely single-handedly bringing law and order to the upper reaches of the Nueces Strip. He was momentarily stirred from his fond recollections as a knock at the door interrupted his idyll. He quickly gathered his thoughts. "Enter."

The corporal entered, came to attention, and saluted.

"At ease, Corporal. What is it?"

"There's a fellow called Angus Moncrieff wanting to see you, sir. He claims to have some cattle he wants to sell."

"Thank you, Corporal. I'll be along shortly."

The corporal didn't move.

"You're dismissed, Corporal."

He still didn't move.

Belknap recognized the uncomfortable expression on the

soldier's face. "Is there something more I should know, Corporal?"

"If I may speak freely, sir?"

"Go ahead, Corporal."

"He calls himself a baron, sir…and…and he wears a lady's skirt."

Belknap raised his eyebrows. "Skirt?"

"Yes, sir…a skirt."

"You're dismissed, Corporal."

The corporal saluted awkwardly and exited.

Belknap shook his head. The image of a man in a lady's skirt selling cattle rattled through his brain. It was an image he simply couldn't get wrapped around. He walked over and grabbed his kepi and saber, checked himself out in the mirror, took a last sip of lukewarm coffee, and left the safe confines of his office to face whatever this man in lady's clothing had for him.

He stood on the landing and looked down at a burly Scotsman in full highland gear. Turns out the lady's skirt was merely a kilt. "I'm Major Gordon Belknap. May I help you, Mr. Moncrieff?" The image painted by the corporal had been shattered.

"Aye, Major. I've got a couple of hundred head of what you Americans call prime beeves. I understand that your men are partial to steak, sir. And sir, if you don't mind, it's Baron Moncrieff…Baron Angus Moncrieff."

Belknap tried to gauge where this apparition was coming from. He recalled seeing some of the local immigrants from Ireland wearing kilts for special occasions, but this man seemed to wear his colors as a regular thing. "We could use some beef, Baron Moncrieff, but not two hundred head or more. Fifty head might be more like it."

Moncrieff was in a bit of a quandary. Many of the beeves in his herd were likely stolen from Mexico. He didn't feature having to head south of the Rio Grande to sell his beeves.

Belknap was plenty savvy enough to sense the man's situation. "You might find some interest upriver at Fort Ringgold, Baron Moncrieff. As to your current inventory, I assume they've all been legally obtained?"

Moncrieff figured there were likely as many as fifty legitimately purchased cattle in his herd. "I'd only sell you legal beeves, major. I'm asking five dollars a head."

Belknap blanched inwardly at the price. He hated negotiating, but recognized it as a necessary evil. "We can't afford more than half that." He'd developed a pretty fair sense of people, partly at having observed his friend Luke Dunn and his cousin Nicholas. Nick had established a reputation as a skilled speculator.

Moncrieff had purchased half his herd at two dollars a head and picked up another hundred head or so of what he figured were free-range beeves on the drive from Corpus Christi. He'd make a profit at two-fifty a head but was confident he could do better. "I can't be losing money in these tough times of prolonged conflict, Major. Can you up your offer a bit?"

Belknap recognized Moncrieff's cagey bartering tactic of not responding with a price. He'd have none of that. "If I check with our kitchen, the chef is going to tell me we have plenty of dried beef. Leaves me to wondering what fresh beef on the hoof is truly worth, Baron. Seems a bit of a luxury." His eyes penetrated through Moncrieff.

There was a silence.

"You're a tough man, Major Belknap. You must be a fellow Scotsman by heritage. What do you say to four dollars a head?"

Belknap was by now coming to the quite logical conclusion that not all of Moncrieff's cattle were obtained by legitimate means. "It's been a pleasure to meet you, Baron Moncrieff. I hope you have better luck at Fort Ringgold." Belknap gave Moncrieff a sort of half salute and turned to go back inside.

"Three dollars?" Averaging in the free-range cattle he'd added to his herd, Moncrieff was going to make a heady profit of nearly a hundred percent.

"Done, Baron." Belknap smiled before he turned back to face Moncrieff. "Cull out that fifty head and run them into the corral over yonder. I'll have my men verify brands and ownership. We'll have your payment ready after we've done that. Pleasure doing business with you, Baron Moncrieff." Belknap rightly reckoned that the Scotsman had made a handsome profit, but lifting the morale of the garrison with fresh steak was worth it.

Moncrieff gulped reflexively. He'd now be taking extra care with the beeves he culled from his herd. Belknap was a bit more savvy than he'd reckoned.

★★

Luke decided to surprise Elisa. He'd approached the barn stealthily, stabled Big Horse, removed his spurs, washed trail dust from his face and hands, and made his way to the house. He climbed the stairs to the gallery so quietly he could almost hear the butterflies flapping their wings. He held a bouquet of Indian Blankets behind his back. As he reached for the latch, the door opened.

"Thought I heard you coming, Lucas Dunn." She was in his arms before he had a chance to offer the bouquet. The flowers scattered to the gallery floor.

"Lisa…Lisa." He held her so close as humanly possible. She felt incredibly wonderful as she pressed to him.

"The children are asleep."

It was a signal. In a heartbeat, they found themselves in the bedroom,   hands…mouths…bodies…searching…yearning. Their passion knew no bounds, but then, it never did. Their lovemaking was always unbridled, a free flow of their senses. Soon, they were basking in afterglow.

"Lisa...how did you know it was me at the door?"

She smiled fetchingly. "Lucas, never ask a woman how she knows these things." She ran her hand across his muscular chest. "Thank you for the flowers."

He gazed deeply into her crystal blue eyes. "Have to gather them later." He moved over her and began to kiss her...beginning with her toes. In moments, she was ready to scream in ecstasy. He was soon within her body and soul again, raising their passion to new heights.

They lay back, once again having been lost in the wonderful but too often fleeting moments of intimacy.

"Are you hungry?" Elisa's eyes danced along the well-muscled but lean body of her rancher lawman husband.

"Not anymore." A broad smile spread across his face. No question, she'd recovered from the yellow fever.

"Eggs, bacon, and cornbread?" She caught the look in his eyes. She wasn't certain she was quite ready to take him again.

Luke grabbed his shirt. "Only if you insist."

"One more thing." She looked ever-so-sweetly at him.

Luke was already seated on the edge of the bed pulling on his boots. "What's that, Lisa?"

"I missed my bleeding."

Luke fell back. His head landed in her lap. "I love you, Lisa Dunn. Dang, but life is good."

Her hands lovingly stroked his wavy red hair. No words were needed.

Moncrieff wiped his brow. Despite the fact that air was free to flow under the folds of his kilt, the wool was not so forgiving of the heat. He dared not hike it up, as his sensitive white skin did not take kindly to the harsh rays of the South Texas sun. He had undergarments and a pair of trousers in his bag but was not especially inclined to wear them regardless of their practicality. His beard and long thick hair actually offered a degree of insulation, but not so much as he noticed.

To make matters worse, the remaining herd of nearly a hundred and fifty beeves was kicking up a lot of trail dust. The particles stuck to his sweaty skin, giving it a rusty-red patina.

He'd had the good sense to hire a trio of competent *vaqueros* and a trail cook, so was mostly able to focus on simply accompanying the operation and handling the buying and selling. Along the way toward Fort Ringgold, he'd even managed to buy a half dozen horses from a couple of Mexicans who assured him they'd been obtained legitimately. He doubted that, but the price was too good to pass up. Better than three-fourths of his livestock were stolen from somewhere, so the horses didn't matter much so far as legal purchasing was concerned.

They'd driven the herd roughly halfway between Fort Brown and Fort Ringgold, when he looked up to find himself in the midst of a Lipan Apache ambush. They seemed to have materialized out of nowhere. Moncrieff had the foresight to have armed his *vaqueros* with repeating rifles and bought plenty of ammunition. He nevertheless found himself outnumbered three to one and facing determined Apache warriors also armed with guns.

He'd heard tales of how the Apache stole cattle on one side of the border only to sell it on the other. They even had the temerity to sell beeves back to the folks they'd stolen them from. He'd heard about the notorious Chief Costalites, so figured these were likely part of his band. But all that didn't especially matter at this particular moment.

By good fortune, Moncrieff was pretty fair with guns. He could hit most anything he pointed a gun muzzle at if it presented a big enough target. The *vaqueros* were mostly decent marksmen. The Apache rode in whooping and hollering with rifles blazing. They were terrible marksmen generally speaking. They divided their forces, as part of the raiding party tried to peel off a few beeves from the herd.

Moncrieff and his men kept returning fire, sending salvo after salvo at the attackers who finally hightailed it back to cover upon losing a half dozen warriors. Moncrieff took stock of his situation. A horse had been shot from under one of his *vaqueros*. Other than that, no one was harmed. He cursed that a bullet had ripped through his kilt, though missed both he and his mount.

"Pedro, lad, be sure your men reload quickly."

"*Sí, Señor Moncrieff...probablemente regresarán.*" Pedro was sure the Apache weren't finished.

Moncrieff got the general drift of what the *vaquero* was saying. It confirmed his own belief that the Apache weren't likely to quit after only one attack. He had the men form a defensive perimeter. They waited.

By some luck or divine providence, it soon appeared that the savages had lost their taste for battle. It was more likely attributable to facing the repeating rifles and losing too many of their warriors that dissuaded them.

"Pedro, let's hustle these beeves to Fort Ringgold." The Scotsman saw no point in hanging around waiting for the Apache to find reinforcements.

He looked down at himself. If he had thought he was sweaty and dirty before, the heat of the attack had significantly added to his discomfort. He craved a bath and some clean clothes. In any case, he wanted to present a professional image to the officer in charge at the fort. As the *vaqueros* drove the herd along a route about a half mile inland from the Rio Grande, Moncrieff turned his horse southward. He had a body and soul cleansing dip in mind.

In but a few minutes, he found himself along the Rio Grande's north shore. He looked around but saw no one, so proceeded to peel off his clothes and prepare to bathe. The water was refreshing to say the least, though not quite so cool as he'd have preferred. With the trail dust washed away, he put his mind to cleaning up his wardrobe as best he could. He mostly shook it out. He'd just begun dressing when a rattling sound caught his attention. He froze at first, then cautiously looked about. There, perhaps seven or eight feet away, a rattlesnake was letting him know to stay clear. Trouble was, the serpent was coiled on Moncrieff's kilt. There he stood clothed except for his buck-naked posterior and manhood. His revolver was lying on a rock halfway between him and the snake.

He locked eyes as best he could with the threatening reptile as though to will it not to strike. In his desperate mind, he sought to hypnotize the nasty critter. But the big question rattling through his mind was whether he could reach the gun, secure it, aim it, and fire with accuracy before the snake could strike? Moncrieff felt as though his heart was going to beat itself out of his chest. Sweat seemed to flow from every pour of his body.

Just about the time the Scot had decided to go for the gun, the rattlesnake apparently figured he'd made his point and slithered off. It seemed a sort of professional courtesy.

Moncrieff looked at his now thoroughly wet shirt, shrugged at the futility of getting cooled off, and finished dressing. He rode on back to the herd, not saying a word of his adventure to the cook or *vaqueros*.

As Luke relaxed on the gallery with a cup of coffee and Elisa tended to children and house chores, he heard the telltale sound of hoofbeats approaching up the entry trail to Heaven's Gate Ranch. The sound indicated an easy trot, so Luke figured there was no threat and eased his rifle alongside the bench.

Sheriff Bill Meaney came into view soon enough. As he passed the old cabin on his way in, he tipped his hat to Jaime.

Apparently, Meaney's views toward Mexicans had changed a bit. He saw Luke lounging on the gallery and rode on up to the main house. "Luke, great to see you back from chasin' Comanche." He dismounted and hitched his horse.

"Come set a spell Bill." Luke started to get up to greet him and fetch Elisa, but she'd had already appeared with a cup of coffee.

"Thanks, Mrs. Dunn." He gratefully accepted the coffee and parked himself in the chair beside Luke.

"You're welcome, Sheriff. You men chat, I've got children to tend to. You're welcome to join us for midday meal."

"Why, thank you. I may just do that."

"What brings you out from Corpus, Bill. I figure it's more than checking on that ramshackle place in Nuecestown you call a jail." Luke smiled as he referred to the dilapidated condition of the town jail. "Is money so tight?"

"The war has cramped our budget, Luke. We'll fix it up when this internal conflict is ended." He gave an aw-shucks shrug. "We've had some excitement round these parts of late. I expect your wife told you about the attack on Corpus Christi and the Yankee foragers that Captain Rucker's troop captured here at Heaven's Gate."

"Yep. I actually ran into a sharpshooter from Rucker's unit a couple days back near San Diego. They were wiped out— Rebs and Yanks both...almost to a man up near Victoria. Any word on Horace Rucker's son?"

"Yes, but not good. He made it home but died from his wounds. Hit the Ruckers pretty hard, Luke. I think Rex is on his way home from Washington. Hear tell the Yankees promoted him to Colonel. He's got some sort of desk job in the War Department."

Luke was immersed in thought about the splinter band of Quantrill's Raiders led by Cole Yopunger that might still be rampaging about. He shook his head so as to better focus on Meaney's stories. "What else, Bill?"

"There's a new fella in town who's running some sort of scam that I haven't been able to pin him with. He's a Scotsman who calls himself Baron Angus Moncrieff. He wears what the locals are calling a lady skirt. The Scots and your Irish kin call them kilts."

"What do you suspect he's up to?"

"More than suspicion, Luke. I'm pretty darn sure he's selling stolen livestock. Just haven't caught him in the act. I lost my deputy to the war, and there's too much lawbreaking in Corpus to devote time to Moncrieff."

"Wears a kilt, you say? What's he look like?"

"Bit shorter than you, Luke, but burly. Has dark hair and a full beard. The man has steely eyes that can penetrate right through you. He packs a Colt 1861, and the barkeep at the Longhorn Saloon says he knows how to use it. I've also heard that he owns a strange-looking sword, sorta broad blade. Never seen him sporting that. Word has it that he's a tough negotiator. Some say he could sell horns to a longhorn."

"The sword is called a claymore. I fought with one of those back in Ireland." Luke smiled momentarily and thought back to those days. "Any idea where he might be found?"

"Last I heard, he was headed south toward Fort Brown with a couple hundred head of mostly stolen beeves. He's savvy enough to only deal in gold and silver. He doesn't want any part of Confederate or Union paper. Like I said, he seems savvy."

Luke pondered the dilemma at hand. Would he chase Quantrill's men, where he'd be seriously outnumbered, or head south to try to find Moncrieff?

Meaney sensed which way Luke was leaning. "And there's a reward of three hundred dollars…gold, of course."

Elisa emerged as if on cue. "May I join you fine gentlemen? The children are napping, cornbread is baking, and brisket will be ready in less than an hour." She smiled as she watched the hungry expressions of Luke and the sheriff as they nearly licked their lips raw at the thought of savoring her cooking. "I couldn't help but overhear your talk."

Luke was always one to value his wife's views. "I expect you joined us, because you have a thought or two, my sweet."

She nodded at Luke. "I'm of the opinion that you'd need a sizable number of armed men to chase down the Quantrill gang. I'd leave them for our military." She offered up an expression that assumed the matter of the marauders was settled. Elisa had a way of expressing the obvious. "That leaves our Scottish Baron friend. Seems it would take a burden from Sheriff Meaney, if you brought Moncrieff to justice, my loving Texas Ranger husband. You and Mr. Barber should be more than capable of that. Oh, and three hundred dollars might come in handy."

Luke and Meaney nodded affirmatively in unison. Luke smiled. "Makes sense to me. What do you think, Bill?"

"The way things are going, the war may be over before we know it. Meanwhile, I could use your help with Moncrieff, Luke."

"If he has a couple of hundred head of beeves, I expect no single fort is going to buy all of them. Plus, the forts change hands regular-like between Yanks and Rebs. I'm thinking he'll follow the line of forts up the Rio Grande until he's sold off his beeves. Just maybe, we might catch up to him in San Ygnacio or Laredo." Luke was clearly warming to the task ahead. "What's Walker Carson up to?"

Meaney was quick to respond. "He's pretty much finished repairing their house from that Yankee cannon shelling. I'd figure he'll be headin' back to join up with Colonel Ford."

"Wish I could persuade him to join up with me and Jake. Guess I'll resort to some other help. Wouldn't mind getting Jubal Strong or maybe that sharpshooter fellow Clay Bell to join me." Luke stroked his mustache, as he tended to do when having to think on something, then paused as though in an ah-ha moment. "I know."

Elisa and Meaney looked quizzically at Luke.

Luke smiled. "One Arrow."

"The Comanche?" Meaney raised his eyebrows.

"Guess I have a way of making friends with the savages. Three Toes helped me. Why not One Arrow? The chief said he wanted to hunt with me. He wasn't referring to hunting varmints. I expect he heard tales from Three Toes."

"What if Moncrieff doesn't oblige you and show up in Laredo?" Meaney wasn't fully buying into Luke's plan to link up with One Arrow. "He might hear that you're hunting him and change plans. He's no fool from what I hear."

"They get that telegraph line run to Laredo?" Luke had gotten to thinking that he might save himself some time.

Meaney shook his head. "They started building it, but soldiers and redskins keep cutting the lines. One side or the other, don't matter. Result's the same. I expect we won't see a reliable line until this confounded war is over."

Luke shook his head resignedly. He was still considering the feasibility of recruiting One Arrow. "I could take a northern route to Laredo, visit his village, and see whether he's interested." Luke stroked his mustache again as he pondered the possibility. "Don't think it'd take much to persuade him."

Elisa's eyes met Luke's. "Lucas, I think you've got the wagon ahead of the horse."

Luke knew that he could wind up running all over the Nueces Strip vainly trying to find Moncrieff. It would waste their time. "Guess I am jumping the gun."

Elisa appreciated Luke's enthusiasm to put another lawbreaker out of business and was pleased that her husband wasn't going off half-cocked.

Meaney chimed in. "I'd just be patient, Luke. Let the good baron come to you."

Luke accepted all the advice, although he remained just a tad begrudging of not taking immediate action. "Well, that leaves us with that Quantrill bunch."

"You said it yourself, Luke. That's going to take more than a couple of Texas Rangers…and they could be long gone by now."

Luke fidgeted.

Elisa knew her husband well. She sensed how anxious he was to resume his lawman efforts. Despite that, there was plenty he could be doing around Heaven's Gate. It seemed to invariably devolve to his dilemma between lawman and rancher. Both held similar challenges of danger and hard work. The common denominator was his role as husband and father. "You might…" She held her tongue.

Luke smiled. "Might spend time with the children, especially Peter and John."

"You promised Andrea Anne a horse."

She had him there. She'd lassoed him, and there was no way he was shaking off the rope.

Luke looked at Meaney who nodded in response. Luke sighed. "Let me know if you hear anything of Moncrieff's whereabouts."

With Luke's near future seemingly settled, they relaxed with small talk about family until Elisa arose in a semi-panic upon smelling well-done cornbread.

"Seven dollars a head, lieutenant. That's my final price." Moncrieff was a sight to behold. He'd taken to wearing a broad-brimmed cowboy hat to protect his fair skin from the intense Nueces Strip sun. He stood before the lieutenant in full Scottish regalia save for having forgotten to swap out the cowboy hat for his traditional Balmoral. The error was almost comical, though the Confederate garrison was likely clueless to the cultural faux pas. There he stood with cowboy hat and kilt.

The lure of fresh beef was hard for the lieutenant to resist. Chicken, occasional venison, and dried beef were getting tiresome for a unit whose morale was existing on fumes. They'd eaten a lot of beans. He had only paper money which accounted for Moncrieff pushing for a higher price. The Scotsman was assuming some considerable risk as to the value of the Rebel dollar. Had either man known what was happening to Confederate forces in central Virginia, they wouldn't have been dealing at all. The lieutenant had fifty troops and roughly a hundred dollars of nearly worthless Rebel currency. "Can't afford more than a half dozen, Baron."

Moncrieff rolled his eyes. A half dozen beeves was hardly worth bartering for. He had to get rid of his inventory, as it was becoming costly to maintain. "Buy ten at eight dollars and I'll throw a horse into the deal, Lieutenant."

The three soldiers standing behind the lieutenant were about ready to eat a longhorn raw. They so longed for fresh-killed beef. The lieutenant looked over his shoulder at the men. Their expressions told him not to mess around any further. "Okay, Baron Moncrieff. You've got a deal." He counted the money out for Moncrieff. The paper was likely losing value with each passing moment, but the Scotsman had ten fewer beeves to worry about.

Moncrieff and his outfit were soon back on the trail now headed further up the Rio Grande past Rio Grande City, on to San Ygnacio, and thence to Laredo. Moncrieff was wrestling with how best to rid himself of most of the cattle. He got to thinking that selling to the military was increasingly a losing proposition, as their money wasn't worth the paper it was printed on. Perhaps Mexico was the answer to his dilemma. *"Pedro, um...donde vender. ¿Donde vender en Mexico?"* Where indeed should he go in Mexico?

Pedro tried to be patient with Moncrieff's halting Spanish. The Scottish accent was amusing and made it hard to keep a straight face. *"Quizás Camargo, señor."* He knew that Cheno Cortina still lurked around these parts. Cortina had abandoned his mother's ranch near Brownsville until things settled down in Texas. The Mexican bandit crossed the Rio Grande back and forth with impunity.

Moncrieff thought on his vaquero's answer. Maybe Camargo? He'd heard about the Mexican bandit revolutionary Pedro mentioned. Cortina might be promising. The greater question would be whether the Mexicans would buy beef, especially from stock mostly rustled from Mexican ranches. He didn't figure to get top dollar, but the peso was likely more stable than Yankee or Rebel paper despite the influx of French francs. Cortina might even have gold coin. *"Vamos a Camargo, Pedro."*

Luke expected that Moncrieff would eventually show up back in Corpus Christi. Might take a while. After all, the man would be slowed by his trail drive up the Rio Grande. He wasn't inclined to hunt the man down. Besides, hanging around Heaven's Gate was enjoyable for the most part, as he was reconnecting with the children and especially spending time with Elisa. Nevertheless, patience remained a difficult virtue to maintain.

As he walked to the barn one morning, he continued to think on eventually having One Arrow join him to hunt lawbreakers. He got to recalling his teaming with the Comanche Chief Three Toes in taking on the Mexican bandit Carlos Perez, battling Roy Biggs, and eventually bringing Horatio Thorpe to justice. The more he cogitated upon it, the more attractive it became. He missed Three Toes, but One Arrow seemed willing to assume the mantel of the mutual respect and friendship the chief had fashioned with Luke.

Luke saddled up Big Horse and soon headed out early with

Jaime to check cattle along the southern boundary of Heaven's Gate. They'd managed to find a few strays, but had a sense that the herd had become short enough head to make it noticeable. "Jaime, you sense what I sense? I'm thinking we're missing a few head. Seems we've been rustled."

"Yes, *Señor* Dunn. I was seeing fewer beeves."

As they reached the eastern-most boundary of the southern property line, Luke found a spot where several head had been gathered in a *parada*, a temporary corral, before being driven south. There was evidence of a fire appropriate to heating branding irons. He and Jaime looked knowingly at each other. The **-HG** brand would be easy to spy from any larger herds and tough to overbrand by even an experienced brand burner. One thing for sure, those beeves would have to be moved outside Nueces County. The tracks were fresh and the rustlers' horses shod. The shod hooves ruled out Apache. That narrowed the choices of perpetrators to foraging soldiers or bandits. Not really so narrow a choice. From what Luke could figure, there weren't more than three rustlers. That was about right for handling a couple of dozen cattle. "Let's go get 'em, Jaime."

The two checked to be certain their weapons were ready for whatever lay ahead. They rode alternately at a walk and a canter trying to keep dust to a minimum. With any luck, they'd close the gap right quickly. There was always the possibility that the rustlers would be overconfident given the vastness of the Nueces Strip, and they'd be driving the cattle at a slower pace.

The trail was easy to follow, which gave credence to Luke's perception that the rustlers were overconfident. Roughly an hour into their stalking of the rustlers, Luke spotted a distant live oak motte. They thought about the possibility of a little shade, but as they got closer realized a body was swaying in the breeze from a rope knotted around its neck. There seemed to be far too many lynchings these days. A couple of buzzards were circling and occasionally diving to their feast. Luke sighed and motioned to Jaime to follow him to the trees. The victim was a Mexican, not unusual for the area or the times. The man could have done something terrible or might have simply looked crossways at some Anglo or his woman. Luke had long since stopped apologizing to Jaime for this sort of thing, as it was all too common and never pleasant.

Luke cut the man down, and they dug a shallow grave and buried him. There was no identification on the body, and the scavengers had already done enough damage as to make the man unrecognizable. It was regrettable that he could be someone's husband or father and even worse that it mattered not.

They'd ridden for about another two hours, when dame fortune smiled upon them. They rode to the top of a gentle rise and saw smoke from a small cooking fire not more than a half mile away. Given there were not a lot of travelers in this part of the country, they felt confident that the rustlers they were tracking had stopped for the night. There were at least another couple of hours of daylight remaining, so they'd have to be patient. But Luke didn't feel patient. He slipped the spyglass out and scanned the source of the smoke. From what he could make out, there were no more than three men. They looked to be White men so far as he could tell. Luke didn't recognize any of them. He saw no uniforms so that likely ruled out foragers. He could see the cattle just beyond.

They moved perhaps a quarter mile closer before hobbling their horses, something Big Horse didn't exactly cotton to but endured for his beloved owner. With Henry rifles in hand, they removed their spurs, ducked below the level of the grasses, and began to stalk their prey.

Luke and Jaime were walking hunched over moving along about ten feet apart, when Luke signaled his *vaquero* to stop. He put his finger to his lips to emphasize the need for quiet.

One of the rustlers was headed in their direction. Given Luke's six-foot-three height, it didn't take much for him to peek above the grass and see that the man was intent on answering nature's call. The man stopped not more than ten feet from Luke. The grasses afforded an effective concealment. The Texas Ranger didn't breathe, didn't move a muscle until the man had dropped his pants, squatted, and begun to strain and grunt. Taking advantage of these sorts of opportunities to catch folks at their most vulnerable tended to enable easy evening of the numerical odds when outnumbered. They were stock in trade for lawmen and lawbreakers alike, depending on hunter versus hunted and assuming the patience to wait. Luke had turned it almost into an art form.

The rustler was clueless as to his pending fate. Luke snuck up from behind. There was no thought given to taking the man alive. With rustlers, it was most often a matter of kill or be killed. Luke resisted the urge to cover his nose and mouth given the overwhelming stench. He closed on the rustler, held his breath, and plunged his Bowie knife deep into the man's ribs. The man opened his mouth to yell, but Luke already had the knife back in play as he slit the man's throat. A gurgle replaced any hope of a warning yell. Now there were only two rustlers. The odds had been evened considerably.

Luke covered his nose with his bandanna in what amounted to an almost humorous signal to Jaime and waved the *vaquero* forward toward the remaining men.

The two rustlers were engrossed in lively conversation when Luke and Jaime broke into their clearing. Luke's Texas Ranger badge was on full display. "Freeze and raise your hands. I'm Texas Ranger Captain Luke Dunn, and you men are under arrest for cattle stealing."

The men stood in unison with hands held high and mouths agape. They'd been totally taken by surprise.

"Jaime, unstrap their gun belts."

"Wait, we're just a couple of cowboys droving cattle on through these parts. Honest."

Luke rolled his eyes and held in his Irish temper. "Problem

is, boys, the brands on those beeves are mine. You've messed with the wrong rancher."

"Where's John?"

"If you mean the fellow out yonder who hoped to take a crap, he won't be seeing the sunset. Now keep those hands high." Luke kept the muzzle of his Colt aimed at the two.

As Jaime went to unbuckle one of the rustler's gun belts, the other lowered his hands and went for the revolver at his hip. He'd barely touched his revolver when a blast from Luke's Colt echoed off the rolling hills and a bullet cut clean through the man's chest. He was as good as dead before he hit the ground. Luke turned and pointed his Colt at the remaining rustler. "You want to try your luck doing something stupid?"

While still keeping his gun aimed at the man, Luke reached to his side and grabbed a set of manacles. "Here you go, Jaime. Do the honors. Let's be sure this man's no trouble." He tossed the manacles to the *vaquero* who promptly cuffed the man.

Luke was now confident that all was under control. "What's your name?"

"Gowdy Durham."

Luke figured the name was too unusual for it to be made up. "What were you going to do with my beeves? You tell the truth, and I might recommend they not hang your sorry butt."

Having seen Luke in action, the man was properly scared and didn't see any point in lying. He'd already peed in his pants at the moment Luke had shot his partner. "Gonna sell them to some Scottish fella named Moncrieff."

Luke's eyes grew wide, and he couldn't suppress a smile. "You willing to help us catch this Moncrieff fellow?"

The rustler looked around furtively. He wasn't exactly in a bargaining position. "What do you have in mind, sir?"

"Your Scottish friend Moncrieff has been buying and selling stolen livestock, but we need to catch him in the act. He's stolen a lot of cattle and been cheating the military. You help us get him, Mister Durham, and you surely won't be doing the dance at the end of any noose."

That offer had a certain appeal to the rustler. "What do I have to do?"

"Well, we've got to get these cattle back to my ranch, then we'll figure how to lure this Moncrieff fellow. Enjoy the fresh air, as I'll likely park you in the jail until we figure how to nab the Scotsman. Your testimony will likely serve to hang him."

The rustler looked from Luke to Jaime and back. "Okay, I'll help you get Moncrieff."

Jaime smiled at witnessing his boss exercise the practical deal-making side of delivering justice. He fetched their horses, and he and Luke soon had the prisoner mounted and the dead rustlers draped over their horses.

"You mind that we drive this little herd in the dark, Jaime? I think we pretty much know the countryside, and there's plenty of moonlight. I expect we can be at Heaven's Gate by sunrise."

The *vaquero* smiled and nodded agreement as they began the drive northward.

SIX
WORTHY PREY

JUAN CHENO CORTINA sat at ease on a rickety old Windsor chair in front of the little hacienda he called his temporary home. He had an urge to laugh at the apparition before him. It was all he could do to simply suppress a smile, a condescending one at that. He had considerable difficulty accommodating a man wearing a skirt.

Moncrieff sensed he'd likely met his bartering match in the wily Mexican. He quickly judged that Cortina was no rube to be trifled with. The rebel leader exuded the confidence that comes with knowing he had the upper hand in any negotiation, especially in his home country. Moncrieff looked to his *vaquero* Pedro for some sort of encouragement. After all, the man had guided him to Cortina. Might the *vaquero* hold any sway at all with the Mexican leader.

"*Es un hermoso dia, señor Cortina. Me llamo Baron Angus Moncrieff.*" A beautiful day? That was rather obvious and a tad trite. Moncrieff felt he had to start somewhere. The language was awkward for him. He felt a rivulet of sweat run down his back. He lamented that South Texas was so God-awful hot.

Cortina smiled with a touch of admiration at the pale

foreigner having attempted to address him in halting Spanish laced with a heavy brogue. *"Yo hablo Inglés, yanqui."*

The Scotsman was struggling to read Cortina's expression and hoped it was other than the patronizing air that he sensed. It was a relief that Cortina admitted to understanding English. Moncrieff at least grasped that. "Very good. Thank you for the opportunity to offer you prime cattle, *señor* Cortina."

"Cattle?" Cortina shook his head emphatically and laid an incredulous look on Moncrieff. "You want me to buy my own cattle?" He laughed far too heartily for Moncrieff's liking. The Mexican made no bones about his position. He'd already had his men scout Moncrieff's herd.

Moncrieff's disappointment showed for a fleeting moment at being so readily exposed for what he was. It took a moment before his face returned to a more confident persona. "Ah, but many are Texas beeves." The Scotsman bent down and started to reach into a satchel.

At Moncrieff's move, the hands of Cortina's bodyguards grabbed at their guns.

Moncrieff paused. "Just a gift, *señor*."

Cortina waved his hand to put his men at ease. "My apologies...my men are simply looking out for my safety. They have what you Anglos call itchy trigger fingers."

With that, Moncrieff drew a bottle of Scottish whiskey from the satchel. He displayed it to Cortina, whose eyes widened with pleasant surprise. The Scotsman next produced two crystal glasses, set them on the table next to the Mexican, and was soon pouring the smooth liquor into them. "Let's toast to making a bargain, *señor* Cortina."

Cortina took several sips of the whiskey, his taste buds thoughtfully savoring the bold liquid as it flowed smoothly over his tongue. In but moments, he'd finished the contents of the glass. "I admire your taste in whiskey, Baron." He waved away his bodyguards. "Please sit." He pointed to a nearby chair. It was hardly better than the one Cortina was sitting upon. Once his men were out of earshot, he turned back to Moncrieff. "How goes *la guerra*, Baron?"

"Won't last much longer. The Federals are winning."

The Mexican nodded. "I think you are right. Soon enough, Texas will be crawling with United States troops and Texas Rangers. Our business will change."

Moncrieff was taken with the rebel leader's thoughtful summation of what was soon to come. "All the more reason to make a bargain between us, *señor* Cortina."

"You have two hundred and fourteen head, Baron. Half are Mexican cattle." He gazed intently at Moncrieff. "My *vaqueros* have already cut them out, and they are mine."

Moncrieff rather expected this and made a point of showing no surprise. "I expected no less. I was going to gift them to you, anyway."

Cortina's smile became a bit mischievous. "I like you, Baron Moncrieff. I'm feeling generous today. I will give you two dollars a head for the remaining cattle."

"Gold or paper?"

Cortina smiled broadly. "United States paper is risky and Confederate is riskier, Baron. I only deal in gold and silver."

"Two dollars a head in gold works for me. We have a deal." Moncrieff already figured he'd met his match and might ruin the deal if he tried to negotiate a higher price. Cortina held all the aces in this deck.

"You must stay and enjoy our hospitality, Baron Moncrieff. Tonight, we have a feast with music and women. You can rest afterward and depart tomorrow."

Moncrieff decided it was likely best not to spurn his host's offer. He saw an attractive *señorita* walk across the clearing beyond Cortina's house. He figured he could use the company of a woman or two. It had been a long time, and lascivious longings easily crept into his mind. "I'm pleased to accept your invitation. And you can call me Angus?"

Cortina was momentarily surprised at the Scotsman being

named after a breed of cattle. He did lean forward and lowered his voice in a mischievous tone. "One more little thing. Why do you wear the skirt?" He laughed before Moncrieff could answer. "And what do you wear under it?" His eyes filled with genuine curiosity.

Moncrieff laughed heartily in turn. "We call them kilts. They're very comfortable, very practical…and convenient with the ladies." He winked knowingly. The final phrase answered Cortina's question as to what was worn beneath the kilt, at least, in Moncrieff's case.

"You will truly enjoy our celebration, Angus."

Luke and Jaime had strapped the rustler to the saddle as best they could. Despite the darkness, the short drive of two dozen head back to Heaven's Gate was uneventful. By the time the sun crested the eastern horizon, they were securing the prisoner in the barn.

"Try to catch a little shuteye, Mr. Durham. We'll be moving out in a couple of hours." They left him manacled to one of the heavy support timbers.

"What are you going to do with him, *Señor* Dunn?"

"I'll run him down to Corpus in the morning. Sheriff Meaney can hold him there until I decide if he might lead us to Moncrieff. The Nuecestown jail is closer, but not fit for occupancy, even for a rustler."

"We need to move beeves to market, *Señor* Dunn."

Luke recognized that he still had some duties at Heaven's Gate, and rounding up beeves for market was one of them. Creatures like Moncrieff had driven down prices in the market as impacted by the war, but Luke had been of a mind to join with a larger herd heading north to Kansas. The herds were still being run north, skirting the wartime hostilities such as they were. Luke found himself once again torn in his near-constant dilemma between home and lawman duties.

"If I run this man to Corpus first thing, I should be back by late morning, Jaime. With the beeves our rustler friends helped gather, we need to add another fifty or sixty head. If our *vaqueros* work hard, we should be able to get a decent herd to Victoria in a couple of days. We can pay them a bonus from the reward for Moncrieff."

"Reward?"

"Yep, there's a reward." Luke smiled. "Guess, we can figure to give a little bonus for getting those cattle up to Victoria. Of course, we have to catch that low-down rustler first."

"Thank you. Julia is expecting again." Jaime smiled at revealing the news.

"Must be something in the drinking water around here. There's going to be another Dunn, too."

The two hugged at the good news.

They were distracted from the barn. "Hey, a little help. Nature's calling."

Luke shrugged resignedly. "Always something. Keep a gun aimed on him, Jaime. I'll let him do his business, and then we can be about ours."

Luke was still uncertain as to whether to pursue the Scotsman. He kept reminding himself to be patient.

Moncrieff was pleasantly surprised at the unbridled passions with which the Mexicans celebrated. Cortina held court at one end of the hacienda courtyard. Candles lit the scene, casting flickering reflections on a fountain in the midst of it all. Men and women were eating and drinking as though there'd be no tomorrow. Festive music blared from guitars, trumpets, and voices, as a small mariachi band strolled about. Liquor flowed in plenteous quantities and merriment abounded.

Cortina whispered something in the ear of an especially attractive dark-haired young woman. She was the woman Moncrieff had briefly spied earlier. She made no delay in seductively dancing her way across the courtyard, dodging revelers before arriving at the Scotsman's side.

"Me llamo Carlotta, señor." Her luscious deep-red lips had a certain sexy pout to them. Her black hair flowed over the silken white skin of her bare shoulders. Her hand found its way to Moncrieff's knee just above the hem of his kilt. *"¿Te gusta?"* There was nothing subtle about this woman.

Did Moncrieff like her? He liked her like a bull in heat. *"Sí."* An excited yes was all he could muster.

Carlotta looked down at the Scotsman's kilt. His arousal had become obvious. She sunk to her knees, and her head disappeared beneath folds of wool.

Moncrieff was oblivious to the curious eyes that were now enjoying watching his fully ecstatic pleasuring. She'd confirm what was beneath the kilt.

A smiling face soon reappeared. *"Muy grande, señor. Muy grande."* She sidled up against him, now giving him a closer view of her ample breasts and the aroma of sweet perfume. *"¿Nosotros iremos a la cama?"* She wanted more. A bed awaited.

Moncrieff took no persuading. He smiled fleetingly at Cortina, as Carlotta led him to a convenient bed in a semi-hidden side alcove. The booze was beginning to affect him, but it mattered not to his libido. With the cattle deal done, he was in no hurry to leave Camargo and Cortina's hacienda. He was more than willing to share a convenient feature of his kilt with the lusty Mexican maiden.

"I'm told this Angus Moncrieff fellow is headed to Laredo. One of the men who stole our longhorns works for the

Scotsman and will testify against him to avoid the hangman. Moncrieff has a handsome price on his head."

Elisa sat beside Luke on the bench overlooking the now picket-fenced front yard. Her head leaned against his chest. She heard his words about a reward and knew that he concluded with that information so she wouldn't protest so much. He'd just returned from chasing Comanche and hadn't been home but a couple of weeks. Part of that time had been retrieving Heaven's Gate beeves from a trio of rustlers and more of it was spent getting a larger herd together and moving it to Victoria to join a larger trail drive. She knew Luke had already used precious time, but she selfishly wanted him to herself. She relished the fact that the Texas legislature had won a concession from the Rebel government in Richmond to defer men serving in what amounted to Texas Rangers. Luke wouldn't be going off to some far away battlefront, so long as Confederate conscription officers followed the law. She prayed that he'd continue to avoid such a confrontation.

"I'm running out of patience over this Baron Moncrieff business, Lisa. I am thinking of going by Nuecestown to get Jake. Figure to leave day after tomorrow." Luke's words lingered. They'd have another day before he'd be leaving.

"I hear tell the Yankee ships haven't been seen on the Gulf for several days." She shifted the conversation.

Luke thought on that a moment, stroking his mustache as was his habit. "Sheriff Meaney told me that Rip Ford is preparing to launch an assault on the federal forces near Brownsville. If hostilities are anywhere close to ending, the word sure hasn't yet arrived in South Texas."

"I hope and pray we might all return to some sort of normal life, though I fear there'll be a lot of resentment, Lucas."

Luke had long ago learned to respect Elisa's perspectives on their world. He couldn't help but agree that she could well be right about resentment. "Forgiveness is difficult for many folks, Lisa." He gently stroked her hair. He looked down lovingly into the liquid pools of blue that were her eyes. She'd borne him five children, and now another was on the way. He took in how beautiful she was—how lucky he was.

Elisa could feel the beat of his heart as she returned his gaze. "I love you too."

"I wouldn't be heading to Laredo, Angus. *Seria peligroso*...very dangerous." Cortina wore a sincere expression as he doled out fatherly-like advice.

"How do you know this, Cheno?"

"I know most everything in Texas. I've heard that a Texas Ranger will be hunting you."

Moncrieff shot back a questioning look. "One Texas Ranger? I should worry?"

"You should worry very much if Texas Ranger Captain Dunn is on your trail."

"I thought there were no Texas Rangers."

"*No es verdad*, Angus. Not true." Cortina's expression turned darker. "This one is a favorite of famed soldier and Texas Ranger Rip Ford. Dunn has never failed to get his man. Never. If you are his prey, you will surely be captured or killed."

"By just one man?"

Cortina smiled sardonically. "I think Carlotta would like you to stay alive." He chuckled at the visual that crossed his mind. "She likes your kilt." The implication was that she liked what was under Moncrieff's kilt.

On the one hand, Moncrieff was determined to head to Laredo. He wasn't one to be put off by what he considered fairy tales. Then again, dallying a while with Carlotta was tempting. Indeed, Laredo could wait. He had to replenish his supply of livestock at the least. If the Texas Ranger was hunting him, the Scotsman was bent on making him wait. He grinned at Cortina. "Perhaps you are right, Cheno." His grin broadened. "¿Dónde está Carlotta?"

SEVEN
NO PREY, NO HUNT

LUKE'S PATIENCE had worn thin. For all his love of Elisa and Heaven's Gate, he yearned to hunt down the Scotsman.

"What do you think, Jake? You up for finding the Scotsman?"

Having been rejected by the Confederate army mostly by virtue of a somewhat checkered past and borderline marksmanship, Barber never had to be asked twice to join Luke on a mission. He was a loyal and enthusiastic supporter. "You think that Comanche chief will be a help?"

"Having One Arrow along can't hurt us. He's an experienced tracker and deadly with bow and arrow. And, he's smart as Comanche go."

"Sounds good to me." Barber turned serious. "Kinda gettin' to feelin' sorry for the savages, Luke. Disease is killing some, the buffalo are dwindling, and White folks are eating away at the frontier."

Luke sighed. He fully grasped what Barber was saying and appreciated the man's perspective. "It's a tough world, Jake. I recall back in Ireland, the British ruled through exercising their military might over us. More men...better weapons...fear... terror. They tried to destroy the heritage, the language, the stories that made us who we were as Celts. The Comanche and other tribes face a power that is taking away their culture. It doesn't matter if they held the land for hundreds of years, they will yield to the power of the White man just as they did to the Mexicans." Luke paused thoughtfully. "The Indians understand power, too. It's always been about power and control with them, as tribes made war and conquered other tribes. They even enslaved their prisoners. The strong consume and rule the weak, Jake. Recall, the Karankawas on the Texas coast practiced cannibalism against their prisoners. That made their enemies think twice about fighting them. But now they're dying off from White man's diseases." Luke looked off at the vista of grasses of the Nueces Strip that lay before them. "Now and then, a Three Toes or One Arrow comes along. They are trying to understand how to survive against a far stronger power. They know they must adapt to change, but are striving to figure out how. Doesn't help that trusts are built and broken. It's a vicious cycle, Jake."

Barber hadn't quite expected a culture lesson from Luke, though it didn't surprise him that the Texas Ranger had thought on and likely even studied these sorts of things. After all, he couldn't forget that Luke knew the names of nearly every flower and shrub in South Texas. "I see your point, Captain. It's like the savages spent centuries frozen in time. They're tough fighters, but it's like the Yanks and Rebs. The Federals have more resources an' are wearin' the Confederates down."

For all their riding together on the trail, Luke and Barber had never had this sort of deep conversation. The Texas Ranger gazed appreciatively at Barber. "You ready to ride, Jake?" Conversation ended. Time to tend to business.

One Arrow stood silently in front of his teepee. His senses absorbed the beauty surrounding him. The sights and sounds of the hills were as a symphony of life to him. It saddened him that his days of enjoying his cultural heritage were inexorably disappearing. He felt in his bones that the end was growing near for his people, for life as they had known it. He almost resented the responsibility thrust upon him by the death of Three Toes. One Arrow had become responsible for the well-being of more than three dozen Penateka Comanche. He had found it necessary to mature quickly. And just the night before, Cactus Flower had borne him a son. Part of him yearned for the freedom of roaming the trails of the high hill country hunting animal and human prey.

"What has captured your mind, my chief?" As if on cue, Cactus Flower appeared beside him. She stood expectantly while nursing their newborn son, a new Comanche warrior to be.

"I fear we must soon move north to land White man is giving us. The old ways are dying." He looked at the child in her arms. "He will grow up in different world."

Cactus Flower looked at the bundle in her arms. His world would indeed be far different and yet the same in many respects. She shared One Arrow's doubts about Comanche acceptance into the White man's world. "When must we go?"

"Soon...too soon."

Dallying at Cortina's hacienda in Camargo was wearing thin on Moncrieff. Carlotta was more than willing to explore the inner reaches of his kilt most any time the opportunity afforded itself. There was seemingly no slaking of her thirst for his Scottish virility perceived or otherwise.

He gave serious consideration to heading up to Laredo if for no other reason than to see if the Texas Ranger was awaiting him. He had no beeves remaining that he might sell at Fort McIntosh so had no business reason to justify heading north. He yearned to leave Cortina's hospitality, but the question at hand was to where? It was a given that he needed to rebuild his inventory. With Cortina close at hand and given the bandit leader's iron-fisted grip on the region, Moncrieff wasn't going to be taking Mexican beeves anytime soon. He was resolved to bid his goodbyes to Cheno Cortina. The sooner the better.

Barber and Luke rode slowly along the Pedernales River looking for sign. The Texas Ranger finally paused beneath an escarpment that he recognized. "Remember this, Jake?"

Barber scanned the area. "Looks as though someone spent some time making it look like nobody ever lived here."

Luke dismounted and kicked at a low mound of dirt. Soon enough, he was kicking up clouds of charcoal dust. He walked toward a break in the trees to the north. "They couldn't hide the tracks from the travois or horses, Jake. From the looks of this place and the trail, I'd guess they left three or four days ago. There's been no rain to wash away their sign."

"Maybe One Arrow decided to rejoin his people up north, Captain."

"Likely right, Jake. With that infernal renegade warrior Crouching Lion gone, the chief had no reason to delay. Even if he had a couple of hundred warriors, he knew he'd only put off the inevitable."

"We gonna go after him, Captain?"

Luke mounted Big Horse and sat for a moment in the saddle. He gazed up the trail One Arrow and his band had surely followed. Part of him longed to pursue the chief and renew their partnership, but common sense told him One Arrow had made his decision and Luke should let he and his

Penateka Comanche find their way unencumbered. "Maybe we'll meet him another time, Jake. Let's go see whether there's any news in Laredo."

"*Siento verte ir, Angus.*" Cortina was genuinely sorry to see Moncrieff leave. He'd enjoyed the Scotsman's company. Cheno sat at his favorite spot under a shady overhang beside the entrance to the hacienda. The sun was high, and the midday heat was stifling. "And Carlotta will miss you." He winked emphatically.

Moncrieff couldn't help but smile at that. The Mexican whore had exhibited an insatiable appetite for the baron. "Perhaps I should leave her my kilt."

The two men laughed heartily at the baron's humor.

"*¿A dónde vas, Angus?*"

"I'm heading back to Corpus Christi, Cheno. If what you say about that Ranger is true, perhaps I'd better avoid him."

"If you find more beeves, visit me again, my friend." He smiled with just a hint of arrogance. "Next time, be sure none of them are mine." He smiled again, but the implication was anything but friendly.

Moncrieff would be traveling alone, as he'd let his *vaqueros* go. There was no point in paying them further until he settled into his next venture. He told Cortina that he'd be heading to Corpus, in case the Ranger showed up in Camargo and inquired as to his whereabouts. His plan was to travel to Brownsville, cross to Matamoros, and catch a boat to New Orleans. With the war apparently grinding to a halt, he calculated that there'd be great opportunities abounding to make money from a defeated Confederacy.

It didn't take long for Moncrieff to gather his belongings. He even found time for a brief but satisfying dalliance with Carlotta. By mid-afternoon, he was mounted up and ready to ride. He wanted to get to Rio Grande City on the Texas side before sundown. He waved to Cortina and a weeping Carlotta who was hugging the kilt he'd given her.

"*Vaya con Dios, Angus.*"

"Sorry to have heard of Sheriff Stills demise," Luke uttered grimly. "Glad to see you're still alive and well, Sheriff Thornton." Luke and Barber sat on their horses in front of the Laredo jail.

"You ain't brought no stinkin' dead bodies for me like ya did fer Stills, have ya, Ranger?" Thornton was a tobacco chewer like Stills had been. He chewed thoughtfully, smiled, and spat into the dust in front of the horses, eliciting a snort from Big Horse.

Luke chuckled. "Not this time. We're just passing through."

"Lookin' for a particular troublemaker, Captain Dunn?"

"You heard anything of a scoundrel named Angus Moncrieff?"

Thornton gave Luke's information a second or two to sink in. "Couple of them Mexican *vaqueros* were said to be talkin' at Texas Jack's Saloon of herding beeves to Camargo for a fella by that name. They had plenty of money, so beeves must've been sold."

"Camargo?"

"I doubt y'all will catch them *vaqueros* now. Hear tell they be headed to Nuevo Laredo."

Luke glanced at Barber. "Doesn't look like Moncrieff has plans to come to Laredo. Those *vaqueros* say anything else?"

"Not especially. There was rumor of the Scotsman headed to Corpus, but I doubt he'd be tellin' folks where he'd be headin'. Them *vaqueros* said he was carrying on with Cheno Cortina and one of his whores."

"Thanks, Sheriff. Guess we'll have to wait for Moncrieff to

pop up again. A man like that will surely find some way to rob and cheat the good citizens of Texas. He won't lie low for long. Not in his nature." Luke felt a bit self-righteous as the words left his mouth. He felt confident that there'd be plenty more Moncrieffs in the coming months.

Moncrieff decided it was time to blend in with the scenery. He had another kilt, but decided he'd bring less attention to himself with more traditional western garb. There'd be time for breaking out his Scottish finery again. Could be, there was another Carlotta lurking in South Texas who'd be curious about what lurked under his kilt.

He'd spent an uneventful night in Rio Grande City. If he could keep a steady pace and avoid Apache, rogue bandits, and soldiers, he'd likely arrive in Brownsville in about three days.

With any luck, the Scotsman felt confident he'd be enjoying Bourbon Street in New Orleans in another week or so. He planned to link up with some old friends and see what sort of new venture they could conjure up. He'd left a storage trunk with an acquaintance and would be able to swap out clothes he'd been wearing off and on for weeks. He yearned to get them properly cleaned of Texas trail dust. Moncrieff also sought the comfort of the soft wool of the kilts he'd left in that trunk.

Major Gordon Belknap looked out beyond the walls of Fort Brown. He sensed trouble but as yet his scouts had brought no especially untimely news.

"What you looking for, Major Belknap?"

The voice from his rear startled Belknap. He turned and executed a salute. "Sir?"

Colonel Theodore Barrett was newly assigned to the Brownsville post. "At ease, Major. You looking for something in particular?"

"Just a gut feeling, sir. I know for sure there's a lot of Rebel cotton sitting out there awaiting transport to Matamoros."

Barrett shrugged. He was anxious for battle but unsure as to whether a shipment of cotton might be enough to trigger a fight. "Our job is to guard the Port of Brazos Santiago, Major. I'm not so sure we should be worried about a storehouse of Confederate cotton."

"The Rebs seem to think we just might try to take their cotton, sir." Belknap wasn't especially anxious for a fight. Talk was that the end of the war was near at hand. He turned to the colonel. "You brought a lot of green recruits, sir."

"They're all colored men, Major. I've been told they can fight, but I've seen no proof." Barrett didn't want to let on that he was frustrated that after four years of war he had not yet had an opportunity to lead troops in battle. "We'll see what our patrols have to say, Major Belknap."

"Yes, sir." Belknap saluted.

"You're dismissed, Major."

Belknap strode off wondering what made this new commandant tick. He sensed that the man wanted to do battle but wasn't sure how to instigate it.

EIGHT
LIVE ANOTHER DAY

HOT AND DUSTY were fully inadequate to describe the conditions. Luke and Barber sought shade during the day and traveled in the early evening and morning to avoid the sweltering heat. It was as much to conserve the strength of their horses as themselves. They'd had the foresight to carry plenty of water. It was warm but refreshing. They soaked their bandannas from time-to-time and wrapped them around their necks in an effort to cool off. Now and again, they'd pour a little water into their hats and let the horses guzzle.

Ever since Luke had opened up to Barber's question about the conquest of the Indians, the two managed occasional probing conversations. Mostly, they rode along keeping their thoughts to themselves. This day, as they sat in the sheltering shade of a lonely live oak motte and leaned back against their saddles, Barber figured it was time to pose another heavy question. It was nearly hot enough to not need to boil the water to brew the coffee. Sometimes it can be so hot that simply the exertion of talking can be too much. Barber decided to talk anyway. "Captain?"

"What's on your mind, Jake?"

"What do you think our lives are gonna be like after the war?"

Luke scrunched up his eyes, tipped back his hat, and stroked his mustache. He looked over at Barber. "You been conjuring up that question for a while, haven't you?" Luke removed his bandanna and wrung it out before placing it back around his neck. "Dang, but it's hot."

"Lotta blood good and bad been shed on both sides, Captain."

Luke sighed. He was going to have to answer the question. He looked up thoughtfully at the sky. "Been thinking about it myself. Worst case, the Yankees declare what they call martial law, Jake. By that, they'll likely be telling us what we can do and when we can do it. They might keep that up for a couple of years until the politicians figure they've beaten us into submission."

Barber looked incredulously at Luke. "You really think they can do that, Captain?"

Luke chuckled in a wry sort of way. "They will have won the war, Jake. They can do as they please." Luke picked up a pebble and threw it out into the grasses. "Remember Lincoln suspended that *habeas corpus* thing. He threw newspapermen that opposed him into jail with no speedy trial. He can plumb well do whatever he wants."

"*Habeas* what?"

Luke smiled. He loved teaching opportunities even in the oppressive heat of the Nueces Strip. "It's about having a right to appear before a judge, Jake, and know what crime you're being charged with. Lincoln jailed folks he saw as his enemies just for disagreeing with his views on the war and slavery. *Habeas corpus* is supposed to protect folks from that sort of behavior." He smiled. "But back to your question. I don't know that life on the Nueces Strip is going to change much when the war ends. At least, my cousins won't have to run cotton down to Matamoros." Luke offered up a guarded snicker. "Eastern Texas with its plantations is going to feel the full weight of any post-rebellion federal agenda, and I expect it'll be pretty harsh. You can count on some lily-livered snake-spined politicians in Austin cozying up to folks sent from Washington."

"What do you figure to do, Captain?"

"My guess is they won't want Texas Rangers running around the countryside. I've got a loving wife, passel of children, and a ranch to tend to. What's Jake Barber going to do?"

Barber wasn't used to Luke turning the tables on him. "Hadn't thought much about me, Captain. Maybe I'll try to start a business in Corpus."

"Maybe so." Luke scanned the sky. "Sun's getting lower, Jake. Let's mount up."

Moncrieff's strategy was to avoid that notorious Texas Ranger he'd heard about and live another day. He still thought of Texas as his land of opportunity. With the distinct possibility of the rebellion ending soon and the Confederacy being on the losing side, he instinctively knew that opportunities would abound. With slavery ended, the plantations in east Texas would be great targets for land deals. As he drew ever closer to Brownsville, he wondered how many times he might sell the same piece of land multiple times to speculators living outside Texas...or maybe even simply living in western or northern Texas.

"Halt! Who goes there?"

Moncrieff had by good or bad luck encountered a pair of Confederate pickets. He had no idea that an encampment might be near. "Baron Angus Moncrieff, late of Corpus Christi and traveling to Brownsville. I mean no harm."

One picket turned to the other. "He could be a spy, Seth."

Seth looked Moncrieff up and down. "Let's take him to Captain Robinson."

"I only wish to pass through and catch a boat to New Orleans, kind sirs."

"Dismount and hand over your guns and whatever that is hanging at your side." The picket pointed to the claymore that Moncrieff was half tempted to use on them. The only thing holding him back was not knowing how many more Rebel troops he might yet encounter. The rifle pointed at him also tended to emote persuasive powers over him. But he was determined to not be delayed.

Stepping forward to relieve Moncrieff of his pistol, Seth crossed the line of sight between the Scotsman and the other picket. The baron seized the moment to draw out the claymore and deliver a sound thwack aside the Seth's head. Before the second picket could react, Moncrieff pushed Seth into him, leaped forward, and brought the full weight of the weapon down on the man's head. It was a skull-splitting blow. The baron pulled back. One picket was dead and the other out cold. No shot had been fired. It was unlikely anyone had heard the skirmish. Moncrieff bent down and tied and gagged the unconscious picket.

Now that he was aware of Confederate troop activity in the area, the Scotsman decided he'd need to be far more cautious. While it might add a day to his trip, he decided to head due south, cross the Rio Grande, and follow the river to the Gulf. He felt he'd just as likely find a boat headed to New Orleans from Matamoros as from Brownsville. Importantly, he wouldn't be at risk of being accused of spying and wind up hanging from some Rebel noose.

The soft glow of lamp lights shone through the windows of the sparse population of stores and dwellings in San Diego, as

Luke and Barber rode easy-like into town just before sunset. The deep golden-orange sky behind them hinted at a beautiful tomorrow. One building caught their attention, as it was lit up especially bright. Turned out to be a church.

"What's going on, Captain? It ain't Sunday. Lot of cayuses tied at the rail…seems to be quite a few folks gathered."

"I kind of expected we'd run into someone back near the outskirts of town. Now, we know where folks went. I've got a feeling something big is brewing that's got folks riled up."

They pulled up easy-like in front of the church, dismounted, and hitched their horses.

Luke led the way to the front door and slowly eased it open. He scanned the room. No one even noticed his entrance. Every pew was full. The atmosphere, well, it was decidedly somber. Luke turned to Barber and whispered. "I'd guess someone important died, Jake."

Luke moved slowly and placed his hand on the shoulder of an elderly man seated closest to the exit. When a six-foot-three mountain of a Texas Ranger puts his hand on your shoulder, it gets your attention. Luke motioned the man to join him outside, took one more look back at the weeping mass of people, and exited with the elderly man. Barber took a final look and followed.

"Pardon my interrupting you, but what's going on, sir?"

The old man looked at Luke and Barber through tear-reddened eyes. "Who are you? Didn't you get the news?"

"Been on the road from Laredo? What news?"

"General Lee surrendered at Appomattox." Tears streamed down the old man's cheeks. "And some man named Booth killed President Lincoln. Coward shot him from behind." The old man was now sobbing such that he struggled to breathe.

Barber stood back aghast at the news. "This ain't good, Captain."

"Deeply sorry, mister." Luke tried to console the old man. He urged the man back inside the church. As he stepped back inside, Luke scanned the place. He spotted someone he recognized, but the man was sitting on the far side away from his and Barber's position. Luke had already risked disrupting the scene and decided discretion was in order. Given his own mixed feelings about Lincoln and his ambivalence about the war, Luke figured he'd have to wait patiently until the wake or whatever they called it broke up. He was of a mind that the citizens of San Diego were more upset about Lee's surrender than Lincoln's assassination. He whispered to Barber. "Jake, I see that sharpshooter fellow Clay Bell over yonder. I want to talk with him." He looked around and saw an old gnarled empty pew against the back wall. "Let's sit over there and wait."

Once they were situated on the rickety old bench, Barber leaned over to Luke and whispered, "what you have in mind, Captain?"

Luke put his finger to his lips and gave Barber a wait and see sort of look.

Long toward midnight, the crowd began to break up. The sniffling and tears had pretty much stopped even among the women. Not much had been said. Given the mixed reasons for the sadness, it was probably just as well. Some were sad the war had ended, others upset that they'd lost. There were equally mixed feelings about President Lincoln, as much over how he'd died as over him having died at all. Luke saw Bell moving toward the exit. By now, he'd spotted Luke waiting for him.

Bell moved toward Luke. "Captain Dunn. Tough circumstances."

"When did you hear the news?"

"Just yesterday. A courier brought flyers from San Antonio. I happened to be in town getting supplies."

"Sad news, Clay. Sad news indeed. I worry about how the country will react. There'll surely be some who'll blame every southerner for Lincoln's death."

Bell shook his head knowingly in agreement.

"You going back to the ranch?"

Bell squinted at Luke. It was late, and he was tired. "Whatcha got in mind, Captain Dunn?"

By now, Barber was getting especially anxious to learn what Luke was thinking.

"I've got a little post-war cleanup in mind. There's a gang of cutthroats wreaking havoc up on the northern reaches of the Strip…up toward Uvalde."

Barber raised his eyebrows. He had a fair idea of the sort of thing Luke had in mind, but he wondered at how the Ranger had heard about the gang's activities.

Bell eyed Luke and Barber appraisingly. He'd recovered physically, and to a lesser extent, mentally from the Cole Younger ambush near Victoria. "What sort of cleanup, Captain?"

"I learned about this gang from some folks back in Laredo who'd managed to escape the gang's killing and stealing. Thought you might like to join us in bringing those Quantrill outliers to justice."

"Justice? Dead or alive?"

Luke offered up an unusual expression. He wasn't generally of a mind to seek revenge. "I expect mostly dead."

"Just three of us?"

"I have another couple of men in mind to throw in with us, Clay."

The thought of getting back at the gang that had wiped out his unit had considerable appeal for Clay Bell. "When we leaving?"

"We've gotta resupply back at Nuecestown. Got a bit of recruiting to do." Luke smiled wryly at the thought of the former Rebel sharpshooter joining his pursuit of Younger. "See what you can muster from your folk's ranch. I expect you'll want that Sharps rifle with the scope. We'll meet back here day after tomorrow." He nodded goodbye to Bell and turned to Barber. "Let's get some shuteye."

For Luke's part, he figured that everyone around Corpus Christi likely knew about Lee's surrender and Lincoln's assassination. He was pretty confident there'd still be residual fighting, if not outright mayhem owing to the temporary chaos. Keeping order would be tough. Perhaps Luke's biggest personal challenge would be convincing Elisa of the need to pursue Cole Younger and his remaining outliers from Quantrill's Raiders.

★★

Just a tad before sunup, Luke was awakened by a strange moaning. Opening one eye, his hand reflexively moved to gently grasp the handle of one of his Colt revolvers. He heard the moan again and sat bolt upright. He surveyed the campsite once and realized that Barber was awake and he was the source of the moaning. "Jake…Jake…What's the matter?"

Barber gave Luke a squinty-eyed pained expression. "Didn't want to bother you yesterday, Luke, but it's getting worse."

"What? What's getting worse?"

"I broke a tooth…damn but it hurts."

"Well, we can't have you moaning all morning, Jake. You'd scare away most any varmints with that pitiable sound. Let's head back into San Diego. I saw a smithy shop…"

"Smithy shop!?" Barber interjected. Then he moaned again, as though the words had hurt as air passed his broken tooth.

"We're going to trade a moment of pain for long-term relief. Trust me." Luke had already begun to break camp.

They rode back to San Diego, Barber following reluctantly. Only the great pain and Luke's promise of relief kept him on the trail and following his Ranger boss right on up to the smithy shop. Luke rang the chime outside the shop.

"Dadnabit, who the hell is it at this ungodly hour?" The smithy was none too pleased to be awakened from his booze-induced slumber from the previous evening's pity party over losing the war. The sun was barely pushing at the horizon.

Luke was his nonplussed self. "I'm Luke Dunn, and we've got an emergency here. You got some horseshoe pullers and a bit of whiskey we could borrow?"

Barber threw in a moan for emphasis.

The smithy cooled a bit. "Well, I'm no goldarned dentist."

"No problem. If you have those shoe pullers and a slug of whiskey, I'll do the nasty work."While the smithy fetched the requested pullers and liquor, Barber reluctantly slid from his saddle.

The smithy returned with the pullers and handed them to Luke. "Sorry, I couldn't find no whiskey. Drank it all last night." He then stood back to watch.

"I don't need the booze, Captain. Just get this over with quickly." He moaned again as punctuation.

The sun had just crested the dark skyline to the east, so there was pretty much enough light for Luke to see what he was doing. Barber laid back and opened his mouth wide. "Which tooth is...oh, I see..." It was obvious and not going to be easy, as it was an upper tooth on the side. Luke hovered above Barber and twisted around so as to see better and get the shoe pullers into position. The jaws of the pullers were broad, and he only wanted to yank the broken tooth, not half the teeth in Barber's mouth. "Now, don't you move, Jake." He guided the jaws so as to get a solid grip on the busted molar. The Texas Ranger tried to appear confident as he clamped and pulled hard in one motion. Luke fell back into the dirt, pullers and tooth in hand, as Barber let out an unearthly yowl likely to awaken the entire town.

Barber sat a moment wide-eyed, then blinked.

"You okay, Jake?"

"Don't hurt so much anymore."

The smithy wiped some soot from his arms then handed Luke the dirty cotton rag. "Put this in his mouth, Ranger. It'll stop the bleedin'."

Luke got up and dusted himself off, then handed the pullers back to the smithy. "Thanks for your help," he said nonchalantly. He looked at his still bewildered friend who was managing to lift himself to a semi-steady standing position. Luke looked at the sooty cotton cloth, shook his head, and tossed it aside. He grabbed his own bandanna and handed it to Barber. "You'd best chomp on this for a bit, Jake...at least until any bleeding stops."

Barber rubbed his jaw and stuffed the rag into his mouth. He mumbled an unintelligible thanks to Luke.

"You ready to head to Nuecestown?" Luke was already easing on over to Big Horse. "We have some work to do and can't be lollygagging over busted teeth anymore."

Barber stood for a moment beside his horse and grasped the saddle horn. He knew he'd have to tough it out for a bit. The pain had mostly disappeared and had been replaced by dull throbbing. He managed to get his foot in a stirrup and swing his big frame into the saddle to the patient stares of Luke and the smithy. "You gonna wait all day, Captain, or are we ridin' to Nuecestown?"

Luke offered up a broad sheepish smile. Never underestimate a Texas Ranger.

NINE
QUANTRILL'S GANG

COLE YOUNGER HAD JUST ABOUT HAD ENOUGH of his little side adventure into Texas. With the rebellion over, what was left of Quantrill's Raiders would be called to disband. Quantrill was dead anyhow, victim of a bullet to the spine in a shootout with federal troops up in Kentucky. Younger was now of a mind to join up with the James brothers and do a bit of bank robbing. He had to make ends meet financially somehow or other.

His problem now was what to do with his dozen or so remaining hangers on from the escapades he led through Texas. In any case, Younger was of a mind to head north. He rather missed Kansas and the violent opportunities it had afforded him. Time seemed to be on his side. The south was mentally shell-shocked and economically devastated in the aftermath of the rebellion. He'd be able to move northward easily, as he even figured to do a bit of robbing and pillaging along the way.

For now, Younger's raiders had found a comfortable place to relax in the hilly, relatively cooler region around Uvalde, a spot that had been mostly isolated from the ravages of the war.

✯✯

Luke permitted himself a hint of a smug smile. He'd successfully recruited Walker Carson and Jubal Strong against the ardent protests of their wives. Carson's wife, Scarlett, had been especially livid at her man being lured away despite Luke's history of kindnesses to her husband, and while Strong's wife, JD, protested there was a sense of envy that she'd have loved to join the mission. She actually might have tagged along had she not been pregnant again. The surprise addition to the group was Rex Rucker. Rucker had finished up his assignment in Washington DC and wasn't fully ready to settle down. His left arm wasn't much use, but he felt passionate about avenging the Younger gang's murder of his brother. Pastor Rucker had blessed his son's intentions, though he deeply feared losing his only remaining son. It would surely be in God's hands.

Luke persuading Elisa had been another matter altogether.

"Why?" Elisa narrowed her eyes to more fully communicate just how serious she was. She'd never before really questioned her husband's decisions to pursue the lawbreaking dregs of society. It wasn't about money, as the ranch brought in far more than the bounties Luke still collected as an unauthorized Texas Ranger. And she knew that it was a moral issue for Luke with his intense focus on bringing justice and a safer environment to the Nueces Strip, to Nuecestown, to their home. She stood before him now, hands on hips, her baby bump thrust out slightly. "The war, the rebellion...whatever it was...is over, Lucas. We need you here."

What could he say? Luke looked directly into her eyes and didn't say a word.

Ever so slowly, her hands dropped to her sides. Her expression began to soften. She knew this was an argument she would never ever win, assuming it even was about winning. A tear found its way down her cheek, her arms reached out, and she buried her face in her husband's chest. "Darn it, Lucas Dunn. Darn it. I love you." Then she froze and stepped back. Promise me one thing.

Luke looked down, gave her a disarmingly loving smile, and nodded. "You name it, Lisa. Whatever you want."

"Promise me this will be your last mission."

Luke flinched almost imperceptibly. He was quiet. Her eyes, the penetratingly heartfelt look she was giving him was melting any resolve he held. He nodded.

"Say it."

"I promise."

She shook her head slowly. "Promise what?"

"I promise this will be my last mission." He pulled her close and prayed silently that he could be good to his word.

"The children are asleep, Lucas." She looked up at him with an invitation she knew he could never ever refuse. She pressed tightly against his well-muscled, range-hardened body. The contours of her body fused with his, she felt his manhood rise, his kiss coursed to her inner core. The bedroom was too far.

They never parted from their ardent embrace, as they slowly slipped down on the mountain lion skin laying before the fireplace. Elisa hoisted her dress just above her hips and pulled Luke's trousers to his knees. He smothered her with his lips and caressed her pregnancy-swollen breasts. They'd disrobed just enough to enable the sating of their intense passions, as she locked him with her hips.

Bathed in exhaustion, Luke enjoyed lying with her after they'd satisfied their passions. These seemed like the most honest moments in their lives. An aura of warmth and vulnerability lay on their minds and bodies. The flickering flames from the fire shed a light that danced across her bare belly as she lay back in his arms. After a few moments, Luke whispered softly. "No more missions. But I'll defend you and Heaven's Gate against the fires of hell."

Elisa turned from the fire and brought her crystal blue eyes to bear on him. "I'm counting on that Lucas Dunn."

So it was that Luke, Barber, Strong, Rucker, and Carson found themselves saddled up and ready to depart from Heaven's Gate. Elisa had cooked up a huge breakfast replete with eggs, bacon, cornbread, peaches, and plenty of coffee. Full bellies were essential to sending men off on any such worthy venture. The aromas lingered seductively, and soon the five fully sated men were saying their goodbyes. Scarlett had come up from Corpus Christi, though Strong had spent the night with JD at Bernice's boarding house in Nuecestown. Luke was the last to mount up, as Peter, John, Andrea Anne, Michael, and Alma each had to be picked up and hugged in turn and his embrace of Elisa was an almost uncomfortably lingering one from the perspective of the men.

Luke leaned from the saddle to kiss Elisa once more. "I love you, my sweet Lisa." He gazed into her eyes. A Texas ranch woman was often expected to do the work of a man while never forgetting that she was a woman. Elisa was all that to Luke. He knew he was richly blessed.

She savored his kiss and then lightly patted his hand by way of silent farewell.

Scarlett walked over and stood beside Carson's horse. She placed her hand on his as it hung against his thigh. He doffed his hat, bent down, and kissed her...deeply.

Luke was finally ready to go, and that meant it was time for all five men to move out. They'd be heading northwest, as word had it that the remnants of the Quantrill Raiders outliers were camped at Uvalde not far from what had been Fort Inge.

They followed the road up to Nuecestown along the south bank of the Nueces River. They hoped to reach San Diego and hook up with Clay Bell before nightfall.

"Dammit, Cole, this sitting around is killing us. Why ain't we headed back north. You know Quantrill needs us."

Younger knew that William Quantrill, the leader of their guerrilla band of Confederate partisans, had been on the run after they'd attacked Lawrenceville, Kansas. He also knew that Quantrill had been shot and killed, and he was intent on keeping that information secret for as long as possible. It gave him a measure of control. During the recent rebellion, Quantrill's Raiders had killed better than 150 citizens and Union-sympathizing Kansas Jayhawkers. They had spent the winter of 1864 in Texas. While Younger had remained in Texas, Quantrill headed north to wreak more havoc upon Yankee sympathizers. They were desperados by any measure, but living under the guise of being a Rebel unit. He looked at his questioner. "I understand your frustration, John, but the war is over. Lee surrendered...Lincoln is dead. We'll wait for Quantrill to contact us. He knows where we are. Maybe Frank and Jesse will join us." He knew there was a risk to not telling the men of Quantrill's demise, but trust was the least of his worries.

The raider spat into the dirt. It wasn't the answer he sought. "We're sittin' ducks here, Cole. We're damned sittin' ducks."

Younger knew that eventually there'd be federal troops out looking for them, if they weren't already. Fort Inge sat empty for the present, and Uvalde afforded ready access to supplies, booze, and women. Their basic life necessities were being met. It was comfortable...perhaps too comfortable.

"Good to see you, Clay. You know Jake here. I'm pleased to introduce Jubal Strong, Rex Rucker, and Carson Walker."

Bell nodded to each in turn.

"I've known these men long enough to hold deep respect for their fighting abilities." He felt no need to explain in any detail his connections with the men. That really didn't matter for now.

Bell took a deep breath. "Do they know I'm the reason for this mission?"

"Pretty much. But Rex here's brother was your unit's captain. Stephen succumbed to his wounds." There was need to elaborate on Rex's stake in this mission.

Bell and Rucker exchanged nods. "Your brother was a fine officer, Mr. Rucker. Sorry for your loss."

Luke looked from man to man. "Y'all want to lollygag around San Diego tonight or head north now?"

Barber knew better than the others that it was foolish to resist Texas Ranger Captain Luke Dunn when his passion for a mission had been aroused. "I'll ride to hell and back for you, Captain. Let's ride." He spurred his horse and turned northward.

Luke followed, and the others took the cue and joined in. Six heavily armed men with a couple of pack horses made a sight for any passersby. Rifles, revolvers, and Bowie knives let the world know they had serious intentions. They were obviously out to take the measure of an enemy they all despised. Luke and his men had five days of hard riding ahead.

Younger awoke to find that two men had deserted the encampment during the night. He was down to eighteen battle-tested veterans. That they were the lowest dregs of society mattered not. They were loyal to him and shared his lust for booty and killing. They'd hung around Uvalde for better than two weeks. That was far too long for a gang used to being on the move, but he had decisions to make. He called his gang together, as he felt it was time to finally head north. He'd received a confirming message that Quantrill had indeed been mortally wounded up in Kentucky. He marveled a bit that these sorts of messages had a way of reaching him at different times from different sources, as the fledgling telegraph and the trains were mostly out of service.

"We've waited around long enough. Tomorrow morning we're heading north to join the James brothers. Y'all can go enjoy a final night in Uvalde." Little did he know how prophetic the use of the word "final" was, as he had no idea what was about to descend upon him. "Y'all should know that Quantrill was shot and killed by Yankees up in Kentucky. God rest his soul." More correctly, it was likely the Devil taking care of Quantrill's soul. "Y'all, do your drinkin' and whorin' to his memory."

If you were a barkeep or a whore in Uvalde, you never had it so good. Younger's men spread booze, money, and man juices like there'd be no tomorrow.

Luke and his outfit eschewed sleep during the final day of their ride. They shoved on through the night intent on reaching Uvalde before sunrise. The glow of the sun was just about teasing the horizon when Luke was first to make out a faint silhouette of a figure in the lingering pre-dawn shadows. They were upon it before they even realized it was a man staggering along the trail. "Whoa! Who goes?"

A gravelly voice moaned back, "Ike McGurdy." He quickly saw that he was facing six very heavily armed men. "Ain't got no guns." He almost fell, as he tried to raise one arm. "Just tryin' to get home."

"Where you coming from and how'd you get so beat up?"

"Younger gang."

"They close by? We're looking for them."

By now, McGurdy managed through swollen eyelids to spot Luke's badge. "Yes sir, Mr. Ranger sir. They be camped 'bout a mile due south of town in a shady spot 'longside the Leona River. They did some hell raisin' in Uvalde last night. I can vouch fer that. Said somethin' 'bout movin' on today. Yer only a mile or so from where they be camped."

Luke looked down at the man. It was clear from his appearance that he'd taken the worst part of a fight. His eyes were nearly swollen shut and a long welt ran across his cheek. One ear was covered tightly with a bandanna, likely to keep it —the ear—from falling off. "We appreciate the information, Mr. McGurdy. Sorry about your condition. Happy to share a canteen, but we best be moving on if we hope to put a whipping on the Younger gang."

"Bless you, Mr. Ranger. Them sonsofbitches can all go straight to hell."

In the dim light, Luke could barely see his men, but he knew they were anxious to get to doing what they'd come to do. He looked again at the bruised and battered man. "You strong enough to show us the way, Mr. McGurdy?" It almost pained him to ask.

McGurdy looked up through the slits that served as his eyes and growled, "Y'all can count on that. I'd walk through a nest of rattlers to see them meet the Devil that made 'em."

Luke stood straight in the saddle and took a deep breath. "Look to your guns, men. We'll approach from the southeast, so the rising sun will be behind us. Don't be doing any shooting until we get close." He knew that he needn't have told them to hold fire, but it never hurt to say so as adrenaline tended to overwhelm common sense.

Younger's men had found their way back to their campsite in groups of threes and fours. It was a blessing that they had horses, as their walking was more akin to staggering. That they had climbed into their saddles and found their way back to the campsite at all was likely a miracle of sorts. As they'd dismounted, a few leaned against their fellow revelers, lurching and careening into camp to find the sanctuary of their bedrolls. None could anticipate that most of them would never see the coming sunrise. There was a cacophony of cursing, groaning, pushing, and shoving not to mention a few dry heaving their guts out. They were a sorry sight, as they collapsed into orbs atop bedrolls.

The horses remained saddled in the natural ravine that formed a remuda. By the time the hints of sunrise had begun to sneak above the eastern horizon, most of the men slumbered around the dying embers of a couple of near-dead campfires. Peace for sure. Younger and a couple of his men made a vain attempt to set a watch, but all quickly succumbed to sleep. Their snoring was enough to drown owl hoots, coyote howls, and even frogs croaking beside the nearby creek. It was a stark contrast to their revels of just hours before. An aura of death lurked in the shadows, but they were oblivious to it.

Luke appreciated the faint pinkish glow creeping up from the horizon behind him. The sun would not crest the horizon for a few minutes yet. Luke had his spyglass in hand. He was ever grateful at having had the foresight to acquire that wonderful invention: the telescope.

McGurdy had led them to a rise looking down at Younger's camp a bit less than four hundred yards away. The gentle downward slope had plenty of tall grasses and brush that would serve as cover. Luke saw no pickets. Far as he could tell, no watches had been set. He permitted himself a guarded smile, as he noted the still-saddled horses milling about near the passed-out revelers. There were virtually no signs of life. In the still early morning air, he could just barely hear snoring above the chirp of crickets and occasional howls. The fires had yet to be stoked for breakfast. To Luke's thinking, this would be like shooting varmints in a barrel.

Luke motioned his band to dismount, figuring to move forward on foot to within a hundred yards. Luke turned to McGurdy and whispered, "Thanks, Mr. McGurdy. You just wait here while we take care of business." He scanned the five seasoned fighters standing before him. "Hobble your horses and leave your spurs here. We've got a bit of ground to cover as quietly as possible." It wouldn't do to have jingling spurs, squeaking leather, or snorting horses, even with their prey mostly passed out.

Bell carried his trademark Sharps rifle with its telescopic sight. In his mind, this was going to be a far better use of his skills than picking off Yankee officers and cannoneers. At a mere hundred yards, he'd likely get at least three kills before anyone stirred in defense. Barber and Strong were primed for action. Rex Rucker seethed inside to avenge his brother, while Carson displayed a maturity built in pitched battles against Apache and Comanche hostiles, Mexican bandits, and Yankee troops.

Luke had marked the pattern of the sleeping raiders on a slip of paper and given each man his assignment. There was no point in having six bullets plow into a single target. If they did their job properly, they'd eliminate at least half the enemy before they could react. The sun finally began its ascent above the horizon and caste shards of blinding light onto the camp from behind Luke's position. The enemy would be looking up hill and directly into the sun, if they were alive to look up at all. Finally, the bright rays bore full on into the encampment.

Luke nodded. Bell fired the first shot. The booming report of his Sharps echoed across the clearing and its slug tore into a body with enough force to lift it several inches off the ground. Quickly the air was shattered with gunfire. They could see the flinching of bodies as bullets shredded through blankets, skin, and bones. The Sharps rifle echoed above all. Those who survived the initial fusillade awoke confused and panicked. A second round of gunfire startled some of them into action that entailed opening an eye and squinting into the sun. To add to the resulting fright, Carson and Strong had cut notches in the ends of their bullets, resulting in an unearthly whining sound as they rained in upon their targets.

"Damn! Horses! Get to the horses!" There was no hesitation from a groggy but now awakened Cole Younger. He was wounded and bleeding, but grabbed his guns and lit out half naked on a dead run for his horse. The only fortune for the three near the remuda was a product of their own drunken laziness in not having removed the tack from the horses and sacked out near the campfire embers after their return from Uvalde. Younger and the two gang members with him mustered the strength to climb into their saddles, spurring their mounts to a near instant gallop away from the direction of gunfire. Younger had seen nothing of the attackers owing to the sun's blinding glare in his eyes, but the carnage wrought by whomever was out there dictated a hasty and decidedly desperate retreat.

Luke couldn't identify Younger specifically. He watched three men reach their horses and manage to bolt away. At least two appeared to be wounded. "Cease fire! Cease fire!"

There'd been virtually no return fire from Younger's camp. With the shooting stopped, an eerie stillness enveloped the scene.

Luke cautiously led his men forward. He looked back to see McGurdy staggering along behind, his strong spirit willing him to glory in the deaths of his tormentors. As they walked into the camp, they remained ever vigilant in case those that escaped returned.

"Captain, there ain't a single one of these men breathing."

Barber was amazed and almost horrified at the carnage they'd delivered in mere seconds.

Luke scanned the camp. He counted thirteen unmoving bodies. He couldn't help but offer a wry smile at their success. "Walker and Rex, y'all stand sentry. The rest of you look for personal effects, then grab a shovel." Luke placed a bag near one of the campfires to collect personal items from the deceased. "Mr. McGurdy, do you have the strength to stoke a fire?"

McGurdy forced a smile. "I'll do that, Mr. Ranger." He looked up admiringly at Luke. "I do thank you from the bottom of my heart, sir."

Luke nodded. Stroked his mustache, and blushed a bit. He wanted to say it was just another day's work, but that didn't seem to fit the occasion. "It was our pleasure, Mr. McGurdy. These men had it coming, and we delivered justice."

Luke pulled a sketch of Cole Younger from his pocket, and then examined each of the dead men. "Appears that we missed Younger," he stated with a tone of regret tinged with frustration. He sighed and looked over at the remaining horses. "I expect these folks won't be needing their horses. When we're done here, you can take a couple home for your trouble. I think the folks in Uvalde might appreciate a few as payment for the sufferings the Younger gang likely inflicted on their town."

Bell walked over to Luke. "Don't see Younger, Captain. I think I saw him escape, though he was surely wounded."

Luke shook his head regrettably. "Well, I expect Texas has seen the last of him. Sorry, we couldn't put him to rest."

Rucker joined them. "Yes sir, Captain. I saw him escape, too. No sense pursuing. I've lost any need to avenge Stephen's death. In a way, this is a sort of hollow victory. Killing Younger wouldn't have brought anyone back."

Luke stared off gravely and once again thoughtfully stroked his mustache. "Wise words, Rex. Wide words indeed."

Cole Younger rode like no tomorrow. While part of him desperately wanted to go back and see what army had descended on his gang, the pain of his wounds and the sense that going back would be a losing cause drove him to move on. Better to cut his losses and join up with the James brothers. With the war ended, there'd be opportunities to rebuild his gang far away from Texas. He was determined not to test Texans resolve again any time soon. Perhaps one day he'd learn what unearthly force had been unleashed on he and his gang.

TEN
LICKIN' WOUNDS

"*¿SEÑOR?*"

Moncrieff looked to his side. His day had already been filled with one frustrating event after another. There seemed to be no boats heading from Matamoros to New Orleans. It was incredibly inconvenient. He looked at the disheveled Mexican who'd shuffled up beside him. He gave the peon an insufferably condescending look. His response sounded akin to a rattler's hiss. "*¿Sí?*"

"*¿Quieres un bote?*" The man offered up a toothless smile as though ignoring the Scotsman's holier-than-thou attitude, as he asked whether he was looking for a boat.

That got Moncrieff's attention. He knew that *bote* translated to boat. "*¿Tienes un bote?*" Did this swarthy little excuse for humanity actually have a boat? Now, he wondered at the price. "*¿Cuanto hombrecito?*"

The man flinched ever-so-slightly at the insult. "*Nada, señor.*"

"*¿Nada?*" Instinctively, Moncrieff knew there had to be a price. Nothing was free—especially now.

The little Mexican nodded to a nearby alley. "*Ven conmigo, señor.*" He grabbed the Scotsman's elbow and pulled him toward the corner of a beige-colored stuccoed hacienda that led to the alley. "*Ven aquí.*"

Moncrieff's curiosity had been aroused. He permitted himself to be pulled. As they rounded the corner, he saw his price. Standing fetchingly against the wall with her hands cradling a growing belly and lips luscious as ever was none other than Carlotta. A piece of paper stuck from her cleavage. Moncrief was desperate. "*Er...Carlotta...maravilloso verte.*" He could at least pretend to be delighted to see her.

"*¿Nosotros vamos a New Orleans, Señor Moncrieff?*" Her eyes dropped to his pants. "*Dónde esta...*" She searched for the word. "Kilt?"

Moncrieff slipped a couple of pesos to the Mexican who scurried off as the Scotsman turned his full attention to Carlotta. He went to grab the paper from between her ample breasts. She pulled away, leaving him grasping a handful of thin air.

"Okay, I'll take you to New Orleans."

Carlotta smiled and handed him the note. She pointed to her belly. "*Yo embarazada.*"

Moncrieff could see that. He figured he could deal with it in New Orleans. He began to read the note. It was handwritten by Cortina and apparently directed one of his people to see to the baron's passage to Louisiana.

"*Nosotros nos casamos.*" She oozed the words out wantonly. She was proposing marriage.

Moncrieff's mind raced. No way he was going to marry this whore, pregnant or not. "Marry? Sure...but not until New Orleans."

"*¿Llevas* kilt?"

"Wear my kilt. Aye, lass. I'll wear it." He still had dreams of her wondrous explorations in Camargo.

Carlotta looked around. The two of them were hidden in the darkness of the alley. She unbuttoned his pants and lifted her skirt. She whispered passionately, *"hacer el amor."* Her voice trailed off as she wrapped herself around him.

A couple of hip thrusts, and he was done. What was he to do? It had been but a couple of minutes. It hadn't taken long to recall just how good she was. Yes, the kilt would have to once again be worn.

The frustrations of Moncrieff's day were now behind him. Passage out of this godforsaken place was assured. Moreover, his carnal passions had been satisfied. He pulled himself together and followed Carlotta to the docks and the boat that Cortina had arranged. It looked barely seaworthy, but it would have to do.

They found a room for the night, as the boat would depart at dawn. Carlotta was a more-than-willing companion.

Luke and his men finished up their business in Uvalde and began the ride home. The weather seemed to be getting ever warmer. Luke wasn't especially inclined to rest during the heat of the day, but the horses needed it more than the men. "Getting hot, men. Let's take a break next to those trees down by the Nueces. It's hot enough we might not need a fire to heat up some coffee." He spontaneously laughed at his little touch of humor.

They pulled up under the trees and unsaddled the horses to help them cool down. Luke let Big Horse take a long drink from the river. Soon enough, the men were eased back resting against saddles, chewing on dried venison, and sipping coffee.

Barber was first to break the near silence. "What you gonna do now, Captain?"

The other men were all ears anticipating Luke's response.

Luke leaned back against his saddle, stroked his mustache ever so slowly, and looked off at the silvery ripples of the meandering river. "Promised Elisa this would be my final mission. Guess, I'll be running the ranch and spending time with my family." He looked at each of the others in turn. He felt a desperate need to turn the attention from himself. "What about you, Jubal?"

"Expect I'll be followin' in yer footsteps, Captain. I got a family to care for, and yer cousin was talkin' about a cattle drive."

Carson picked up a stick and thoughtfully traced a random pattern in the dirt. "Scarlett and me...well, we haven't given up on the haberdashery, Captain. Got two young'uns to care for." He smiled broadly, "Just maybe we can grow our family a bit more." He looked off wistfully, as he thought on his beautiful wife with her silken alabaster skin and ravishing red hair.

Luke looked over at Rucker. "Rex, your father and mother likely need your help."

Rucker rubbed his chin a bit. "Got a great offer from the War Department, Luke. It had been the colonel's dream to take mother to Washington. I think I owe it to them and to Stephen's memory to take the offer. The colonel has his faith, and I'd rather be making him proud."

As Rucker's words trailed off, Bell got up and walked over to the river away from the others.

Luke wasn't going to let him off that easy. He stood and slowly ambled over to stand near Bell. He skipped a flat stone across the water. "Clay, I hope you satisfied what had stuck in your craw."

Bell looked out over the river. "Pretty much licked my wounds, Captain. Glad the damned war is over."

"You going back to the ranch?"

"Figure I can now. My conscience is clear, Captain. Rex there pretty much nailed it about vengeance being hollow."

Luke figured that was at least partly so. He wondered at how Bell had managed to deal with picking off often-unsuspecting enemy soldiers during the war. There had to be a moral conflict raging deep within Bell's psyche. "You ever feel a need to talk, Clay, you're welcome to come see us at Heaven's Gate."

"Appreciate that, Captain."

Luke walked on back to the campsite.

Barber chuckled. "Ain't you wondering about me, Captain?"

Luke allowed himself a good laugh. He'd rarely felt so at ease. "Should I, Jake?"

"Lots of work to do around Nuecestown, Captain. Bernice and Agatha are gettin' on in years and needin' help at the boardin' house."

"And?" Luke felt like he was pulling teeth to get information.

Barber smiled sheepishly. "Well…well, there's this half-breed daughter of a homesteader up the other side of the Nueces. Kinda caught my eye, Captain. I think the feelin's mutual."

Luke nodded. "Seems like everyone is pretty much returning to what folks call a normal life. I sure pray it'll be that way."

Bell returned to the campsite just as Luke spoke. He poured himself some coffee. "You think it'll be rough, don't you, Captain?"

"Lots of folks have axes to grind. And there'll still be lawbreakers and savages. I expect the Black folks will struggle with their new freedom. Likely some resentments will show themselves."

The little caravan stretched out over better than a mile, as it wended its way ever northward. Travois and horses kicked up plenty of dust that was inhaled in turn by squaws and children. One Arrow's entire village finally found its way to the banks of the Clear Fork of the Brazos River. What had been

Camp Cooper lay in decaying ruins. The scene was dismal, but the beauty of the surrounding countryside was enough to lift their spirits. The Comanche had been moved to the Indian Territory up just north of the Red River that marked part of the northern border of Texas.

One Arrow surveyed his little band. His people were hungry and tired of travel. He fought back the instinct to salve his sorrow with senseless raids. They had been defeated, but not in battle. It would not do to fight battles against an enemy that could muster great strength. Such suicide was not an option.

The band of Penateka Comanche gathered together and made camp for the night. As One Arrow curried his favorite pony, he was distracted by a figure that appeared seemingly from nowhere.

"You Comanche?" The White man was a grizzled old trapper with a long white beard and only a couple of service-able teeth. He wore a coyote-skin hat and buckskin shirt and leggings. He used a Kentucky long rifle as much as a crutch as a weapon. He was a throwback to another era.

One Arrow's look of surprise seemed to have been expected.

"Pretty damned good sneaking up on ya, ain't I?" The trapper slipped off his hat to reveal a bald head. "No scalp here. Sorry." He allowed himself a crackling chuckle and went on talking. "Yer brother Comanche gone north a couple of years ago. Call it Indian Territory." He pointed a gnarled hand northward. "Expect you'd best be followin'."

One Arrow shook his head slowly, as he stood trying to absorb the trapper's chatter. "You go Indian Territory?"

"Been there. Ain't too bad fer yer people." With that he whipped out a knife and threw it past a startled One Arrow. The blade pinned a rattlesnake to the stump that the serpent was coiled upon a mere five feet away. "Damned nasty critters. Sorry 'bout the surprise. He was given ya the evil eye."

One Arrow collected himself as best he could. "Me grateful."

"Name's Bear Wills. Who you be, Chief? You speak some English." The trapper cocked his head inquisitively.

"One Arrow. Me Penateka Comanche chief."

Wills surveyed the gathered assemblage of savages that didn't look especially savage. "Yer people look tired and hungry, Chief."

One Arrow looked at the apparition before him and nodded.

"Kilt a deer couple hours ago...maybe a short walk back yonder. I got plenty food for me. You can have the deer in exchange for a horse." The trapper had the good sense to make his charity part of a trade, lest he wound the Comanche pride.

One Arrow urged the trapper to follow him toward several horses nearby and placed the lead of one of his very own ponies in the man's hands. It was a sacrifice he felt that he must make. "You show me deer?"

Within an hour, One Arrow's people were feasting on venison. The trapper had been invited to stay and in a reasonably proficient Comanche tongue offered stories of his hunting exploits to the children.

One Arrow's facial expression revealed the intensity of deep thought as he observed the White man interacting with the Comanche. It confirmed to him that there could in fact be peaceful coexistence despite being culturally conflicted.

Come morning, Wills and the Comanche would part ways. For One Arrow, the chance encounter had kindled hope.

Moncrieff wasn't especially impressed with the rickety old sailboat, but it was hard to complain. The single-masted craft had seen many a day at sea, but he'd been assured that it was seaworthy. He and Carlotta would be holed up in a reasonably sheltered corner in the hold. The captain and his single crew member made it clear that they would stay out of their way.

The Scotsman had caught a glimpse of the cargo and was concerned that there were a couple of quite obviously heavy crates. Through cracks in the sides, he could see cannon balls. Contraband! There was at least one barrel of black powder, a chancy cargo if it should either be ruined by moisture or be ignited. It was strange, but discretion dictated that he not question it.

Moncrieff stood at the bow with his legs akimbo and his back leaning against the mast. He'd acceded to Carlotta's wishes and donned his kilt. As the boat approached the mouth of the Rio Grande as it spilled into the Gulf, he looked off to his left and saw a massing of troops to the east of Brownsville. He thought it strange, as he thought everyone would know of Lee's surrender nearly a month earlier.

He'd just begun to relax, when he felt a soft hand on his leg. Carlotta had crawled up from the hold and found her way forward unsteadily on the slightly rocking deck. She was already a bit nauseous from the pregnancy, so the yaw and pitch of the smallish sailboat added to her woes. She looked back to be sure the captain and crewman had gone below deck. She ran her hand up under Moncrieff's kilt. She wasn't disappointed.

Moncrieff looked about. "*Ahora no, Carlotta.*" It was neither the time or place.

She continued her exploration, nearly causing him to fall as the rocking of the boat in the waves caused it to pitch. Her head ducked under his kilt just as the captain reemerged. He looked away but couldn't help but peek and finally stare at the performance before him.

The baron was too caught up in the moment to worry about what the captain might see.

The captain guided the boat about a mile out into the Gulf of Mexico before turning to port and beginning the voyage up the coast. He lashed the tiller in place and decided to nap. It'd be an hour or so before his crewman took over the helm.

As Luke headed eastward with his men, they peeled off and departed one-by-one. Only Carson was still alongside, when they left Nuecestown.

Each in his own way had been wondering what a post-war Texas might be like. The cold reality of the war's aftermath was settling in. A couple of folks in San Diego had mentioned that newspapers were reporting that President Johnson was at odds with Congress over how to treat the states that had seceded. Johnson was apparently inclined to be more forgiving, but that flowed against the political winds which sought retribution. The South wouldn't be given time to lick its wounds.

Luke pulled up at the entrance to Heaven's Gate. "Give Scarlett our best, Walker. Y'all should be making a good life in Corpus. Do come by and visit."

The two exchanged the all-too-common cowboy sign of a couple of fingers tapped against the brim of their hats. Nothing more needed saying.

Luke turned up the trail toward the main house. Big Horse picked up the pace as he sensed his home stable. Somewhere deep in his equine brain lurked memories of apples from small humans.

Luke was soon dismounting and leading Big Horse into the barn. He threw the tack over its rail and hung the halter before giving the steed a much-deserved currying.

"You lovin' that horse more than me, Mr. Texas Ranger?"

Luke froze.

Elisa eased up beside him.

"You need some currying, ma'am?"

The brush fell to the floor as they fell into the deep embrace of lovers. "I missed you, Lucas. I missed you so."

"Won't be missing me anymore, Lisa. I'm hanging up my badge."

Elisa pushed back from him and stared deeply into his eyes. His expression confirmed that he was true to his promise. She wanted to have him right there in the straw, but that was not to be.

"Pa...you're home!" Peter had interrupted the homecoming. "Brought an apple for Big Horse."

"Whoa! What's with the crutch, Peter?"

Elisa smiled uncomfortably. "That new horse gave him a toss the other day. Tell your dad what happened, son."

"We were racing up the trail when a javelina dashed out. Wasn't the horse's fault, Dad. He turned sudden like, and I was thrown sideways from the saddle. Doc says I didn't break any bones, but my ankle is plenty sore." He looked expectantly at his father. "And I didn't cry, Dad...and I got back in the saddle."

Luke was more interested in how well Peter was explaining the incident than the event itself. The boy could talk a blue streak when he wanted to. "What happened to the javelina?"

"He run off. Scared likely."

Luke gave an approving smile. "Well, give Big Horse that apple, and let's all go see your brothers and sisters."

Elisa couldn't take her eyes from Luke as they walked arm in arm to the house. Was he serious about hanging up his Texas Ranger badge? Relief swelled through her body.

ELEVEN
PALMITO RANCH

"COME ON, big fella. Let's find some beeves." Luke had mounted up and given Big Horse his head, as they left the barn. The big gray stallion sensed the day ahead, putting an extra bit of a prance into his step as he added a snort or two for good measure.

Luke was about to head out when hoofbeats and the rattle of sabers caused him to halt and pivot toward the noise while simultaneously grabbing for his Colt revolver. The lone rider quickly came into view, and Luke let the revolver slip back into his holster.

"Easy Luke. It's just me, Gordon Belknap."

"Major?"

"Colonel now." Belknap eased up and dismounted. "Heading up to Austin to meet my new command. Thought I'd stop by and visit my old friends."

"Great to see you, Colonel. We just finished up breakfast, but I'm sure Elisa has biscuits and can whip up a little something for a friend."

"Between us, do call me Gordon, Luke. No point in formalities. I learned from Sheriff Meaney down in Corpus that you've hung up your Ranger badge. Wouldn't mind knowing what's with that, if you're up to sharing." Belknap relaxed in his saddle.

Luke thoughtfully looked off into the distance beyond Belknap. He decided to ignore Belknap's question. "You traveling in hostile territory without an escort, Gordon? I mean, a saber, Henry rifle, and Colt do have limits."

"Sent my escort on to Nuecestown. I'm reasonably brave but not crazy."

"Well, come on, Gordon, and bring your horse along. If you've got time, I'd be pleased to show you the latest improvements around Heaven's Gate." Luke dismounted and led Big Horse up toward the house with Belknap following. As they drew close, he shouted out, "Lisa, set a place. We've got a guest."

Elisa emerged on the gallery drying her hands on her apron and offering a warm welcoming smile. "Well, Major Gordon Belknap, I do declare. We haven't seen you in a bit." She laughed at a fleeting thought back to the early days of the war when Belknap struck a face-saving deal with Luke for horses while on a foraging expedition. "You had breakfast?"

"Good to see you, Mrs. Dunn." He tipped his hat. "I'm about as hungry as a newborn puppy searching for its momma, especially for your cooking. Why I could likely eat a deer, antlers and all."

Luke chuckled a bit at Belknap's attempt at local folk humor. "Sweetheart, Gordon's been promoted to colonel and is on his way to a new command in Austin. I figure to show him around a bit after he chows down on your delicious biscuits and fixings."

Soon enough, they were seated around the kitchen table with Belknap enjoying eggs, bacon, a stack of biscuits, and a cup of the all-important coffee. "Dang, but this is absolutely scrumptious, Mrs. Dunn."

Blushing, she refilled his coffee cup. "It's Elisa, Gordon.

And no disrespect taken at using my first name. We do like to be comfortable around these parts."

Luke slowly sipped a bit of coffee but didn't eat, as early breakfast had left him uncomfortably full. "Last I heard, you were down in Brownsville. How'd it go down there?"

Belknap squirmed a little and smiled sheepishly. "Not too well I'm afraid."

Luke knew what had happened but wanted to hear it directly from Belknap. "How's that?" He feigned ignorance.

"You enjoying this, Luke?" Belknap couldn't help but grin, especially with the expectant faces of five children gathered around at the possibility of a story.

Luke looked at Elisa and her growing belly and then at the children. "Not to worry. The one in Lisa's belly can't hear your story." Laughter tended to take away any discomfort.

"Let me tell you the truth behind the Battle of Palmito Ranch." Belknap tried to look deadly serious, as though he had some deep dark secret to share. "It really began back in February, when a new commander showed up at Fort Brown. Colonel Theodore Barrett arrived with about four hundred Black soldiers. Buffalo soldiers, they call them. They were all what you'd call green as a fresh-cut tree branch, but it brought the command up to a little more than a thousand troops."

Luke held in another chuckle at Belknap's attempt to work in some more homespun humor. "Y'all likely didn't expect much trouble with the war seeming to be winding down."

"That's what I figured. But Barrett had other ideas. He had pretty much bought his rank and hadn't seen any battle action. He was itching for a fight. He'd been given command of the 62nd United States Colored Troop mostly to get him off the backs of the high command. He tried desperately to be a spit-and-polish officer, which annoyed most all the other officers. He was also convalescing from a bout of malaria." Belknap leaned back in his chair and took a long sip of coffee.

Elisa topped off his cup again, and the children began making signs of losing interest.

Luke offered encouragement. "So, how did y'all wind up fighting Confederate troops, Gordon?"

"The colonel had a habit of strolling up a hill overlooking the city and the Port of Brazos Santiago. One day in early May, I arrived at his favored spot ahead of him. As he came alongside me, he peered through his telescope and let out a squeal of surprise. He handed it to me and exclaimed that Rebel troops were setting up battle lines. I looked and looked again. Turns out your Colonel John Ford was indeed readying his forces for an attack." Belknap turned in his chair and pretended for the children's benefit that he was looking through a spyglass. Giggles followed.

Luke shook his head. "Didn't anybody know the war was ended? Hadn't they heard about Lee's surrender?"

"I think most everybody knew Luke, but nobody was backing off from a possible fight. We found ourselves well to the east of Fort Brown. We'd moved from a place called Brazos Santiago and dug in as best possible in the boggy ground with Palmito Ranch behind us. The landscape was challenging, Luke. Salt flats, marshes, shallow bays, dunes of wind-blown clay. I'm sure you've been there." Belknap eased from his chair and slipped down onto the floor. He grabbed some table implements and laid them out on the floor to demonstrate Union and Confederate positions. The children kneeled expectantly beside him. "We had this Colonel Branson who took it upon himself to lead a couple of hundred men in an attack against the Rebels. They somehow managed to slog through the godforsaken terrain." He pushed part of the Union line forward. "I was in the rear with Colonel Barrett's 62nd US Colored Troops and my own companies. Well, Colonel Branson was successful at first and it began to look like we might press on to Brownsville and a big supply of cotton that

Richard King was trying to ship to Mexico. The colonel even captured some Rebs."

Luke smiled. "I recall helping with a caravan of my cousin's cotton down to Matamoros early in the war. Must have been a big stockpile of cotton to have the Union troops so anxious to capture it."

"I know it was a considerable quantity, Luke." Belknap looked back at the children squirming to hear the end of the story. "Well, Rebel troops led by a fella named Captain Robinson counterattacked and drove Colonel Branson back." Belknap moved the implements on the floor as though they were attacking troops. "Branson had those captives but was embarrassed at having lost the day. About that time, the troops had lost any advantage and with sunset nearing stopped fighting for the night." Belknap took another sip of coffee. He hunkered down toward the children. "Now guess what happened?"

Little Peter couldn't contain himself. "The Rebels won?"

Belknap tried to look surprised. "Well, Colonel Ford brought up six French cannons and the 2nd Texas Cavalry." He moved spoons across the floor as though they were cannons. "He counterattacked in force. He captured most of Colonel Barrett's unit and pushed us all the way back to Brazos Santiago." He swept the Union forces back with his hand. "Some of our retreating Union soldiers drowned in the Rio Grande or were shot by French border guards from the Mexican side." Belknap shook his head sadly and pretended to cry to the delight of the children. He smiled and winked mischievously. "Lots of folks got involved when the end was nearly assured. I expect they could boast of being in battle and there's surely a lesson in that."

"Then what happened?" Little Peter pressed Belknap toward a conclusion. Luke and Elisa sat back watching Belknap interact with the children.

"It turned out to be what folks call anti-climactic. A false ending, and quite unexpected. The Rebels had won the battle but already lost the war. They officially learned of General Lee's surrender, so they released their prisoners and surrendered. The Rebel officers headed to Mexico to seek protection from President Benito Juarez." Belknap climbed back into his chair, and Peter, John, and Andrea Anne laughed with glee as they dutifully picked up the battle formations from the floor. "That was pretty much it. I soon received an unexpected promotion to colonel and orders to head to Austin to help with what they're calling reconstruction."

Luke turned serious. "What happened to Colonel Ford?"

"I hear tell that General Steele recently persuaded him to return from Mexico and serve as a parole commissioner for disbanding Confederate units. Colonel Ford was concerned that there be no mean spirit of revenge for the war. He made it clear to his men that the negro now had a right to vote." Belknap looked around the room. "Elisa, this was one very fine breakfast. I'm so full up I may not be able to get back on my horse."

That brought more laughter to the room, especially given that Belknap was rather slim and likely would have no trouble mounting up.

"You ready to take a ride around Heaven's Gate, Gordon?"

"Wouldn't miss it, Luke."

Luke kissed Elisa and the children and was soon heading out with Belknap.

The cramped quarters in the hold were made barely tolerable by the liberal use of straw and blankets. With the captain asleep at the wheel, the moment was ripe for Moncrieff. He stroked Carlotta's hair and ran his fingers across her bare breasts. *Pity*, he thought. She responded to his touch by reaching down to his crotch.

Carlotta was always ready for him. Her wanton smile stoked his ardor. He couldn't afford to waste time. She embraced his body as he slid on top of her. They seemed to both be quickly caught up in the rhythm of their passions. But it was not so for the Scotsman, as his hand grasped her throat. He began to squeeze. Her eyes grew wide with this new direction to their ardor. Any realization as to her possible fate didn't occur to her. Her excitement reached new heights. Was he adding a new game to their lovemaking? His hand closed ever tighter. He exploded inside her while squeezed her beautiful milk-white throat with all his strength. She grew suddenly fearful. Panic set in, but it was ever so fleeting. He felt her body grow tense, her breathing stop, her body relax, grow still.

Moncrieff looked at her for only a moment. He closed her eyes. What was done was done. He took two cannonballs from a nearby crate and tied them in her skirt. He rolled Carlotta and the cannonballs inside a blanket.

He peeked through the hatch. The glow on the horizon called for Angus Moncrieff to move quickly. He eased up the ladder to the deck above. He saw that the captain was still napping, and he could hear the snoring of the crewman in the cubbyhole below. He shifted the burden wrapped in burlap and now slung over his shoulder, made his way to the rail, and let precious bundle slide into the waves. It floated a moment before sinking from sight. The weight of the cannonballs did their job. At sunrise, he could explain that Carlotta had grown very seasick, said she went up on deck to get fresh air, and apparently fell overboard.

Life would now be simpler in New Orleans. Moncrieff stood on the deck watching the horizon.

The boat captain had awakened as rays of the sun danced across his face. He saw the Scotsman standing at the rail and made his way over to him as the Scotsman stared out across the Gulf waters. "Dónde *está la mujer, gringo?*" He was curious as to why the Scotsman was on deck by himself.

"*No la he visto, capitán.*" Moncrieff was telling the truth. He hadn't seen her, at least, not since he'd dumped her body overboard. "*Estaba enferma.*" Indeed, Carlotta had been sick the last time he saw her.

The captain showed deep concern. "*Ella era prima de Cheno Cortina.*"

Moncrieff had no idea she was Cortina's cousin. No wonder she'd been able to secure a boat for them. With her pregnancy, she'd likely persuaded Cortina to let her rendezvous with him in Matamoros and help get a boat. Moncrieff sighed and shrugged. "*Tal vez, ella cayó por la borda.*" To say that she might have gone overboard was a truthful possibility. After all, she actually had gone overboard.

"*Que lástima, Cheno no será feliz.*" The captain was right with that observation. Cheno would not be happy when he got the news.

Moncrieff reached into his vest pocket and fished out two gold coins. "¿Nosotros *vamos a New Orleans?*"

The captain couldn't help but smile. "*Sí, señor.* New Orleans."

Luke and Belknap rode easy-like among the grasses and mesquite of Heaven's Gate. They could hear a few varmints, but there mostly wasn't much animal life to be seen. Luke finally broke the ice.

"You have to be on the lookout mostly for coyotes, javelina, and rattlers out here." He stated the obvious. "So long as you stay mounted, you're mostly pretty safe."

Belknap looked over at Luke, measuring his words. "So, how come you managed to not be conscripted into the Confederate cavalry, Luke? I expect you'd likely have been given a command."

"Fair question, Gordon. Governor Lubbock was a strong proponent of conscription. Ben Terry was heading up a unit called Terry's Texas Rangers and prowled the Texas frontier. Rip Ford was given a commission and headed up the 2nd Texas Cavalry. Despite their presence, the Nueces Strip was vulnerable to all sorts of threats. Guess I held some sort of special place in Rip's heart, because he asked me to do what I could to bring law and order to the region as a Special Ranger. So, I recruited a couple of folks and did what I could. We were a ragtag crew at best, but we managed to do a pretty fair job against savages and bandits. I was able to spend time at Heaven's Gate, too."

"Yeah, Luke. I recall when we made that deal for horses, when I'd been sent out to forage for fresh mounts?"

"But that was just common-sense haggling, Gordon. Nothing to do with being a Texas Ranger."

"Ever think you'll go back to Rangering, Luke."

"I've got to keep my promise to Elisa." He set his jaw firmly and caressed his fiery red mustache. "Life is pretty much about choice, isn't it?"

"I heard that you went after Cole Younger a piece back."

"Word gets out, doesn't it?" Luke smiled as he thought of that final mission. "Rip Ford would've been proud of us. Younger and some others from Quantrill's Raiders had ambushed a troop of Confederates with Union prisoners up around Victoria. Only two Rebs escaped, and one of them, Horace Rucker's son Stephen, later died of his wounds. The other was a sergeant named Clay Bell who'd been a sharpshooter for the 1st Texas Cavalry. He joined us in the hunt for Younger. We finally found the outlaw up around Uvalde."

"What happened?"

"I'm getting to it." Luke looked out thoughtfully across the Nueces Strip prairie and its bounty of flowers as though savoring the memory. "Seems Younger was figuring to head north to join with the James brothers in Kansas. He and his gang celebrated with a final wild night in Uvalde. I had five men with me. Darn, but we were armed to the teeth, Gordon. We could have taken on an army." Luke grinned at the thought. "We ran into one of the previous night's victims of Younger's gang. The man had been beaten up pretty badly. He showed us where the gang was camped."

"So, you were able to surprise them."

"That's an understatement, Gordon. The rising sun was at our backs when we crept to within a hundred yards and laid down a withering fire on their camp. That Bell fellow unlimbered his Sharps rifle with a telescopic sight. Devastating. We delivered the wrath of God on those sorry excuses for humanity. Most of them never moved from their bedrolls. Out of sixteen gang members, only Younger and two others escaped. They never returned fire. From blood on the ground near where Younger's horse was tethered, he was likely wounded. That was it, Gordon."

"Amazing." Belknap looked with incredulity at Luke. "You'll be a huge loss to the Texas Rangers, Luke. You think Elisa will ever let you rejoin?"

"Look over there, Gordon." Luke pointed to a buck prancing along a nearby arroyo. "Get your rifle out. That's tonight's dinner." He'd effectively ignored the question.

Belknap didn't waste time pulling out his Henry and dispatching the buck. After silently field dressing the deer, they turned back toward the house. A few coyotes cast hungry eyes on the pair from a respectful distance, as they salivated over the carcass tied behind Belknap's saddle.

"Quite a spread you've built here." Belknap mentioned the obvious as he rode along beside Luke.

"Couldn't have done it without Elisa, Gordon." He threw a mischievous smile at Belknap. "You ever think of finding a good woman?"

Now, it was Belknap's turn to divert a question. "If you were still a Ranger, you'd likely be interested in a fellow I met down in Brownsville. He was a big Scotsman selling stolen cattle. He even wore a kilt, or what my soldiers called a man skirt."

Luke pulled up and got dead serious. "You talking about Baron Angus Moncrieff?"

"That was his name. Word sure gets around. Sold us a few head and moved up the Rio Grande toward Camargo. Lost track of him."

"Sheriff Meaney down in Corpus Christi has a serious interest in Moncrieff, Gordon. He's up to no good for certain. I can't help but feel that we haven't seen the last of him or his kind in Texas. Fools like him tend to repeat their evil deeds even if they've only had a hint of success."

"You think Elisa would let you chase him down, if he were close by, Luke?"

"Well, it's not really up to her. I love her, but I'm my own man. And I'm good to my promise. However, if the man were threatening me or my family directly, no question I'd bring him to justice." Luke saw that he hadn't satisfied Belknap. "Think of it this way, Gordon. Out here on the ranch, there's all sorts of dangers that my family must be protected from. Whether lawman or not, I must defend my home. If...and that's a big if...if Lisa were ever to free me from my promise, I'd likely be sore tempted to rejoin the Texas Rangers. Of course, that's a moot point for the present, as it doesn't appear that any Rangers are going to be authorized again."

The two rode the rest of the way making small talk about raising cattle and horses. They soon pulled up at the house. "Can you enjoy some venison with us, Gordon? Pleased to have you spend the night. You can head for Austin in the morning."

"I'll take you up on the venison dinner, Luke, but y'all have a full-up house. I'd as soon find my way up to Bernice's and

Agatha's boarding house just up the road in Nuecestown and rejoin my escort."

Luke was just a little hurt but didn't show it. "Shucks, Gordon, we were going to bed you in the barn anyway."

They laughed awkwardly, as Belknap realized his unintended slight of Luke's hospitality. "I'm sure it won't be the last time I visit at Heaven's Gate."

"*¿Ella desapareció?*" Cortina couldn't believe his cousin had disappeared.

"*Sí jefe. Desapareció.*" The man shuffled his feet. He hadn't wanted to be the bearer of bad news. "*El capitán dijo que se ahogó.*" Casting the captain as the originator of the news made him a little more comfortable. Bad enough it was hot, and he was sweating profusely.

Cheno Cortina seethed. "*¡Ahogó!*" Drowned. "*¿Moncrieff la mató?*"

"*Él no sabía, jefe.*" The captain wouldn't have admitted to knowing whether Moncrieff killed Carlotta.

Cortina spat into the ground. "*¡Maldito gringo!*" Damned indeed. He'd bide his time but figured to get his revenge at some point. With Moncrieff in New Orleans, he'd have to fully test his own patience. He calculated that Moncrieff suffered from overconfidence and would eventually revisit Mexico. Finally, Cortina cooled off. He waved the messenger away. "*Basta, gracias.*"

Now that the Union and Confederate troops had departed from Brownsville, Cortina was determined to see how his mother's hacienda had fared during the war. He'd received word that soldiers from both sides had stopped there on their travels, but little damage was done. He'd also been amused at news of the Palmito Ranch battle. The irony of the fact that the

Confederates won the battle but then had to surrender wasn't lost on him.

Cortina had his own set of problems. Emperor Maximillian I, crowned back in 1864 by the French, was defending against forces loyal to ousted President Benito Juarez. The US government was preparing to arm Juarez's supporters. In an effort to remain consequential Cortina offered to help transfer weapons from former Union General Herman Sturm, fresh from his actions in the War of Northern Aggression and now an agent for the Mexican government. Controlling arms gave Cortina a modest degree of power.

"Why I remember you now, honey. You helped Luke Dunn out a few years back." Bernice had her ah-ha moment, as she placed the breakfast platter in front of Belknap.

The colonel looked up and smiled. "Yes, ma'am. In fact, I spent yesterday with the Dunn family. Luke was kind enough to show me around Heaven's Gate and Elisa cooked up an incomparable feast." It wasn't lost on Belknap that Bernice and Agatha were the eyes and ears of Nuecestown and beyond. He looked up at the sergeant sitting opposite him and winked.

Bernice prattled on. "I hear tell that there's looting in Galveston, and they sacked the munitions building in Houston. Folks are afraid they'll run out of supplies. They're desperately trying to get their stuff out before the Yankees move in."

"Afraid they'd be too late, Miss Bernice. General Granger has things under control."

Bernice put that piece of information away in her bonnet. She sighed resignedly. "Well, Colonel Belknap, around these parts we're glad the war is over. It's been nothing but trouble for us folks trying to get on with our lives. There's still bad people out there and nobody to protect us."

"I truly do hope I can help keep folks safe, Miss Bernice. I'm headed to Austin to get my orders to round up malcontents and troublemakers. Of course, Texas is a big place. But we'll try our best."

"I do pray that you are successful, Colonel. You seem to have a good heart and are a friend of Luke Dunn." Bernice was a pretty fair judge of character, but the connection with Luke cinched her opinion.

The polished dark mahogany-paneled walls surrounding the trio gave off an undeservedly sophisticated patina, as they sat around a table and enjoyed the fine Scottish whiskey that Moncrieff had been good enough to provide. The patter of rain on the roof provided enough noise to mask their conversation from any prying ears. The heat and humidity of New Orleans were only partially relieved by hand fans provided to patrons. The baron made use of a silk scarf to wipe his brow frequently.

A young woman whispered in Moncrieff's ear. "Seriously? Palmito Ranch?" He acted as though he had just received news of the battle at Palmito Ranch. He vaguely recalled having seen the troops forming up for an attack on Brownsville. "I should have stayed to watch." He and his two business partners enjoyed a hearty laugh. After all, the war was over and opportunities to ply their illicit trades abounded.

"I heard that someone robbed the Texas treasury in Austin of $17,000 in gold. Somebody is spending the bounty right handsome-like about now. Been plenty of looting, too." The speaker was a swarthy man with a wide-brimmed hat worn low over his forehead. His nickname anachronistically was Scrub. He was one of those types who was physically clean but never looked it. "They're saying that better than half the Texas Confederate forces have already deserted or been disbanded. I expect we'll have no trouble hiring any help we might need."

The table rocked a little, just enough to annoy Moncrieff. The heat and mugginess were the result of it raining off and on for days. He looked forward to heading to higher altitude and slightly drier weather in Texas.

The second man, Robert, had a gleam in his eye. "I've got to believe there's all manner of contraband to be acquired and sold at a handsome profit."

Moncrieff took a swig of whiskey and leaned back in his chair. "Not big enough."

Robert glared back defensively. "Your cattle scheme wasn't exactly a huge flaming success, Baron."

"Aye, I'll allow as to that. No luck there. Couldn't avoid happening on to the very man in Mexico that my *vaqueros* stole the cattle from." Moncrieff smiled inwardly at the fleetingly perverse thought of having gotten even with Cortina by murdering his floozy of a cousin. He took on a more serious demeanor. "I think the money to be had will be in land. Always has been...but now more than ever."

Scrub leaned forward. "Now yer talkin', Baron. Whatcha got in mind?"

"I've been traveling through what they call the Nueces Strip. There's acres and acres to be had, lads. And that means, acres to be sold and resold and resold again." Moncrieff relished the thought of the art of land swindling. They would sell the same property to multiple buyers and let them haggle over who was the rightful owner.

"What about the law?"

"The Texas Rangers are gone. We just keep setting up land offices in different places throughout the Strip. If we feel any heat from local sheriffs, we simply move our operations."

Scrub sipped a bit of whiskey. "They're talkin' in Austin 'bout some sort of state police. Gonna hire a bunch of them nigras. Could be a problem."

"Lad, don't forget the almighty power of the dollar. I

expect we'd be making them our friends. Besides, it's going to take them a while to organize."

Robert nodded. "Still, I'm thinking they might hold a vengeful nature."

Moncrieff sighed. "I've got that worked out, Robert. Recall those Rebel deserters that'll be looking for work. We'll have our very own enforcers."

"When do we start?" Scrub was anxious to head for the Nueces Strip.

"The sheriff knows me in Corpus Christi. He's not my friend. You two will go on ahead. There'll be homesteaders ruined by the war and looking to leave Texas. You'll buy up a few of their holdings dirt cheap to get us started. I'll join you once you have the operation established."

"Where you goin' to hole up 'til then, Baron?" Scrub was fearful that the Scotsman might enjoy New Orleans overmuch and never join them in Texas.

"Thought I might make a few friends in Austin. Could come in handy later." He saw the apprehension on Scrub's and Robert's faces. "Once they get the telegraph back up, I'll stay in touch." Moncrieff poured another round and raised his glass. "Here's to striking it rich in Texas."

Their touching of glasses served as a signal to the barkeep. In but another moment, three comely, elegantly dressed, painted ladies of New Orleans had joined the three swindlers in toasting to future success.

"So, you were at Palmito Ranch, Colonel Belknap?" General Andrew Hamilton had been appointed by President Johnson as provisional governor of Texas.

"Yes, General." Belknap stood tall before the general's desk.

"Seems you managed to earn a promotion in spite of that

debacle, Colonel." Hamilton seemed to enjoy dangling the Palmito matter at anyone that he knew had been involved. "Good thing Lee had already surrendered. No telling what Rebel prison you'd be in."

"Yes, General. Good thing." It wasn't Belknap's most comfortable moment.

"I expect you know that we've granted amnesty to all ex-Confederates who swear allegiance to the United States?" He eyed Belknap cautiously. "And there'll surely be a few that will refuse our generous offer."

"Yes, General. I expect there will be a few."

Hamilton stood and leaned slightly toward Belknap. "Welcome to your new assignment, Colonel Belknap. You will lead the effort to hunt down those who refuse."

"Sir?"

"Is there a problem, Colonel?"

"No sir, but may I have permission to speak freely?"

Hamilton snorted. "Granted."

"Many may be unwilling, sir. They may resist violently. Do we have police authority to use deadly force?"

Hamilton smiled. "As provisional governor, I'll be establishing a state police force. You'll have a company of federal soldiers. There will be no Texas Rangers as such. Any further questions, Colonel?"

Belknap considered how a company of a hundred and fifty men would work out to cover all of Texas. It was clear that the general hadn't the vaguest notion of just how big Texas was. There wasn't much he could do about for the present. "No sir. Thank you, sir."

"One more thing, Colonel." Hamilton selected a cigar from the humidor on his desk.

"Yes, sir."

The general clipped the end of the cigar, lit a match, and took a few drags to be sure it was lit. He exhaled smoke that a draft swept quickly to the ceiling. "Stay clear of Pendleton

Murrah. He's settling down in Mexico trying to rile up Texans to continue the fight."

"Yes, sir." Belknap knew Murrah had been the governor of Texas at the time of the Confederate surrender, and the man was an ardent secessionist. He interpreted the general's comment as indicating that a lot of his attention should be focused on the vast region from Austin to the Rio Grande, as Murrah stirred up Texans in that neck of the woods.

"You're dismissed, Colonel."

TWELVE
RECONSTRUCTION BEGINS

THE ROAD to the big house was deeply rutted, and the magnolias lining either side suffered for lack of care. But the sight that troubled Edward Thorpe most was the big house itself. It failed to even remotely resemble the home he grew up in.

Shutters had long since been stripped for firewood. What remained of furniture lay in various states of disrepair around the grounds. One of the four Georgian columns had been pushed over with the result that the section of portico it had supported hung at a decidedly sharp angle from the roof. Grasses and weeds seemingly sprouted from every foundation crack. The entire west wing was mostly a burned-out hulk, likely a miracle that the entire house hadn't been engulfed in flames. What the fire had not accomplished, rapid decay had. Such was the formerly magnificent hub of Magnolia Plantation.

"Where is everybody?" To Thorpe, this was a logical question. He'd freed his slaves but expected a few might be sufficiently appreciative of his acts of kindness and stay on at Magnolia until he returned. Of the better than seven hundred that remained when he departed for France, he could see perhaps two dozen hanging around the house and the former slave quarters beyond.

"They done gone north, massa."

"Dammit, Frederick. I'm not your master and never have been. I'm not my father." Thorpe gazed with deep consternation at the former slave. It distressed him that the man's eyes bore an eerie resemblance to Horatio Thorpe's eyes. Too many of the inhabitants of Magnolia featured characteristics tracing to his father's biological legacy. "Well, gather everyone around that you can find." He watched the man strike a *yessir massa* pose and run off head low and shoulders hunched over to do his bidding. The former slave's abjectness disgusted Thorpe. It harkened to past treatment, thus, a harsh reminder sooner forgotten.

It turned out there were closer to three dozen former slaves still calling Magnolia their home. Thorpe stood on the steps of the big house and gave a short speech about how they were free and would have the opportunity to sharecrop on sections of the plantation. He offered some income to get them started, but they'd be responsible thereafter for raising crops and making a living from their labors. He knew that sharecropping was tantamount to indentured servitude, so promised that after only three years he'd give them the opportunity to purchase the sections they worked at a fair price. There were collective smiles and nods of approval. Thorpe had thusly released a lot of the tension that typically accompanies an uncertain future. In closing, he told them that he'd make the same arrangement for any of the former slaves who'd left Magnolia and were willing to return under his conditions. He'd leave it to Samuel back in Austin to work out the details, while Frederick would manage the day-to-day operations at Magnolia.

After the now free laborers headed back to their quarters, Thorpe turned to Frederick. "There are a lot of memories good and bad around this house, Frederick. I'm inclined to tear it down, but I'll leave that decision to you. Perhaps you can find enough materials to build a more modest dwelling to live in and manage Magnolia from." He was pleased to see the former slave quite obviously pleased at what lay ahead.

The former slave stood slightly more erect. Just a tentative touch of pride had seeped into his psyche. "I be grateful, but where you going, Mr. Thorpe?"

Thorpe was pleased that *massa* had disappeared from Frederick's lexicon. "I'm going to stay in Austin a bit. On my recent trip to France, I reestablished my father's trade arrangement. I'll be watching over shipping operations in Galveston. That's also why I've asked Samuel to set up the operations that you will manage here."

"My people are grateful, Mr. Thorpe. You be a godsend."

"It's our people now. I'm counting on you, Frederick." Thorpe stepped forward and grasped the Black man's hand. He nodded graciously to Frederick, strode over to his horse, and grabbed the reins. He had one more thing to do before he departed.

A hundred yards or so behind the big house was a small fenced-in plot with the family graves. He led his horse over to the wrought-iron fence. Even the little fence around the graves was rusted and had been bent in places. Weeds grew along its base. Thorpe stood at the gate and scanned the headstones, thinking on the memories that yet lingered. There was a part of him that would have plowed the graves under, but he'd rather enjoy knowing that his father was likely turning over in his coffin at the thought of what his son was doing to his plantation masterpiece. Thorpe said a prayer for his mother, but could only smile wryly over his father's and brother's graves unkempt as they were from overgrowth. He cleared the weeds as best he could from his mother's and sister's headstones.

He mounted up at last, took a final wistful look at Magnolia, and began the journey to Austin.

★★

"I'll do what I can, Colonel Belknap. I support what Governor Hamilton is doing, though I'm afraid he doesn't fully appreciate our stretched resources." General George Armstrong Custer stood. He was headquartered in Austin for the present and was Chief of Cavalry of the Department of Texas. His outsized ego and flowing golden locks made for a dashing persona, though his words belied his flair for drama. He once again scanned the document outlining the colonel's orders.

"I understand, sir. Whatever you can spare." Belknap was hoping for at least four hundred men.

"I'm not sure what you might be able to recruit, Colonel. We're also lean on money to pay troops. The upheaval in Washington caused by the unexpected transition to President Johnson's administration is still a problem." Custer looked off thoughtfully. "I expect you want cavalry, as you must be highly mobile. I'm sure you can appreciate how much of a lover of horses and sabers I am, Colonel." He turned his gaze on Belknap. Custer was every bit the dashingly handsome officer and seemed to know it. "I can spare a hundred and fifty men and perhaps two hundred horses. I'm sure you'll need more mounts."

Belknap exhaled. He thought he might fare better given rumors of mutinies among Custer's cavalry commands in parts of Texas. It was nevertheless a beginning. "Thank you, sir. I can find more horseflesh."

"Where has Governor Hamilton asked you to focus your efforts, Colonel?"

"The governor says that Texans down south are being stirred up by Pendleton Murrah, the former Texas gov—"

"Yes, I know Murrah," Custer cut off the colonel's sentence. "Good luck to you. My adjutant will give you the unit transfers you'll need."

"Er, thank you, General." Belknap saluted smartly and was

relieved to leave Custer's presence. He had the sense that the general was intent on protecting his own troop strength and could have cared less about Texas except as it might serve his own ends. The colonel made a mental note to avoid future association with Custer if at all possible. He'd be out fulfilling his assignment soon enough. He much preferred the challenge of hunting down the troublemakers that lurked on the wide expanses of the South Texas frontier. As to more horses, he figured to make a visit to his friend Luke Dunn.

Luke was saddled up and ready to head out. Jaime, his lead *vaquero*, would join him momentarily. With banditry run amok throughout the Nueces Strip, it remained their sense that it was best to patrol the far reaches of Heaven's Gate Ranch in pairs. The brief wait gave Luke a few moments to think on the future. With a sixth Dunn child on the way, a growing ranch, and a reviving Texas economy, he had his hands full. Stuck away in the deep recesses of his psyche was a longing for a return to being a Texas Ranger. Seemed that longing would ever lurk in those inner parts of his mind. He was nevertheless committed to his promise to Elisa.

"*Señor* Dunn. Good morning." Jaime broke Luke's train of thought.

"Oh, Jaime. Yes, good morning." He shook off the cobwebs that come with daydreaming. "How's Julia?"

Jaime laughed. "Fine. She has what you call the morning sickness."

"My condolences to you and hope she gets past it." Luke well knew how that could be, though Elisa was one of those very fortunate women that rarely had the problem. "Let's head west, today. Haven't been down in those parts for a while."

"The creek is running strong, so we should find a few stray beeves gathering, *Señor* Dunn."

Luke waved to Elisa and the children standing on the gallery, as he and Jaime headed out. Big Horse offered up a snort as if to sense possible adventure ahead.

Elisa couldn't miss the fact that her husband was carrying more guns than usual. What could he be sensing?

He patted the butt of the 1861 Army revolver at his hip as though to acknowledge what she already suspected. With the war ended, troubles were ever more likely to be lurking.

Thorpe pulled up at the hotel, dismounted, grabbed his duffel, and handed the reins over to the eager Mexican livery boy. A coin widened the young man's smile.

He looked up at the building. The Magnolia main house in its heyday was more impressive. But this was Austin, and he had no intention of staying for long.

Thorpe had the good sense to hire a couple of men as armed escorts. His generosity assured their loyalty. He could take no chances given his reputation for having freed slaves. There were plenty of holdover malcontents around that harbored deep anti-Black sentiments and would take pleasure in exacting retribution on him for his actions during the war. Far too many throughout the south held firm to their prejudices, and this would trouble Thorpe no end.

He walked into the lobby and was greeted by Samuel. It was clear from the former slave's demeanor that he was thoroughly enjoying the responsibilities Thorpe had given him.

"Mr. Thorpe, I've been looking forward to your return. How was France? Your visit to Magnolia?"

The rapid-fire questions caught Thorpe off guard. The questions were sort of rhetorical, as he'd been in regular contact with Samuel during his travels. The two men shook hands. "Good to see you, too, Samuel."

Samuel noted the two bodyguards who stood several paces

away. He nodded toward them. "Difficult times, Mr. Thorpe." He motioned toward a cluster of plush chairs. Two steaming cups of coffee sat on a small table between them. "I have you checked into Driskill."

Thorpe followed him over and sat. The trip had been strenuous enough that he fully appreciated the soft upholstery. "Have you arranged the meeting with Hamilton?"

"Yes sir, Mr. Thorpe. Tomorrow at ten in the morning." He smiled at his own efficiency. "I also have the paperwork for the folks back at Magnolia."

"Thank you, Samuel. We'll see how Hamilton reacts to my proposal." He took a long sip of coffee. "Hmmm. Good coffee, Samuel." He savored a second sip. "As to Magnolia, it's imperative that we deliver on my promises. I know Frederick is excited at the prospect of running Magnolia. To tell the truth, I'm glad my father's overseers left. They would have posed a problem. It's difficult to give up power once you've held it."

"Will you be heading to Houston, Mr. Thorpe?"

"Actually, I'm planning to head to San Antonio and Corpus Christi. I understand there's very affordable land available. Unfortunately, many folks have pulled up stakes as a result of the war. The economic hardships combined with a bit of drought were too much for many folks." He paused thoughtfully. "Maybe I'll visit the man who brought my father to justice."

Samuel's eyes grew wide. "You're gonna visit with Mr. Dunn?"

"I've met him. He seemed like a fair sort. I understand he has a good sense of the nature of the Nueces Strip and especially the area around Corpus Christi. He's got a reputation as an honest man. I expect he'd be a good person to consult before I make any purchases."

Samuel gazed admiringly at Thorpe. He was surely a far better man than his father had been.

Thoughts of the future weighed heavily on One Arrow. The chance meeting with the trapper Bear Wills had brought with it a rude awakening.

He found himself determined to find a different way. First, he had to settle his people in the Indian Territory. For reasons he was unable to fathom, he had come to the realization that he was unlike other Comanche. Perhaps it was some legacy from Three Toes, perhaps the influence of that Texas Ranger, Luke Dunn. One Arrow had three wives, a son, and at least two children on the way. He had plenty of horses. He was a wealthy Comanche. But could he absolve himself of the responsibilities of family and tribe? Should he?

One Arrow felt as though he had no choice. No matter for himself or his people, he felt called to take action. As he strove to bring his future into focus, it increasingly came to him that his answers might be found in reconnecting with Ghost-Who-Rides. For now, however, there was no point in unnecessarily alarming his Penateka Comanche brethren. They'd cross the Red River and be in Indian Territory soon enough.

He thoughtfully stroked the cross on the necklace he'd purloined from Three Toes's grave. It had been a gift from Luke Dunn's squaw to the Comanche chief. He still wondered at the supposed strength of the God worshipped by the White man. Moreover, Three Toes and the White lawman had become blood brothers. What drove such an unlikely relationship? It made for more reasons to find the Texas Ranger.

⭐⭐

Thorpe strode through the hotel lobby with its handsomely lacquered mahogany walls and rich golden-framed paintings and climbed the stairs toward his room. He took a final glance at his two escorts dutifully watching for trouble. On the second-floor landing, he turned up the dimly lit hallway toward his room.

"Edward Thorpe?"

The voice wasn't loud, but it demanded an answer as it echoed in the hall. "Who's there?"

"We must talk."

As his eyes adjusted to the shadows, Thorpe could make out a broad-shouldered form wearing what at first appeared to be a skirt and brandishing a pistol. "Who are you?" Thorpe suddenly felt vulnerable. He had no weapons on him.

"We must talk." The voice was firm.

Thorpe fumbled with the key but managed to unlock the door to his room and push it open.

Moncrieff followed him into the room, slipping his pistol into his belt as he did. "I am Baron Angus Moncrieff."

Thorpe was beginning to feel less threatened, though the man had yet to state his business.

"I apologize for meeting this way. Your two friends downstairs necessitated this wee bit of intrigue."

As he listened to the man's Scottish brogue and reasonably intelligent use of the king's English, he found himself increasingly curious and certainly ever less fearful. "What is the nature of your business with me, Baron Moncrieff?"

"I appreciate your directness, Mr. Thorpe. I understand you may be interested in property. Is this true?"

Thorpe was taken aback. "How did you learn of my interest?"

"No matter, Mr. Thorpe. Am I correctly informed?"

"Possibly." Thorpe was gaining confidence and moving his thinking into business mode.

"Then, we have a mutual interest, sir." Moncrieff took the liberty of sitting in the chair beside him. "I understand you are partitioning your holdings at what you call Magnolia Plantation. But I'm not interested in that. My interests lie far to the south."

Thorpe began to relax despite the personal invasiveness of the man having done his homework as to Magnolia Plantation and his property acquisition intentions. "You have a proposal, Baron?"

"I am experienced in matters concerning the trading of properties, Mr. Thorpe. I believe I could be of considerable assistance to you in acquiring land."

"You propose to be my agent?"

"Exactly. You could go on and concern yourself with your interests in Galveston and Houston and leave your land dealings to me."

Thorpe quickly saw that he needed to buy time. He knew better than to make rash decisions. "Baron Moncrieff, I would be pleased to consider your offer. For now, I am tired and prefer to rest before dinner. Perhaps, you could return tomorrow afternoon." In the back of his mind, Thorpe was already wrestling with the need for what was called due diligence. Who was this Baron Moncrieff? What was his reputation?

Moncrieff nodded. "Certainly."

"Good. Meet me downstairs at mid-afternoon tomorrow."

"You may do well to post a guard at the hotel rear entrance, Mr. Thorpe. I had no trouble finding my way up here." Moncrieff offered a decidedly serious expression and found his way out.

"Samuel, ain't seen you in a coon's age. How be that new massa of yers?" The grizzled old man offered up a toothless grin, as he teased the Black man.

Samuel was annoyed but tried not to show it. Old Crookshanks knew every nook and cranny of Austin. "I do work for Mr. Edward Thorpe. He's a gentleman."

Crookshanks shrugged. "Whatever you say." The old coot

was such a dark white man that he made Samuel look like a light-skinned mulatto. He scratched his head with gnarled fingers, roughened by years of all sorts of manual labor. He'd worked for just about anybody in Austin who had money. Importantly, he kept his eyes and ears wide open. "So, how come you be lookin' up old Shanks?"

Samuel pulled back his coat to reveal a bulge in his vest. "Mr. Thorpe needs some information, you old coot." He tried to ease the tension and pressed a gold coin into the old man's palm.

Crookshank's eyes widened just a tad. "Hmmm...gold?"

"You know anything about a Scotsman named Angus Moncrieff who's new to Austin?"

The old man was going to milk this for all it was worth. He made like he was deep in thought for a few moments. He stroked his chin and rubbed his forehead feigning deep thought.

Samuel waited patiently.

"You talkin' 'bout Baron Angus Moncrieff?"

The Black man nodded with studied anticipation.

"Yer Mr. Thorpe done got hisself messed with a bad one." Crookshanks stroked his chin again. "He done some rustlin' down south a bit an' been known to kill as he feels led. But that not be the bes' part. He in deep trouble back where be from. Murder fer sure. An he be no baron. It jus' soun' important."

"What's he doing in Austin?"

"Got a fren' in New O'leans say he be doin' land deals."

"Land?" Samuel fished out another gold coin, but held it hostage to the answer to his question.

"He be lookin' to buy land cheap an' sell it." Crookshanks paused. "An' sell it again...an' again."

Samuel stepped back. "That's fraud."

The grizzled old man squinted his eyes as if to say of course it's fraud. "An' he's got partners."

"Partners? Where?"

Crookshanks waited to feel another gold coin touch his palm. "Hear tell, they be settin' up bizness down in Corpus."

Samuel gave up a third and then a fourth gold coin. It had been a banner meeting for both and well worth a little gold. "Thank you, my old friend."

"Take care yerself, Samuel. Enjoy yer newfoun' freedom." Crookshanks gave a light tip of his hat and waddled off to whence he came.

★★

Thorpe sat back in one of the plush chairs in the hotel lobby. Smoke from his cigar curled up toward the ornately decorated ceiling. He glanced up, as the filigrees and gold leaf stood in stark contrast to the simpler but decidedly rich mahogany décor of the rest of the lobby. He shrugged and allowed his mind to wander back to the big house at Magnolia as it used to be. His respite was all too brief.

"Mr. Thorpe, good to see you." Moncrieff presented himself in all his Scottish glory, full regalia with best kilt included.

Thorpe stood and greeted him. "Please do have a seat, Baron."

Both men sat, as an uncomfortable silence began to envelop them.

"Have you considered my offer, Mr. Thorpe?"

Thorpe looked intently at the Scotsman. "You want to be my agent to buy distressed properties."

"That's the essence of my proposal, Mr. Thorpe. What say you?"

It was important that this not go too easily. "How can I trust you, Baron? You show up unannounced and offer no *bona fides*."

Moncrieff had anticipated this sort of challenge. He had a

sheaf of forged documents attesting to a stellar moral and business reputation. "I hope these might properly answer your concerns, Mr. Thorpe." He handed them over.

Thorpe took his time looking through the papers. He'd seen enough documents from his lawyer days to recognize when documents supposedly from different sources were written with the same ink. He'd ignore that for now. Now and then, he stole a glance at Moncrieff to see how he was handling the interminable care with which he was shuffling through the Scotsman's papers. He took a long drag on his cigar and blew smoke directly at Moncrieff. It was done to observe the Scotsman's reaction to the annoyance as much as anything else.

Moncrieff endured the smoke. He badly wanted a deal. He began to doubt that Thorpe was the easy target he'd expected.

"Let's try a couple of deals, Baron. We'll see how that works out. Call it a test, if you will."

Moncrieff wasn't fully happy, but he saw this as a beginning. He figured to leverage his connection with Thorpe to make deals with other folks in Austin. "A test? That's fine, Mr. Thorpe. Let's do this."

"I'll have the papers drafted for us, and you can meet with Samuel in the morning to sign them. I'd say a ten percent fee for you?" Thorpe smiled at his own generosity. "I look forward to the first land purchase opportunity, Baron Moncrieff."

Moncrieff was momentarily taken aback by the lower-than-expected fee, but figured he'd more than recoup as he sold and resold any properties.

The two shook hands, and Thorpe watched as Moncrieff departed. He was shaking his head slowly, as Samuel emerged from behind a nearby curtain.

"What did you think of that, Samuel?"

"You've set the trap, Mr. Thorpe. We'll see if he takes the bait."

Thorpe ran his fingers through his hair. "Governor

Hamilton had best keep his end of the bargain. He was supposed to send a messenger to Luke Dunn this morning."

"Are you still going to Galveston?"

"I'd love to go out of my way, Samuel, and visit in Corpus Christi as I'd planned, but that would surely give us away. We need to appear to trust Moncrieff, if we hope to catch him at his game." He shook his head resignedly. "Best I head to Galveston."

THIRTEEN
HANGING

"I COUNT EIGHT, Jaime. There's one trying to hide in the catclaw, but those horns are hard to miss." Luke stifled a grin, resigned himself to the task at hand, turned Big Horse, and rode at the reluctant longhorn while swinging his lasso. The beast shot from behind the bush and took off at a run. Luke wasn't inclined to do any tailing, so figured to let the longhorn run himself out a bit before lassoing. Besides, catclaw was thorny and could be nasty to go charging through especially at a gallop. Chaps had their limits and Big Horse wouldn't be especially appreciative. Jaime held the other longhorns while Luke headed out at an easy trot.

As he rounded a bend in the creek, he drew up short at a live oak motte. "Jaime! Jaime, get over here!" He dismounted and stood aghast. A priest had been tortured and staked out over an ant hill. From the appearance and odor, it had likely happened four or five days previous. Luke thought back to the murders of priests he'd dealt with a couple of years back, but they'd been shot and the killer captured. This was far different.

"¡Oh, Dios mío, Señor Dunn!" Jaime was also shocked at the brutal savagery of the hanging. "Who would do this thing?"

They tied bandannas over their faces so as not to suffer inhaling the noxious fumes of death.

Luke's Texas Ranger experience kicked in, as he dismounted and began to search for clues. "Been at least three horses around here recently. They're shod, so this wasn't likely done by Indians."

"Looks like they had a fire over here, *Señor* Dunn."

Luke shook his head with dismay. "Expect that accounts for the burns on the corpse. These were angry men." He walked an ever-wider circle around the scene as he searched for more clues. "Grab my shovel, Jaime. We'll need to bury this fellow. I'll spell you on the digging." Luke hadn't walked but another few feet when the glint of metal caught his eye. He strode over to it. "Looks like a watch over here, Jaime." He picked up the timepiece and opened the cover. He smiled.

Luke had Jaime's attention. He stood from his digging. "You have a clue, *Señor* Dunn?"

"Big clue. This watch belongs to T.J. Sparks. I know the man. Expect I'll have to pay him a visit." Luke knew that Sparks had endured some tough times. Were they enough to take out his frustrations on a clergyman? Enough to torture a man and a priest at that?

Jaime watched the former Texas Ranger at work and shook his head knowingly.

Luke walked back to the body and began the distasteful task of rifling through the deceased priest's vestments. Other than an engraved crucifix, there was no identification on the man. "Perhaps someone in the diocese will recognize this cross."

Jaime was well aware of Luke's promise to Elisa not to do any Texas Ranger duties. "Er... *Señor* Dunn...maybe you should ask Sheriff Meaney to talk with *Señor* Sparks?"

Luke gave Jaime a hard glare then had to smile. He knew his *vaquero* was right, but he didn't especially like being called on it. He sighed deeply. "Dang it, Jaime. Dang it, you're right."

He took the shovel from Jaime and worked out his frustration by digging.

Just as they finished up the task of burying the priest, the reluctant longhorn appeared. He looked at Luke and seemed to smile before heading past at a trot and rejoining the other beeves. Luke shook his head and mumbled to himself, "Can never figure what goes on in these beasts' heads." Burial completed, he mounted Big Horse and turned back toward the herd. "Let's get these critters back to the main pasture, then I can go see the sheriff."

The Red River was flowing a bit heavier than normal, carrying more of the red soil that gave the Mississippi tributary its name. The small band of Penateka Comanche had searched for as shallow a crossing as possible. Small children were hoisted up and carried in the laps of mounted warriors. As many belongings as possible were tied to pack horses, as the travois would tend to sink and drift downstream. It took several hours to cross, but all arrived safely in the Indian Territory.

One Arrow was well aware of their vulnerability. He and two warriors had crossed ahead of their people and chased off some hunters from other Comanche bands. Caution was paramount.

Once across the Red River, they still had several miles to journey before they'd reach their destination just south of what were called the Wichita Mountains. As the Comanche traveled further from their home hunting grounds, they found themselves ever more fearful. This was less an adventure and more a stark cultural shift brought on by unfamiliarity with the new territory. There were buffalo to be sure, but there was plenty of evidence of the white man's presence. Much of the ground had been crossed by cattle drives. Discarded wagon parts and sun-bleached longhorn skulls dotted the landscape. An occasional cross-marked grave evidenced the memory of some soul who didn't make it to Kansas or Missouri.

One Arrow was already having doubts about his decision to bring his people north. He also felt the pull of the yearning to reconnect with Ghost-Who-Rides. He had a sense that there was much more to learn from the Texas Ranger. At first opportunity, he would make a vision quest and commune with the Great Spirit about his decision.

He stood at the mirror fully admiring himself. He looked every bit the part of a Scottish nobleman from tam to kilt to boot. Angus Moncrieff was ready to cut himself a swath of land fraud through the scions of Austin. He took extra time to groom his beard and mustache. With signed agreement from Edward Thorpe in hand and his impressive collection of forged papers, who could possibly resist his proposals.

He counted on the combination of slow communications plus the ability of his South Texas operations to move quickly to work his sleight-of-hand scheme, take his profits, and avoid the long arm of the law.

He reckoned to be long gone before they figured him out.

Luke rode easy-like up to the Corpus Christi jail. He'd had a long conversation with Elisa and had assured her that he'd let Meaney handle this situation. He fought the deep-in-the-belly urge to investigate the priest's murder. He was in the saddle thinking on his dilemma, when Sheriff Meaney emerged from the jailhouse.

Meaney's appearance broke Luke's trancelike state. "Luke? Luke, what brings you here?"

"Oh, yeah...Bill...I want to report a murder."

Like pretty much everyone else, Meaney was aware of Luke's pledge to Elisa. He didn't even ask why the now former Texas Ranger wasn't pursuing the killer. "You want to come in and tell me what you've got?"

Luke reluctantly dismounted and hitched Big Horse. He slowly followed Meaney into the jailhouse and pulled up a chair. He glanced longingly at the rack of Henry rifles mounted on the wall. A tempting stack of wanted flyers sat on Meaney's desk. "Jaime and I were corralling beeves yesterday, when one lit off and I had to give chase. As I rounded the bend in a creek, I came upon a motte of live oak with a priest spread across an anthill. He'd been beaten and tortured pretty badly, Bill. Figured he'd been staked out there for maybe three or four days." Luke placed a small cloth containing the priest's personal effects on Meaney's desk. "Anyway, Jaime and I buried him after I did some investigating. There was evidence of at least three shod horses and a spot where a fire had been used to heat whatever the priest was tortured with. I searched the area as best I could and came up with this watch." Luke passed the watch to the sheriff. "Flip it open, Bill. It's got T.J. Sparks name engraved in it."

"You thinking he might have killed the priest, Luke?"

"Don't know. Guess that'll have to be your job to find out." Luke sighed and caressed his mustache as he was wont to do when deep in thought or about to deliver a serious message. "I understand that Sparks was struggling. Lost two sons in the war, was deep in debt, wife left him, and he was going to lose his ranch. Could be the priest happened to be in the wrong place at the wrong time and paid the ultimate price for it."

"Sounds plausible, Luke. My deputy and I will ride out to Sparks's place today and check his story." He watched Luke still staring longingly at the rack of rifles. "Sorry you can't join us, my friend."

"Be sure to let me know how it turns out. You know I miss being a lawman. Miss it terribly much."

Meaney resisted the temptation to tease his friend. This was far too serious. "I'll be sure to let you know, Luke. And thanks for sharing your thoughts on Sparks."

One Arrow closed his eyes in prayer to the Great Spirit, as he sat cross-legged on the blanket. Beside him to his right were his travel pouch with pipe and tobacco and beside that his ever-present bow and arrow, knife, and lance. The chief had removed the bone necklace with its cross and gently laid it to his left. A feeling deep inside told him that the vision quest with the Great Spirit might offend the White man's God. His arms were spread at his sides, his hands barely touching the blanket.

He felt a tingling sensation course through him and then heard the telltale sound of the rattlesnake. He slowly opened one eye. The reptile wasn't more than six feet away, and he was a big one. One Arrow strove to breathe as slowly as possible. He opened both eyes and stared intensely into the slit-like eyes of the rattler. There was no time to reach for a weapon. The snake was looking ever more irritated.

His left hand moved toward the bone necklace. It wasn't a conscious move. He maintained eye contact with the rattlesnake. It was as though he could feel the spirit of Ghost-Who-Rides envelop him protectively. He had no idea why a mind image of the Texas Ranger should come to him at that moment. The chief's hand made contact with the necklace, and he cautiously wrapped his fingers around it.

Just as the rattler was about to strike, One Arrow whipped the necklace out at it. By some miracle, it landed directly around the rattler's mouth. Distracted and surprised, the angry reptile bit the cross and spit it out before uncoiling and slithering away. One Arrow would forever swear the snake shuddered when it bit the cross.

As though the spirits were not finished, *kwihnai*, the eagle, swept from on high and snatched the snake away in its talons. One Arrow was incredulous. What had just happened? Had the Great Spirit spoken? Was an even higher power at work? He had to find the answer. His vision quest was obviously ended. The answer made clear. He would seek out his friend Ghost-Who-Rides.

"Tom Sparks! It's Sheriff Meaney. We need to talk." Meaney and his deputy sat their saddles out front of Sparks's humble cabin. They were greeted by silence.

"Tom?"

A rifle muzzle appeared through a slit in the front door.

"Don't want it to go down like this, Tom." The lawmen slid rifles from their scabbards and slowly dismounted, keeping horses between them and the cabin.

The rifle was withdrawn from the door. Still silent.

"You know anything about the killing of a priest, Tom?"

A single shot shattered the air.

It came from inside the cabin. Meaney ducked low and ran for the door. He put his shoulder to it and crashed through. Sparks lay sprawled on the dirt floor of the cabin, blood pouring from a gunshot wound to his head. Meaney kicked the rifle away and kneeled beside the man. "What? Why? Dammit, Sparks."

Barely conscious, Sparks tried to focus his eyes.

Meaney tried in vain to stop the bleeding.

"I done it. Got nothin' to live…" Sparks's words trailed off, and he breathed his last.

"Hey, Sheriff. We got company!" The deputy called from outside.

Meaney went to the door. A dark-haired teenage girl riding a black horse had appeared. "Who are you?"

A desperate expression swept across her face. "Who are you, and where's my father?"

Meaney saw that she was unarmed. "I'm Sheriff Bill Meaney. I'm sorry, but if the man inside is your father, he's gone."

The girl slid from the saddle and ran past Meaney into the cabin. "No! No!" She fell to her father's side.

Meaney stood helplessly in the doorway. He couldn't come up with any words to ease the young girl's obvious pain. All he was capable of doing was watching her in the agony of loss.

Tears streaked down her dust-caked face. She'd been riding hard only to come upon this grim scene. "Why?"

Finally, Meaney had to become the sheriff he was. "What's your name?"

Through sobs and sniffles, the young girl responded. "Emma. My name is Emma Sparks."

"We're sorry for your loss, Emma. We tried to stop him." Meaney instinctively walked over to her. "Do you know why he might have done this?"

Emma grabbed a nearby blanket and slipped it under her father's head. She slowly stood and faced the sheriff. "I told him not to do it."

"Do what?"

"The priest. Father James."

"He killed the priest?"

"Saw him do it." Emma hung her head. "I couldn't stop him." Once again, she started sobbing. "Father James tried to pray for him. He promised forgiveness...that everything would get better. It made my pa angrier."

"I'm sure Father James's soul is in heaven, Emma." A part of Meaney felt like joining her in her grief, but he had a job to do. "Do you have any kinfolk around these parts?"

She looked off forlornly. "Got an uncle in San Patricio."

"We can see that you get there safely."

"No...no, I can't go there." She shuddered uncomfortably.

Meaney sensed there was far more to this. He shifted the conversation. "You have a burial plot around here?"

"Ma's buried out back. Donny, too. Billy's buried at Gettysburg."

Meaney recalled Sparks's sons dying in the war. "Shall we bury your pa with them?"

"I expect so. He loved my ma. Nearly killed him, when she left him and then passed." Young Emma grew serious as though reliving some vivid memory. Staying at the cabin was not an option. "My ma had friends in Laredo. That's where she was from."

Meaney could feel some not-so-pleasant unspoken story in her words. There was terrible trauma in this family. It made him uncomfortable and was not easy to shake off. Try as he might, words of comfort seemed inadequate. He wrapped his arms around her trembling body as she once again began to sob uncontrollably. He caught the deputy's eye and made a nod toward a shovel leaning near the fireplace. He'd tend to T.J. Sparks's body himself once he calmed Emma.

The sheriff did his best in the ensuing hour to comfort the young teen while conducting a funeral of sorts for her father. Seeing the three neatly aligned graves, one fresh dug, was sobering of itself.

Emma seemed to have gotten her emotions under control at least for the moment. She strove to put on a deceptively strong demeanor given her youth. "Thank you, Sheriff. I'm much beholden."

"How about you come back to Corpus Christi with us for now, Miss Sparks." He purposely used a more formal form of address. She was going to be growing up sooner than most. "You can stay the night with me and my wife, Clara. We can come back in a day or so and gather any personal effects."

Emma wiped a tear and nodded. She grabbed a few essentials in a satchel, and they were soon mounted up. She didn't look back as they headed toward Corpus Christi.

★★

It had been a long day. Luke sat on a bench on the gallery beside Elisa. He was distracted, wondering how the sheriff had made out investigating the murder of the priest.

"You've got something on your mind, Lucas?" She knew.

They'd had a long conversation that morning about what Luke and Jaime had found on the southernmost reaches of Heaven's Gate. Finding a priest tortured and murdered deeply affected her husband, but his frustration at not bringing the killer to justice was taking a far greater toll. He'd been true to his promise to her to hang up his Texas Ranger badge and reluctantly but dutifully reported it to Sheriff Meaney. Had she coerced him into making an impossible promise? The ranch was already rebounding from the war. With Jaime and three part-time *vaqueros*, the livestock duties were under control. She and Julia did the gardening, and her three oldest, Peter, John, and Andrea Anne were beginning to be ever more experienced, hard-working helpers. Did she dare release him from his promise?

"Just wondering how Bill made out." Luke gazed off thoughtfully across the grassy prairie spread before them. He slipped his arm around Elisa's shoulders. He tried to shake off wondering what he might have done to pursue Sparks. "This is a great life, Lisa." The words didn't seem to spill out comfortably. Yes, he loved her and Heaven's Gate, but part of his heart was delivering justice, was helping keep folks safe from lawbreakers. Darn but he was a Texas Ranger to his core.

A fully-unexpected wave of recognition crashed over Elisa. She felt the truth coated in hollowness as Luke spoke. She was sitting beside half a husband. "Lucas…" Her words trailed off. She suddenly felt the wetness beneath her. "Oh my. Lucas, it's time!"

Luke scooped her up and carried her to the bedroom. He lay her on the bed and went off to heat some water and call

Julia to help out. Talk of promises made and promises forgiven would wait.

One Arrow had crossed to the south side of the Red River. There'd be no going back—at least not now. He'd bade farewell to Cactus Flower, Bird Woman, and his newest wife Blue Feather. The most difficult were goodbyes to his young children. None were yet old enough to understand his parting much less the adventure he was undertaking. He could only pray that he'd return with stories they'd be ready to understand. He left a trusted warrior, Bear Killer, in charge until his return.

He didn't linger at the river's edge but turned southward. He had two ponies in tow, one a pack horse. With the intense heat and humidity, he carried plenty of water. His bags were filled with venison jerky. He chose to rest wherever he could find shade during the day and travel in the relative cool of the night. For now, One Arrow's path would be under the light of a full moon. Assuming no unexpected delays, he was confident he'd reach Heaven's Gate midway between the new moon and next full moon.

Sheriff Meaney had settled poor Emma in with Clara's help and was on the road to Heaven's Gate to fill Luke in on what had happened to Sparks. In a way, he relished the escape. The poor waif of a girl undoubtedly had a rough night. Clara had done her best at breakfast to cheer the teen, but Emma's eyes were near swollen shut from crying. Whatever meager future she had seemed to have died with her father's suicide. The Meaneys would be tasked with trying to kindle new hopes for her. Such was the ongoing aftermath of war, but this was more the obligation of community reaching out to those in need.

Meaney paused at the entrance to Heaven's Gate Ranch. Looking up at the arched gate, he admired Luke's handiwork. The gateway was a work of art with the ranch name spelled out in an ornate wrought-iron scroll. There was a permanence to it, and permanence was much needed in these post-war days.

As he rode past the barn and approached the house, he was taken aback by the silence. It was as though no one had yet awakened. Then he heard the plaintive cry that a newborn makes. "Damn. Well, I'll be. Another Dunn," he thought to himself, as a wide grin spread across his face.

He dismounted, tied his horse to the post, and climbed to the gallery. He was about to knock when the door opened. He looked down.

Peter was playing greeter. "Howdy, Mr. Sheriff. Mom and Dad are..." He was at a loss for words. He laughed with glee and thrust out his chest pridefully. "I have a new brother!"

Luke appeared from the bedroom. "Come on in, Bill. Fix yourself a cup of coffee. Be with you in a minute."

Meaney looked at young Peter then at the coffee pot.

Luke strode down the stairs looking like he'd been the loser in a battle with a pack of coyotes.

"Sorry about the timing. Congratulations," offered Meaney.

"Peter, please pour a cup of coffee for Sheriff Meaney."

Peter found himself in a race with John and Andrea Anne to fetch a cup. After a little jostling, he managed to secure a grip, carefully pour the coffee, and hand it to the sheriff.

Meaney was impressed by their eagerness. "Thank you, Peter. Thanks to you all." He knew to give wide credit. He was glad they hadn't all been told to pour the coffee, as there was no knowing what mayhem might have ensued.

A smiling Julia soon emerged from the bedroom, waved friendly-like at Meaney, and departed.

Luke smiled. "Back in a minute, Bill. Make yourself comfortable." He headed back upstairs. He stood in the bedroom doorway for a few seconds to smile at wife and newborn son. He kissed her gently and took up the baby in his strong arms. "Back in a minute, Lisa."

Luke headed downstairs with their new son. He proudly thrust the newborn forward. "Matthew. His name is Matthew, Bill."

"Good strong name, Luke."

"Yep. Yes, it is. It means gift from God." He paused thoughtfully as he scanned the room full of children, including a couple hanging on Meaney. "Shucks, they're all gifts from God." Luke took Matthew upstairs and reconnected him with Elisa. He kissed her again, then headed back to the kitchen, grabbed a cup of coffee, and joined Meaney at the table. "What news brings you out here this fine morning, Bill?"

"Figured you might want to know about Sparks."

"Should we take this conversation outside?"

Meaney looked around. "Might be best, Luke."

That didn't bode well so far as Luke was concerned. "Peter, John, watch after your brother and sisters." He led the way out to the gallery.

"I'll get right to it, Luke. Sparks did it. Confessed as such."

"Did you arrest him?"

"Killed himself. Stuck the rifle barrel in his mouth and shot himself clean through the head as the deputy and me approached the cabin."

"What a shame."

"Gets worse. His young daughter came on us just after he'd killed himself. She'd seen him kill the priest."

"Oh my, Bill. How'd she handle it?"

"She grieved, though I think it was as much loneliness as loss of her family." Meaney toyed with his watch fob. "She stayed with Clara and me last night. Says she has friends in Laredo."

"You going to help her get there?"

"Thinking on it. Laredo's rough. Her ma was from there."

Luke tried to think the best, but couldn't deny reality. "You're right about Laredo. Easy to get into a bad crowd."

"Thought I'd ask Scarlett to chat with her."

"Makes sense. Scarlett sure experienced the seamy side of Laredo. Reputation followed her for a long time."

"True. By-the-by, she and Walker have their haberdashery open. I think they'll do quite well." The sheriff stared off, as he sought to phrase a lingering question. "Miss it, don't you?"

Luke shook his head. "It's the way it is, Bill. No point in you keeping on asking the question."

"Well, best I be getting back to Clara and young Emma. Much obliged for the coffee. While I'm out here, I'll take a quick ride out to Nuecestown and see how bad a condition the jailhouse is in. Congratulations again on your new son." Meaney stood, patted Luke on the shoulder, and turned to go. "Enjoy your family, Luke. You're a special breed, and you're breeding a special family."

Luke laughed. "Thanks, Bill. Looks like it's going to be a horse day."

"Horse day?"

Yep. I promised a while back that I'd give Andrea Anne her own horse. Got to deliver on my word. I think every kid in Texas age four and up ought to have their own horse." He laughed. "The Dunn gang will all be riding into Corpus before you know it."

Meaney mounted up. "Y'all take care now, ya hear?"

Luke headed back to the bedroom.

Elisa was awake and nursing Matthew. "Did Bill leave?"

"Yes."

"Did they catch the killer?"

"Sparks killed himself." Luke knew he was being abrupt. He really didn't want to talk about it, as it reminded him of how he yearned to be bringing justice to the Nueces Strip.

Elisa couldn't stand the somberness written large across Luke's face. They should be focused in on the joy of their newborn son. She knew they needed to revisit his promise to her. "That's so sad, Lucas. Here. Take your son. He needs to know his father." She handed Matthew up to Luke.

Holding the tiny babe in his huge arms softened Luke a bit. Meaney was right. He was a special breed. "I love you, Lisa Dunn." He sat on the edge of the bed, leaned over, gently stroked her hair, and kissed her.

The feel of his manly presence contrasted with the fresh aroma of newborn life. Luke was her man. He was committed to her. He loved her, the ranch...loved it all. But part of his heart, a part she missed, was in being a lawman. She nestled her face into his shoulder, then pulled back and looked softly into his eyes. "I forgive your promise, Lucas."

He held her as tightly as the baby would permit.

FOURTEEN
FIGHTING AGAINST CHAOS

"DON'T KNOW ABOUT THIS." General Custer was clearly upset.

"There's been a lot of talk about it. That duty they gave to Colonel Belknap is mostly a stopgap. Those idiots in Washington need to come here and see first-hand." Crime had begun to spiral out of control. Hamilton waffled between his being provisional Texas governor as juxtaposed to his role as an army general.

"You say, they don't want to reauthorize the Texas Rangers?"

"I think they're afraid. So many Rangers fought with the Rebel cavalry during the war. They're fearful that hostilities would begin again."

Custer shook his head. He was an egocentric man, intensely disliked by many, but was no one's fool. "I think they're looking to punish Texas. It's like an extra kick in the teeth."

"You've got a point, George. I've heard rumors of forming up a state police."

"Where will they get their lawmen from?"

Hamilton ruefully shook his head. "Colored troops. They'll use mustered out colored troops."

Custer was speechless, but not for long. That wasn't his nature. "That'll be mighty interesting, Andrew. Mighty interesting indeed. Sorta like pouring oil on a fire. Some folks are likely to get burned." He took a long sip of whiskey.

★★

"Pleased to meet you, Emma." Scarlett welcomed the teen into the "Cacti & Boots" haberdashery she and Carson owned. She extended her hand.

Emma hesitatingly shook her hand. "Thank you, ma'am."

"You can call me Scarlett, honey. Everyone does."

"Yes, Scarlett, ma'am."

Scarlett couldn't help but smile. It was as though she could read deep into Emma's mind. From what Clara had told her, this girl was living on a razor-sharp edge and could too easily fall into the abyss of a dark life. As Scarlett well knew, abuse wasn't always physical. "Hear tell, your ma was from Laredo. Spent time there myself."

Emma looked distracted, as she scanned the dresses, hats, and shoes before her. "Yes, ma'am...I mean Scarlett...my pa met her in Laredo." She turned an appraising gaze toward Scarlett and her flowing waves of red hair. "My but your hair is so beautiful, Scarlett." She hesitantly touched her own forlorn locks.

Scarlett judged Emma at about 14 or 15 years old, so her mother likely would have predated her own time in the town. "We'll just have to fix up your hair, darling." She offered a kind smile. "What was your ma's name, honey?"

Emma thought on that. "I just always called her ma."

"What did your pa call her?"

"It wasn't nice." Emma hung her head. "He called her bad names."

Scarlett was beginning to get an ever-clearer picture of the teen's upbringing. "How would you like a dress, Emma?"

"Ain't never owned a dress. Can I ride a horse in a dress?"

Scarlett smiled compassionately. "How about we start with a cup of tea?" She led her to a small side table with a couple of comfortable chairs. "My daughter Margaret likes to sit here and drink tea." Scarlett rightly figured that a hairdo and fresh clothes might begin the teen's healing.

"Is she my age?"

"She's barely seven years old, Emma. You'd probably like her though. And you might like my assistant, Martha. She's closer to your age." Scarlett thought long and hard about her next question. She didn't want to jeopardize the line of communication she was opening with the now-orphaned waif. "You been bleeding regular every month?"

Emma looked at her quizzically. "Did until a month ago."

Scarlett stifled a gasp. "None last month?"

"No."

"Any men touch your privates, honey?"

"Just my pa." She was fully innocent as to her father's perverse lechery.

"Did he put himself inside you?"

"Yes, Miss Scarlett. He said it felt good. It made him happy, so I let him."

Old memories flooded Scarlett's mind. This young girl was in trouble and didn't yet know it. Who should tell her? What was she to do? Scarlett shifted her line of thinking almost in self-defense. She began to comb out Emma's hair. "Do you have family in Laredo?"

"None that I know of."

"Let's drink some tea, do up your hair, and get you that dress, then we'll go back to Sheriff Meaney's house."

"I like you, Miss Scarlett."

Scarlett fought the urge to break down in tears.

★★

The buzzards were circling lazily above. "Damn, Cal. Ain't them birds got no sense? We be alive an' well."

Pablo looked upward. "Likely waitin' fer ya, ya stupid sonofabitch."

"We don't git some grub soon, we all gonna be buzzard bait." Cal poured the last of the coffee into his tin cup. "Whatcha think, Silas?"

The third man sat silently. "Damn hot day."

They were a swarthy trio sitting in the shade of the live oak motte. The tree offered little relief from the sweltering prairie heat.

"I heard somebody in San Diego talkin' 'bout a ranch near Nuecestown. Called Heaven's Gate. Maybe we send 'em to their maker."

Silas swiped his forehead and neck with his bandanna and then wrung it out. "Near got us kilt at the last 'stead we set on."

"Mexicans fight tough, Silas. ¿Como esta tu dedo gordo?" Pablo laughingly teased his friend about having his big toe nearly shot off.

"Ain't funny. Hurts like hell."

Cal stood and looked off toward the east. "Sun's sinkin', boys. Should be able to ride soon 'nuf."

"How's ammo holdin' up?"

Pablo checked his own supply. "Bit low here."

Turned out they were all low on ammunition. And food. Hunger tends to make desperate men even more dangerous and perhaps not too smart.

"Better make every bullet count." Silas looked at the others. "Could make it by daybreak." He wiped more sweat from his brow. "Gotta get water fer the horses, too. Dead horses ain't gonna git us anywhere."

✩✩

Luke stretched easy-like, as he sauntered down to the barn. He had a premonition that morning, so had packed both his Colt revolvers and brought the new Henry instead of the Colt rifle. He froze at the sound of a horse's snort somewhere off to his right.

"Hey, mister! Can we water our horses?"

Luke turned to see the foulest-looking trio of men he'd seen in a long time. His thinking immediately went beyond their appearance. They were heavily armed despite their disheveled condition. One wore a beaten old gray Rebel tunic, and one of the others sported a belt buckle emblazoned with CSA. "Trough's over that way. Help yourselves. I'm fixing to saddle my horse." Luke continued into the barn.

Cal, Silas, and Pablo took their time sizing Luke up. It was easy to see that their prey was a big man. Nor could they miss the firepower Luke was packing.

Luke felt the hairs on the back of his neck stand up. Something was out of sorts with these men. In the first place, they had no pack animal. If they did, it was hidden away somewhere. He saddled Big Horse and slipped the Henry into its scabbard. He left one Colt holstered but some weird sense told him to keep the other at the ready.

The three men were busily watering their mounts as Luke emerged leading Big Horse. He tried to appear relaxed and friendly, but he was coiled tight like a wound-up spring.

Silas whispered. "Damn, he's a big man. Wonder if he can use that peashooter?"

"If we're gonna get any grub, we'd as soon find out." Cal was ready to do whatever it took to get food and money. "Wonder if there be any women aroun'?"

The men stepped away from their horses and stood about twenty feet in front of Luke, effectively blocking his path.

Luke had already figured the order in which he'd drop

these men. He knew their all-too-familiar game. In a calm voice that should have warned them that he'd been in these sorts of situations before said, "You men need something else?" Luke stepped clear of Big Horse.

In the blink of an eye, Pablo raised his rifle and took a bead on Luke. But an explosion rocked the air, as Pablo's heart burst in shreds from his chest. Luke dropped Silas with a single shot as the man had just pulled back the hammer on his Colt. Cal dropped his pistol like a hot potato and raised his hands high. Luke looked around to see where the shot that stopped Pablo came from.

At the sound of gunfire, Jaime and Julia emerged from their cabin. He had rifle in hand, but the action was over. "*Señor* Dunn, you okay?"

"Yes thanks, Jaime. Keep that rifle on this man."

Luke kicked Cal's gun out of the way. "Get your hands up and step back." He glanced at the other two. They weren't breathing. Luke looked up to see Elisa walking toward him, newborn Matthew in one hand and the Sharps rifle in the other.

"Doggone, Lucas. I'm going to have another bruise on my shoulder."

Luke swelled with pride as he looked down at her. "Lisa Dunn, have I ever told you how good you are with that thing?" He kept an eye on the remaining outlaw. "Don't move a muscle, mister." Luke pulled a piece of rope from his saddlebag. "Put your hands behind you."

"Did I hear Dunn?"

"Yes. What's that to you?"

"Never woulda showed here had we knowed."

"We all make bad choices, mister. Now, what's your name?"

"Cal Stimson."

"Your friends have any next of kin?"

"Not sure. Met up in the Rebel army. Didn't talk much 'bout family."

"Well, Cal Stimson, we're going to load up my buckboard with your friends and take a ride into Corpus Christi to hand you over to Sheriff Meaney."

"Ain't you a Texas Ranger?"

"Not right now. Can't arrest you, but I can and will turn you in for attempted robbery and murder." Luke turned to his *vaquero*. "Jaime, be kind enough to hitch the buckboard. We've got some folks to deliver to Sheriff Meaney."

"Comes back right quick, doesn't it, Lucas." Elisa chuckled wryly. How could anyone miss the expression of lawman's pride on his face, as he did what any self-respecting Texas Ranger would do. Her man was back, every inch her man. She gave him a light kiss before walking on back to the house with baby on her hip and Sharps under her arm, as though having conducted some normal course of events on Heaven's Gate. Five little awe-struck faces pressed against the windows, having watched their momma do what she had to do.

Luke watched her admiringly, as she walked away. Sexy little stride to be sure. He thought on how no one could ever tell from looking at her that she'd given birth to six babies, six Dunn children. He shook his head and turned back to the business at hand. It had been but a momentary but rewarding distraction. His day was already disrupted and none too pleasantly. He pushed Cal toward the wagon and hoisted him up. Luke stood a head taller and maybe forty pounds heavier, so it barely took any effort. He tied the man to the side of the wagon bed. "You sit real peaceful like and keep your mouth shut. This ride won't take all that long, Mr. Stimson." Jaime helped load the blanket-wrapped bodies of Cal's two deceased partners-in-crime into the bed of the buckboard. The *vaquero* drove the wagon while Luke rode alongside and kept an eye out for any more trouble. The trio's horses were hitched to the back of the wagon, though they wouldn't be needing them anymore. Luke figured their sale would likely pay for Cal's hanging. It made for quite a sight, as Luke waved to Elisa and headed east.

The ride to Corpus gave Luke time to think. Was the attack on Heaven's Gate by these men just the beginning of greater lawless chaos? He wondered what the provisional government in Austin was going to do and whether his old friend and mentor Rip Ford would have any influence?

★★

The small entourage pulled up in front of the Corpus Christi jail to find Sheriff Meaney sitting on the front stoop. With all the jingling, jangling, and creaking of the wagon, it was hard not to miss the arrival. "Dang, Luke. What on earth you got there?"

Luke dismounted and walked over to the sheriff. "New tenant for your jail, Bill. Crime is attempted murder and robbery. His friends already paid the price for their crimes."

Meaney stood, smiled at Luke, and walked to the wagon, nodding a greeting to Jaime as he walked past and gazed into the buckboard. "You're in luck, Luke. Just sent a couple of men to the prison at Huntsville. How'd these two meet their maker?"

"Elisa killed one as he took a bead on me, and I got the other just as he was yanking out his gun. The one that's hogtied is Cal Stimson. He surrendered peacefully after his partners had been killed. Jaime here witnessed it all."

"Elisa got one, you say. You have quite a woman there, Luke Dunn."

"She used the Sharps." Luke chuckled. "I expect she'll be getting a bruise on her shoulder."

"If you don't mind, I'd appreciate it if Jaime here could dump those bodies out back. We'll get a couple of boxes and have them planted in the cemetery." Meaney looked at the horses tied behind the buckboard. "These their horses."

"Yep. Figured they would pay for the boxes and maybe a hanging...or at least a cell at Huntsville." He saw Stimson flinch at the mention of hanging.

"You seem to be acting like your old self, Luke. You're not backing off on your promise are you?"

"Elisa forgave me my promise to her, Bill. Guess that makes me available to wear a badge again. Happy to help when and if you need me."

It was almost too much for Meaney. Here was one of the most famous lawmen to wear a badge in South Texas seeming to beg for a job. "I'll keep that in mind, Luke. I got a telegram yesterday that our old friend Colonel Belknap is heading our way. Seems he's gotten new orders and may be looking for help."

"He stopped by at Heaven's Gate a couple of weeks back. We'll see if he shows up." Luke paused and thoughtfully stroked his mustache. "Say, Bill, what became of that Sparks girl you mentioned?"

"Emma's been staying with Clara and me. Sort of like having a daughter. She's been talking with Scarlett."

"That helping?"

"I think Emma has pretty much decided not to go to Laredo. Poor girl has had a rougher life than we'd thought. Scarlett thinks her ma may have whored in Laredo. Turns out her pa had his way with his daughter, and she's pregnant."

"So, you thinking of letting her stay with y'all for a while?"

"I expect. Sure wouldn't do to turn the poor girl out."

"Let me and Elisa know, if y'all need any help.

"Thanks. Let's park this Stimson fellow in a cell, write up the paperwork, and go grab a drink down at the Longhorn." Meaney looked over at Jaime. "You, too, Jaime." The sheriff's anti-Mexican bias had apparently eased quite a bit.

★★

Belknap sat high in the saddle as he surveyed the men assembled before him. The heat and humidity were already oppressive at mid-morning. Dismay would be an understatement to describe his mood. He who had dutifully led men into battle, journeyed over mountains and through impenetrable passes, suffered ignominious defeat at Palmito Ranch, now found himself leading a ragtag collection of war veterans most of whom had never seen battle. Instilling discipline would be the first order of business. He had two captains and three lieutenants under his command. He tried to be optimistic as to their abilities. Belknap had historically relied on non-commissioned officers and figured he'd be doing a lot of that.

Something Luke had suggested still hung with him. He was nearing thirty years of age and hadn't taken the time to even consider finding a woman and marrying. Life seemed to be speeding by, and he was increasingly aware of a certain loneliness that shrouded itself over him. He didn't want to become some disgruntled old bachelor. His musings were interrupted.

"Colonel Belknap, sir."

He looked down and returned the sergeant's salute. "Good to see you, Sergeant Brown. What do you think of this motley group?"

The sergeant was surprised to have his opinion solicited. "Sir?"

"You heard me. Any hope that we can make some fighting units out of these men?"

The sergeant nodded with a wry smile. "Yes, sir. I do believe we can. Some might not endure the discipline and training, but we'll have them ready to fight, sir."

"I think we'll get along just fine then, Sergeant." Belknap's eyes glanced over at his group of officers as he offered up a wry grin. "Can you work with them?" He nodded in their direction.

The sergeant simply smiled. "Yes, sir. We'll have 'em all working like a fine machine, sir."

"We'll be heading south in two weeks. Have them ready as you can." He looked back out at the nearly hundred and fifty assembled men. "Carry on, Sergeant."

Deserters, wounded, former prisoners of war, Yankees, Rebels, Black, Hispanic, Anglo…they were as diverse in individual history as in appearance. Belknap's plan would be to divide his force in two companies so as to cover more territory. The companies would be organized to enable smaller patrols to begin the labor of cleaning up the Nueces Strip of former Governor Murrah's troublemakers. As to his personal goals, he aimed to meet up with Luke Dunn sooner than later and get his advice—maybe even persuade him to join in the mission.

FIFTEEN
TROUBLE THIS WAY COMES

MONCRIEFF CLIMBED the marble steps and knocked with his cane on the large oak doors, and soon heard the quick treading of feet from within. The doors were highly lacquered, but not so as to give away their history as evidenced by the many nicks, gouges, and even a bullet hole or two. They spoke volumes of their owner, but the Scotsman wasn't listening.

"You are Baron Moncrieff, sir?" The Black man was clothed as befitted a house servant with his white shirt featuring, red coat with gold buttons, black breeches, white stockings, and black shoes with silver buckles. He seemed a throwback to another era.

Moncrieff nodded.

"You are expected. May I take your hat?"

"I'd as soon keep it, lad." He played his Scottish accent for whatever advantage it might afford.

"Follow me, sir."

Moncrieff was led to a library that featured as many books as he'd ever seen in one place. An ornate mahogany desk dominated one side of the room. A pair of comfortable reading chairs with brass kerosene floor lamps were situated on the opposite side.

"Please have a seat here, sir. Mr. Burnett will be with you in a moment." He was offered one of two straight-backed cane-seat chairs facing the desk. The servant exited the room, closing the door behind him.

Moncrieff looked longingly at the reading chairs as he took the seat he'd been directed to and waited with his back to the door. And waited. A clock ticked. Ticked again. He waited.

The door opened after what seemed like an hour but was likely half that. A short ruddy-complected man dressed in cowboy hat, pale-blue cotton shirt, heavy dark blue cotton trousers, and brown leather boots with jangling spurs strode in and took a position behind the desk. "Trying out these new-fangled pants, Mr. Moncrieff. Some haberdasher in California is experimenting with a heavy fabric for work pants. Seem pretty durable." Burnett gazed intently at Moncrieff. He looked down at the kilt and smiled. "Hrumph. Seems pants aren't your concern, Mr. Moncrieff." Burnett sat and leaned in toward his desk. "Sorry to be late. Horse was a bit skittish this morning. Maybe didn't like the smell of the dye in the fabric." Burnett arose enough to reach across the desk and extend his hand. "Pleased to meet you, Mr. Moncrieff."

The baron ignored Burnett not using his faked title, as he stood and took the man's hand. "My pleasure, Mr. Burnett. Thank you for seeing me."

Burnett looked at the clock. "Damn, it's ten thirty. Time for my whiskey and cigar." He walked toward a nearby side-boy. "Care to join me, Moncrieff?" He didn't wait for an answer but proceeded to pour a glass of the liquor and snip the end of a Cuban cigar he'd taken from a thermidor. He offered them to Moncrieff who had the good sense not to refuse the hospitality. He motioned Moncrieff to the reading chairs. "You familiar with San Jacinto?" He saw the Scotsman's face go blank. "No matter." He leaned back and blew a column of cigar smoke straight up. "Now, what is this opportunity you referred to in your inquiry, Mr. Moncrieff. While I respect Mr. Thorpe's judgment, I do make my own business decisions."

Moncrieff was taken aback by Burnett getting right to the business at hand. These Texans didn't truck with delay, as though time were some enemy to be defeated. However, the whiskey and cigars were as close to niceties as he was likely going to see. "I am in the land business, Mr. Burnett. Mr. Thorpe and I have reached an agreement whereby I serve as his agent purchasing distressed properties in South Texas in exchange for a small fee."

"You're from Scotland, Moncrieff?" Burnett laid a penetrating squinting gaze on the Scotsman. "Where in Scotland?"

"Glasgow, sir."

"You ever boat on the River Warren?"

Moncrieff blinked. Burnett was actually testing him. "Pardon, but I've not heard of that river, sir. I have boated the River Clyde."

Burnett took a long drag on his cigar and blew circles of smoke that dissipated in the rafters above. "What is your fee? Are the titles clear?"

"The fee is a mere ten percent of the purchase price, sir. And yes, the titles to any land I purchase on your behalf will be clear. There'll be no encumbrances."

Burnett nodded. He knew that Thorpe had agreed to a similar arrangement. "I don't know you well enough to do business just yet, Moncrieff." He glanced again at the Scotsman's kilt. "Let's go for a ride and get better acquainted. I assume you can sit a horse in that thing."

"The kilt? Yes. Yes, I can ride, Mr. Burnett."

Burnett quaffed the last of his whiskey and ground out his cigar in a dish. "Very good. Let's go to my stable."

Moncrieff disposed of his own drink and cigar and followed Burnett to a pair of horses conveniently saddled and awaiting them. As he climbed onto the horse he'd been directed to, he noted the Henry rifle in the scabbard beside his saddle. "Do we plan to hunt, Mr. Burnett?"

"Can you shoot, Moncrieff?"

"Of course."

"I meant, can you hit what you're aiming at?"

Moncrieff smiled. "I get lucky." It was an honest answer.

"Mr. Dunn?" The courier handed a sealed envelope to Luke.

Luke took it tentatively. "Thanks." From the heavy lather worked up by the horse, the courier had clearly pushed hard. Luke wondered why the sender hadn't used the telegraph, as it had been mostly repaired through to Corpus Christi. "You're free to water your horse down there at the trough. I'd rest him right good before you head out."

"I'm supposed to wait for you to read the message, sir."

"Well, water your horse while you wait. Curry him a bit, too."

Luke watched the courier lead the horse to the trough before dutifully opening the envelope and drawing out a letter written on US Army stationery. He thought it rather interesting, though understood that Texas stationary—if any remained —was likely out of the question. It actually bothered him more than it likely should have.

Elisa heard Luke talking with the courier and joined him in the gallery. "What did he want, Lucas?"

"Let's find out." The letter was from General Hamilton, the provisional governor, and asked Luke to cooperate in rooting out a land fraud scheme led by none other than Baron Angus Moncrieff. The letter revealed that the Scotsman had apparently been so confident in his scheme that he'd set up a land office in Corpus Christi. Luke was pleased that Colonel Belknap would be available to assist if needed. In fact, Belknap would be arriving to explain in greater detail the trap being set for the Scotsman. Luke couldn't hold back a grin. He shared the letter with Elisa. "What do you think?"

She was pleased that he'd asked, but rightly figured his decision had already been made. "You know you're going to do it, Lucas."

Luke turned to the waiting courier. "Tell them I'll help."

The courier rode off with the response.

"Looks as though that Moncrieff fellow just can't stay away." Luke chuckled as he wrapped his arm around Elisa's waist and walked her back inside. "Let's eat breakfast." Luke could hardly wait to share the news with Sheriff Meaney.

Moncrieff lounged in his hotel room. He now had five agency agreements in hand. His overconfidence was beginning to cloud his judgment, as every Austin patron he'd approached had come to terms with him. He felt great, even unbridled joy at his successes. Assuming his men in Corpus Christi were doing their job, he felt poised to make a lot of money. By the time his clients figured out the scam, the Scotsman planned to be long gone from Texas.

Each client had given him a small cash advance to retain his services. But for the likelihood of increasing the cash many-fold, he was half tempted to abscond with the retainers and leave his partners holding the bag in Corpus Christi. Matter of fact, he did need to see first-hand how his partners, Scrub and Robert, were progressing with setting up their first office. Moncrieff's overwhelming greed won out, and the prospect of much larger rewards dissuaded him from taking the retainers and running off.

A couple of worries did remain. He had to hope that Cheno Cortina held no grudge about his cousin and, more importantly, that Sheriff Meaney had a short memory.

Moncrieff stood and examined himself in the mirror. He

thought himself a handsome devil decked out in his kilt. He'd dally a bit in Austin before heading south. A winsome Texas whore and some fine champagne would suit his fancy for the evening.

★★

"Colonel Belknap's on his way?" A bemused Elisa was confirming what Luke's expression told her. She'd made the right decision in forgiving him from his promise. She was happy to have her man back. It'd already been proven in their bedroom last night.

"Yep. He ought to be here in a couple of days. I expect I'll head into Corpus this morning and give Bill a heads-up. That Moncrieff fellow has a couple of co-conspirators, and the sheriff will need to keep an eye on them until the trap is sprung."

Elisa laughed a confident laugh that only a woman with six children and a ranch to keep up, a woman who'd shot and killed savages and outlaws, could express. "You're really enjoying this aren't you, Lucas?" It was almost a rhetorical question.

Luke gave a sort of aw-shucks smile and rubbed his fingers easy-like over his mustache. "Could say...yep, could say I am." He looked lovingly at her with grateful eyes that melted to her very soul.

"I'm thinking you have one more thing to do before you head off to Corpus." She nodded her head toward Andrea Anne.

Luke looked over at his daughter, then turned to Peter and John. "Hey, boys. How about helping me with a bit of work down at the corral?" He looked at Andrea Anne and nodded, pretending it as an afterthought. "You can come help, too."

Andrea Anne hesitated, then put on a determined expression and followed Luke and the boys toward the corral. She didn't need to be asked twice, as her competitive nature and desire to be treated like her brothers kicked in. She wasn't what you'd call a tomboy, but she wasn't a dainty girly sort either.

Elisa stood with Matt at her breast and watched from the window. Excitement coursed through her.

Peter and John ran ahead and reached the corral first. They turned to Luke as he strode up with an easy grin across his face. "Dad, where'd this filly come from?" A beautiful dappled gray pranced around the corral showing off for her visitors.

About this time, Andrea Anne arrived. "What's all the commotion?" She peered between the fence railings, and her eyes grew wide.

Luke turned to Peter. "Son, grab that saddle and bridle over there. Let's see how this filly rides."

Peter retrieved the tack, and Luke readied the filly for a ride. He offered soothing words to the horse. "Easy little girl. You know what's coming. You've done this before." He stroked her gently and patted her nose. "So, who'd like to be first to ride her?"

The boys eagerly pushed toward their father to ride first. Andrea Anne hung back, as she still admired the beauty of the horse.

"It's ladies first this morning, boys. Don't y'all agree that Andrea Anne should ride first?" He watched the boys reluctantly nod and back off while an ear-to-ear grin spread across Andrea Anne's face. "Come on, darling. Let's introduce you." He slipped her a couple of sugar cubes.

The filly for its part seemed to sense something special was afoot. She stood perfectly still other than a few tail swishes. Andrea Anne approached cautiously, finally arriving alongside and reaching up to pat the young filly's neck. She offered up the sugar, bringing a snort and an affectionate nuzzle. Andrea Anne moved to the side and prepared to take on the task of mounting. She was tall for her age, but still only five years old. The stirrup was a challenge.

Luke let her work it out. The filly was patient. Once she managed to get into the saddle, she was all smiles again.

"What are you going to name your horse?"

The last two words didn't sink in at first, but then tears of sheer joy rolled down her cheeks. "Mine?"

Elisa still stood in the window watching her daughter's reaction. She burned to be at the corral but wanted this to be a binding between father and daughter.

"Yep. She's yours, darling."

Peter and John were all smiles. "We all need to go riding!" was the refrain of the morning.

Andrea Anne couldn't have stopped her gleeful grinning if her life depended on it. "I'm naming her Bluebonnet. She's pretty as any flower."

Frontier-tested lawman and hardy rancher that he was, Luke felt a warm heartfelt surge and a couple of tears seep into the corners of his eyes as he experienced his daughter's sheer joy. "Y'all want to ride into Corpus Christi with me this morning?" Luke reflected a few seconds on what he'd just said. The vision of a six-foot-three cowboy with three half-pints trailing along was a humorous one to say the least. "Shoot, maybe we can hitch the buckboard, and we all can go."

Soon enough, a Dunn caravan was wending its way to the city.

The arrow's aim had been true, as it delivered on its shooter's purpose. The doe stopped, eyes momentarily revealed panic and pain, legs buckled, and her body unwillingly toppled over. She was now dinner and more meals for the journey ahead.

One Arrow acted swiftly to field dress the beast. Spending

time now would likely pay off later. He cut thin strips of venison, retrieved the salt he'd brought with him, and began the
process of making jerky. He wouldn't have time to stretch,
scrape, and fully tan the hide, but he'd do the minimum
required to keep it pliable for future processing. Only after
he'd completed these tasks did he afford himself the luxury of
a venison steak dinner. Now and again, he'd stand still to scan
the horizon, sniff the air, and listen for threats.

An exceedingly warm breeze wafted through the flowers
and meadows. One Arrow was grateful for having stalked the
doe to a grove of trees. He welcomed the shady relief from the
burning rays of the mid-afternoon sun.

He allowed himself to think back on the day he'd earned
his name. He was but sixteen summers of age at the time. His
name at the time was Laughing Crow. Upon passing the
rituals of manhood, he'd be given his new name. The hunt
with his adoptive father and Peneteka Comanche Chief Three
Toes had been not unlike today so far as the weather: clear and
hot. They'd hunted for the mighty buffalo for perhaps two
hours, finally coming upon a lone bull on a rise overlooking
his domain. The beast's cows milled about feeling safe under
his vigilant guard. But he wasn't vigilant enough. Laughing
Crow had ridden to the edge of a grove of trees not unlike
those he was enjoying now. He had been perhaps a hundred
yards from the massive bull. Ever so slowly, he urged his pony
forward. The bull raised its head and sniffed the air. Laughing
Crow knew that the buffalo's eyesight was terrible, but he had
to be wary of its sense of smell. The Comanche approached
from downwind, but that was no guarantee the bull wouldn't
detect enough of his scent to be alerted. He kept an eye on the
tail. So long as it hung low, he was likely safe.

He stole a glance back at Three Toes. The chief nodded his
approval.

Laughing Crow had edged to within fifty yards. The line of
sight between them was mostly level and quite open. Of a

sudden, the bull came to full alert. He snorted, raised his tail straight up, and turned to face the threat. Laughing Crow kicked the sides of his pony. The steed leaped into action, charging straight at the buffalo. It took barely a split second for the buffalo to decide to charge. If Laughing Crow had hoped to get the bull to turn and run, he was mistaken. A bull buffalo in full charge was not to be trifled with, plus the beasts were amazingly agile. The Comanche teen turned his mount at the last moment to dodge the bull's charge, bringing the buffalo to a skidding halt that brought it into perfect position. In mere seconds, the hunter paused, nocked an arrow, and fired it deep into the bull. It bellowed in pained surprise but was never to regain his footing. The huge bull sunk to its belly, quivered, and rolled on its side, as it took its final breaths. Laughing Crow's aim had been exceptionally true. A single arrow, a lone shaft had delivered on its shooter's purpose.

Laughing Crow looked back at the wood line. Three Toes hadn't moved, but sat astride his pony admiring his adopted son and warrior. The chief had already decided the new name for this brave young man. The Comanche naming ceremony would be a memorable one. And it was.

One Arrow's musings over the buffalo hunt were interrupted by sounds of which he had to suddenly be more concerned. A pair of coyotes were flirting with savoring the warrior chief's venison prize. They were somewhat put off by the cooking fire, but too close for comfort as their hunger was apparently enough to cause them to ignore the threat posed by One Arrow. Not being inclined to waste arrows on the carrion lovers, he grabbed his spear and moved aggressively toward the pair. The cowardly beasts snarled a bit, but at least one of them had apparently tasted the wrath of humans before as they reluctantly backed off and were soon lost from sight.

One Arrow resumed his efforts toward replenishing his food supply. He dared not tarry further on his travel toward Nuecestown, so having a plentiful supply of food was critically important. He could ill afford hunts for small game along the way, and given all the potential human dangers, building cooking fires was not especially advisable. As night fell, he enjoyed his venison steaks, ever grateful to the Great Spirit who'd provided for him. He drew the bone necklace with its cross adornment from his bag and fondled it. It had been a gift to Three Toes from the squaw of Ghost-Who-Rides. It was now his, and he wondered at its significance and still more at what power it might hold. He felt the need to stand as if to honor it, as he placed it around his neck. He did credit it with saving him from the rattlesnake. The young Comanche chief committed himself to learning more of the meaning of the cross that dangled from the necklace. If it was a higher power, how did that sit with the Great Spirit who'd sent him on this mission? There seemed to be so much to learn in this ever-changing world.

"Quite an entourage you've got there, Luke." Meaney stood in front of his house with Clara and the young Sparks girl, Emma, seated nearby.

"Andrea Anne got a new horse, and everyone was anxious to go for an adventure, so here we are."

"She's a pretty one, Andrea Anne. Does she have a name?"

"Her name's Bluebonnet, Sheriff Meaney," she gushed.

Luke looked back at Elisa. "Lisa, sweetheart, how about taking the children over to Scarlett's and Walker's place for a bit while I talk with Bill? Maybe Clara and Emma here can join you." He watched them amble on up the street toward the Carson's haberdashery.

"What's so all-fired important, Luke?"

"You recall that Scotsman, Angus Moncrieff?"

"The one we knew was rustling but couldn't pin it on him?"

"Well, he's found a new game. I received a note from Governor Hamilton. Moncrieff and two partners are fixing to do a bit of land swindling. Somewhere in our fine city, his partners have set up an office to conduct their affairs. I just wanted to give you a heads-up so you can be on the lookout."

"You figure to be setting some sort of trap, Luke?"

"Folks in Austin are involved. I'm waiting for Colonel Belknap to arrive with whatever plans they're cooking up."

"Gordon survived the war?"

"Yes. Good man. He deserved his promotion." Luke was ever a supporter of Belknap. "From what I've been told, he's heading what might be called a police unit of mostly colored men from those so-called buffalo troops. He'll be trying to head off the aftermath of lawlessness that often accompanies defeat."

"Can't say as I begrudge Gordon his duty." Meaney averted his eyes, then looked back at Luke. "I hear tell there's some Apache stirring up in Mexico. Not sure how far north they'll range. They're not so nasty as Comanche, but I'd as soon not have to mess with them."

"Well, first things first. I'll let you know what Colonel Belknap has in mind." Luke turned Big Horse. "I'd better catch up with my brood and be sure to get back home before dark."

SIXTEEN
APACHE AGAIN

COSTALITES FOUND HIMSELF IN A QUANDARY. No friend of Mexican or Anglo, the Apache chief sensed increasing restlessness among his warriors. He'd ventured into Texas regularly while the White men were distracted with their war. His scouts now brought tantalizing information about apparent post-war confusion. He knew the gray coats were being disbanded, and most of the bluecoats had left Texas. Union General Philip Sheridan had begun to keep a wary eye out in South Texas, but was spread far too thin. There were no Texas Rangers to be seen, and the dreaded Comanche had been pushed far north to the Indian Territory. The ranches throughout South Texas, however sparsely located, were now more vulnerable than ever.

Even more important to the Apache chief, Cheno Cortina was tied up dealing with the turmoil created by erstwhile Mexican President Benito Juarez. Juarez was in conflict with Austrian Archduke Ferdinand Maximillian who'd been installed as Mexican emperor by Napoleon III. To make matters worse, the Mexican president was under pressure from the United States to confront the French and oust Maximillian.

All of this meant that Costalites was free to wreak havoc throughout the Nueces Strip. Unlike his brethren Mescalero and Chiricahua Apache to the west that trafficked in cattle rustling, the Lipan Apache chief preferred raids producing less labor-intensive benefits like weapons, whiskey, and money. Counting coups and lifting a few scalps were a side benefit that kept his warriors happy. The downside was that while beeves were restocked, the Lipan Apache prey was rarely replenished. Dead people didn't breed more people.

Nevertheless, Costalites was determined to make a few exploratory attacks across the Rio Grande. He'd stay clear of Camargo, Cortina's stronghold on the Mexican side, while venturing into McAllen further to the east. The chief figured to make exploratory attacks on a few small ranches and home-steads that yet survived after the war and then see what sort of response those raids attracted.

Belknap felt confident that he could count on the leadership of the troop he'd left behind in Austin. They'd be conducting daily patrols to root out lawlessness in the region between Austin and San Antonio. He'd sent a token troop of forty mounted men eastward to patrol the region around Galveston. He personally led a second troop of forty of arguably the best of those soldiers he'd been assigned. They weren't up to the standard of troops he'd led before the war, but he figured they'd comport themselves reasonably well in any fighting.

As he neared the entrance to Heaven's Gate, he halted and directed his men to bivouac along the shore of Nueces Bay. His second in command, Captain Richards, was given orders that they could venture into Corpus Christi but had to return by sundown. Belknap cautioned Richards to be wary, as many citizens might not especially cotton to Black men having free rein in their town.

Belknap exchanged salutes with the captain and turned his mount to the archway entrance to Luke's ranch. "Sergeant Brown, please join me." The men watched with a touch of envy as the sergeant joined Belknap but soon took to the tasks of bivouacking, so they might enjoy the nearby city sooner than later. Brown was cut from a different mold. He reminded Belknap a bit of Bol Richards, the tough-as-nails throwback frontiersman turned Texas Ranger leader that he'd had the pleasure of meeting before the man's untimely and dastardly demise.

"May I speak freely, sir?" Brown was curious as to why Belknap was bringing him along instead of an officer.

"Yes, but make it quick, Sergeant."

"Why me?"

"Frankly, Sergeant, if my observations are correct, I should trust you more than most. I feel it's important for you to hear my exchange with Mr. Dunn."

"Who is this Dunn fella?"

Belknap smiled broadly. "Expect you've never run into him. If you were ever on the wrong side of the law and in his path, most likely you wouldn't be here at this moment in time. You'd be in jail, dangling from a tree, or six feet under. He's one of the most famous Texas Rangers that's ever lived."

"And he's a rancher?"

"Oh yes. Has a lovely wife, big family, and plenty of long-horns and horses."

The sergeant shrugged and half saluted. "Thank you, sir."

"Here we are, Sergeant. You'll see for yourself."

"That him standing on the gallery, sir?"

Belknap nodded.

The sergeant's jaw dropped. "Dang, but he's a big man. Tough you say?"

"As Texans are fond of saying, Dunn is so tough he'd fight a rattlesnake and spot it the first bite. Yes, Sergeant, he's a man of grit, character, and faith."

The two slowly rode up to the house.

"Colonel, welcome to Heaven's Gate." Luke tipped his hat and offered up a broad grin. "Been expecting you."

The men dismounted. "Luke, I've brought along Sergeant Brown here. He'll be integral to our scheme. Sergeant, meet Luke Dunn."

Brown reached up to shake Luke's hand. As the rancher's hand wrapped around the sergeant's, the poor man was nearly brought to his knees by the strength of the grip. He managed to stammer a pleasantry while wrestling free of the bone-crushing hand. "My...my pleasure, Mr. Dunn."

"Come on and join us for some coffee, Colonel, Sergeant." Luke was using Belknap's title in deference to the presence of the non-commissioned officer present.

"What's that you got growing on your face, Gordon?"

"Disguise. Tell you more later."

"Did I hear Gordon Belknap arrive?" Elisa appeared in the doorway. "Why, I sure did. Y'all are welcome. Grab a seat and I'll bring y'all some coffee." She didn't add that she'd be offering up her famous cornbread as well. Surprises were her specialty.

Soon enough, the men were enjoying coffee with cornbread on the gallery that ran the length of the front of the house and now wrapped around the western side to afford a better view of their land holdings. Belknap elaborated on the deals that Moncrieff had struck with some of the wealthy folks in Austin and how Thorpe, Burnett, and others were in on trapping the Scotsman.

Brown yearned to learn more about this new acquaintance but had to defer to Belknap.

"So, Colonel, do tell me about your thoughts on this Moncrieff matter?"

"I was going to defer to you, Luke."

"Well, I do understand that a family named Sparks recently had a family tragedy, and the land might be up for purchase."

Luke didn't add the fact that he'd set the events in motion that led to that situation by instigating the investigation of the hanging of a priest.

"So, you figure the land might be bait to set in a trap?"

"We should get Sheriff Meaney involved, as he'll have the power to arrest the swindlers."

Belknap grinned. "Actually, we're like an interim police force, Luke. The folks in Austin would like to make an example of the Scotsman to discourage others from land fraud. I'll be pleased to take him off the sheriff's hands."

Brown couldn't suppress a chuckle.

That grabbed Belknap's attention. "Something I say concern you, Sergeant?"

"If I may, sir. My family was swindled out of some land years back in Louisiana by your revered Alamo hero Jim Bowie and his brother. Sold the same tracts of land to multiple buyers. Likely this Moncrieff fella has a similar scheme."

Luke nodded. His hand went to his mustache, but he folded his arms instead. "I'd heard rumors as to that less savory part of Bowie's background. Still, he died a hero defending the indefensible Alamo. Pleased you can appreciate what we'll be trying to do, Sergeant."

Belknap interrupted. "Further thoughts, Luke?"

Elisa had been eavesdropping and stepped from the doorway. She'd just finished nursing baby Matthew and had set the other children to playing. She was never one to hold back her thinking. "Doubt you're going to trap this fellow with a bunch of soldiers hanging around. He'll smell a trap right quick."

Luke always appreciated her thoughtful perspectives. "Lisa's right, Colonel. I suggest we set a couple of your men in civilian clothes so as to set a believable trap for Moncrieff. From what I've heard, the man has an outsized opinion of himself and just might be a tad overconfident."

Elisa always appreciated her husband's recognition of her

wise counsel. "You're going to need a woman to make it look more like a family."

Belknap nodded. "Makes sense, but it might be risky."

Luke gave Elisa a look of concern.

"Doesn't sound as though these men are hardened thugs. With our friend Scarlett coming to visit, perhaps I could play the role."

Luke shook his head vigorously. "No. I'm not taking kindly to that idea, my sweet."

"This from my husband who's appreciated my killing Comanche and outlaws and standing up to invading soldiers?" She smiled so as to lessen the bite of her words. It was far too easy for men to overlook the toughness and self-sufficiency of frontier women, especially when put into a pretty and petite package such as Elisa.

What was Luke to say? "You're every bit a frontier woman Lisa Dunn, and a braver woman I've never known. Far be it from me to deny your earnest desire to help." Luke was thinking. His trademark mustache stroking came a bit more animated than typical. Elisa stared at him expectantly. "Just don't take any undue risk."

"Then that's settled. Now, pardon me gentlemen, as I have dinner to make." She laughed almost too giddily and ducked back into the house.

Luke sighed. "Well, Colonel, we seem to have our trap ready to be set."

Brown sat in wonderment at what he'd just been witness to. A truly sensical plan had come together as though part of the normal course of the day. "If I might ask, Mr. Dunn, will you have a role?"

Luke understood. "I'll be around, Sergeant. You won't see me, but be assured I'll see you."

The sergeant wondered at how a tall, broad-shouldered man could accomplish that very effectively.

Belknap interrupted. "You and I will be the bait, Sergeant.

We must keep this to a very small circle lest word of our trap should accidentally be revealed." He looked over at Luke. "It'll assure double protection for Mrs. Dunn, as well."

With plans set, the trio engaged in the details of the trap, making small talk, and finishing their coffee and cornbread. Belknap and Brown offered their thanks and were soon headed back to the bivouac site.

With close to fifty well-armed warriors, Costalites permitted himself the luxury of joining in the excitement of what lay before him. The small ranch that lay before his eyes would be a worthy prize.

The sun behind the savages was just peeking above the horizon, emanating a soft pinkish glow that bathed the prairie with its promise of a clear day. The cabin below still lay in shade, and there were not yet any stirrings of life.

Costalites was patient. He was waiting for the first puffs of smoke to rise from the chimney. It would then be easy enough to use the old trick of blocking the chimney, forcing smoke into the cabin and flushing the coughing inhabitants outside. Out in the open, they'd be easy targets for the Apache. It was an outcome worth the wait.

There it was. The first trickle of smoke wafted from the chimney. Costalites motioned two of his warriors to circle behind the cabin where the roof nearly met the ground. They could climb up easily, blankets in hand to do their work.

As fate would have it, even the best laid plans can run afoul of unexpected events. Two cowboys emerged, stretching and yawning to take in the fresh air. It was a refreshing contrast to the stale stench within the cabin. They headed to the privy behind the cabin to answer nature's call. As they rounded the corner of the cabin, they were met with two Apache looking about as fierce as they could muster.

"Damn! What the hell!" The first cowboy reached for the gun that wasn't in his holster. He'd neglected to grab his weapon before leaving the cabin. His companion's situation wasn't much better except for a knife. Essentially unarmed, fight-or-flight instincts took over. The cowboy with the knife charged the first of the Apache. The savage neatly sidestepped the awkward rush, hitting the cowboy on the back and causing him to dive headlong into the dirt. The other cowboy had taken about two steps toward the cabin door when a half dozen rifle shots echoed across the landscape.

"Indian sonsofbitches! Apache! It's an attack." He managed to shout out as bullets riddled his body. He staggered back into the cabin and fell to the floor where he quickly bled out and breathed his last.

One of the men inside had the presence of mind to douse the cooking fire. The cabin had now become a fortress.

Costalites cursed. He knew better than to charge, as rifles began to appear in most every window and door. The Apache to his right was shot by pure dumb luck given the range at which they stood.

The two Apache beside the cabin were at a momentary advantage. They'd managed to kill the first cowboy with the knife and now stood tightly against the cabin wall next to a window. They quickly grabbed the first rifle to poke out beside them. Its owner followed and met the same fate as the first cowboy.

Costalites directed half his warriors to lay down a covering fire, while he led the rest in a full-bore attack. War whoops, shouts, and gunfire made it seem as though all hell had broken loose. Warriors opened the corral gate and freed a half dozen horses, though a couple of savages paid the price of eating lead.

The Apache chief had no idea how many men might yet be inside the cabin. From its size and the number of horses, he figured it couldn't have been more than seven of eight at the start. There were likely no women or children, as this ranch was all about raising beeves not families. With at least three warriors killed or wounded, he thought about waiting them out. This was getting to be an expensive attack. Conducting a siege wasn't his style, but he figured to let the men sweat at least for a while. He signaled his warriors to retreat to the hill out of range of the cabin.

As Costalites observed the cabin, he realized he'd over-looked one of its features. The roof was thatched. With any luck, he could set it afire. He'd smoke out his enemy yet.

Torches were fashioned, and the chief sent a small contin-gent of warriors forward from behind the cabin. The back of the cabin was windowless and thus afforded no view of the outside, so the Apache easily snuck up and threw their torches onto the roof. In the dry near-desert heat, the straw quickly went up in flames. It didn't take long for the desired effect.

Coughs quickly filled the air, and three men emerged through the front, choosing to be shot rather than burn to death. The Apache laid down a barrage of gunfire that left no doubt as to the outcome.

Once the smoke cleared, the Apache rode to the cabin and took their time scalping the victims and stealing anything they considered of value. The entire attack, despite the early change of plan, had taken a mere half hour to complete.

Costalites gave his men a bit of time to enjoy the fruits of their savage labors before leading them back to the south.

Luke slowly rode Big Horse into Corpus. He'd gotten up extra early to beat the late summer heat and humidity. As he approached the jail, he glanced up the street and waved to Walker Carson who was unloading a wagon with merchandise for their increasingly thriving haberdashery. He dismounted and knocked on the jailhouse door.

"Y'all come on in." Meaney called out friendly-like, though his Colt sat before him on the desk ready to grab as needed.

"Bill, you're usually waiting for me out front." Luke strode in and glanced around. The cells were empty and rifle rack full. Nothing out of the ordinary other than Meaney seeming out of sorts. "You're looking like you got a bit of a hitch in your gitalong this morning."

"I found your land grabbers. They got a store front up the way calling themselves Liberty Land Company. The two rascals worked up a drunk last night at the Longhorn. I had to break up a ruckus. Was going pretty well until someone hit me across my back with a damned chair."

"Do you know who hit you?"

"Nope. 'Bout a dozen folks in the saloon at that hour, and no one was talking. Those two land grabber fellas got out while the getting was good."

"You go after them?"

"No point. I didn't want to run them out of Corpus knowing y'all were setting a trap."

"Sorry you're sore, Bill." Luke pulled up a chair and turned the barrel of the gun away from both of them. "I just wanted to stop by and let you know that Moncrieff left San Antonio, and we'll be setting the trap in a day or so."

"Thanks, Luke. I look forward to arresting him, though I expect I'll be turning him over to the Austin folks." Meaney took a swig of coffee. "Dang, I'm sorry Luke. You up for some day-old coffee?"

"Doggone, Bill. You must really be sore to be letting coffee sit overnight." Luke got up and eased over to the coffee pot. A quick look and sniff, and he decided he'd get some fresh brew later. "Thanks. I'll pass."

Meaney stretched out his sore shoulders. "You heard 'bout the goings on in Mexico?"

"That Cortina fellow still stirring up rattlesnake nests?"

"Not quite. President Johnson's apparently pushing President Juarez to overthrow that Maximillian fellow that the French put in charge. Result is that Cortina is showing signs of making more trouble on the Rio Grande, and the Apache have begun making raids again."

"Guess that'll keep General Sheridan busy. I don't think there's a prayer of Texas Rangers being authorized any time soon, or I'd be hell-bent-for-leather to get down there."

"I'm sure you would, Luke." Meaney was getting back to his old self. "You going to check out the land company office?"

"Does a javelina have tusks? Darn right I'll check it out." Luke followed with a laugh. "Feels good to be chasing lawbreakers again, Bill. Feels right good for sure."

"I can see it in you, Luke."

"Everything good with you and Clara?"

"Yep. That Sparks girl, Emma, is still with us. Scarlett's been teaching her to sew, though she seems too feisty for that sort of womanly business. I expect she'll come into a little money when her pa's place is sold, though it was heavy in debt. Have to wait till after y'all have caught Moncrieff, of course."

"Have you talked with Emma about the colonel's plan to use her pa's property as bait to trap Moncrieff in his land fraud scheme?"

Meaney offered just a hint of a smile. "She supports the plan. She may still be a bit tender-minded from her pa's suicide, but she got right upset at the thought of someone like Moncrieff taking advantage of troubled folks."

"Hopefully, it'll all end well. I'm going to mosey on up the street and say hello to our land fraud friends." Luke's sardonic smile revealed how he relished being back, as he prepared to bait the hook of the scheme to bring Moncrieff to justice. "Seems appropriate to let them know a prime piece of real estate has come on the market. Should put them in good spirits with the Scotsman coming to town."

The Apache were flush with their recent victory at the small ranch north of McAllen. Flush with victory meant they tended to be not quite so vigilant. Costalites noticed first. There was an eerie silence, as they approached the north shore of the Rio Grande. A sort of intuition held him back for a moment, as most of his warriors descended the riverbank and began to urge their ponies across.

The warriors were no more than fifty feet from shore, when a fusillade opened from the Mexican side. A troop of regular Mexican Army had opened fire.

Costalites cried out to retreat, but not quickly enough to save a dozen or more of his Apache. He was treated to the sound of bullets whizzing by, as the Mexican officer in charge spotted him and directed fire. Horses thrashed about, warriors shouted and sought escape, and gore and mayhem seemed ever-concentrated in that little space of river.

The chief managed to escape with slightly better than half his warriors. Only after his band had bolted a mile or so back into Texas did he stop to assess his situation. Then, the thought occurred to him that those same Mexican soldiers might have attacked his village. Were his people safe? He had to get back into Mexico.

As the remaining warriors rested, tended to their wounded, and took stock of who was still alive, Costalites let it be known that they'd ride a few miles toward Brownsville, wait until nightfall, cross the river into Mexico, and then double back. The Apache were desperate to know the fate of their loved ones. Some were already talking vengeance if anyone was hurt.

Moonlight cast a faint glow over the Lipan Apache village, as Costalites cautiously approached. The smoke from a half dozen fires wafted skyward. The chief pulled up a short distance from the huts. Something wasn't right. It was far too quiet. A few forms could be seen sitting around one of the fires. They weren't moving.

One of his warriors pulled alongside and whispered. "What is it, my chief?"

"Where are the ponies? Why no life? Is trap!" Costalites's practiced eye saw that the figures they saw were dead Apache propped up and posed to draw him into an ambush. He wheeled his pony.

At that moment, a cannon exploded its deadly charge and a dozen red-coated Mexican dragoons with sabers drawn and guns blazing rushed the Apache seemingly from nowhere.

The warriors fought back in vain, as the dragoons had the element of surprise and used it to full advantage. Two...three Apache fell. Shouts...chaos...rattling of sabers. Costalites strove to rally his Apache to no avail. He kicked his pony's sides hard and led the tiny remainder of his band at a gallop toward the north and relative safety of Texas.

The chief had not ridden more than a mile when he found himself overwhelmed with anger at what the Mexicans had done to him and to his people. He'd seriously misjudged his enemy. He pulled his warrior band to a stop.

With their fast ponies, the Apache had long out-distanced the dragoons. Costalites realized he must act quickly. The Mexicans surely wouldn't expect a counterattack. Splitting his depleted force of warriors into two bands of five warriors each, his strategy would be to attack the Mexicans from two sides so as to reduce the effect of their cannon.

The Apache turned and headed their ponies south. Far ahead, they could see the dragoons laughing as they returned to the village.

Under the dim light of the moon and stars, they would be

able to draw close to their enemy. As they drew near to the village, Costalites directed his warriors to dismount. The dragoons and a small group of Mexican soldiers were gathered around celebrating their success in chasing off the Apache.

Rifle fire broke the night air. The Mexican cannoneers and dragoons were riddled with bullets. Moving with a speed and ferocity inspired by vengeance, the Apache were on top of the troops, scalping some even before they'd breathed their last.

The gunfire had stopped, replaced by a silence broken only by the occasional groans of the few remaining dying Mexicans. Costalites looked at the carnage around him, then slowly walked to his hut. He swept aside the buffalo skin covering the entrance and looked inside. The stench of death was strong. He stepped back, looked again at the scene, and wept.

SEVENTEEN
MONCRIEFF'S SCAM

LUKE EASED from his saddle and draped Big Horse's reins over the hitching rail. He stood back a moment and took in the big freshly painted sign before striding up and knocking on the door of the Liberty Land Company.

A groggy voice from within responded. "Yeah? Who's there?"

Luke thought a second on how unwelcoming that sounded before opening the door and letting himself in. "Howdy, gentlemen. I hear y'all are new in town. Thought I'd drop by a moment and say hello."

Scrub and Robert shook off hangovers best they could, as they scrambled to slick back their unkempt hair, straighten their wrinkled clothes, and generally appear presentable. They stood unsteadily, as they looked at the big stranger who'd just entered. Scrub blinked first. "Sorry, partner. Rough night."

"I've heard." Luke stifled the urge to laugh. The stale aromas in the office were likely to give a skunk pause to retreat. Luke resisted the urge to cover his face with a bandanna, as he tried not to breathe too deeply. "You open for business?" He'd rarely seen two scruffier-looking individuals.

Robert dragged himself over to the only desk and made a

show of shuffling some papers. "My name is Robert Dunlevy. We are in the business of buying and selling property. You have some land to sell, sir? Or perhaps you're looking to buy?" A couple of papers slid from Roberts nervous fingers to the floor.

Scrub picked up the papers and balanced himself as best he could against the side of the desk. He tried to give Luke a head-to-toe once over through blood-shot eyes. Of a sudden, his eyes bulged. His hand went to his mouth, as he turned just a tad green and bolted for the back door.

Luke and Robert could do naught but watch.

Scrub returned in a moment seeming none the worse for the incident save for some telltale dribbles of something on the front of his shirt. "Sorry about that. Guess somethin' I ate didn't agree with me."

"Apparently not," Luke drawled as he glanced around the office. "Just figured I'd give y'all a heads-up as to some property about ten miles west of here that might be looking to sell. Owner's name is Sparks. Family hit on a rough patch."

"We're grateful to you for that, Mr. Er...what did you say your name was?"

"Smith. George Smith." Luke forced a smile. The trap had been set and baited. "Well, I must get on with my day. Good luck with your business." He tipped his hat and exited. It was great to get outside and take in some hot but fresh air.

Baron Angus Moncrieff fanned himself in a vain attempt to ward off the heat, as he rode slowly into Nuecestown. Even the natural venting of his kilt wasn't much help in what seemed like a damp oven. It being late afternoon, he decided to seek shelter for the night and continue on to Corpus Christi in the morning. He pulled up in front of Bernice's and Agatha's boarding house.

Bernice answered Moncrieff's knock, opened the door, and stood back in momentary amazement at seeing a man in a skirt.

"Lass, have you a room for a weary traveler?" Moncrieff put on his best Scottish brogue.

Taken aback at first, Bernice was quick to gather her wits and realize she was dealing with a Scotsman in full flower as it were. "Yes sir. Please do come in." She ushered him to the guest register and watched as he wrote his name. "Baron? Is that some sort of title, sir?"

"Apparently not of particular concern here in Texas, lass."

"You can take your horse up the main street to the livery, Mr. Moncrieff. We'll be serving up dinner in about an hour." She led him up the hall to a guest room and handed him the key. "Do make yourself comfortable, Baron." She said it as though it connoted some sort of nobility. She wasn't sure whether to bow or laugh. Bernice had her brain in high gear. Something about this new guest was more than unusual.

Moncrieff dropped his satchel in the room and locked the door behind him. "I'll be back shortly, ma'am."

As soon as the Scotsman had begun heading to the livery stable, Bernice roused Agatha.

Agatha looked at the signature in the register and watched the Scotsman leading his horse up the street. "Guess he's a foreigner. Strange to be wearing a skirt."

"Oh, Agatha, they call that a kilt. Wear them in Scotland and Ireland." Bernice's intuition was at work. "Something's not quite right about our guest, Aggie. Do you not sense it?"

Agatha joined in staring at the Scotsman. "Cute legs." She laughed. "Wonder what's under…"

"Oh, you stop that now. We'll have none of that sort of talk." She cast a playfully stern eye at Agatha. "Maybe we'll send Jody off to check with Luke at Heaven's Gate." Bernice's intuitive thinking on these sorts of things had proven right before, and sending the stable boy off with a message might be justified.

Elisa, Belknap, and Brown did their best to look poor and downtrodden, as they conducted simple chores around the front of ramshackle cabin. Luke hid himself behind a stand of live oaks with an aim to providing security.

Wasn't long before Scrub and Robert drove up in a rickety old buckboard. They at least looked far more presentable than Luke had found them a couple of days earlier. They both wore plain but professional-looking coats, and Robert even sported a new-fangled bowler atop his head. "Howdy neighbors. Passing out this way and thought we'd stop by. My name's Scrub Smith and this is my partner, Robert Dunlevy."

Belknap took the lead, looking as desperately forlorn as possible. "Welcome. My name is Tom Sparks. Folks call me TJ. What's your business around these parts?"

Scrub and Robert exchanged glances. "We run the Liberty Land Company in Corpus, kind sir. We purchase and sell properties. Pay cash money. Curious. How're you making out in these post-war times?"

Belknap hung his head. "Sam, Connie, y'all go inside." Elisa and Brown went into the cabin but kept an ear to the goings on outside. Belknap turned back to the men and lowered his voice so as to sound as though he was passing on family secrets. "To be honest, y'all might have come by at just the right time. This ranch...well, it's not making us a living. Got too much debt. Still holding Confederate paper. Like to get out from under and move on."

Scrub resisted the urge to leap from the buckboard and hug the man. This was to be their first deal, and it seemed to be coming quite easily. "If yer serious, Mr. Sparks, we do have a buyer agent. He'll be in town early tomorrow, if you could find your way to our establishment in Corpus Christi in the morning."

"I'll talk with my wife and brother here, but I expect y'all will see me in the morning, gentlemen." Despite his being accustomed to a more rigid military bearing, Belknap managed to keep the hangdog body language about him.

"Please do be sure to bring your land title with you, Mr. Sparks." He hesitated. "Just in case we reach an agreement." Scrub and Robert could barely contain their joy. It was all they could do to keep from rubbing their hands together with glee.

Luke came out from hiding once Scrub and Robert were out of sight. "Appears that went well. You're a pretty fair actor, Gordon. Maybe you missed your calling." Luke couldn't help but chuckle.

Elisa emerged from the cabin with Brown close behind. "Guess we'll be seeing if that Scottish fellow takes the bait." She hadn't had much of a role, but was ready had there been any trouble. It was then that Luke noticed she'd hidden a Colt Army revolver in the folds of her dress.

"Proof's going to be tomorrow morning, Luke." Belknap addressed Elisa and Brown. "We appreciate your help Elisa, but I think it best that only the sergeant accompanies me to Corpus. Once the deal is completed and Moncrieff works his scheme, I expect the matter will be in Sheriff Meaney's hands. We'll just be escorting the prisoners to Austin."

Luke saw the disappointment on Elisa's face. "He's likely right, Lisa. No point in unnecessarily exposing yourself to further danger."

Elisa was tempted to go into a pout. Being a prop for setting a trap hadn't been very exciting. "Mind if I go visit with Clara Meaney and young Emma while you men are conducting your business?" She gave Luke a mischievous wink.

Luke sighed and looked over at Belknap before answering her. "You must promise to stay clear of the land office."

Elisa nodded.

"Colonel, how do you propose to catch Moncrieff in the actual commission of his fraud?"

Belknap smiled. "We had that figured out in advance, Luke. While the miscreants were out here getting acquainted, we had a couple of spy holes drilled into the ceiling of the office. We can watch and listen to whatever the inhabitants do."

Luke shook his head. "Better hope nobody sneezes or coughs."

"Morning, lads! You making acquaintances of the fine citizens of Corpus Christi?" Moncrieff was in good spirits. He'd had a great night's rest at Bernice's and Agatha's boarding house in Nuecestown. He hadn't a clue that the stable boy had left a message for Luke at Heaven's Gate Ranch confirming that the Scotsman was close by.

Scrub and Robert had tidied up and aired out the office, and it could almost pass for a place of professional business. "We done better than just get acquainted, Baron." Both men were all smiles. They'd as soon forget the carousing two-nights back at the Longhorn Saloon.

"How's that, lads?"

"We're expecting a landowner to be dropping by this morning. He's had hard luck and is looking to sell his ranch." The men looked smugly at each other. "Did you complete yer end of our deal?"

"You gentlemen are looking at the holder of five agency agreements." Moncrieff puffed his chest out and smiled broadly. "So, you say this rancher will be stopping by this morning?"

"He seemed to be inclined to visit us, Baron."

"Good. It's early. I can take some time to make the duplicate titles I'll need. You do have the details?"

"He'll be bringing it with him."

A slight scuffle sound emanated from above.

Moncrieff tensed. "Anyone on our roof, gentlemen?"

"Birds, Baron. There are plenty of seagulls about these parts. They seem to like it up there." Scrub shrugged as though it were no big deal. "Larned not to look up when them birds are flyin' about." He chuckled at his humor. "Likely some wharf rats, too."

"Well, clear out of that chair, Dunlevy. I've got work to do."

"You ready for this, Bill?"

Meaney stood, strapped on his gun belt, and straightened his vest. "About as ready as ever, Luke. My boys tell me Moncrieff has the false titles ready to be filled out with the title particulars." He pulled a badge from his desk drawer.

"Raise your right hand."

Luke grudgingly stood and raised his hand. "Forgot about this part," he sighed.

"Do you solemnly swear to obey the laws of Corpus Christi in Nueces County, Texas as directed by the duly appointed sheriff therein? So help you God."

"I do." Luke pinned the badge on his shirt.

"I think Clara's got some coffee while we wait."

"Fresh coffee?"

Meaney took the ribbing well. "I don't always let it set out overnight, Luke."

"I brought Elisa along. She wanted to see us in action."

"Well, I do hope she stays put with Clara and young Emma at my place, Luke."

Scrub suddenly rose to attention. "I hear a wagon, Baron."

Belknap pulled the buckboard up in front of the Liberty Land Company office with Brown seated beside him. The two climbed down and knocked on the door.

"Come on in."

It was a moment of truth for the colonel, as he hoped his beard coupled with loose-fitting ranching duds would be sufficient disguise given that he'd dealt with Moncrieff over that cattle purchase weeks earlier in Brownsville. He stepped in with Brown close behind. Belknap hung his head in apparent abject failure and meekly opened the business at hand. "I'm here to talk about maybe sellin' my ranch. Nice to see you Mr. Dunlevy."

Moncrieff stepped forward. "You must be Mr. Sparks. My name is Angus Moncrieff, and I am the agent for the possible buyer of your property. It's a pleasure to meet you, sir." The Scotsman deferred to Scrub and Robert. "Gentlemen, do as you will."

"Are you ready to sell your property, Mr. Sparks?" Scrub smiled ear to ear, then turned serious.

Belknap pulled an official-looking piece of paper from his pocket. "If the price be fair, this be the title." He held it up but didn't offer it just yet.

Scrub looked over at Moncrieff. "What's your buyer offering, Mr. Moncrieff?"

"Why he's feeling quite generous. He authorized me to offer five dollars an acre." Moncrieff knew the going rate post-war was around ten to twelve dollars an acre, even more around Austin and San Antonio.

Belknap was actually momentarily taken aback by the

miserliness of the offer. But he figured he needed to legitimize the proceedings by haggling a bit. "I was hoping for nine dollars, sir. I got a sick mother back east." He strove to look as humble and aw-shucks as he could muster.

Scrub eased back in his chair. "What say you, Baron Moncrieff?"

Moncrieff knitted his brows and rubbed his forehead as though in deep thought. "My client would truly love to have your property, Mr. Sparks. How about if we split the difference, and I'll buy at seven dollars an acre."

Belknap turned to Brown. "What say you, brother?"

"It's your property, Tom. Sounds like a fair deal."

Belknap turned to Scrub and Robert. "Sounds like we have a deal. I'll stop by in a couple of hours and sign the papers."

"Oh, we can do that right now, Mr. Sparks. We just need to transfer the property description, insert the date, and have you and Baron Moncrieff sign the new title."

In the space of ten minutes, the papers were ready and signed. Belknap used a smooth signature that would be easy to forge. Moncrieff handed over a bank draft for three thousand dollars. "Pleasure doing business with you, Mr. Sparks. I'd appreciate it if you could clear my property within the next two weeks. Are you amenable to that?"

Belknap and Brown nodded and shook hands with Moncrieff and departed.

The Scotsman quickly went to work completing multiple copies of the title and forging Sparks's signature on each. He had no idea that he was being observed from above.

A lanyard had been strung from the land office and attached to a small flag. One end was within easy reach of the spy in the attic. As Moncrieff completed the final title forgery, the line was pulled. It made the flag hop up and down. Meaney saw the silent signal. It was time to move in.

Scrub was leaning against the front doorjamb, smoking. Robert was sitting in a chair near the office desk. He drummed his fingers on the desk much to Moncrieff's annoyance.

Meaney climbed the steps of the wooden sidewalk with the sheriff's badge on full display. Luke approached from across the street. "Mr. Scrub, I presume?"

"Yes, sir. Can I help you?" Scrub glanced over and recognized Luke. He immediately saw the badges. He just about soiled his trousers.

"If you don't mind coming quietly, you are under arrest." Meaney kept his hand on his gun.

Luke moved forward with the manacles in hand. "Let's go nice and quiet like, Mr. Scrub."

"Dammit. You stopped by a couple of days ago. Didn't know you were the law." At that, Scrub spun away and crashed through the office door. He grabbed a rifle that had been leaning against a side chair.

Meaney and Luke hugged either side of the doorway as bullets spit hot lead from inside.

"Sonofabitch, Moncrieff, we been set up!" Scrub was in a panic and hollering as loud as his lungs would permit.

Moncrieff's hand was quickly filled with his own pistol, though he wasn't the greatest marksman.

"Don't be stupid, Moncrieff. Surrender peacefully." Meaney peeked around the doorjamb and almost caught a bullet for his trouble. He nodded at Luke who by this time had both his Colts ready.

Just as they were about to rush inside, Robert came charging into the street with his gun blazing wildly. Bullets narrowly missed Luke.

Luke turned, calmly aimed, and dropped Robert where he stood. He looked back at Meaney. "Anyone else in there stupid enough to come out shooting?"

"We surrender, Sheriff. We're coming out."

Luke and Meaney heard the footsteps approaching the front door. A rifle and a pistol were thrown into the street.

Scrub emerged first followed by Moncrieff, who walked to the middle of the street and turned to face the lawmen. A sneer swept across his bearded face. "You lads don't know whom you're dealing with."

"Keep your hands high." Called the sheriff, as he holstered his revolver and headed toward Moncrieff.

For a split second, Meaney's move toward Moncrieff screened the Scotsman from Luke's view.

A gunshot rang out. Then a second.

Meaney ducked reflexively.

The revolver fell from Moncrieff's hand as he fell. His eyes went down to the piece of his evil heart hanging from where the 44-caliber ball had exited his chest leaving a gaping hole. A second bullet had torn off his nose. His eyes glazed over as he crumpled headfirst into the only mud puddle on the street, suffering the additional ignominies of drowning in three inches of water and his own blood and of his kilt having flipped up over his waist to reveal his bare posterior.

Luke stood calmly at the office door. He holstered his Colt. "Dang, Bill. Sounded sort of like a Colt 1861 Army." He looked over with a wry grin at Elisa standing across the street with a smoking gun in her hand. The irony of her seeming to always be in the right place at the right time when trouble brewed wasn't lost on him. And dang, but he was grateful that her aim was ever true. But from where had the second bullet come? His eyes shifted to Emma. Tears streamed down her cheeks, as she shook uncontrollably beside Elisa and dropped the old 1851 Colt Navy that had belonged to her father. Elisa and Clara moved quickly to comfort her.

Scrub didn't move a muscle. "I...I surrender. Don't shoot."

Meaney looked over at Elisa, then to Luke. "Guess we only get to arrest one. Ole Scrub here will make as good an example as any."

Belknap emerged from beside the land office, slipping on his uniform jacket replete with colonel's shoulder bars as he walked toward Scrub. He stood beside Moncrieff, reached down, and flipped the kilt down over the dead man's butt. "Guess we've seen enough of that." He smiled at his own humor in the midst of what had been a stressful situation.

Scrub's jaw dropped. "Damn! Y'all set us up!"

"Sheriff, if you'd be kind enough to manacle this man, we'd be pleased to take him off your hands." Belknap straightened his coat.

Meaney smiled. "I'm thinking Elisa Dunn ought to do the honors." He dangled the manacles in her direction while winking at Luke. He faced Scrub. "As for you Scrub, move a muscle and you'll join your friends."

Luke turned toward where the women were standing in front of the Meaney's house a mere twenty feet away. Emma was recovering from the emotion of the shootings. Luke nodded comfortingly.

Elisa released Emma to Clara's embrace and pranced on over with a special bounce in her step. She was quite delighted to perform the honor of putting the manacles on the prisoner. "It's my pleasure," she offered up in as smoothly silken a Texas accent as she could muster. She secured the shackles and stepped back to admire her work.

Meaney grabbed Scrub's elbow and began to walk him over to the jail. "I'll have him ready for you shortly, Colonel Belknap."

Elisa walked over to Luke, gave him one of her more winsome smiles, and kissed him lightly. "Guess, you won't be needing this. I like the Texas Ranger badge better." And she proceeded to unfasten the deputy badge from Luke's shirt, examine it thoughtfully for a moment, and hand it to Meaney as he walked by with the prisoner. She smiled again at Luke. "I think Clara has some coffee waiting." She turned then paused and looked back over her shoulder. "Didn't you ever wonder what those Scots wore under their kilts?" Elisa laughed and marched herself back to the sheriff's house.

What could Luke do? He watched his wife with a mix of pride coupled with the disappointment at having been mostly a peripheral observer of all that had happened as concerned the land fraud scheme. He watched Meaney escort the prisoner into the jail for processing.

"Luke...Luke." Belknap was trying to get his attention. "Luke, you're looking like your best horse died."

Luke snapped to. He was proud of Elisa, but his lawman pride was a tad hurt at having to be bailed out of a situation. "Did it show?" He shuffled his lanky frame over to where Belknap was standing.

"Well, I might be able to help temporarily. Oh, and you did nail one of them."

"You have something in particular in mind?" Luke had now completely shaken off his funk.

"You know I've been assigned to support General Sheridan's campaign in South Texas to protect citizens from the Apache savages and the post-war malcontents. I could use a special operator, a scout of sorts. I need trusted eyes and ears out there on the Strip."

"Sounds like a sort of state police, Gordon."

"I think that's what it'll eventually become, Luke. They seem opposed to reauthorizing Texas Rangers just yet. Guess they think it is too closely associated with the Rebels in the recent conflict."

"You want me to be like one of those hunting dogs pointing out the prey?"

"Bit more than that. I trust your judgment, Luke. I think the dog needs to be able to bite."

Luke's broad grin betrayed his excitement at getting back into the lawman action. "I'm grateful, Gordon." The two shook hands.

"*Au contraire*, my friend. I am the one who is grateful. You underestimate your value to Texas and the nation."

"Let's go get some of Clara Meaney's coffee while we're waiting for Bill."

"I could use some coffee about now. My men will clean up this mess. I'm sure the good citizens of Corpus Christi don't appreciate bodies lying around their streets."

It seemed as though there were more lights than the last time One Arrow passed through the region. The White man's predations were indeed expanding like so many tentacles, gobbling up territory over which the Indians had once roamed free. Of course, the tribes never actually owned the land, as private property wasn't part of their way of thinking. Traveling at night as he was, the lights served as beacons around which he rode a wide distance. He had no interest in meeting up with any Anglos and testing their attitudes toward his race, much less Comanche in particular. He'd seen enough bodies swinging from trees or staked out to be understandably wary of the unpredictable White man.

He did covet one of those Henry rifles he'd seen the bluecoats carry. The bow and arrow had served him well, but he recalled how Three Toes had made use of the Colt revolver. Having a gun of any sort offered a clear advantage. The question was how to best acquire one.

Colonel Belknap still wore the scruffy beard he'd grown for his recent assignment, as he strode in with Luke to enjoy Clara Meaney's coffee. Nevertheless, he looked every inch the confident, battle-tested military officer.

"Clara Meaney, I'm pleased to introduce my good friend Colonel Gordon Belknap."

"I'm pleased to make your acquaintance, Mrs. Meaney. I

am quite impressed with your husband, as he was most helpful in my recent mission." Belknap neatly doffed his hat as he was introduced. As he took the cup of coffee offered by Clara, his eyes scanned the room and came to rest on Emma Sparks. "And this pretty young lady must be Emma Sparks." There was a certain electricity in his words.

Emma stepped forward to shake Belknap's hand. Even as their hands barely touched, an unfamiliar feeling coursed through her. It was a far different sensation than that she'd felt when her father had his way with her. And this man was quite a bit younger than her father.

Belknap was momentarily taken aback by her, but quickly shifted his thinking to ward off whatever strange feeling he'd sensed emanating from her. "It's my understanding that one of the folks that our ill-begotten friend Mr. Moncrieff had engaged is seriously interested in purchasing your property, Miss Sparks. Edward Thorpe is a man of fine reputation and will give you a fair price, if you're still of a mind to sell the ranch."

Emma finally found her voice. "I'm deeply grateful, Colonel Belknap."

Elisa stepped up as though on cue. "Why don't you sit down, Colonel? We'll be serving up our midday meal here shortly, and I speak for the Meaney's in inviting your company."

Emma's eyes remained boldly locked on Belknap.

Clara reinforced Elisa's invitation. "She speaks for me, Colonel. We'd love to have you join us. The sergeant is welcome as well."

Belknap looked again at young Emma. Luke's words a few days back about finding a wife had settled in the recesses of his subconscious mind. Now, he had become all-too-aware of the hole in his life. He judged Emma to be around sixteen years, about ten years his junior. She was attractive in a plain sense, as well, though not nearly so pretty as Luke's Elisa. He distractedly shook off his momentary musings. "I'd be pleased to accept your hospitality."

The energy exchanged between Belknap and Emma wasn't lost on Luke. "Sit tight here, Gordon, I'll tell Bill Meaney to put Scrub in a cell and let your troopers know that you've got a social engagement to attend to. I expect, they might be entertained down at the Longhorn Saloon, if that meets with your approval."

"Long as the men don't tarry, Luke. I should begin my journey back to Austin after our midday repast."

As Luke's strode out the door, Elisa excused herself and took him aside. "Lucas, I think there's something in the air between Colonel Belknap and Emma. I fear that may not end well, when he discovers that she's with child. Would you be good enough to take him aside later and explain? I'd hate to see the poor girl's heart broken."

Luke nodded with a hint of a rueful look. "Don't think it's gone so far, Lisa. The colonel hasn't shown any interest in courting that I can see."

"Oh, Lucas Dunn, you men just don't often see the signs we women catch. Emma just about swooned over him, and the look on his face...well, I'd say it was mutual."

"I'll inquire as to Gordon's intentions, Lisa."

Elisa gave him a hug and went back inside.

Luke could but sigh and resign himself to seeing whether the colonel had any intentions toward Emma. As to figuring women...he'd have to work on that.

Costalites was raging mad. He had thought the arrangement with Cheno Cortina was iron-clad toward keeping the Mexican military away from the Apache. He vowed to confront the Mexican rebel at first opportunity. Meanwhile, he had to mourn his dead and assess his situation. Word of his defeating the dragoons would spread quickly, so he needed to move on, likely into Texas and northwest of Rio Grande City. The Apache chief knew that the Yankee General Sheridan was also roaming the region for the purpose of eradicating any threats to frontier settlements. With war experience under their belts, the bluecoats would be very tough opponents. Costalites had to be cautious that his emotions didn't override common sense.

"I sure appreciated your help, Luke. Goes without saying that your lovely wife proved her worth. Dang, but she sure can shoot." They had left Meany's house and were walking up toward the jail. Belknap was looking forward to a shave and a bath, all the more to be a more presentable officer.

"I expect we're in for some tough days ahead, Gordon. With the countryside swarming with desperate men and women, we're going to be kept right busy. I'm afraid we've barely seen the beginning." Luke nodded toward the Longhorn Saloon. "I'm surprised that your men haven't stirred up any trouble being Black and all. There's still plenty of prejudice."

Belknap nodded. "Troubles we have aplenty. I liken it to a dog with fleas, Luke. The poor beast bites one while a bunch more are itching him. I'm looking forward to delivering our prize to meet his justice in Austin. I expect to get back to these parts as soon as I can."

"You were catching a few smiles from Miss Sparks back there at the Meaney's place," Luke chided

Belknap blushed a bit. He'd never really taken much notice of women before now given how caught up he'd been with his military duties. "She seems sweet. Guess something you said a while back made me more conscious of the fairer sex, Luke."

"Well, before you decide to pursue any interest, there's something you ought to know."

Belknap pulled up short. "What's that?"

"Her father was in a terrible way. With the war and the passing of Emma's mother, he became crazed. Recall that he killed a priest."

"Okay. I appreciate that. Is there more?"

Luke gazed intently at his friend. "Her father had his way with her, and…well…she's carrying his child, Gordon."

An expression of shocked surprise momentarily spread across the colonel's face. Pregnant single women were not exactly well-respected in any times and especially these times. The fact that she'd been defiled, been raped by her own father, only added to the dilemma that Colonel Gordon Belknap must now face. He looked off in deep thought. "Poor woman." He said it in a near whisper. "I'll have to think on that, Luke. I'll surely have to think on it."

Luke dug deep. "I expect you might think on what was going through Joseph's head when he learned that Mary, to whom he was betrothed, was with child. I grant it's not nearly the same given Emma's not carrying the Savior of the world, but Joseph did honor Mary." Luke rather was surprised at himself, as it wasn't common for him to use biblical references. He actually often found himself struggling with his own faith despite the strong Catholicism to which he'd been born and raised. Out on the frontier, church wasn't a regular thing, so reinforcing one's faith often became a very individual, very personalized journey. He and Elisa said blessings at family meals and they occasionally carved out a Sunday to visit his cousin John Dunn's ranch for worship. Now, he looked at Belknap as if to fully judge the colonel's reaction.

Belknap turned back to Luke. "Anyone know?"

"Far as I know, just the Meaneys, Scarlett, and us. I mean, you didn't even notice, so I expect no others would."

The colonel was not an impulsive or emotional man, but he

was obviously touched by Emma's situation. "I'm thinking we might spend another couple of days here in Corpus, if the sheriff doesn't mind keeping Scrub locked up. My men can bivouac up the road a piece." Belknap's message was clear.

"Guess I'd be correct in thinking you're of a mind to get better acquainted with Miss Sparks."

What could Belknap do but smile and blush just a bit? "Mind you, Luke, it's not out of pity. My father taught me to never make decisions too quickly, and to be especially careful with important decisions. I'd hate to see the young woman find herself in a situation not to her liking."

"Well, Gordon, I expect we'll have to find some accommodation for you here in Corpus. Elisa and I will be headed back to Heaven's Gate. You might stay over in Nuecestown at Bernice's and Agatha's boarding house. We'd be happy to let you borrow our wagon, if you'd like to find some private time with Miss Sparks. On the other hand, she does sit a saddle quite well."

Meaney stepped from the jailhouse. "Say Colonel, your man is ready to go."

Belknap responded with a command of himself that barely hid his ulterior motive. "I do appreciate your speedy processing, Sheriff. However, I've decided to spend a few days here, if you'd be good enough to hold Mr. Scrub for a time?"

Luke winked at Meaney. "The colonel has some new business to look after, Bill."

Meaney gave a look of understanding. "No problem, Colonel. I assume the government can feed Scrub here in the jail for a few days."

"Thanks, Sheriff." He turned absentmindedly. "Luke, I'm going to head up to Nuecestown." He took a step and stopped. "Thanks for all your help, Sheriff. I hope you wouldn't mind if I were to stop by tomorrow and visit the young lady in your charge?"

"I expect that can be arranged, Colonel. Do enjoy your evening."

EIGHTEEN
ONE ARROW RETURNS

UNDER THE CLEAR STARLIT SKY, there was no mistaking the silhouettes of men sitting around a campfire. One Arrow had spotted it from a goodly distance. Three men were doing enough boastful talking to drown out the natural sounds of the night. Owls, crickets, coyotes, wolves...none could ever hope to raise their voices loudly enough to compete with the men's blustery braggadocio. One Arrow's knowledge of the White man's tongue revealed that these men were not friends of anyone, white or red. He hunched low in the grasses and crept to within a mere hundred feet of the campfire. He listened intently.

"You see the 'spression on his face, when I put that slug in his belly, Croc?" The man took a swig of whatever they were drinking. "Went down whimperin' like a dog."

"Weren't watchin'. Too busy stickin' my rod in that whore wife ah his." The man smiled as he reminisced. "Damn good woman, Billie. That sodbuster had it good."

"She weren't too bad, Croc, 'cept I had her after you."

"Looked like she was preggers. Ya think?"

"Don't matter none now. 'Spect the varmints are feastin' on her now."

One Arrow knew very well how Comanche tortured and killed their victims, but it was somehow different hearing it articulated by three drunken White men sitting around a fire as though describing some sport. A shiver of disgust found its way up his spine. To his thinking, this was more than about coveting the Henry rifle that leaned against one of the saddles. The Comanche chief would provide a service by ridding the world of these dredges of society. He knew that he could nock and shoot arrows quickly enough. He'd have to be deadly accurate, too. Vigilante wasn't in the Comanche lexicon, but he was about to become one.

The chief decided to wait until they'd liquored up some more. With a bit of luck, one might leave the camp to pee. One Arrow wasn't disappointed.

"Gotta take a piss, Croc. Back in a minute." One of the men by sheer chance walked to within twenty feet of where One Arrow crouched behind a clump of grasses. As the man began to relieve himself, the Comanche silently and swiftly covered the few feet between them. The chief slit the man's throat. There was no sound but for the gurgle of the dying man drowning in his own blood.

"What's goin' on out there? You okay..." Croc's sentence was punctuated by a whooshing sound, as an arrow found its way into his cold black heart. He looked down at the shaft protruding from his chest, looked at his partner pleadingly, and breathed his last.

The third man dove for his rifle but was not nearly quick enough. Another arrow had found its target.

One Arrow entered the campfire circle. He picked up the liquor bottle the men had been sharing and took a sniff of its contents. He threw it down and rubbed his itching nose. He decided he wanted no part of this water that smelled like fire. He glanced over at where the third man had dived before tasting the chief's arrow. The Henry rifle still leaned against the saddle, seeming to glow with the reflected flickering light of the campfire. He strode over and picked it up, admiring its finish, the beauty of the wood stock and blueness of the barrel. Now, he'd have to figure out how to shoot it. He'd watched others but had never fired a rifle before.

He reached into the saddlebag and found a heavy leather pouch. It contained bullets that looked to be the right size for the Henry. Recalling what he'd seen other men do, he slipped one cartridge into the breech to be certain. It fit just right. He smiled and slung the pouch strap over his shoulder. He saw that a scabbard was attached to the White man's saddle, but he had no saddle, thus making it of no use to One Arrow. Then he glanced at the bridle and reins hung near the horses. It occurred to him that he could attach a length of the leather reins to the scabbard and sling it over his shoulder just as he did with his quiver of arrows.

The young chief's eyes carefully surveyed the scene. There were more guns, but he didn't want to be weighed down with them. He nudged each outlaw with his foot to be sure each man had breathed his final breaths. His Comanche instincts inclined him to scalp his three victims. Given the heinousness of the crimes they'd boasted of, they deserved to be defiled. Had any one of them been captured alive, he'd have taken pleasure in torturing them to the limits of their endurance. One Arrow looked at his hands and the knife he held in one. Despite his nature, he struggled to bring himself to touch the hair of these evil excuses for humans. His nature won. He deftly scalped each, then thought on how they'd boasted of raping their latest female victim. All the more reason to slice off their private parts and stuff them in the dead men's mouths. It was a Comanche practice, and these men had earned it. The chief thoroughly wiped the blood from his hands.

The chief fetched his pony and pack horses and began to load what seemed useful. He slipped the Henry into the scabbard and slung it over his shoulder. It would serve to keep the weapon protected from the elements. He mounted his pony and resumed his southward journey despite the darkness. At dawn's light, he'd strive to learn how the White man's weapon worked. He felt a certain relief in his soul as he departed the boundaries of the campsite. In his communing with the Great Spirit, he had felt uncomfortable at times. One Arrow was of a mind to believe that those were forebodings of what he'd just encountered. He especially wondered at *kwihnai* having taken the rattlesnake.

Luke and Elisa enjoyed the wagon ride back to Heaven's Gate. Luke had Big Horse hitched to the back, as he much preferred sitting alongside Elisa. They were looking forward to hearing whether romantic sparks had flown in Corpus Christi after they'd departed. As they drew within a couple of miles of Heaven's Gate, they'd felt confident enough to send the children on ahead. It gave them some much-needed privacy.

"What do you think, Lucas? Did it seem that Gordon might look past Emma's condition?"

"The colonel's an honorable man. He's not experienced in the ways of the heart, and Emma's pregnancy complicates the situation. There did seem to be attraction between them."

"Do you think their sparks were anything like we felt?" She smiled broadly. She knew she'd thrown out a loaded question.

Luke gave a you're-not-going-to-trap-me-with-that grin and looked over at her. "Nothing could ever hope to match the sparks that flew between you and me, Lisa Dunn." He paused. "And fly to this day."

"Took you long enough to realize it, Lucas."

"Not fair. I was and am an honorable man. I respected you far too much to take advantage."

Elisa offered a mischievous smile. "I knew that, Lucas. I

just like hearing you say it. We'll see how honorable you are, when we reach Heaven's Gate."

Luke could do naught but give a thoughtful stroke to his red whiskers, smile, and give the team a bit of a snap to the lines to hustle them along.

Elisa slipped her arm over Luke's. "Take it easy, love. We'll get there."

Of a sudden, Luke steered the rig off the road and artfully placed it behind a sheltering stand of pecan trees. He gave her a look that likely would have put a mating longhorn bull to shame.

"What are you doing, Lucas?" She feigned bewilderment.

They embraced passionately and tumbled gently back into the bed of the wagon.

Big Horse's eyes grew wide, and he shook his head. The stallion gave a few snorts mixed with neighs. Whether he was expressing alarm or approval likely will never be known, but he had a close-up view of the action unfolding under his nose.

Elisa guided Luke to her. His lips melted to hers. Her fingers clawed at the rippling muscles of his back, while his hands caressing her breasts coupled with rhythmic thrusts that sent her into transcendent orgasmic spasms. Nothing around them existed. Their pleasure gripped heart and soul, awakening the impassioned beasts within. She pulled him closer as her legs wrapped ever tighter around his hips. Their lovemaking exploded in a euphoric crescendo. They lay breathless.

"Lucas?"

He looked over at her with that languid look that accompanies a fully satisfied man.

"You…you are…" She couldn't find the words.

"Pretty much." He kissed her.

Late August in Corpus Christi was about as hot and humid as any place on the face of the planet. The old image of frying an egg on a rock was about right. Nevertheless, the colonel had dressed in full uniform to escort young Miss Sparks to dinner.

It would be a huge understatement to suggest that the romantic fires stoked between Gordon Belknap and Emma Sparks were hot and growing hotter. It had become a whirlwind courting that tended to leave the girl breathless.

Clara and Scarlett kept a watchful eye and offered the dear girl advice as needed. Back in Nuecestown, Bernice and Agatha quickly figured out what was going on and offered helpful counsel to Belknap. Luke and Sheriff Meaney mostly stepped back and watched dumbfounded. Belknap was woefully inexperienced at these things and Emma equally naïve.

For Emma, this was the first military man she'd ever made any acquaintance of other than to see soldiers march by in parades. There was a slight soldierly stiffness about her suitor that his years chasing Indians and Rebels across the Texas frontier hadn't quite softened. As to Belknap's part, the mere fact that he was within close reach of a woman for whom he had some romantic feelings was totally new ground. For her, there was both a hardiness of spirit borne of growing up on a working ranch and a softness that came with being a naturally nurturing woman.

Belknap now found himself walking arm in arm with Emma along the Corpus Christi pier. They had enjoyed a fine dinner, and the colonel was surprised at how easily they conversed. Thus far, they hadn't discussed her condition, though it would soon become obvious to most anyone. Her pregnancy simmered just beneath the surface of their chats. Now, they were enjoying a romantic post-dinner walk. Clara and Scarlett were some distance away perhaps unnecessarily making sure the colonel did nothing untoward.

Belknap stopped and turned to Emma, then gazed out over

the Gulf before looking down into her eyes. He cleared his throat. "Dear Emma, you should know that I'm aware of your situation. I've thought and prayed upon it, and it is of no concern to me."

A tear ran down Emma's cheek, then another. "I'm so ashamed, Gordon."

"It wasn't your fault, dear Emma. Take no shame in it." He smiled endearingly, looking full into her crystal blue eyes. His sincerity totally disarmed the young woman.

There was a heavy stillness between them. Of a sudden, Emma was startled to have him drop to one knee. His eyes never left hers. He swept his saber aside and reached into his tunic pocket.

Further up the pier, Scarlett and Clara gasped in unison.

"Emma Sparks, would you be my wife?"

Clara and Scarlett were too far off to prevent what happened next, as Emma pulled the colonel up and wrapped her arms tightly around him. "Oh Gordon. You make me so happy."

Belknap pulled away ever-so-slightly. "Is that a yes?"

Tears of joy streamed down Emma's face. "Yes...yes...yes, I'll be your wife."

Belknap shook his head in wonder at why women cried when they were happy and while sad. No matter, he'd surely found a life partner. "Emma Sparks, I love you."

No one had ever said those words to the young woman. They brought more tears.

There were more joyful tears being shed further up the pier.

Shots rang out across the vast expanse of scrub brush. One Arrow had pretty much mastered the Henry. The chief was even reasonably confident that he could hit pretty much whatever he pointed the rifle at. By now he'd managed to cut away a strip of hide from a buckskin cape and fashion a more comfortable strap than the makeshift one he'd fashioned from the reins.

He roughly calculated that he was perhaps no more than two days' ride from Heaven's Gate. He'd passed the place on the Pedernales River where his small band of Comanche had camped weeks ago. He hadn't lingered but a few moments before moving on.

As he journeyed closer to Nuecestown, the landscape became ever flatter. He hoped he wouldn't encounter any further trouble. He'd learned of the end of the White man's war over enslavement of the Black man. He'd never encountered a Black slave, though his Comanche brothers were known to keep captive whites and other Indians as slaves. One Arrow recalled Three Toes's story of having killed a Black frontiersman but having been frustrated at trying to scalp the man. The old chief had also been startled at the heavy scars across the dead man's back. One Arrow became ever more vigilant for threats along his route that might try to take advantage of the post-war chaos.

Belknap wasn't certain how long he'd be tied up with the bureaucracy in Austin as he delivered Scrub to the provisional governor. It made sense to him to wed Emma, before departing. Given her pregnancy, speed had been of the essence.

For Emma's part, she was committed to her future with the colonel. It could well have been the naivete of her youth that had enabled the putting of her fully abhorrent introduction to sex behind her. Her attraction to Belknap was strong and more than sexual.

She readily looked for counsel to the women who'd

befriended her. Scarlett was teaching her to sew, and Clara Meaney shared cooking skills.

Now came the question of who'd officiate and where they'd hold the ceremony. Emma was at a total loss. She was beholden to so many folks, she feared any perceived offense.

Belknap was ever one to act, when action was required. "Emma, I believe that Sheriff Meaney can preside over our wedding. I don't think we have time to find a proper church. Horace Rucker in Nuecestown is visiting friends in San Antonio and the local Corpus Christi clergy are out on the trail making rounds."

"Whatever you say, Gordon." She was in no position to argue and surely didn't fancy waiting weeks or even months for the colonel's return to Corpus.

"I don't want to offend Luke and Elisa, but we'll celebrate with everyone when I get back. Sheriff Meaney says you can stay with them until I return. Then, we'll get us a proper home and raise our family."

Emma simply nodded. It was likely going to take a while before she rebuilt the inner spirit by which she'd contribute meaningfully to their marriage decisions. So much had happened so quickly for the teen. Had it not been for Scarlett and Clara, she'd undoubtedly have been at a loss. Even the incident with Angus Moncrieff contributed little to her healing. She was in the midst of a life tempest of sorts, and it took all she had to cope. She was happy that she hadn't decided to seek her fortune in Laredo. It'd been her first inclination, and she had the retrospective sense to understand its folly.

That afternoon, Colonel Gordon Belknap wed Miss Emma Sparks at the sheriff's home. Scarlett and Walker Carson served as witnesses, Margaret and Martha strewed flower petals about, while Clara played some wedding-type music on the old piano that graced their parlor. Scarlett even found a white dress for the young lady, so she'd be properly matched with her uniformed beau.

As the couple received congratulations after the ceremony, Belknap whispered in Emma's ear. "I have a suite at the hotel for us tonight. We'll have dinner and then enjoy our first night of marriage." He tried hard not to reveal his total nervousness at the prospect of spending the night, their first night together.

She smiled nervously. "Whatever you say, Gordon." She glanced furtively at Scarlett and Clara. They had tried their best to prepare her for this. She'd strive for her part to push away the images that played through her head of her father's clumsily painful assaults.

The colonel was not exactly lily-pure in matters of the opposite sex. While the powers-that-be at the military academy would deny it to their deathbeds, students were known to steal away on occasion and avail themselves of a bawdy house or two in New York City. The camaraderie among young men was such that all partook of the whores of the big city at one time or another. It may not have been not the optimal sexual introduction for the now married Colonel Belknap, but at least he had some vague idea what to do.

Everyone put on the happiest faces they could and waved genteel-like, as Belknap led his bride up the street toward the hotel. He hoped a romantic dinner would hold promise of leading to a mutually enjoyable consummation of their marriage.

Jaime Sanchez had ridden out at dawn to check cattle on the northern reaches of Heaven's Gate. He was on the lookout, as Luke was planning to ride out and join him. The *vaquero* looked out appreciatively over the vast reaches of the ranch. He and Julia had a good life working the ranch, and he was especially pleased that Luke had begun adding an addition to their cabin. A part of him itched to have his own spread, but life was so good he struggled with venturing to risk buying his own spread.

As he looked to the west, away from the soon-to-be burning rays of the rising sun, he caught sight of a lone rider off in the distance. He slipped his rifle from its scabbard and held it across the saddle pommel, as he headed his mount in the direction of the rider. Out here on the Nueces Strip, it simply made sense to be cautious.

The approaching rider began to draw close enough for Jaime to make out what manner of human it was. The grasses weren't so tall that he couldn't see a couple of horses trailing. The figure was bare-headed, so wasn't likely to be a cowboy.

One Arrow was going through the same recognition process. Was the rider he was approaching a friend or foe? He'd met Jaime twice, the first time under the quite stressful circumstances of the ill-fated Comanche attack with War Cloud and Three Toes. He'd likely had one or two of Jaime's bullets whiz by, though the event was marred by the death of Three Toes at the hands of the traitorous War Cloud. The second meeting had also been at Heaven's Gate but under decidedly better circumstances.

Jaime had drawn to within perhaps 200 yards. By now, it was clear that he was facing not only an Indian, but a Comanche at that.

One Arrow realized that the man he was drawing near to was not a White man but one of the brown skins, the ones that were called Mexican. He raised his hand as a sign of peace and could only hope that the man understood.

Jaime pulled up and returned the sign. He kept the rifle handy across his lap just in case. As if to add to his concerns, he heard distant hoofbeats behind him. His experienced *vaquero* ear recognized the sound as a shod horse. A quick glance over his shoulder confirmed that his boss was heading toward him. He looked back at the approaching Comanche and saw a smile spread hesitantly across the savage's face.

"Me One Arrow!" the chief hollered out, as he thumped his chest. "Me friend."

Jaime relaxed enough to slide the rifle back into its scabbard. He waved at One Arrow to approach.

Instead of pulling up alongside Jaime, Luke rode on by. "One Arrow! Welcome, my friend!"

The big man on the big stallion was certainly easy to recognize. "Ghost-Who-Rides!"

Luke pulled up alongside the Penateka Comanche chief, and they grasped hands. "You have traveled far, brother."

Jaime gave a shrug and rode over. "Welcome One Arrow. Peace to you."

"Jaime, I think we should take the day off and welcome our friend to Heaven's Gate." Luke grinned from ear to ear. There'd be a lot of catching up to do. "We can check the range tomorrow."

The three turned their horses toward the ranch house and headed eastward, chatting and laughing as they rode.

The report of the rifle echoed across the landscape. A bullet whizzed past Luke's ear.

"What the…!" In one motion, Luke grabbed his rifle and dove from the saddle. He slapped Big Horse on his hindquarters to send him off.

Jaime dismounted a split second later.

One Arrow? He kicked his pony into a gallop, let out a series of wild war whoops, and charged in the direction of the gunshot.

The gunman was totally surprised by this turn of events. He fumbled to insert a second cartridge into his rifle. Too late.

One Arrow leaped from his pony onto the unfortunate gunman. The shooter was a bigger foe, but the Comanche had the element of surprise coupled with the momentum from leaping from a galloping pony. One Arrow quickly subdued the attacker, sitting astride the man's chest with a knife to his throat.

Luke retrieved Big Horse and rode over to where the chief held the gunman captive.

The gunman strove to wriggle free to no avail. He saw Luke approach. "Don't let him scalp me! Please don't scalp me!" he called out desperately.

One Arrow held the knife at the man's throat until Luke had the ambusher's hands tied behind his back. "Me want scalp." He gave a crazed wild look and made a cutting motion before the cringing man's eyes. Then he laughed. He'd had his fun.

Luke smiled as he pushed the man down to his knees. "Who are you, mister and what are you doing trying to bushwhack me on my own ranch?"

"Don't let him scalp me."

"You don't answer my questions, I'm going to do the scalping." Luke gave him an angry glare.

Jaime pulled up. "I saw this man near Nuecestown yesterday, *Señor* Dunn. Doc had stitched up that cut on his arm."

Luke pulled out his own knife, a Bowie knife. "Maybe he needs a fresh cut?"

The gunman looked furtively from Luke to One Arrow to Jaime and back to Luke. "You...you be that Texas Ranger."

"Not any more. What's it to you?" Luke waved the Bowie knife and flashed the most evil smile he could muster. "And you still haven't told me your name." He stared down at the sorry excuse for manhood before him. The man stunk to high heaven, likely hadn't shaved in days, wore barely serviceable clothes with trousers that hinted of Confederate butternut gray, and had a hole in the toe of one boot.

"The Kid." He said it in a sniveling but defiant manner.

Luke moved the tip of the Bowie knife to within an inch of the man's throat. "The Kid?" It seemed laughable to Luke.

One Arrow stepped forward swiftly and pulled Luke's hand away. He simultaneously grabbed a handful of the man's hair and waved his own knife inches from the hairline. "Me scalp now!" The chief had put on that wild look in his eyes again.

The gunman peed in his pants. "Carlson. My name's Dev Carlson. Please, please...not my hair!"

The Comanche chief stepped back and offered a self-satisfied smile to Luke. "He need dry pants."

Jaime was taking this all in. "He was asking questions about you, *Señor* Dunn. Boasted of making a name by killing a Texas Ranger."

"You don't know what yer talkin' 'bout, ya damned Mexican."

"Watch your mouth, Carlson, or I'll lend my knife to my *vaquero* here."

"I'd a got ya, Ranger, but fer my bent gunsight. They was gonna pay me."

"Well, Mr. Carlson, seems you missed your chance. You're going to be making a name for yourself by doing some time in the Corpus Christi jail." Luke looked around. "You got a horse?"

Carlson hung his head. "Damned beast run off when I fired the rifle."

"You've got a long walk ahead."

Carlson looked at One Arrow's pack ponies.

Luke gave a wry look. "Not a chance. The chief would take your scalp for sure."

"Who's the Injun?" Carlson was resigned to his fate.

Luke began to string out the lead to the rope now tied around Carlson's neck. "This here is One Arrow, Chief of the Penateka Comanche. You're lucky he's a friend of mine or your scalp would surely be hanging on his lance." Luke mounted Big Horse and held the end of the rope lead. He'd try to maintain just enough slack to avoid choking the prisoner. "You just walk on ahead. We have a few miles to cover."

Jaime and One Arrow fell in behind Luke.

Luke nodded to One Arrow. "That was the craziest move I've ever seen, my friend. But it sure worked."

One Arrow nodded his agreement. "Ghost-Who-Rides good friend. Three Toes...he do same."

"Yeah. We miss him." Luke briefly looked off at the horizon. "He was a good friend." Luke suddenly pulled up and yanked on the rope. Carlson nearly fell. "How were they going to pay you? Who was paying?"

Carlson put on a defiant expression as though momentarily forgetting how close the chief's knife had come to his hairline.

Luke looked over at One Arrow. "Mr. Carlson, are you familiar with Comanche torture?"

"You'd never do that."

"They stake you out naked. Then the fun begins...for the Comanche."

One Arrow smiled and pointed to his privates.

"No! No! It was a fella with a black beard. Think his name was Cogburn. Yeah, that's it...Cogburn. Said he'd pay two hunert dollars."

"Two hundred dollars! I've brought outlaws to justice for bigger bounty." Luke glared hard at Carlson.

"I be desperate, Mr. Ranger. Got no pay from the Rebel army."

"So, you'd kill for money? You're a sorrier excuse for a human being than I'd first guessed. Maybe I ought to let the chief here have a go at you after all."

"I...I...I'm sorry."

Luke shook his head. "Keep walking." And he flipped the rope just hard enough that once again Carlson nearly fell.

NINETEEN
TROUBLE ON THE RIO GRANDE

NO SOONER HAD Belknap arrived in Austin with his prisoner, but he was alerted to the rumblings on the Rio Grande about what General Sheridan was dealing with. Cheno Cortina was frustrated by the power games in Mexico City so was taking his resentments out on Texans. He was deeply irritated by Benito Juarez sending dragoons to Camargo to attack the Apache with whom Cortina had a long-standing mutually beneficial relationship with. The Apache chief Costalites was licking his wounds while trying to figure a way to vent his anger while avoiding Sheridan's troops and the Mexican dragoons.

Leaving Scrub and his report of the Moncrieff affair behind with the authorities in Austin, Belknap headed his troop south. He figured that Sheridan just might be able to use his help. The colonel decided that along the way he'd stop briefly in Corpus Christi to spend time with his new wife. He had thought some on the whirlwind nature of their courtship, but was comfortable in the outcome. He'd never loved a woman in the way he'd begun to feel for Emma, and he was rather enjoying it. He found himself missing her company.

Scrub had spilled the beans on the land fraud deal and

would be doing serious time at the prison in Huntsville. The men like Thorpe and Burnett who'd help bait the trap by signing agreements with Moncrieff didn't lose any money and could enjoy the satisfaction of having helped stop a crime. It didn't hurt that it earned them political points.

★★

It was quite a sight. Luke, Jaime, and a Comanche chief riding into Corpus Christi with a prisoner staggering before them like some mangy dog on a leash.

"Keep walking, Carlson. We're almost there."

A few passersby whispered furtively at the sight, especially of the wild-looking savage with scalps hanging on his lance and a Henry rifle in his arsenal. One Arrow made a point of avoiding any eye contact, as he sensed the uncertainty and fear especially resident in the ladies' faces. He felt a passing urge to let out a war whoop just to see what would happen. Fortunately, his better judgment prevailed.

The entourage finally reached the jail. Luke dismounted and knocked on the door. "Sheriff Meaney?!" The door was locked. "Bill?"

"Dang it, Luke. Can't a man eat a meal in peace?" Meaney emerged from his house nearby. He pulled up sudden like upon catching sight of One Arrow. "Uh oh, what have we got here?"

"Little present for you, Bill. This fellow took a shot at me." He paused for effect. "Obviously, he missed."

"Well, I can dang well see that he missed, Luke. How'd you get to wrangling him like some wayward yearling?"

Luke glanced over at One Arrow. "My friend One Arrow caught him."

"Friend? You seem to be making a few Comanche friends."

"Well, Bill, turns out Three Toes adopted this fellow. He's chief of the Penateka Comanche these days and by God's providence happened to come for a visit to get better acquainted with me."

Meaney stared at cross hanging from the chief's neck. "He know what that there cross means?"

"We're working on it." Luke pushed Carlson toward the sheriff. "This here is Dev Carlson. You have a cell for him?"

"Sure. You have witnesses?"

Luke looked to either side. "Seems like."

"Guess Jaime will stand up all right. The chief here not so much." It was a sad part of justice that the word of an Indian wasn't worth anything in a courtroom. The word of a Mexican wasn't much better but would have to do in this case. "You have any idea why Mr. Carlson took a shot at you?"

"He said a black-bearded man named Cogburn offered a couple of hundred dollars to kill me. You run into this Cogburn, fellow?"

"Can't say as I have, Luke. Let's get this ne'er do well registered in our fine jail. Then, we can concern ourselves with Cogburn."

Costalites was licking his wounds, hiding out among the Texas ebony, mesquite, and elm trees of the Rio Grande valley while using the growths of sage as dense cover. His scouts kept a watchful eye for Sheridan's patrols and dared not cross into Mexico with its ever-present threat of dragoons. He hoped that Cortina might venture north where the Apache chief could renew their arrangement. He was frustrated at his luck against the bluecoats and grateful that the Texas Rangers were not to be seen.

Once again, his warriors were getting restless. Costalites would have to organize another sortie, victimize another Anglo ranch. And he'd need to do it soon. A few Lipan Apache stragglers had found their way to his encampment, and it was enough to swell his band to better than a hundred warriors. A few women and children who'd escaped the wrath of the Mexican dragoons had even managed to join them. The tribe had invested effort in constructing a few dugouts to dwell in, but they weren't elaborate. The Apache weren't quite ready to make any great effort for the long-term. Their relationships with outsiders were far too rocky and fleeting to establish roots.

The chief had to satisfy his warriors while adopting a nomadic strategy. He knew intuitively that his encampment would soon be discovered, if it hadn't been already. Staying on the move was integral to his existence. Keeping a hundred or so Apache on the move was challenging. They needed to travel light and leave as little evidence as possible. The temporary answer was to divide into smaller bands, gathering at regular intervals. Such would be their lives until they could establish roots of some sort.

As Costalites thought on these strategies, a pair of scouts arrived. "What news do you bring?"

"Bluecoats far to south."

The chief saw this as too easy. "How far?"

"Two-day ride."

"How many?" Costalites felt as though he was having to drag information from his scouts. It was irritating, but he strove to be patient.

"Many." The Apache didn't have a word for five hundred. "Like grass on prairie. Many horses, many cannon."

Costalites would have to be satisfied. Knowing the troops were far to his south bought him time to feed his warriors' blood lust while preparing to move his village farther north along the Rio Grande.

★★

"¿Lo de banco en Rio Grande City?" Cortina's men huddled around the table. The room held a musty feel owing to the rain that morning. Camargo didn't see much rain, so they'd filled water cisterns as best they could. But water and food were the least of their worries. They desperately needed cash to pay for more weapons, if they ever hoped to realize any revolutionary dreams. The rebel leader saw Benito Juarez as a lackey of the United States, as Washington pressured the erstwhile president of Mexico to overthrow Maximillian, the man the French had installed as emperor. So, they needed resources. His question about the bank in Rio Grande City as a target made sense.

"El banco tiene mucho dinero."

"¿Hay guardias?" A bank with lots of money would logically be well-guarded.

"No hay guardias en la noche."

Cortina pondered that. Why would they have no guards at night? He knew that nearby Fort Ringgold was not garrisoned, and the region lay vulnerable despite the roving patrols of General Sheridan's troops. *"¿Así, atacamos el banco en la noche?"*

The men around the table nodded agreement. They'd rob the bank at night and employ a plan they'd used successfully before, positioning a few men around the bank late in the day to be sure there were no guards. They had to work out moving as many as two dozen men across the Rio Grande and into position to carry out a successful mission. That would be accomplished by traveling in small groups of three or four men with weapons hidden beneath serapes. Bandoliers and rifles would only be carried by the men conducting the main attack.

One of the men stood back. *"Tienen una bóveda."* This was not good news. A new vault, and a large one at that, posed a problem.

Cortina shrugged. *"Vamos a robar la bóveda."* It made perfect sense to the rebel leader. They'd simply steal the vault. It would be a matter of bringing a wagon and hoisting the heavy vault into it. There would be increased risk from a slower escape, so they'd have to rob the bank as stealthily as possible. Were they not so desperate, he likely wouldn't have accepted the risk.

The troop comprised mostly of colored soldiers with a few Anglos and Mexicans rode easily if not noisily. While many of the blacks had been slaves, several had been born free and never tasted an overseer's lash. They were of good spirits and had come far under the guidance of Sergeant Brown. Belknap rode smartly out front, focused on the business at hand. He had the foresight to have sent a courier to General Sheridan advising of his intention of heading toward Rio Grande City in support of the general. The colonel rightly assumed Sheridan was aware of his policing mission. Meanwhile, he planned to bivouac his men outside Corpus Christi while he ventured into the city. He had visions of spending a couple of days and especially a couple of nights with Emma before answering his call to duty.

As they rode past the entrance to Heaven's Gate, the colonel was sorely tempted to visit with his friends. On the other hand, he didn't want to miss a precious minute with his new wife. He decided to stay the course.

The troop was soon setting up camp on the outskirts of the city. Belknap was pleased with the efficiency and discipline displayed by his men. He was confident that this would serve them well in the weeks ahead.

"Sergeant, I'm going to head into Corpus. I'll be back tomorrow. If you need me, go to the sheriff's office and inquire of Bill Meaney. I don't anticipate trouble here, though we dare not be overconfident. Set some pickets tonight." Belknap was set to dismiss the sergeant, when he had a second thought. "I'd give the men leave to do some relaxing in the city, but I'm uncertain as to the attitudes of the townfolk toward coloreds these days. We ought not be stirring up trouble." The lingering prejudices would be an ongoing problem. They'd been fortunate thus far, as the region still reeled from the aftermath of the War Between the States. Soon enough, there'd likely be trouble brewing.

Sergeant Brown nodded. "Yes, sir. I understand, sir." He was as apprehensive as Belknap.

"Dismissed, Sergeant."

Brown saluted but then paused. "Sir. Permission to speak plainly, sir?"

Belknap was anxious to be getting on to Corpus Christi, but valued his sergeant and his opinions. "Yes, Sergeant, but be quick."

"Sir, there be rumblings in Austin by some fella named Edmund Davis. Word is that he hid away in Mexico during the war. He be stirrin' up folks 'bout takin' rights away from freedom-lovin' Texans an' givin' Nigras the vote." Brown hesitated.

"Go on, Sergeant. I'm listening." He now commanded the colonel's full attention.

"Yes sir. Well, I think a few of our colored troops have heard 'bout some of those rumors, sir. I'm thinkin' it don't bode well. Nope, don't bode well at all."

"Sergeant, I appreciate your concerns. Appears we must keep a watchful eye on our own soldiers as well as for any possible external enemy. Select your pickets with extra care."

"Yes sir, Colonel."

As Brown departed, Belknap shook his head with just a touch of bewilderment. A new dynamic seemed to be developing. He wasn't surprised given what he'd seen already in the aftermath of the war. He now seriously considered shortening his stay in Corpus despite his personal desires. He feared the citizens of the city might not take so kindly to any extended bivouac of colored troops near their city.

★★

A wagon pulled by four horses was hard to hide even in a small Texas town after dark. The thing was noisy, a jumble of creaks and squeaks of wood on wood coupled with sixteen hooves beating the hard-packed streets of Rio Grande City. Cortina's men were overconfident, loudly overconfident. Any hint of a surprise bank robbery was quickly lost once they entered the town.

Cortina was even foolhardy enough to accompany his men on this mission. They had to grab that heavy vault and high-tail it for Mexico. There'd be a lot of ground to cover between Rio Grande City and the raft that waited on the north shore of the river. "*Prisa, hombres. Debemos hacer esto.*" Hurry indeed.

Eight armed outriders accompanied the wagon. Cortina rode behind giving orders as needed. "Rápido. *¡Entra al banco!*" The men weren't moving nearly quickly enough. Time was of the essence, and they were making themselves easy targets of anyone with an inclination to defend the bank.

Just as they pulled up, Cortina spotted a man walk from a nearby house. The man paused, when he saw the wagon in front of the bank. Cortina called out, "*Juan, tómalo antes de que pueda hacer sonar la alarma.*" The man had to be stopped before any alarm was sounded.

Juan swung a rifle around and shot the man. Naturally, the shot echoed far-too-loudly among the buildings.

Cortina was horrified at Juan's stupidity. "*¡Estúpido! ¡Demasiado ruido! ¡Tenemos que darnos prisa!*" Again, he urged speed.

Four of Cortina's men were soon dragging the vault from the bank. It was still going far too slowly. Noise should have been their enemy. Why was there no resistance, no guards, no defense?

Of a sudden, all hell broke loose. Cortina had ridden into a trap. He pivoted and shouted to his men. *"Hombres, abandonen el banco. ¡Corran por sus vidas!"* Ride for their lives indeed!

The men dragging the vault were cut down in a fusillade of gunfire. Those on horseback, including Cortina, fared better. They turned and retreated at a gallop behind their leader. Only a hundred yards or so ahead, a second ambush awaited. Cortina clung low in the saddle and charged on praying he'd not be introduced to a bullet with his name on it. He and five of his men managed to break through and ride hell bent for the Rio Grande. They had not even returned fire, such was their desperation to escape. Cortina's brain already throbbed with the shock of who among his supposedly loyal followers was a traitor.

"Luke. I hadn't expected to run into you here in Corpus." Belknap half saluted his friend. He was distracted, as he'd filled his ride to the city with thoughts of Emma mixed with concerns over the politics in Austin and his own policing mission.

"Just checking on a new prisoner, Gordon. Bill and I were fixing to look for a man named Cogburn who offered up a bounty on my head. What brings you here?"

"Well, I thought I might spend a little time with Emma."

"You'll find her over at Scarlett's place."

"Much obliged, Luke. When you've finished your business, I have something for you to look into west of here. Seems Cheno Cortina stirred up a hornets' nest of trouble down in Rio Grande City where I'll be headed, but that confounded Apache Costalites is wreaking havoc among settlers further up toward San Ignacio. Might like to have you check it out. Your friend Jake Barber might be some help." Belknap glanced behind Luke and did a double take, as he noticed One Arrow astride his pony just behind Jaime. "You cavorting with Comanche again?"

"One Arrow? He helped corral the man we just locked up in Meaney's hoosegow. One Arrow here was a protégé of our dearly departed friend Three Toes."

Belknap nodded to One Arrow, who stoically returned the nod. "Still some ill feelings around as concerns Indians, Luke. There are folks who'd as soon see him dead, not to mention anyone who befriends them."

"Most of the Comanche are up north these days, Gordon. One Arrow is just visiting. Might say he's on sort of a mission. We'll be careful." Luke was a bit taken aback by Belknap's concern.

"I don't mean any disrespect to your friend, Luke. It's just that emotions seem to be running high with so much uncertainty ahead. Folks don't seem to distinguish between tribes or friend or foe. Shoot, all the dang prejudices about Indians, blacks, and Mexicans, it's a wonder anyone can get along these days. Right now, there's Apache to deal with." Belknap nodded apologetically to Jaime.

Luke understood that the colonel meant well. "Well, go find your Emma, Gordon, and maybe we can discuss our Apache friend Costalites at the Longhorn before I head back to Heaven's Gate."

"I'll look forward to it."

Luke watched the colonel walk away smartly toward Scarlett's and Walker's Cacti & Boots haberdashery. He turned to One Arrow. "My friend, how about you and Jaime here ride on out to Heaven's Gate. I've got business to finish up here with Sheriff Meaney."

"You need help?" One Arrow clearly was intent on hanging around Luke.

"I can handle this. Just want to figure who this Cogburn fellow is. I should be out to the ranch right quickly enough."

With that, Luke bid them farewell, and went off to connect with Meaney.

The ranch the Apache were targeting was nestled along Solomoneno Creek, now an extended arroyo that meandered its way along toward the Rio Grande near Bellville. It provided a fine habitat for raising longhorns along with numerous incidental indigenous varmints including coyotes, rattlesnakes, and javelinas plus their nasty cousins the wild hogs. The setting sun cast a warm orange glow on the landscape.

Costalites warriors gazed down on their prey. His scouts had reported that four women and seven men lived on the ranch along with a couple of children and assorted dogs and chickens. There were several horses and plenty of food to be had. The best news was that the ranchers had Henry rifles. Those were prized by the Apache, as they afforded them a significant advantage in firepower to couple with their mobility.

The chief watched as a few of the residents milled about. They'd apparently enjoyed dinner and were partaking of the Anglo habit of post-dinner smoking and drinking. When he saw a couple of musical instruments appear, he let out an audible sigh of resignation. It could be a long wait, depending on how much drinking occurred. Drunken prey was easier prey, though any shooting could get wild.

It took all of a bit more than an hour for the sun to sink below the horizon and the drunken festivities to become even more festive. The women were dancing, with or without the men. If his scouts had reported correctly, all of the inhabitants were now in full view.

Costalites decided the best attack would be on foot. They'd approach silently under the cover of darkness to deliver their wicked evils upon the unsuspecting whites.

The chief personally led four warriors from one side while another dozen approached from the opposite direction. As they drew close, he saw a man and woman leave the gathering and head behind some brush not more than a dozen yards from his position. The couple quickly stripped from the waist down and embraced in carnal passions. The man wasted no time mounting the woman, and she began moaning softly. They were virtually oblivious to anything around them. Costalites snuck up such that he could have reached out and touched them. Instead of touching, he raised his rifle and fired into the man's naked butt. At such close range, the bullet passed through both lovers. The chief smiled as the man collapsed onto the woman.

The firing of the shot was also a signal to attack. Costalites warriors were efficient and effective. The men and one woman were quickly shot and killed, and two of the women were bound and held captive. Three young children appeared from the cabin.

Costalites paused before joining his brothers. He slipped out his knife and swiftly scalped the man and woman he'd just killed with the single bullet. He'd let their still entwined bodies rot in the Texas sun or be devoured by scavengers. No matter. He strode over to where the women were being held. He grunted and sneered. "Strip them."

The Apache needed no prodding. They knew what was to come. The recent near-massacre attack on their village by the Mexican military had resulted in the savage butchering of several Apache women and children. The warriors had a considerable amount of vengeful anger not to mention pent-up sexual energy to release.

Some warriors grabbed furniture from the cabin and lit a bonfire. In the raging light of the flames, the two women were tied side by side to corral posts with their feet spread and tied to stakes. The Apache next turned to the children. Each child was to be brought before the women as though as a sacrifice.

Costalites himself would decide life or death. One young girl, perhaps ten years old, held a defiant look. The chief liked her spirit. She could be broken. "We keep this one."

"Sarah?! Please! Not..."

An Apache slapped the woman across her already bloodied cheeks. The little girl was scuttled away out of sight of the proceedings.

Two tearful younger boys were brought forward. They couldn't have been older than five or six. Costalites nodded to two warriors. Swipes of rifle butts crushed the boys' skulls, while the women strained in horror against their bonds.

Costalites stepped forward. He would have first honors at raping the women. The others would follow until all were satisfied. A few would partake more than once.

The women were totally spent from the ordeal. Their fully dispirited expressions revealed that they'd given up any hope of surviving.

The Apache proceeded to ransack the cabin and choose the best horses from the corral. The prized Henry rifles were snatched up along with plenty of ammunition.

As the warriors gathered to depart, Costalites turned to the women still bound to the corral posts. They were slumped over in total despair. Costalites would now execute the full evil of his psyche. He no longer held any tolerance of the Anglo invader of his lands. He would mutilate the women and leave them hanging. Cuts to their breasts and abdomens were complemented by slices across their faces. The chief recalled how the Comanche would cut off women's noses to further disfigure them, but instead he chose to slice an ear off each woman. The wounds would not kill them—at least, not imme- diately. Scavengers might hasten the work or starvation, if no one happened upon the ranch.

One of the women found some spirit of defiance within her. "You bastard heathen. May God strike you down!"

Costalites had begun to walk away but stopped dead in his

tracks. He turned with an angry sneer, brandished his knife, reached into the terrified woman's mouth, and cut out half her tongue. The other woman watched in total horror. The now nearly tongue-less woman struggled to make sounds of hatred toward the chief. He was done with her. His knife plunged deep into her chest with the full force of all his anger at the White man and at the Mexican dragoons that murdered his people. He stepped back, as she breathed her last. He looked around at his Apache band and motioned to the horses. "Let's go. This place has bad spirits."

The warriors rode off toward their camp without a second thought as to the horror they'd just wrought. They'd fulfilled their needs and possibly discouraged the advance of the Anglos on the frontier.

Cortina finally caught his breath as he sat astride his horse on the south side of the Rio Grande. By quick count, he and five others had escaped the ambush. He was tired and angry. Who was the traitor in his midst?

TWENTY
MURDER & MAYHEM

LUKE AND MEANEY stood before the entrance to the Longhorn Saloon. Luke looked left and right for any potential troublemakers and then tilted his head questioningly. "You say there's a poster on this Cogburn fellow? Murderer you say?"

Meaney nodded. "I recall seein' it a few days back. Likely still in the stack on my desk." Both men checked the loads in their guns. "Sorry, I didn't pay it more attention, Luke."

The lawman duo clearly meant business to the crowd inside the Longhorn, as they strode purposely through the doors. Meaney found his way over to the bar to their left, while Luke turned to the right, stood with his back to the wall. They scanned the room.

Meaney tapped on the bar to get the keeper's attention. "John, you seen a man around here named Cogburn?"

The barkeep knew better than to hold back information from the sheriff and seeing Luke meant that this was likely extremely serious business. "He was here last night, Sheriff. Drank a bit. Talked real boastful like."

"You hear him make any threats about killing a Texas Ranger?"

The barkeeper thought on that a moment. "He was

spoutin' off 'bout payin' somebody. Nobody figured he could be serious. Likely, it was the liquor talkin'."

"Where can I find him?"

"I think he has a room up the street, Sheriff. Stayin' at the McDonald's place."

"Much obliged, John." Meaney nodded to Luke, and they took a sweeping look around the room one last time before easing out of the saloon. Once outside, the sheriff turned to Luke. "I don't like the house this Cogburn fellow is staying at, Luke. For one thing, it's more whore house than rooming house. It's got a couple of exits and enough nooks and crannies inside to frustrate a prairie dog. If he decides to resist, we'll be at considerable risk, not to mention the women and any customers."

"What are you thinking, Bill?"

They had ambled up the street until they found themselves standing in front of the rooming house. "Well, first we'll need to get the landlady to tell us which room he's in. If Cogburn has a room, I'm of a mind that he may have bought himself a passing interest of sorts in the enterprise. The barkeep was lettin' on that he was well fixed money-wise. If true, that might make her reluctant to tell us where he is. I'm not especially partial to being ambushed either. Remember what happened to the county sheriff last year. Matt Nolan was arresting a man when the Gravis brothers gunned him down in broad daylight. It was supposedly an accident, but death is sort of final. I find Nolan's murder lingers on my mind when I deal with known killers."

Luke nodded, though such doubts never lingered with him. Likely, his strong faith contributed to that. If it was time, so be it. Most folks would consider that fatalistic, but Luke figured death was God's choosing rather than his. He was always careful in any case. He shook off the mental distraction and brought them back to the situation at hand. "Sounds like we'd best split up. He could run out the back while we're dallying with the landlady out front." The rooming house seemed like it had been constructed randomly with multiple additions built over several years. It was a fairly good-sized two-story structure with all sorts of fancy Victorian architectural gingerbread. Its tasteless purple-colored shingles with cream-yellow window frames and shutters caused it to stand out strikingly among the surrounding buildings. Likely as not, it was the definition of architectural ugly. That having been said, it made for being right easy for a cowboy seeking a bit of lovemaking to find his way to it.

"Better double-check those Colts you're carrying, my friend," said Meaney. Of course, it didn't need to be said. Likely a touch of nerves.

Luke went up the alley to the rear of the building. He noted two rickety-looking stairways from second-floor exits and one exit at ground-floor level. He'd have to stand at the rear corner to be able to keep his eyes on ground-floor exit plus the stairways to have a chance at spotting anyone trying to escape.

Meaney walked up to the front door and knocked. No answer. He knocked again. An explosion shattered the silence and a bullet blasted through the door and just missed the sheriff's head. By the time a second gunshot was heard, Meaney had ducked to the side of the doorway. Two more bullets blew through the door. A window across the street exploded in shards.

Hearing the gunfire placed Luke in a bit of a dilemma. He hoped Meaney was okay.

"Luke, I'm all right!"

The shout from Meaney eased Luke's mind but now had him on high alert. He had both Colts at the ready. Off to his right, he heard a commotion from one of the rooms. A woman was hollering and arguing with a man who was apparently roughing her up. A shot was fired. As Luke rounded the corner of the building, he saw a man's leg emerge from a window along with the muzzle of a revolver. He figured a body would quickly follow. Luke waited to be certain of his target's identity, took careful aim with one of his Colts, squeezed the trigger, and watched the man's gun-hand shatter. The revolver went flying up the alley. The man ducked back inside. Luke could hear cussing and groaning. He hollered out to Meaney. "Bill, he's back inside! He might still be armed, but I hit him."

Meaney kicked open the front door. A trio of scantily-clad women were huddling in a corner of the foyer frantically trying to hide behind a settee. One woman fearfully pointed to a hallway. Meaney cautiously crouched low and stalked his way up the narrow passage. He heard noise in a room to his right. Another gunshot...another...a scream...moans. A door swung open. Meaney raised his gun. A woman was oozing blood from a bullet wound to her arm. The sheriff pulled her past him and stepped to the door. The man who was apparently Cogburn lay in a crumpled heap on the bed.

Luke entered through the rear door and quickly found his way to Meaney's side. "What's going on? I heard more shots."

"Looks like we found Mr. Cogburn, Luke. He appears to be still breathing." He pointed to the whore sitting stunned from in the hallway behind him. "Seems she shot him, but he returned the favor." Meaney noted the blood seeping from the whore's shoulder and motioned to the madam to care for the poor woman.

Luke kept one Colt at the ready as he entered the room to examine Cogburn's condition. "Cogburn, you able to talk?"

The man groaned but managed to bring up his pistol in his good hand.

He was too slow, as Luke slapped the gun from the man's hand. "Not nice, Mr. Cogburn. Not nice at all."

Meaney came up beside Luke. "Dang, Luke. You made a mess of his hand. We can't hardly manacle him." He shook his head and turned his attention back to the outlaw. "Mr.

Cogburn, you're under arrest." The sheriff locked one cuff around the man's hand and held on to the other cuff.

"He's got a nasty chest wound, Bill. Likely ought to fetch a doctor on our way to the jail." Luke pulled Cogburn to a sitting position. "We just wanted to talk with you, Cogburn. Why the shooting?"

One of the women burst in flailing and screaming and began beating on Cogburn before Luke or Meaney could react. "You sonofabitch! You evil bastard! You sonofa...you killed Betsy!" Luke managed to pull her off Cogburn who was now writhing in pain.

"Whoa, settle down. You say he killed one of the ladies?"

"She's in the back room! He done shot her dead!" She shouted, clawing at Luke to get at Cogburn. "Poor Betsy... meant nobody no harm."

Luke restrained the whore, as he turned to Cogburn. "That so, Cogburn?"

"Bitch had it comin'." He snarled through pain clenched teeth. "She snitched on me."

Meaney glared at him. "You got that wrong, Cogburn. Fella named Carlson told us about you."

The woman wasn't finished. "What are you going to do with him? He needs to hang, the sonofabitch."

"He's going to jail, ma'am."

The whore spat full in Cogburn's face.

Luke and Meaney were trying to figure this all out. They had suspected Cogburn of foul play but had simply come to question the man. The shooting rampage had been a surprise. They lifted Cogburn from the bed and began dragging him out. They got to the street and began thinking on having to carry him a half mile or so to the jail.

"Dang, Luke. This guy's a load."

By this time, Cogburn had nearly passed out from pain. "You go open a cell, Bill. I've got this." With that, Luke hoisted the prisoner over his shoulder and headed toward the jail. "Fetch the doctor along the way."

By sheer happenstance, Doc Andrews had journeyed from Nuecestown to visit and do some shopping. Meaney literally ran him over on his way to the jail. Momentarily dismayed at possibly hurting the old doctor, he reached down and helped him to his feet. "Doc! So sorry! But great to run into you."

"Can't quite say the same, Sheriff. What you in such an all-fire hurry about?"

"Luke's coming along with a wounded prisoner. We could use your help."

Doc sighed. He hadn't anticipated any professional duties in Corpus Christi. He dusted himself off. "Okay. Hang on. I've got to fetch my bag."

They settled Cogburn into a cell beside the one housing Carlson, and Doc soon went to work. "Woman's peashooter tore up his chest pretty good, Sheriff, but not so's it'd kill him. He's goin' to be sore for a while."

Luke sat in the chair beside Meaney's desk absentmindedly shuffling through wanted posters. He was about two-thirds of the way through the stack, when he paused. "Hey, Bill. You seen this?"

Meaney had been looking out the window, watching some of the ladies that had walked up the street from the whore house. There was also a passel of citizen onlookers less interested in the jailed man and mostly disapproving of the scantily-clad ladies.

"Looking like trouble brewing outside. What'd you find, Luke?"

"Lookee here. The man described on this poster matches Cogburn's description except for the black beard. Looks as though he stopped shaving. And this is strange...wouldn't hardly know it to look at him." Luke's finger traced down the text until it stopped at a sentence near the bottom.

Meaney walked over and glanced over Luke's shoulder at the poster. "I think you're right. Seems I missed seeing that poster." Meaney concentrated on the poster. "He's wanted dead or alive for murder in Kansas and Missouri. Nice reward, Luke."

"Bill, look at this," Luke insisted, jamming his finger into the bottom of the poster.

Meaney looked again. "Damn!"

"Cogburn is what they call an octoroon. He may have murdered in Kansas and Missouri, but he escaped slavery in Mississippi." Luke looked over at the man lying in the cell as Doc was finishing up digging the bullet out him. "You'd not know it to look at him." Luke reached over Doc, pulled up the back of Cogburn's shirt, and spotted scars on the man's back. "Looks like his overseer was none too pleased. Nasty scars."

By now, Dev Carlson had realized who his jail mate was. He broke the silence enveloping Luke's and Meaney's concerns. "Holy Mother of God, y'all found him!"

"Settle down, Carlson. Finding him isn't going to help you except as you put us on to him. Likely means you won't be getting hung."

They began to hear a chorus of chanting from the street. "Hang him! Hang him! String him up!" The ladies of the McDonald's rooming house were causing a ruckus.

Meaney looked at Luke.

Luke shrugged and smiled wryly. "You're the sheriff, Bill. They're your problem."

Meaney grabbed a rifle and strode resignedly out the front door.

Doc was finishing up bandaging Cogburn. "Sounds like a hornet nest of angry women out there, Luke."

"Yeah, but Sheriff Meaney can handle it."

Doc was nonplussed. "How are you, Elisa, and the children these days?"

"Is that what they call a rhetorical question, Doc? You know everyone is healthy."

Doc smiled. "Just checkin'."

Luke smiled knowingly. "How'd you know?"

"Goes with the profession."

"Guess the new addition will come early next year, Doc."

"I'm proud of you, Luke. Bein' a lawman while running a ranch and bein' a father and husband would be too heavy a load for most men. You're a credit to the Irish race."

"That's credit to the Texas race, Doc." Luke laughed. "I expect Mr. Cogburn here is going to be okay?" Luke had always appreciated Doc Andrews. It hadn't been so long ago that the doctor doubled duty as the town drunk of Nuecestown.

"He'll live, Luke." Doc began to gather his medicinal supplies. "I'm fixin' to leave and finish my errands, Luke, but we should likely not interrupt the sheriff."

Meaney was facing down a very unhappy clustering of the city's prostitutes. They'd been joined by a half dozen whores from the other whorehouse in Corpus and continued their chanting. He looked from them to the onlookers across the street and back to the whores. They were a sight to behold in their colorful professional silken and laced finery, though he dared not take them any less seriously for their clothing. He struggled to overlook the breasts ready to burst from tight bodices and their bare ankles. "Ladies, Mr. Cogburn is in city custody. I'm sworn to protect him no matter how vile a human being he is. So, you ladies please disperse. Go back to your business."

"He must hang, Sheriff!" One of the ladies stepped forward as spokeswoman. She was angry. She breathed heavily, and her ample breasts heaved such that it seemed as though they'd explode from her bodice. "He done us all wrong. He owes money an' he killed Betsy and wounded Sarah."

"Now, that's going to be counted toward his record, ladies. He'll surely hang, but he must have a fair trial. Justice will be served."

"Not soon enough, Sheriff. The judge left the county. Save us all the trouble and let us deliver the justice to that skunk at the end of a rope."

Meaney's mind was racing, as he sought a solution to this dilemma. It came to him of a sudden like a bolt from the blue. "Ladies, ladies. We've got a military officer here today. We're under a provisional government, so I expect he'd be qualified to render a verdict."

The ladies seemed to settle down at that news.

"Let me talk with the good Colonel Belknap. Perhaps we can hold a trial in the morning, if he's willing." He saw with relief that the ladies were somewhat mollified.

"We'll be back tomorrow morning, Sheriff. You'll be needing witnesses for the trial."

Meaney breathed a sigh of relief as he watched the women disperse. He tried to imagine what a courtroom might look like packed with a bevy of prostitutes and a passel of curious folk seated around the periphery judging both them and the accused. The onlookers across the street gave semi-disapproving looks before moving on. The sheriff slunk back inside the jail, threw his back against the closed door, and let out a sigh of relief.

"Nice work, Bill." Luke was chuckling. "Now, you've got to convince our friend Colonel Belknap to break free from his love tryst long enough to hold a trial. You think the ladies were tough, try getting a newlywed husband out of bed." Luke laughed some more.

Doc shook his head mirthfully and moved to the door. "See y'all later. I'll send you my bill, Sheriff. The man ought to be healthy enough for his hanging."

Belknap and Emma had been so caught up in each other that they hadn't even been aware of the commotions going on around them. The colonel had secured a suite in the hotel, and the two immersed themselves in the sorts of exploratory passions with which newlyweds engage. It didn't take long. They lay naked side by side on the bed, breathing heavily from their unbridled lovemaking. Emma had been able to divorce herself from the memories of her crazed father and become an eager student of sexual fervors. As they lay quietly in the after-glow with Belknap's gentle hand caressing the waves of auburn hair falling about her shoulders, she'd already mentally prepared herself for more sex.

Emma's face suddenly contorted. Pain caused her to double up. She reached between her legs. Blood! "Gordon! Help! I'm bleeding!"

Belknap dashed to the window and threw it open. He looked to the street below and hailed a passerby. "Hey, mister! Fetch a doctor quick!"

Doc Andrews had just passed near the hotel and heard the commotion and call for a doctor. He sighed at once again being called into service, turned toward the caller, and headed to the hotel as quickly as his aging knees would allow. He burst into the hotel lobby. He had a fair sense of where the call had come from as he hurried up the stairs. "Who needs a doctor?" he shouted as he huffed and puffed at the third-floor hallway.

A door swung open. "Doc! Doc Andrews! Thank God." He motioned toward the bed. "Over there! Emma's bleeding! My wife's bleeding!"

Doc was at the bedside in a flash and went to work to stem the apparent hemorrhaging. His practiced expertise was quick to find the cause, and he soon had the bleeding stopped. "I'm deeply sorry, sir. Your wife has lost her baby."

For Belknap, it was a moment of sadness at the death of a human mingled with a sort of relief that the issue of the child's fatherhood would need never be broached. "Is she going to be all right, Doc? Is she okay?" He implored Doc Andrews for more.

"She just needs rest. Lost a bit of blood." It was then that he realized he was talking with Belknap. "Sorry to meet on these terms, Colonel. Yes, she'll be all right."

"Can we still have children?"

"I expect so, Colonel, but you'll need to give your love a rest for a few days so she heals in heart and mind as well as body."

Emma looked up woozily from the bed. "What? What happened?"

Belknap looked at her then at Doc and back at Emma. "You…we…lost the child, Emma. I'm sorry."

She closed her eyes as though deeply relieved. Despite her physical discomfort, her exhaustion, she smiled at Belknap. "We'll have to try again."

Belknap sat on the edge of the bed and stroked her hair. She seemed so small and fragile among the bedcovers that had but an hour earlier born witness to their passions. "That we will, my sweet. That, we will. For now, get some sleep. Doc says you must rest to let your body recover. I'll be back in a little while." He kissed her ever-so-gently.

"Gordon?" She reached out weakly with her eyes.

Belknap turned to her. "Yes, Emma?"

"I love you."

He turned and smiled lovingly.

Doc, not knowing the origins of her pregnancy, was somewhat perplexed by the couple's reaction to the miscarriage but decided it was none of his business. In fifty years of being a frontier doc, he'd pretty much seen it all anyway.

"I'll escort you out, Doc." The colonel led the way.

Luke emerged from the jailhouse and saw Belknap up the street a piece seated on a bench. He turned back to Meaney. "If you like, I'll go up the street and ask the colonel if he's up to officiating at a criminal trial?"

"Sure. I'd appreciate that, Luke."

Luke strolled on up the street and was soon standing before the colonel. "Gordon, you don't look so good, my friend."

"Emma just lost the baby." It came out quietly but not with any particular sadness or regret. Luke was one of the few folks he could reveal it to. "She's resting."

"So sorry to hear that."

"I expect it's for the best. Likely means I'll be here for an extra couple of days instead of heading south to join up with General Sheridan."

Luke nodded, looked serious-like at Belknap, and stroked his mustache. "Well, you being here might work out well. We've got a bit of a dilemma that you could help us out with."

"How's that, Luke?"

"We've got a prisoner in the jail. He was wounded in a gun battle."

"I didn't hear any shooting."

Luke flashed a smile. "I expect you weren't exactly focused on anything beyond Emma." He paused. "But this is serious. The man's wanted for murder in Kansas and Missouri. He set another man named Carlson to kill me for a modest bounty. Meanwhile, he was holed up in that McDonalds whorehouse a few blocks away. He killed one of the ladies and wounded another who returned the favor. Now, the city's whores are demanding he be hung. Sheriff Meaney's telling them the murderer needs a fair trial. The judge is away in Victoria and been defrocked by the provisional government anyway. Upshot is, we need a judge and were of a mind that you'd be qualified as representative of the provisional government."

Belknap quietly absorbed Luke's words. "Never featured myself in the role of a judge, Luke. It does appear you're on the horns of a dilemma that could turn nasty." He sighed deeply. "I suppose I could do it. I assume there's a court clerk around that can help."

"Thanks. We'll have it set up in the morning, Gordon. And sorry again for Emma's loss." As Luke turned to go, he paused and turned back. "One more thing you should know given the composition of your troops."

"What's that?"

"The man's a former slave and an octoroon. You'd never know it to look at him, being only one-eighth Black and all. He apparently escaped a plantation in Mississippi and then turned to his murdering ways."

Belknap thought on the seeds of unrest that were germinating among some of his Black troopers. "What's got to be done, has got to be done. We'll just have to deal with it, Luke. I do appreciate your concern."

"We appreciate your help."

"Before you go and given that I'm going to be here for a few more days, would you do me a favor?"

"What might that be?"

"Ride out to the bivouac site and let the sergeant know about the situation. After the trial, I truly do need for you to look into those Apache attacks I was telling you about. Settlers are being murdered by those savages."

Luke didn't look forward to taking on Apache again, but would deal with it. "One Arrow might be up for some adventure, especially against the Apache. You recall, Comanche were not exactly their friends." Luke knew he was making a gross understatement, as the marauding savage Comanche had mercilessly driven the Apache from the Panhandle and deep into the Rio Grande valley.

"Sounds like you're up for it, Luke." Belknap chuckled a bit. Luke seemed to have the effect of lifting the colonel's spirits. "I'd better check on Emma. I'll see you in the morning for the trial."

Dev Carlson and Joseph Cogburn sat and stared at each other through the iron bars for what seemed like an eternity. The morning brought rain with it, making the outlook for the day about as dreary as could be conjured up. Coupled with the prospect of a trial that would send one man to prison and the other to the gallows, there was no cause for the slightest optimism.

Cogburn finally broke the silence. "You got a big mouth, you sonofabitch."

Carlson continued to stare. It began to turn into more of an angry glower.

"You couldn't even shoot that damned Texas Ranger. Look at him. How do you miss someone that big?"

Carlson remained silent.

"You got nothin' to say?"

Carlson finally looked up at Cogburn. "Here tell ya got nigra blood. You ain't worth a pot to piss in."

Despite his pain, Cogburn rose up and angrily shook the bars that separated them. "Damn right. An' I got the scars to prove Black blood runs red in my veins."

Their exchange was interrupted as Sheriff Meaney and Luke walked in. "Settle down. I could hear you plain as day from outside."

"When do I get out, Sheriff?" Cogburn thought he'd at least ask.

Meaney laughed. "You're headed to trial this morning, Mr. Cogburn. In fact, you both are. And you're lucky I didn't let those ladies string you up yesterday. Likely as not, they'd have cut your privates off afore they hung you."

"Trial? You have a judge in this damned godforsaken town?"

"The provisional government of Texas has afforded us the services of a high-ranking military officer to serve as judge."

Cogburn's rightly sensed how truly dire his situation had become. "Do I get a jury?"

Meaney sighed. "We could arrange that, Mr. Cogburn. I doubt that it'll go any better for you. The colonel is a cavalry officer who fought for the Union during the recent war. He's about as fair as they come."

Cogburn sat back resigned to his fate. "Okay. Hell with a jury then."

There was a knock at the door and voice from outside. "They're ready, Sheriff."

"That's our cue, gentlemen. The court is ready to go into session." Luke held a rifle aimed at Cogburn, as Meaney manacled him.

"Damn, that hurts." The manacle cuff chaffed at Cogburn's wounded hand.

"You don't stay quiet, you'll have a lot more to complain about." Meaney cuffed Carlson, and he and Luke escorted the two prisoners.

The rains had let up a little, but made for muddy going. They soon arrived at the packed courthouse. As they entered, Cogburn and Carlson became the targets of spitting and verbal insults as they strode up the makeshift aisle between rows of whores. Meaney finally had enough. He loudly declared, "Y'all settle down or I'm going to send y'all packing. We'll have order here!"

The audience of mostly women twittered on a bit but grudgingly settled down.

"Who is this?" Cogburn wondered who the man in the gray suit seated at the defense table was.

"He's your lawyer, Cogburn. Now, shut up." Meaney removed the manacles from the prisoner's wrists. For each prisoner, he put one end around an ankle and the other to iron loops screwed into the heavy oak table.

Luke was about to take a seat off to one side, when he noticed a half dozen new visitors. He'd not normally have taken particular notice except they wore blue cavalry tunics and were black-skinned. The men squeezed into a back row. Luke caught Meaney's eye and motioned to the rear of the courtroom. There was an intimidating feel in the air. Angry whores, judgmental citizens, and angry Black men made for an unsavory brew. Luke checked his rifle.

Meaney sat behind the prisoners. He leaned forward. "You men keep your eyes to the front. If you turn your heads an inch, I'll put a whipping on you both."

Cogburn felt he had nothing to lose, so chanced a quick glance behind him. He couldn't miss the men in the back row.

"You hear me? Eyes front!"

Belknap presided over a speedy trial. Evidence was overwhelming, and the lawyer for the defense never said a word. Two of the ladies testified, and even Dev Carlson testified as to Cogburn's threats against Luke.

All the while, Luke kept a steady eye on the back of the room.

Belknap excused himself to the judge's chambers, first motioning to Luke to join him.

Meaney slipped his gun from its holster as Luke headed to the judge's chambers.

Belknap took a seat and took a long look at Luke. "You've brought me an interesting situation, Luke. Those men in the back row have been prattling on and off about some sort of colored revenge ever since the troop left Austin. If justice prevails, we just might have a bit of an incident. A lot of innocent folks could be hurt." A knock at the door interrupted them. "Who is it?"

"Sergeant Brown, sir."

"Come in, Sergeant."

Brown entered with four men from the troop. Two were colored troops. "I saw that six potential troublemakers had left camp, sir. Thought they might be up to no good."

Luke and Meaney were relieved to have reinforcements on

hand, if needed. "Good thinking, Sergeant. Position you and our men at the rear of the courtroom behind that last row. If it becomes necessary, don't hesitate to use force to keep order."

The sergeant dutifully led his fully armed men into the courtroom to the curiosity of the audience and the angry glares of the men in the back row. Brown positioned his men as ordered. Meaney slipped his gun back into its holster. Tensions were beginning to lift.

The court was called to order and Belknap entered. He took his place behind the judge's docket and surveyed the courtroom before him. He noted a newspaper reporter scribbling madly in a notebook.

The clerk called the defendants to rise and face the bench. Cogburn strove to look as tall and defiant as possible despite the lingering pain from his chest and hand.

"Mr. Dev Carlson, you are hereby found guilty of attempted murder and conspiracy to commit murder. You are hereby sentenced to imprisonment for no less than ten years at the Texas prison in Huntsville."

Carlson slumped dejectedly but remained standing.

"In consideration of your cooperation with the state, Mr. Carlson, your sentence is hereby reduced to five years."

Carlson tried to appear grateful for the relative leniency and was surely relieved to not be hanging from the gallows.

Belknap looked directly at Cogburn. It was a penetrating look. "Mr. Joseph Cogburn, you are hereby found guilty of murder, manslaughter, and conspiracy to commit murder. The penalty for the crime of murder is death. Thus, you are hereby sentenced to be hung by the neck until dead."

He watched, as Cogburn didn't flinch.

The two rows of prostitutes indicated their approval of the judgment. Only then, did the audience become aware of the attendees in the back row.

Belknap delivered his final order for the trial. "Said execution shall be carried out day after tomorrow."

There was a stir in the back row, but the colored troops stayed seated. They weren't quite ready to give up their lives over the likes of Joseph Cogburn. They'd made their point and had to grudgingly admit that justice was being served.

Belknap exited the courtroom into the judge's chambers.

The prostitute who'd led the protest the day before winked at Luke and Meaney. She put her hand to the side of her ruby-red lips and whispered, "Anytime you boys want a freebee, just come knocking."

The two men simply shook their heads with dismay.

Manacles were placed on Carlson's and Cogburn's wrists, and they were escorted out a side door and back into the rain for a dreary trudge back to the jail.

Belknap sat in the chambers a bit longer, as he pondered the fate of the six colored troopers who'd sat menacingly in the back of the courtroom. Technically, they were away without leave and could be shot as deserters, but that would likely cause greater problems. He'd have to come up with a punishment that would be memorable without damaging the men's dignity. He sensed there'd be plenty enough challenging cultural adjustments ahead here in Texas without adding fuel to the fires.

"How'd it go in Corpus, Lucas?" Elisa seemed especially bright-eyed and cheery, as she placed breakfast on the table. It was as though she had personally willed the rains to stop and invited the warming rays of South Texas sun to bear down on a new day.

Luke was just about busting with news. He'd pulled in to Heaven's Gate wet and bedraggled just before sunrise, and was gulping coffee to warm his insides and keep himself awake. He hadn't even had time to more than nod at One Arrow, who was sleeping in the dry comfort of the barn. Luke looked across the table at Elisa and scanned the room filled with children. It was a good life. He proceeded to fill Elisa in on all the goings on. He soon settled back with a satisfied expression and quaffed a final cup of coffee. "Well, Lisa, I'd best be seeing to One Arrow and getting on with chores."

Elisa stood and took Luke's plate. "And?"

He wondered how she knew. "And what?"

"Your eyes give it away every time, Lucas. Where are you headed?"

Luke couldn't help but smile. She knew him all too well. "Gordon has asked me to check on some Apache trouble down around Bellville and San Ignacio. Reckon I'll get Jake Barber to join me. Maybe One Arrow will be up for some adventure."

"How many Apache?"

"Won't know until we get there. Colonel says they've been pretty much decimated by the Mexican dragoons and United States cavalry. The Apache are desperate and are attacking small ranches and homesteads...killing innocent folks on the frontier."

"Three of you are going to chase all the Apache out of Texas?"

"Well, darling, we don't expect to reason with them." Luke offered a pregnant pause.

Elisa gave him an apprehensive look.

"Actually, we'll be scouting for General Sheridan. It'll be up to him to take them on."

She sat back down. "What's to happen, Lucas? Rumors going around don't bode well for Texas. There's even talk of not rejoining the Union, but that hasn't a prayer. Texas is poor as a church mouse."

"You're likely right, Lisa. Texans still have their fight on, but it's not what it was before that infernal rebellion. We'll come back. There isn't another place on earth with as much strength of spirit."

"That Moncrieff fellow we brought down was probably

only the beginning of what's likely to descend on Texas, Lucas. I have a feeling it's going to get uglier before we start prettifying. A baby warthog is a right ugly thing. Doesn't get any less ugly when it grows up, but it sure gets meaner. I pray Texas doesn't go down that path, Lucas."

Luke chuckled at her metaphor. "You've got that right, sweetheart. Maybe, we can smile them into submission."

"Do what you must do, Lucas. Do come home safe. Peter, John, and Andrea need more from their father, and little Michael isn't far behind. A few months, and he'll be ready for a horse. Matthew is about ready to walk."

Elisa's concerns weren't lost on Luke. There'd surely be hard choices ahead. He looked absentmindedly out the window. "I see One Arrow walking up the path from the barn. I expect he's hungry. With all the troubles in Corpus, I'm afraid I haven't been much of a host to our friend." Luke picked up a plate full of eggs and ham that Elisa had prepared. He knew that One Arrow, like many of his race, wasn't inclined to be confined by four walls. Elisa had set up a table beside one of the benches on the gallery.

"Ghost-Who-Rides, it is fine morning." The chief was all smiles as he bounded up the steps to the gallery.

"Welcome, One Arrow. Indeed, it is a fine morning."

One Arrow dug into the breakfast Luke laid before him. "This good. Lots better than eating deer." He laughed at his little joke. His English language skills were still awkward, but he was trying.

"With all the business with the shooting, I don't recall you telling me why you decided to visit. You traveled a long way from your people."

The chief replied earnestly in even tones. "One Arrow talk with Great Spirit. Found power of cross Three Toes wore. Great Spirit sent sign. Told chief to learn more of White man's ways. Ghost-Who-Rides is only White man One Arrow trust." He smiled. That was the first time he'd heard One Arrow string so many sentences together. The Comanche or most tribes for that matter were not renowned for being especially talkative.

As Luke was about to reply, several wondering pairs of eyes emerged from the open front door. Peter, John, and Andrea Anne recalled Three Toes, but for little Michael and Alma a Comanche chief eating breakfast on the gallery of their house was a huge curiosity. A human being that wasn't white or brown or black conjured an eager interest, especially one decked out in buckskin vest and leggings, beadwork, and moccasins.

One Arrow looked over at the children and grinned broadly. "Ghost-Who-Rides have many children. This good." He looked off with a bit of melancholy to the prairie. "One Arrow have two sons."

Elisa brought two cups of coffee and joined Luke and the chief. She turned to Luke. "Have you shared your plan with our friend?"

"Just getting through the morning formalities, sweetheart. One Arrow has…"

"Two sons. I heard as I came out. I'm sure he misses them."

One Arrow watched the dynamic between Luke and Elisa. He could tell they respected each other, but he sensed more. "You what whites call married?"

Elisa blurted, "Do Comanche marry?"

"Comanche have what you call wives."

"More than one?"

"One Arrow have three…and twenty horses." He held up three fingers, then threw up his hands to illustrate the horses.

Elisa overlooked the inadvertent equating of wives and horses as symbols of wealth. She looked at Luke and said, "We marry one man, one woman." She thought about fetching their copy of the Bible, but rightly figured the words in the book of first Timothy would be lost on One Arrow.

One Arrow shook his head with curiosity. "Why only one?"

Luke figured he'd better step in. "That necklace that you wear, the one Lisa gave to Three Toes? The cross is a symbol, a sign of God. We have a book with words that remind us of how to live. It shares words of God's love and strength. It is like a map. It says that when one man and one woman marry, they must love and respect each other." Luke was striving to offer One Arrow a streamlined version of a much greater and more complex story.

"What is love?"

Luke looked at Elisa. "It is willingness to pledge your life to another person, even to die for them. It is respect, it is honor. It is a feeling of oneness that never dies." He smiled. "Did you love Three Toes?"

One Arrow's eyes widened. "Three Toes was man."

Luke decided he wouldn't touch that again. "Do you love your wives?"

"Cactus Flower. One Arrow love Cactus Flower. Bird Woman like a mother. Blue Feather young. Good in blankets." If a Comanche could blush, One Arrow did so as he realized what he'd just said. He gave Elisa an apologetic glance. "One Arrow begin to understand White man's God." He looked over at Luke and changed the subject. "Did I hear of plan?"

Luke was also grateful for the shift in conversation. "Some old enemies of the Comanche to the south are making trouble. I have been asked to help stop this trouble."

"You talk of Apache?" One Arrow's expression turned to eagerness. He tried to concentrate on what Luke was telling him, though Michael and Alma were now tugging for his attention.

"I do talk of Apache. A chief named Costalites is leading about two dozen warriors." Luke flashed his fingers a couple of times to illustrate the numbers. "Costalites had a treaty with Mexican rebels, but I hear that Mexican soldiers murdered his women and children. He has been killing Mexican and White women and children as revenge. Now, the bluecoat General

Sheridan is hunting for him. I have been asked by our friend Colonel Belknap to help the general."

"You want Apache scalps?" The chief made a cutting motion across his forehead while making a scary face at Michael and Alma. The children ran off unsure of his seriousness.

Luke laughed and shook his head. "There will only be three of us: you, me, and our friend Jake Barber. We're to scout them and report to the general."

"Three of us, many of them. Plenty coups. We kill plenty."

Luke wasn't going to argue.

"When we go?"

"Two days. I must go and get Jake."

"One Arrow play with children. Teach some of Comanche ways."

Luke caught Elisa's apprehensive look. "I think there are Comanche ways that White people should know. I trust you One Arrow." Luke tried to look reassuringly at Elisa.

The chief arose and bowed slightly to Elisa. "One Arrow grateful for food. Wife of Ghost-Who-Rides make great cornbread. One Arrow go care for ponies and then teach older children to shoot bow and arrow and carve wood."

Elisa felt sort of relieved, though she had visions of knife cuts and chickens stuck with arrows.

Nuecestown had survived the war pretty much intact. It was an easy fifteen-minute ride for Luke, and Big Horse was familiar with the route. It gave Luke plenty of time to think on what lay ahead. He didn't relish taking on Apache, but neither was he one to shirk from responsibility. He thought on One Arrow and whether there was really any potential for peace between the Red man and White man. Seemed pretty much everywhere he looked there was cultural and racial tension.

Mexicans, Anglos, Indians, blacks, rich, poor...there needed to be some sort of accommodation of differences. Some folks tried to call it a melting pot, but Luke saw it as more of a witch's brew retaining the very distinct and quite separate flavors of its various parts. He recalled a book on his father's bookshelf back in Ireland. It was called *Utopia* and written by some British statesman named Thomas More. It was about a perfect world, but it too didn't work out. Seemed that one person's perfect world was different from another's perfect world. As Luke had it worked out in his mind, it would take strong over-arching government to keep any kind of peace. Perhaps too strong. Nevertheless, with strong laws, strong faith, and a strong defense, such a government could be small but strong. Texas had survived, and the United States was trying to. So long as people had an equal voice and followed some solid moral code, he felt it ought to endure. It was when folks departed from that moral code and sought to fill unrealistic personal expectations like power and control that it all fell apart. He'd heard some cowboy say riches were the root of all evil, but the way he saw it, it was the love of riches that wreaked of evil. About this time, he arrived in front of Barber's cabin in Nuecestown.

"Jake! Jake, you awake?"

The big man staggered from the dark confines of the cabin, blinking his eyes in the bright mid-morning sunlight. "Luke? Why the ruckus?"

"What you up to, Jake? You ready for some adventure?"

Barber settled down a tad from being so unceremoniously called out. He shrugged and cinched the belt barely holding up his trousers a notch. "What ya got in mind, Luke?"

"Apache are stirring down near Bellville and San Ignacio. General Sheridan needs some scouting help. We've been asked to oblige."

"Just be the two of us? I think JD had her baby and might be ready." Barber chuckled at his own humor. The diminutive

JD had disguised herself as a boy and accompanied he and Luke on an earlier adventure. Now, she was married to Jubal Strong and had become a mother.

Luke caught the joke. "Three of us. Got someone better even than JD, Jake."

"Now, who that be?"

"Friend by the name of One Arrow. He's a Comanche chief —adopted son of Three Toes. You remember him?"

"Whew, you sure know how to pick-em, Luke."

Luke grinned. "Picked you, didn't I?"

"Shoot, I got nothin' better to do. Count me in."

"Come on by Heaven's Gate first thing day after tomorrow."

"There's one more thing, Luke. I got me a woman now. She's a pistol. Cheyenne squaw mind you."

Luke winked. "Well, we'll try to bring you back in one piece to her."

Luke turned Big Horse to begin to ride back to Heaven's Gate. He'd barely ridden a hundred feet, when he passed Bernice outside the boarding house. "Miss Bernice. How y'all doing this fine morning?"

She lit up with a broad smile. "I'm fine, but I hear tell your lovely wife is expecting again."

Luke's jaw dropped, then he grinned. How did Bernice come to know these things? "Well, you're right, Bernice. We try to do our best to keep growing the population around these parts."

"You've got a lovely family, Luke Dunn. You be sure to keep it that way." She knew there'd never be any doubt as to that.

"How's Agatha these days?"

"She's getting better, Luke. Like your Elisa, she had a bout with the yellow fever, but managed to fight it off. They're both strong women. Of course, Elisa is downright beautiful, too. To look at her, one would find it hard to believe she's birthed six children."

"Beautiful and strong indeed, Bernice. Give my best to Agatha."

Luke tipped his hat and headed out toward Heaven's Gate.

About halfway up the road to home, three horsemen loitered along the side of the road. Behind them, a body swayed in the breeze from a rope tied from neck to tree limb.

Luke reflexively slid his new Henry rifle from its scabbard and held it across his lap. He slowed Big Horse to an easy walk. Three men and a lynching weren't something to be trifled with. As he drew closer, he figured them to be strangers, as he didn't recognize any of them. They were well-armed.

He was soon within hailing range. "Howdy, gentlemen. What are y'all up to this fine morning?" It was obvious what they'd been up to, but Luke didn't want to seem overly threatening.

No surprise that one of the three recognized the now famous former Texas Ranger. The big man on the big horse was one to be feared by any lawbreaker. "Damn!" The man pivoted his horse and took off at a gallop toward Corpus Christi. The other two hesitated.

Luke raised his rifle. "How quick do y'all think I can get off two shots? Y'all want to test me?"

Hands raised.

"Get yourselves down from your horses and drop your guns in the dirt."

The men did as they were told. Neither knew of Luke's reputation, but the quick retreat of their henchman gave them a hint.

Luke rode up. "Back away from the guns." He glanced at the man swinging from the tree. The victim was Mexican, and

Luke thought he might still be breathing. He pointed to one of the men. "You! Cut him down." The man hesitated. Luke fired a shot into the dirt at his feet. "Now!"

The man paused in abject fear and peed in his pants. He grabbed a knife and ran to cut the victim down.

Luke looked to the second man. "What'd you hang this man for?"

"He weren't no man. He be Tejano."

Those were not the best words to be using with Luke Dunn. "You didn't answer my question. Why'd you hang him?"

"'Cause he be Mexican."

Luke shook his head in disgust. "If that man dies, I guarantee you'll be on the end of a gallows rope, if you're lucky enough that my trigger finger doesn't get a sudden itch."

The first man had dropped the victim and was untying him. He desperately shook the Mexican to try to get him to breathe. At last, there was a cough.

"Who are you?" It was the lyncher's back-handed way of asking why their partner had run off.

"Y'all are lucky today. I happen to know this man y'all were hanging. He may be old, but Pedro here fought with Houston at San Jacinto. My name is Luke Dunn. I'm a lawman. Used to be a Texas Ranger." Luke let that sink in. "Now, your friend that ran off was smart, but he didn't know I can be merciful. Since my friend here appears to be recovering, I'm going to let you men go free, though a part of me would have you strung up in his place. Being of a different race is no cause for killing another human being. Thought we'd seen enough of that when the war ended. Count this as a life lesson, gentlemen."

Expressions of uncertain relief spread across the faces of the two men.

"Where's Pedro's horse?" Luke had dismounted.

The men were suddenly especially respectful, especially so

when they realized just how big Luke was. He towered over the men. "He had no horse, Mr. Dunn sir. Just an old mule. We run it off."

"Well, seems you're going to pay a small price after all. My friend Pedro here is going to be trading his mule for one of your horses. Sound about right to you?"

"We'll only have one horse."

"Figure y'all can find that mule. Consider yourselves lucky. Pedro loved that mule dearly. Now, take your gun belts off and drop them real careful like." Luke waited until the men's gun belts were lying in the Nueces Strip dust. He proceeded to unload the men's guns.

"Thank you kindly. Now, you two be on your way." Luke watched them as they slunk off leading their one horse and searching for the mule.

"¿Pedro, estás bien?" Luke dismounted and helped the older man mount the horse.

Pedro tried to smile, but he'd been beaten as well as strung up. His neck bore abrasions from the rope. "Muchas gracias, Señor Dunn. Muchas gracias."

"De nada, amigo." Luke gave the horse enough of a pat on the flank to start it on its way. "Via con Dios." He picked up the men's gun belts, pocketed the ammunition, and left the guns and gun belts at the base of the hanging tree before he mounted Big Horse and continued on to Heaven's Gate.

TWENTY-ONE
ROBBERY

SEEMED LIKE AN ORDINARY SUNDAY. Luke figured to get started on chasing down those pesky Apache the next day. For better or worse and by way of trying to educate One Arrow about this powerful God the White man worshipped, they had gathered the family in the buckboard and headed off to Luke's cousin John's ranch. John generally held a prayer meeting on Sunday mornings with or without a priest. If one of the saddleback priests had been available, John would have invited neighbors for a full-fledged mass. He was strong in his own faith, and except for him not knowing enough Latin to shake a stick at, folks recognized him as up to the task of delivering a Sunday message.

The families of the cousins in the region who were able to tear away from ranching and farming duties stuck around afterward for food and to catch up on the latest family happenings. One Arrow quickly became the center of attention. The Dunn family was well-acquainted with Luke's and Elisa's encounters with Comanche as well as cousin Nicholas's having built a reputation as an Indian fighter and Luke's past friendship with the Penateka Comanche chief Three Toes.

Nevertheless, having a very real full-blooded savage in their midst was worthy of considerable accommodation and would be fodder for many a family discussion about the "Indian problem" for months to come.

For his part, One Arrow had donned full regalia save for the war paint. At Luke's suggestion, he left his war lance with its collection of scalps back at Heaven's Gate.

The Dunn entire family did go out of its way in striving to be hospitable to the chief. It was a hot sunny day and featured just enough breeze to cause John to hold the mass outside. That was much to One Arrow's liking given his aversion to being cooped up in four walls. He sat quietly and displayed admirable patience as he listened. He now understood just enough English to catch the gist of John's message. Luke appreciated that the initial titillation accompanying One Arrow's arrival had died down.

As the service ended, the chief watched the attendees as they crossed themselves in the Catholic tradition. He nudged Luke. "Ghost-Who-Rides, what strange sign?"

"It is our recognition of God's will over us. He is an all-powerful God who is three-in-one."

"Three?" One Arrow raised three fingers. "Comanche have many gods." He looked off in thought for a second. "No gods for dogs or women."

"We have what God calls the trinity...Father, Son, and Holy Spirit, my friend. God is the father who sent his Son in the flesh to save mankind by his death and coming back to life and deliver us as a powerful Holy Spirit." Luke wrestled with how to explain the power of the trilogy. "His power in saving folks' souls, Chief, is sort of like triple-struck lightning."

The chief's eyes widened at his grasping the virtual impossibility of triple-struck lightning. His eyes locked on Luke's.

Luke said nary a word.

One Arrow finally nodded just a tad, shaking his head

thoughtfully at Luke's revelation of this tri-partite deity and the idea of anyone conquering death. "Come back to life? Like ghost?"

"We call it resurrection." Luke was unsure how much of this the chief was grasping. "It was a symbol of suffering for man's sins and being reborn to a sin-free life." Luke was trying hard to simplify what even he struggled to fully comprehend.

"You have no other gods?"

"Don't need any others. God is all-powerful. And he tells us to worship no other gods."

One Arrow chewed on that a moment. "We have many gods. One god...simple."

Luke couldn't hold back a smile. "God would like to hope it was simple, my friend." He pretty much rightly figured that One Arrow had taken in about as much as his Comanche brain with all its cultural history was going to absorb for the present. He nodded over to the veritable cornucopia of victuals laid out for family and guests. "Let's get some food. I think there are some of my family that would like to meet you."

As if on cue, Luke's cousins Matthew and Nicholas appeared alongside. Nicholas had shot a few Comanche and Kiowa on trail drives and fended off a couple of attacks on his ranch, but had never been so close to one of the savages on a peaceful footing. He felt a bit of a tingle in his scalp. Nevertheless, he extended his hand, "So, you're the Comanche chief Luke's been telling us about. My name is Nicholas Dunn."

One Arrow took Nicholas's hand. "Pleased to meet cousin of Ghost-Who-Rides. You too have hair like fire." It was his way of observing friendly-like that both Luke and his cousin had red hair.

Nicholas resisted the urge to wipe his now sweaty hand on his breeches. He actually relaxed a bit. "I like your necklace." He'd noted the cross, and it was as close to a compliment as he was likely to offer.

Matthew went through the same routine before asking a

pressing question. "Are your people to the north?" He wasn't sure how to phrase the question so as to not sound as though he was rubbing it in that the Comanche had been defeated and sent to a reservation. "Are they happy?"

One Arrow forced an uncomfortable smile. "Penateka Comanche live to north of what you call Red River. We are at peace." He hadn't said they were happy.

Luke noted the chief's discomfort and extricated him from his cousin's questioning before it got beyond uncomfortable. He guided him to where food was laid out for all to partake. One Arrow filled a plate and sat with Elisa and the children.

John, Nicholas, and Matthew sidled up to Luke out of earshot of One Arrow. "Pretty cheeky bringing a Comanche chief to Sunday mass, cousin."

Luke smiled and stroked his mustache thoughtfully. "Not sure how we should come to peace with these folks, dear cousins. The chief earnestly wants to understand the White man. His adopted father had given him the necklace with the cross, and he's trying to understand the God that the Anglos and Mexicans worship. I just figure I'm doing my part to bring a lasting peace."

"Dang, if you're not optimistic, Luke," ventured Nicholas.

"Shucks, I'm about to head out to track down some Apache raiders, and One Arrow volunteered to help. I trust him as a brother."

John turned to the others. "A brother? Humph. Well, guess that's good enough for me." He smiled and walked off to grab more food.

Nicholas and Matthew shrugged. "Hope it works out, Luke. Red hair sure would pretty-up a savage's war lance." They chuckled and strode off unaware that the chief had heard the comment.

Luke could do naught but smile wryly and rejoin Elisa, the children, and his guest.

One Arrow smiled and whispered an aside to Luke. "Your

cousin with fire hair funny. One Arrow want no fire hair on lance." He laughed nervously at the realization that Elisa had inadvertently overheard him.

"I'm of a mind to trim a lock of cousin Nick's hair and gift it to One Arrow," she jokingly added.

Luke glanced about and licked his lips. "Doggone, but this chicken is downright delicious." He'd had enough of scalp talk even funning around.

★ ★

As the buckboard pulled up near the house, Luke couldn't help but notice that the front door was hanging from a single hinge. Someone or something had violated the place while they were away. He heard a muffled sound coming from Jaime's cabin and leaped from the wagon to investigate. "Stay here, Lisa. Come on One Arrow."

The door to the cabin was unlocked, and Jaime and Julia were on the floor with their hands tied and mouths gagged. Luke rushed over and undid the ropes and tore away the gags. "What the...what happened?"

Jaime coughed and clutched Julia close to calm her. "Dark soldiers, *Señor* Dunn. The Black ones. Four of them."

Luke saw that they were unharmed save for having been tied up. He quickly freed Jaime. "You take care of Julia. I'm going up to the house and see what they've done." Luke sensed they'd been robbed, so the question would be how much of what had been taken.

"*Señor* Dunn, I heard them leave not long before you arrived."

Luke walked back to the buckboard. "Let me check out the house before you and the children go in, Lisa. I must be sure it's safe, and I don't want to disturb any evidence."

Elisa pouted a bit at having to wait but resigned herself to it.

One Arrow was under no constraint and leaped down to join Luke. He quickly examined the horse tracks. "Tracks fresh, Ghost-Who-Rides." That served to confirm to Luke what Jaime had said about them leaving not long ago. It also meant that they might have a good chance of catching them.

Luke made a quick survey of the house. He emerged on the gallery and called out to Elisa, "It's safe to go in. Looks as though they got away with a bit of food, a couple of rifles, and some of my clothes. We only just missed them. One Arrow, Jaime, and I are going after them."

"Shouldn't you alert Colonel Belknap?"

"Don't have time. If we leave now, we'll catch them right quick."

"Tracks fresh. They ride slow. One horse lame." One Arrow rode out front and was proud to be employing his tracking skills. In addition to leaving an all-too-obvious trail, the four deserters had made the mistake of escaping across Heaven's Gate. Luke and Jaime were intimately familiar with the ranch's every nook and cranny.

"Drunk, too." Luke noted a freshly emptied whiskey bottle tossed at the side of their route.

One Arrow's pony's ears suddenly perked up, and he pulled the mount to a halt. He scanned the scrub and live oak mottes before them and waved Luke and Jaime to join him. He pointed to a spot barely visible perhaps two hundred yards away.

Luke saw a dry creek bed to their left. "We know where that'll take us, Jaime," he whispered.

The three-man posse checked the loads in their guns and ventured along the route Luke had pointed out. They soon could hear the troopers carrying on in their drunkenness, celebrating their good fortune. The posse managed to pull up undetected behind a live oak about spitting distance from the colored troops. Luke motioned One Arrow and Jaime to fan out to the left and right respectively, then nudged Big Horse into the clearing where the colored troops lolled about.

Luke didn't say a word, as the Black men came to realize in near unison that they were facing the muzzles of some big-bore rifles. It had an instant sobering effect. Luke recognized two of the men from the group that had attended the Cogburn trial back in Corpus Christi. He finally broke the silence. "You men are under arrest. Raise your hands high."

"Whoa, brudder...we just be havin' fun," spoke up the ringleader of the four. He was a big, strapping hulk of a man with rippling biceps that tested the seams of his shirt.

Luke made a quick scan of the area. "Your fun include stealing from folks?" He nodded toward the Dunn belongings they'd stolen from Heaven's Gate. He saw some goods likely stolen from other victims of the four deserters. "I'm thinking Colonel Belknap's going to be none too pleased with you men." He addressed the trooper who'd spoken up. "What's your name?"

"Coop. My name's Coop."

The others broke into barely disguised chuckles at the name.

"I'm thinking that's not likely your real name, Coop, but it'll do for now. Where are your uniforms?" Luke knew from tracking them that a couple of blue tunics had been discarded along their route. "Do you remember me?"

"You be at the trial of our nigra brother."

"True. Cogburn was a murderer and thief. Guess you know what happened to him. Had nothing to do with his skin. He broke the law and paid the price."

Coop glared at Luke with a certain maliciousness bred of misguided thinking. "Slavery be breakin' the law."

Luke sighed. "True, Coop. Breaks God's law and man's law. But you're not slaves today, are you?" He ruefully shook his head. "To the matter at hand, you broke the law and must pay the price. Colonel Belknap will be deciding y'all's fate."

"You takin' us to the colonel?"

Luke nodded. "Jaime, there are a couple sets of manacles in my saddlebag. The other two will need tying up."

With that, Coop made a break for the tall grass only to find himself blocked by One Arrow. An armed Comanche on horseback was a fearsome sight, and Coop's eyes grew wide as he found his path blocked and the commanding figure of a savage inches away.

"Seems you've met One Arrow, Coop. He's a Penateka Comanche chief. See those scalps on his lance?" Luke smiled and stroked his mustache. "You looking to be scalped?"

Coop cowered, as he resigned himself to his fate and rejoined his fellow deserters.

"Y'all have a lame horse there, so one of y'all's going to have to walk." Luke knew it would slow their travel to Corpus, but he didn't feature the mischief that could occur with any of the deserters mounted double. Besides, the lamed horse was still in good enough shape to carry the goods that had been stolen. "Times a wasting, so let's get started."

As the caravan of posse and prisoners neared Corpus, Luke sighted the bivouac of Belknap's troops. The sun was creeping close to the horizon and an orange glow was already being cast across the landscape. "One Arrow, Jaime, let's head over yonder. We can deposit our prisoners with the colonel's unit. I'll go on to tell the colonel the news while y'all head back to Heaven's Gate."

Coop's and the other deserter's eyes grew wide with fear at the very near-term prospect of facing Sergeant Brown.

They rode right on past the sentry, who wisely decided against challenging them. He merely offered a grim expression and cursory salute. He likely figured that the deserters would give the unit a bad name.

The sergeant and a lieutenant had seen the caravan of riders approaching, so were standing out front of the bivouac to greet them.

Luke led the way, pulling Big Horse up and dismounting. "Lieutenant...Sergeant Brown, I'm pleased to bring these deserters to you. They have stolen goods from at least two nearby ranches, including mine."

The lieutenant stepped forward. "I'm Lieutenant Starke. Sergeant Brown here will take your prisoners, Mr....um, I don't recall your name, sir."

"Dunn...Luke Dunn, Lieutenant Starke."

There was a sudden moment of recognition as though a light had been turned on in the lieutenant's head. "Ah, yes. I've heard the colonel mention you, sir." There was full respect in his voice.

"I didn't want to burden Colonel Belknap directly with this matter, lieutenant. I figure y'all will know how to handle it. I'm going to head into Corpus and do the courtesy of letting him know."

"Thank you, Mr. Dunn, for saving us the trouble of hunting these men down. We'd only a short time ago realized they were missing." He shook Luke's hand. "Sergeant, place these men under arrest."

Sergeant Brown nodded respectfully at Luke as he and an armed guard took the deserters into custody. Coop and his fellow deserters even gave Luke a reasonably respectful though hang-doggy look as they were led away.

Luke bade One Arrow and Jaime farewell, as he headed Big Horse toward Corpus Christi. He wondered how many other similar and even worse incidents like this one would face Texans over the next few years, especially until Texas was accepted back into the Union. So far as he was thinking, it would suit him just fine if Texas became an independent republic again. He rather regretted that such an outcome would be highly unlikely, especially given the economic distress and the sentiments of many of the citizens. While the economic challenges might be readily overcome, he recognized the rawness of the aftermath of the War of Northern Aggression as likely lasting many years.

TWENTY-TWO
TROUBLE COMES

EDWARD THORPE STRODE into what had been his father's office in Austin.

Samuel arose from the desk to greet him. "Welcome, Mr. Thorpe. Good to have you back, sir."

"Good to be back, Samuel. I much prefer post-war America to Europe. Being home in Texas makes it all the better."

"Did you visit Magnolia?"

"Well, you must know that I did. The old house already looks like new, and all the old families seem to be settling into their new ways of living." In his mind's eye, Thorpe envisioned the former slaves thriving as farmers and merchants. "Frederick seems to be managing it well."

"I check on him from time to time, Mr. Thorpe."

"You telegraphed me that all went well in Corpus Christi?"

"Yes sir, Mr. Thorpe. They say that Scottish fella got his just desserts, his partners, too." Samuel smiled that the plan to trap Moncrieff had succeeded. "Colonel Belknap and Mr. Dunn carried the day well, but it was Mrs. Dunn who truly shined. She put the finishing touch to Mr. Moncrieff."

Thorpe smiled. "Mr. Dunn found himself a treasure with her, Samuel."

"Six children worth." Samuel smiled. "And I hear there's going to be another."

It got Thorpe to thinking of a part of his own life that was missing, but he shook off the thought. "How's your family?" It was almost a perfunctory question designed to shift the subject of his own family or lack thereof from his thoughts.

"Missus is fine, Mr. Thorpe. My two boys be off in Montana trying to make a life in the cattle business. Lotsa danger up there, though. Injuns making trouble from what they tell me."

"Good to hear that they're working hard and keeping their scalps. It's great that your sons stay in touch." His genuine expression betrayed his inner sadness at not yet having a family of his own. "You know, Samuel, I think I'll go visit Corpus Christi. I think my business can go on without me for a couple of weeks."

"I'll see to the arrangements, Mr. Thorpe."

Luke was once again leading a motley sort of force aimed at delivering law and order. They looked to be two White men and an Indian finding their way westward across the prairie. They were well-armed and well-outfitted—ready come what may. Justice after all seemed to exhibit an especially capricious nature as concerned the Nueces Strip. Its vast uninhabited expanses lent themselves to an equally vast array of lawbreaking and the sort of mayhem wrought by competing cultural forces. Opportunity basically cut two ways: good and bad. Simple enough. The relative chaos of post-war Texas was a fact, and lawlessness pretty much thrived in the early efforts toward reconstructing the Union.

"How do you like that Henry rifle, One Arrow?" Luke admired the Comanche's rifle but was mostly just making occasional small talk as they whiled away the hours heading in the general direction of Bellville.

One Arrow wasn't much of a conversationalist, especially given that he was still working on understanding the White man's strange tongue. Even the Comanche tongue was best described as lean and efficient. "Is good, Ghost-Who-Rides. Shoot far." He slowed his pony and fell back a bit as if to end the talk.

Luke slowed and kept pace. "Comanche don't like Apache do they?"

The chief resigned himself to having to talk. Then again, he realized it might help him understand the White man better. "Go back many many moons. Apache always outsiders. Bad."

"Your people were not kind. Doesn't Comanche translate in the Ute tongue as enemy?"

"That's what you say, Ghost-Who-Rides. Is Ute word. Ute sometime friend, sometime enemy of my people." One Arrow looked over at Luke. "Question, Ghost-Who-Rides." He stared hard at Luke, as though preparing to find the answer to some profound truth. "Why do bluecoats never keep promises to Comanche?"

That caught Luke a little off guard, not the least of which because he'd thought about that very question himself. "Why did Comanche and Ute fight?"

It took a moment for One Arrow to figure what Luke was getting at. After all, what did Utes and the bluecoats have in common? "Ute break promises."

"Why do they break their promises?"

"Some Ute seek war. Seek power over Comanche."

"That's why the bluecoats break promises. Some Whites seek power to control Comanche lands. They push bluecoats to break promises."

"Humph!" One Arrow grudgingly understood. "Ugly people. What your god do?"

"Folks can be ugly. They can be like rattlesnakes, just fine so long as you don't stir them up. As to God, I think He expects us to work out some things for ourselves based on the teachings he gave us through his son and those Ten Commandments he gave to that Moses fellow."

"Commandments?"

"Yeah...stuff like not murdering or stealing or having another man's wife."

One Arrow chewed on Luke's response. "All people no believe."

"There are bad apples on every tree, my friend. We can forgive their sins, but they must be punished. That's why I have work to do."

"Like Black soldiers who steal?"

"Yes. Those deserters weren't all bad, but they didn't follow God's or man's laws."

"What punishment?" One Arrow was thinking about what Comanche would do to those who broke their code.

Luke gulped hard at the question. There was no avoiding the truth. "Colonel Belknap likely had them shot by a firing squad."

They fell to an agreeable silence.

Barber had been taking in the conversation. "Shucks, we wouldn't have any work, if everybody was at peace."

The sarcastic obviousness of Barber's comment broke the ice. The travelers relaxed. They might not change the world, but they'd give it a try by bringing justice to the Nueces Strip.

★★

Costalites's Apache had at least temporarily satisfied their blood lust. The chief found himself quite taken with the young girl they'd kidnapped in their recent raid. She refused to cry no matter how badly the squaws in the camp treated her. Her feistiness had turned to stoicism, the outward appearance of resignation to her fate. She'd tried to escape once already and suffered a serious whipping for it.

The chief knew a bit of Spanish but almost no English.

"*¿Cómo te llamas, muchacha?*" A name would be helpful toward breaking her down. Beating obviously wasn't going to work. He was fascinated with her long blond hair, as she stood nearly naked before him. She was a skinny waif, as exacerbated by not having eaten much of anything in the several days since the raid. She was just old enough to have just a hint of a swell to her breasts. He drew close and gently stroked her hair.

She punched him in the nose.

Costalites sent her tumbling with a slap to the side of her head.

She got up dry-eyed and delivered a fiery, hate-filled look at the chief.

A nearby Apache warrior nearly laughed but contained it before the chief noticed.

"*¿Cómo te llamas, muchacha?*" Costalites again demanded her name.

The girl finally snarled, "bitch!"

"*Ah, te llamas, Bitch. Muy bien.*" The chief had no idea she was playing upon his ignorance of English.

Now, she smiled guardedly at having put one over on him.

Costalites judged that getting a name from her was enough for now. He'd have her tied up for the night, so she wouldn't escape. He told two squaws to tie up Bitch. He figured with the squaws' help he'd break her will over time.

"From my reckoning, it looks like Bellville ahead, Luke."

The trio pulled up to what they gathered was the edge of town.

Luke turned to One Arrow. "Might be best, if you didn't ride into town. They are likely afraid of my red brother." Had Luke been aware of the festering hate over the recent Apache attack, he'd have sent One Arrow far away. The settlers didn't distinguish among tribes. A Comanche so far as they were concerned was no different than an Apache or Navajo or Kiowa. As it was, the trio set up a small camp hidden near an arroyo among some sage and mesquite. Luke decided to enter the town alone. He'd had the foresight to grab his old Texas Ranger badge before leaving Heaven's Gate. He pinned it to his shirt.

"You impersonatin' a lawman, Luke?" Barber had a bit of fun.

"Have to get some respect somehow. Just so these folks don't recall me riding with Callahan back in '56."

"Yer hard to forget, Luke." Barber laughed again. "See ya in a little while."

Luke checked the loads in his Colts and the new Henry and headed into Bellville. As he rode in, he was especially struck by how quiet it was. No children running in the main street. Hardly any sign of life. He pulled up at the local watering hole, dismounted, and hitched Big Horse. He looked left and right and headed inside the cantina. It was small and gave off a stale stench of fresh woodchips, sweat, piss, and liquor. He strode over to the bar.

"Can a man get a drink here?"

The barkeep slowly eased over to Luke. "Who you be and what's yer bizness in Bellville?" he snarled. Obviously, he wasn't the welcoming committee.

"I'm Luke Dunn, Captain Luke Dunn, formerly of the Texas Rangers. What's going on in your town?"

The barkeep squinted at Luke and noticed the badge. "You ride with Callahan?"

Luke didn't like the tone. "Not as I recall." He'd ask God to forgive his lie later.

"Apache hit the Snider's place a few days back. Killed all but Miz Snider and took her daughter. They cut the poor woman up pretty bad."

Luke sighed. He'd hoped the unrest on the border

wouldn't have been this bad. "I'm scouting Apache for General Sheridan."

"Lotta good that's done."

"I understand how you're feeling, barkeep. Sorry, I got here late." He looked around the room. There were half a dozen men hanging on Luke's words. "Can I talk with the woman?"

"She ain't said much of nothin' since she be found. Sam over there can take you to the Wilson place up the street. That's where she be, Ranger."

"Much obliged." Luke slipped a coin onto the bar. "We'll find her daughter." He tried to look reassuring to the men as they held back their urge to snicker.

"We?"

"I've got a couple of men outside town."

"You get that girl back, you'll be a hero around here, Mr. Ranger."

Luke followed Sam out the door and up the street.

Belknap held a tearful Emma in his arms. He'd stayed a day longer than planned in part for her and in part to witness Cogburn's hanging. The latter hadn't gone well, as the drop wasn't quite far enough and the man didn't die right away. His suffering wasn't very pleasant to see. Finally, a heavy man grabbed the murderer around the waist and yanked down hard. The merciful crack of Cogburn's neck breaking was nearly as bad as watching the slow death.

The crowd dispersed, and Belknap escorted Emma back to their home. He felt distressed, though wasn't certain whether it was from overseeing an execution, having to head back to duty, or leaving Emma and the prospect of enjoying more of her eager lovemaking.

But now, it was indeed time to bid farewell to his wife. "I'll be back soon, my dear." He wiped her eyes with his bandanna, a red civilian bandanna he preferred to the yellow kerchief issued by the cavalry. Her tears touched him, but duty was duty. He felt her tremble at his touch.

"I want you again, Gordon." She pressed hard against him and felt his manhood rise to the occasion. It was hardly the moment for this, especially right after such a grisly execution.

"Folks are watching, Emma. I'll be back in a couple of weeks. I'll stay longer. I promise." Going through his mind was that he'd created a sexual monster, if there was such a thing. For all his inexperience, his performance must have exceeded any expectations she had.

She finally released him.

Scarlett and Clara watched. They'd certainly succeeded at making a match.

Belknap mounted up, gave a final wave to Emma, and rode on out of Corpus Christi.

Luke was warned to be quiet as he was ushered into the parlor where a bandaged Mrs. Snider sat staring blankly into space and rocking rhythmically. Luke walked up to her and knelt beside the bed so as to not appear threatening. "Miz Snider, my name is Luke Dunn. I'm here to get your daughter back."

Snider eyes stole a sideways glance at Luke and returned to staring ahead.

Luke shook his head sorrowfully. The poor woman was in shock. He could never hope to appreciate the trauma she'd endured. He earnestly wished he'd been there to save the woman's family. The war had sure messed things up across the Nueces Strip, and this was just more evidence of it. "I will be back, Miz Snider."

He'd now committed to more than simply scouting for General Sheridan. This was going to be beyond what Belknap had asked him to do, but Luke's sense of justice had kicked in. This was a job that simply had to be done.

Costalites warriors were once again itching for an attack on the evil whites. The chief's efforts to amuse himself by breaking the spirit of the Bitch had about run their course. He gave her to the squaws to serve as a slave, but not before he took her virginity. He felt some perverse satisfaction in debasing the young girl.

Scouts had brought back news of a homestead south of Bellville that was ripe for attack. It was only a couple of dozen miles inland from the Rio Grande so was expected to be easy. The scouts assured him that there were no more than four homesteaders, including two young children.

Costalites decided to strike the next day. In fact, he decided to be bold and attack during the day. He would have liked to have struck a larger target, but he needed to find and recruit more Lipan Apache to join him.

His Apache warriors would spend the evening in dancing and singing to pump themselves up for the next day's adventure.

Luke, Barber, and One Arrow headed south from Bellville. They'd gotten a restful night's sleep and eaten quite well. Luke had waited until morning to tell them about the Snider woman and what he'd promised.

They followed the Texas shoreline of the Rio Grande. It was challenging at times, but they made good progress. From past experience, Luke calculated that the Apache wouldn't camp too far from the big river with its ample water supply and plenty of game.

"Shhhh!" Luke brought them to a halt. "You hear that?" It was the faint vibration of horses' hooves. Luke looked to One Arrow.

The chief nodded. "They're unshod."

They listened some more, as they tried to figure where they might pass.

"Ghost-Who-Rides, they will pass that way." The chief pointed to the north.

"Let's follow. That many horses moving so fast must mean they're up to something."

The terrain was hilly and crossed with dry arroyos and plenty of brush for cover. They hadn't gone but ten minutes and the sounds stopped. It seemed likely the Indians had come upon whatever they were after.

Luke thought back to his days chasing Lipan Apache out of Texas with Texas Ranger Captain James Callahan back in 1856. Callahan was outnumbered but easily put the savages on the run. He'd have whipped them totally had not the Mexican military stepped in.

The three dismounted and cautiously approached the rear of the Apache band. It looked to be about eighteen warriors, though Luke couldn't be positive of the count. He pulled out his spyglass. Off in the distance, he could make out a dugout cabin and a handful of White folks. He motioned Barber and One Arrow to him. "Let's spread out. Lead our horses in until we get closer. When the Apache move to attack, we mount up and ride at them yelling and shooting like all hell had broken loose. If those folks in the cabin can shoot, the Apache will be taking fire from two sides." They proceeded to lead their horses, ever-so-silently following the Apache toward their intended victims.

Of a sudden, there were yells, whoops, and gunshots, as the Apache charged. Luke could hear the homesteaders shooting back. "Let's go!" He leaped onto Big Horse, spurred the stallion, and charged toward the melee with guns blazing.

He shouted at the top of his lungs though was no match for One Arrow in that department.

The Apache were caught totally by surprise. With their overconfidence and blood lust, they'd neglected to post any rear guard. One...two...soon at least half a dozen warriors had been shot from their horses. Costalites turned to face the new threat before galloping headlong toward the Rio Grande. Perhaps four warriors followed him, as more Apache fell to the crossfire. Luke reached the cabin, then turned to face the Apache. They were gone.

One Arrow was already off his pony and busy collecting the scalps of the Apache he'd killed. He dreamed of the stories he'd be telling his sons. He efficiently accomplished his work and rejoined Luke and Barber.

Luke dismounted. "You folks all right?"

"Whoever you are, mister, God be praised for sending you." At that, the man realized there was a Comanche in front of his cabin with fresh Apache scalps dangling from his war lance. He lifted his rifle.

"Hold! He's a friend." Luke was quick to restrain the man's inclinations.

By some stroke, none of the defenders had been hurt. Luke looked to One Arrow and Barber, then turned to the home-steader. "Y'all stay on guard here in case they come back. We still have work to do."

"Who are you?"

"Luke Dunn. Used to be a Texas Ranger. We were supposed to just be scouting those red devils for General Sheridan, but we couldn't let them hurt y'all." Luke tipped his hat. "Jake, One Arrow! Let's go. They won't head back to their camp right away. If it's close by, maybe we'll get lucky and find the Snider girl."

"You gonna save the Snider girl, Mr. Dunn?" The home-steader's expression was of incredulity.

"Going to try, friend."

"You need help?"

Luke looked from the man to his wife to his children. "I think your family could better use your protection, but thanks for the offer." He mounted Big Horse and led Barber and One Arrow in a southwest path toward the river. Instinct told him he'd soon come upon Costalites's camp, if he headed in that direction.

Barber called out as they rode. "Luke, how'd you know to attack like that?"

"Did it with Callahan. My cousins told me they used the tactic on cattle drives to fight off Comanche and Kiowa." Luke nodded as deferentially as he could toward One Arrow as they proceeded at a slow gallop. His goal was to get to the Apache camp before Costalites, grab the girl, and head back to Bellville.

Costalites didn't know how far he'd be followed into Mexico. He certainly didn't expect whoever had attacked to be heading to the Apache encampment. No one would possibly be so foolish as to do that. Again, his overconfidence had clouded his judgment. After about twenty miles, he pulled up to take stock of his warriors. Eight Apache! He was stunned. He'd lost more than half his band. Horses were well-lathered. They'd be forced to rest before heading back to their little village.

On a rise overlooking the north bank of the Rio Grande, Luke came upon the Apache village. Costalites had just arrived with his bedraggled band on well-lathered ponies. There appeared to be a few women and children and but a handful of old men hardly worthy of a fight. He pulled out the spyglass to have a closer look. "She's over by the dugout to the left." He whispered to Barber and One Arrow.

Luke stroked his mustache as he thought briefly on the situation. Finally, he turned to One Arrow. "My friend, here's where you make another great story for your sons. Jake and I are going to cause a noisy ruckus over yonder, while you ride in and scoop up the yellow-haired girl. We'll meet you at the arroyo over yonder." He pointed to a spot perhaps a half mile away. Luke calculated that the Apache chief would still be out of sorts after the failed raid, and any pursuit would be delayed by having to round up fresh horses.

Luke and Barber went charging through the Apache camp whooping and hollering while firing their guns into the air. In the space of perhaps a half minute, the attack was over. The girl was no longer stoic but was screaming and kicking in the arms of her Comanche savior.

One Arrow gladly handed her off to Luke. "Crazy girl!" He rubbed the scratches she'd left on his arms and chest.

They wheeled their horses around at the arroyo. "Let's get out of here. They might try to chase us." Luke thought there'd be some effort at pursuit, but nevertheless off they galloped toward Bellville with Mrs. Snider's daughter clinging to Luke for dear life. He kept looking over his shoulder, but the anticipated Apache chase never materialized. Luke couldn't know that Costalites was tired and felt that losing the Bitch was good riddance.

One Arrow pulled up at the town limits of Bellville, causing Luke and Barber to rein in as well. The chief looked questioningly at Luke. "Is this good, Ghost-Who-Rides?"

"I'm thinking the good citizens of Bellville need to know who rescued Mrs. Snider's precious daughter. Stay close, my friend."

As they rode on into Bellville with Mrs. Snider's daughter, Luke was thinking less about what the folks might think of a Comanche chief riding into town and more on trying to imagine what must be going through Costalites mind about this time. He allowed himself a wry grin and a chuckle. The Apache's days were surely numbered.

People stopped and stared at the little procession. Fingers pointed at the little golden-haired girl. She was dirty and her clothes were but rags, but she still maintained the defiant expression that had served her well resisting Costalites.

Of course, mouths dropped aghast and agape at the appearance of a Comanche savage in their town. One Arrow rode proudly on his favorite pony, erect and in full regalia. No one could miss the still fresh scalps dangling from his lance.

Luke rode up to the house where Mrs. Snider was being cared for. By now, a small crowd of perhaps a dozen curious Bellville citizens had gathered, begun to follow them up the street, and now anxiously awaited the reunion of Mrs. Snider and her daughter. One Arrow was mostly ignored for the moment.

Luke dismounted, took the young girl gently by the hand, and strode up to the door. The little girl's defiant expression was beginning to crack. The homeowner had seen them coming and opened the door before Luke could knock. He humbly doffed his hat and kept it simple. "I brought someone to see Mrs. Snider."

The woman called back over her shoulder. "Harriet? Come see!"

A hush fell over the scene. Seconds passed like hours. Mrs. Snider appeared slowly, hesitantly. She still wore bandages, though they were mostly aimed at disguising the angry scars from the cuts the Apache had made in their attempt to disfigure her. She peered from the doorway. The little girl suddenly burst forward and ran to her mother, nearly knocking the woman down as she wrapped herself around her. Mrs. Snider's face buried in her daughter's hair. "Sarah," she said weakly. She began to weep with relief and joy. She held her daughter tightly. "Sarah." They were the first words she'd said since the attack.

"Mrs. Snider, I'm sorry for your loss. May God be with you." Luke put his hat back on, turned, and then realized that most of Bellville had turned out to witness the reunion. Women were crying and even many men were wiping away a tear or two.

The good feelings were inevitably broken, as a grizzled old war veteran grumbled. "What's an injun doin' in our town?"

There was a mixture of shutting the man down for ruining the reunion and a few guffaws of agreement with his question.

Luke was quick to respond. He figured a few already knew whom he was, so he'd dispense with any introduction of himself. "This is One Arrow, War Chief of the Penateka Comanche. He single-handedly rescued Mrs. Snider's daughter from the savage Apache. He comes in peace. He is my friend." He paused and looked around at the surrounding faces. "And you should be his friends."

The old veteran grudgingly nodded. "Okay, but mostly good injuns is dead injuns." He couldn't quite let go of his prejudice.

About this time, a family in a buckboard pulled into town. The driver saw the gathering and drove on up to see what the commotion was. As he pulled up, the family recognized Luke. "Mr. Dunn! Mr. Dunn! Praise the Lord!"

The crowd's attention was quickly diverted to this unexpected greeting.

The husband stood and addressed the crowd. "Mr. Dunn and his friends defended us against an Apache attack yesterday. Must have killed dozens of the hostiles." The number was an exaggeration, but Luke wasn't going to interrupt with a correction. "They saved our lives."

If it was possible to create legends in a matter of a few

seconds, such a legend had been forged in that very moment. Luke Dunn had come to Bellville, rescued a little girl kidnapped by savages, and saved homesteaders lives by fending off an Apache attack. He'd be written up in Bellville lore for years to come.

Luke nodded to Barber and One Arrow. "We'd best be going." He turned Big Horse.

"Mr. Dunn?"

He looked back. It was a weak but earnest call.

Mrs. Snider still stood in the doorway with her arms wrapped tightly around her daughter. "God bless you, Mr. Dunn."

Luke tipped his hat and led Barber and One Arrow back out of town.

Barber broke the silence as they rode past the town limits. "Where to, Luke?"

"Expect we'll head south until we find General Sheridan. I've got to let him know what happened before I can return to Heaven's Gate. Seems as though we did a bit more than scout, but I don't think he'll mind." Luke looked over at One Arrow. "Well, Chief, you have proven yourself a strong warrior and friend to the White man."

"One Arrow full with spirit of Ghost-Who-Rides." It was his way of saying Luke inspired him. "One Arrow Ghost-Who-Rides's friend forever."

★ ★

They heard the rattle and jangle of sabers well ahead of the sound of shod horses. No question that a military contingent was on the trail ahead. And they were in a hurry. They were hidden from view for the moment by a bend in the trail and dense brush.

Luke was in the lead, as the three rounded the bend and came face to face not with General Sheridan's cavalry but with a troop of Mexican dragoons. Luke quickly saw that their horses were well-lathered. They had been either running to something or from something. For some reason they'd managed to cross to the Texas side of the Rio Grande.

The lead dragoon stopped so suddenly at the sight of the three travelers as to nearly catapult over the head of his horse. The others veered to avoid him.

Luke held back a moment to gather himself. Those red coats dredged up terrible memories of his years fighting the red-coated British oppressors in Ireland and chasing the dragoons with Callahan. In a heartbeat, he found his two Colts in his hands and fired warning shots into the air.

The dragoons came to a halt. Desperation was writ large across their faces. Now, they found themselves looking down the muzzles of an arsenal aimed directly at them. Their dreaded long lances were no match for bullets.

Luke and the dragoons heard more hoofbeats. Sheridan's lead troopers rounded the bend and pulled up behind the dragoons.

The Mexicans were surrounded. Weapons clattered to the ground and hands went up high. There were ten dragoons all together. Sweating and now frightened out of their skin, they awaited whatever fate was to befall them.

General Philip Sheridan soon emerged with the rest of his cavalry. "Who the hell stopped these Mexican sonsofbitches?"

A sergeant rode up to him, saluted, and pointed at Luke, Barber, and One Arrow.

"Sergeant, take those Mexicans prisoner." Without further ado, he promptly rode over with his adjutant to where Luke sat calmly astride Big Horse. Sheridan gave Luke a squinty-eyed appraising look. "Much obliged, but who the hell are you and what are you doing here?"

Luke was taken aback by the general's manner. "Luke Dunn, General. Until late, a Texas Ranger. I was sent down here by Colonel Belknap to scout Apache. Got delayed putting a whipping on Costalites and saving some home-steaders lives. Then, low and behold, I get to capture a bunch of Mexican dragoons. Guess that's what I'm doing here, General Sheridan. Oh, and the colonel should be along right soon."

Sheridan realized he just might have overstepped a bit. "You report to Governor Hamilton, Mr. Dunn?"

"No, General. Just doing a favor for the colonel and a service to you."

"Who are these men? You ride with a damned injun, too?"

Luke knew he had flustered the normally strong-willed general just a bit. "Jake Barber here's from Nuecestown. He's been a Texas Ranger, too. As to this so-called injun, he's One Arrow, War Chief of the Penateka Comanche and a good friend of mine. He's saved my life and rescued a young girl the Apache had kidnapped."

Sheridan's head was swimming with too much information on the backside of his long chase after the dragoons.

"If I might ask, General, what did the dragoons do?"

"Tread on United States soil."

"Chasing Cheno Cortina I'd wager."

"Could be, Mr. Dunn. But we saw no Mexican rebels."

Luke offered a sympathetic smile, although he was near ready to burst with laughter. "I expect Cortina didn't want to be seen, General."

Sheridan caught his drift and immediately sought to shift the discussion. Losing his prey wasn't exactly comfortable for him. "You said you were scouting. What have you learned?"

"Well, General Sheridan, sir, Costalites is licking his wounds in Mexico the other side of the Rio Grande from Bellville. He's also got a small village of mostly women, chil-dren, and old men on Texas soil between Rio Grande City and Bellville. The Apache massacred some ranchers a couple of weeks back and had the folks in Bellville on edge. I think we gave them some relief from that, sir. Other than Cortina and these dragoons, you've likely got a clear trail to Bellville and beyond."

Sheridan stared deeply into Luke's eyes. He acted as though he'd never before seen anyone quite like the former Texas Ranger. "Are you the man that broke up that fraud ring a few years back that was taking inventory from army posts and Indian reservations?"

Luke nodded. "I had some help."

"Well, thank you, Mr. Dunn." The general had completely changed his attitude toward Luke. "I'm much obliged for your help today and will mention you and your men in my report. Now, I must head out with my prisoners. I expect I've got some fool international incident on my hands. You're welcome to join us."

"We'll be moving on, if you don't mind, General. Pleased to have helped."

Sheridan saluted as Luke rode by and led Barber and One Arrow up the trail.

Barber near burst with laughter after they were out of earshot. "That was sooooo sweet, Luke. You turned that general around like a cat chasin' its tail."

"Now, now, Jake. He's a good officer. Very capable for a Yankee. Just doing his job." Luke still couldn't suppress a slight grin.

"Ghost-Who-Rides have powerful medicine." There wasn't much more for One Arrow to contribute to the conversation.

Luke gave Big Horse a light kick into a canter. "Let's get home, men."

The trio didn't see hide nor hair of Belknap and his unit on their journey back to Nuecestown, though that was to be expected given the broad expanses of the Nueces Strip. The summer was coming to an end along with its infernal heat and humidity.

They settled down for a final campfire a day out of Corpus Christi. A rabbit, victim of One Arrow's unerring bowmanship, roasted on a makeshift spit. As they sat around the fire sipping some of the worst coffee imaginable, Luke asked One Arrow of his plans for the future.

"One Arrow return to his people." He thought on that and realized that he really hadn't answered Luke's question. "Ghost-Who-Rides not like other whites. One Arrow learn true friendship. Skin no matter. Learn of what White man God call respect." He wanted to add love, but it wasn't in his way of thinking. The Comanche didn't even have a word for it.

Luke resisted the temptation to expand on the chief's perspectives. The chief would have to learn that over time, if at all. But he didn't totally avoid the subject. "Our God is powerful medicine for whites and for Comanche."

Barber nodded agreement.

One Arrow fondled the cross hanging around his neck. He'd have to give Luke's statement about an all-powerful God more serious thought. He tossed the remainder of the coffee from his cup. "Bad medicine." He smiled longingly. "One Arrow miss Cactus Flower." The chief took a bite from the roasted rabbit leg that he'd been gesticulating with.

Luke smiled at the glimmer of hope for the Comanche chief eventually accepting the White man's ways. At least, the chief had a favored squaw. "I expect we all miss our wives." He thought on One Arrow's three wives. He smiled as he considered that put the other way around, perhaps all the wives missed their men.

"One Arrow leave in morning," the chief stated it matter-of-factly.

"When the sun is high tomorrow, we will be at Heaven's Gate. One Arrow will miss my wife's cornbread."

That gave the chief pause. He patted his taut belly, laughed, and shook his head side to side. "If One Arrow stay…get fat."

Luke stirred the coals from last night's cooking fire. The sun had just snuck its soul-warming rays above the distant horizon. One Arrow was nowhere to be found. Luke touched the ground where the chief had slept. It wasn't even warm.

Barber stirred. "Got coffee ready yet, boss?"

"One Arrow's gone home."

Barber sat bolt upright. "Dang! I'm gonna miss him."

"Didn't realize he'd had such an effect on you, Jake."

"Caused me to think 'bout a lot of things, Luke."

Luke stuck the coffee pot on top of the embers he'd managed to stir up. He bent over to pick up his saddle. "What's this?" A beautifully beaded buckskin bag lay where the saddle had been. Dropping the saddle, he picked it up and unfastened the leather tie.

"What'd you find?" Barber was curious.

Luke closed the bag. "Sorry, my friend. It's between me and One Arrow." He hoisted the saddle onto Big Horse's back and hung the bag from the pommel.

Barber picked up his own saddle. No bag under it. "Lookin' forward to seein' Ameone again."

"Ameone?"

"Didn't I mention my woman's name? Sorry 'bout that. It's Cheyenne for Walking Woman." Barber reflected, then grinned. "I get home, she won't be doin' any walkin' fer a while."

"I know what you mean, my friend." Luke smiled then grew serious. The morning breeze tossed a couple of tumbleweeds across the nearby arroyo. It gave him pause to think appreciatively about Barber and their missions together. "I've appreciated your company, Jake. We sure have worked well together. Put whippings on some bad men, saved a few lives. Justice has its rewards."

"You've treated me with respect, Luke Dunn, when no one else would. I thank you fer that. I'll ever be loyal to you." He paused as he thought on that. "You mention justice, Luke, but you don't talk none of the forgiveness and redemption parts. Not sure you think on it so much, but you do save souls gone astray."

Luke's face turned a deep red. He wasn't one to blush, and he did his level best to hide it. Even pulled his bandanna over his face for a moment. He looked long and intently at Barber. The man was right. Whether he'd intended or not during his delivery of justice, he had indeed encountered folks he'd deemed worthy of second chances, of redemption if you will. Yet, he wasn't quite ready to face his own redemption. He offered a lighthearted response. "We ought to have a picnic. You and Ameone, Jubal and JD, Scarlett and Walker, Jaime and Julia...everybody come to Heaven's Gate. Eat...drink...games. We'll roast up a side of beef."

"Sounds like a great idea, Luke." Barber poured the last of the coffee and kicked dirt over the remaining coals. Soon enough, he was saddled up and ready to head home.

"I've got to reach out to my cousin Nick. Last I heard, he was going to join his beeves with a herd being put together by some fellow named Shanghai Pierce up in Victoria. Seems like Kansas is fetching good prices."

"You going to join the drive?"

"Nope. Just enough to get a few of my beeves joined up with my cousin's herd. You ever drive cattle, Jake?"

Barber smiled. "Only beef I like is settin' on a plate with taters an' biscuits."

They turned their mounts eastward, riding into the rays of the morning sun. The day would likely be another scorcher.

A live oak motte soon came into view. A couple of buzzards cut circles in the sky overhead. The men looked at each other. They'd have to check out what had the birds so interested.

Barber fell in behind Luke as they approached the tree. Luke heard it first, a whimper he could barely hear. Big Horse snorted, as he caught the smell. Something or someone was under the tree. Luke moved in cautiously. "Jake, look here." He dismounted.

"Dang, Luke. It's a dog."

Luke grabbed his canteen and kneeled beside the dog. It had cuts in its neck and deep slashes along its ribs. "He's been in a fight with a cat, Jake. He must have fought well or the cat would've finished him." Luke poured water into its mouth all the while thinking he couldn't let so tough a fighter die.

"He's in bad shape, Luke. You might oughta put him down."

Luke pulled the Colt from his holster and held the muzzle close to the dog's head. The dog whimpered and licked Luke's hand. He re-holstered his gun. "He doesn't deserve to die. I'm going to take him to Heaven's Gate." Luke slipped his bandanna from his own neck and bound the dog's neck wounds. The blood had already dried on the dog's ribs, so Luke just hoped he could carry him without reopening the wounds.

Jake was appreciating observing the sensitive side of Luke, when he caught a glimpse of something on the other side of the motte. "I'll be darned."

"What's that, Jake?"

Barber walked over to what had caught his eye. "Lynx. It's a dead lynx, Luke. That dog bested the danged cat."

Luke lifted the dog across his saddle and climbed up. "Must have been quite a fight. Might have been better than those cock fights I used to guard for Colonel Kinney a few years back. Anyway, we're going to deprive those buzzards of one meal."

"What kind of dog you think he is?"

Luke held the big pup across his lap. "Tough. A fighter."

"I meant breed, Luke."

"Haven't seen one like this before. His yellow eyes are sure different, like maybe he's got some coyote blood in him. I heard about some fellows breeding dogs with coyote to help with rounding up beeves. I think their name was Lacy."

"You're fixin' to make him one of the family, ain't you?"

"Been wanting to get the children a dog for a long while. That confounded war put a stop on so many things. If we can nurse this one back to health, he'd do just fine." Luke nudged Big Horse forward at a gentle walk. "I expect I'll get Doc to have a look at him."

Luke bade farewell to Barber at the entrance to Heaven's Gate. They'd stopped and given water to the dog a couple of times, and the brave pup seemed to be gathering some strength. It was as though he had a will to live. He slept across Luke's lap much of the journey. The rocking motion of Big Horse seemed to soothe him. Luke thought the dog's fate could be likened to the Confederacy, deeply wounded, struggling to recover, and with hope for the future. The pup represented a sort of life truth, a reality.

Luke had paused and grabbed a handful of rock roses and antelope-horns along the last couple of miles. He thought the combination of red and white flowers were right pretty. Certainly, a bouquet worthy of Elisa.

As Big Horse found his own head up the trail to the house, Luke spotted Elisa kneeling at the graves of her parents and brothers. Luke dismounted, unsaddled Big Horse, and left the big stallion to graze. He carried the dog with him over to Elisa and knelt beside her. The pup gave nary a whimper, as though he knew to be quiet.

Elisa looked first at the dog and then up at Luke. A tear found its way down her cheek.

Luke gently spread the bouquet across the graves.

"Wish they were here, Lucas."

"You know they're watching, my love. You know they're with us."

"I so missed you."

Luke wrapped an arm around her and pulled her close. "I miss them, too...for your sake, Lisa. But now...well, you are my life now and ever more."

She buried herself in Luke's chest, sobbing as though finally releasing some long-held, bottled-up feelings. "Dear God, I've missed you, Lucas."

They kneeled there together for a time. In a way, it was a moment to be cherished. Luke had found his ultimate calling, and held it ever so closely.

He helped her to her feet.

The dog let out a soft whimper as if to say he was still there.

"What have you found there, Lucas?" She kneeled beside the dog. She was about to pet him when she saw the wounds. "Oh my!" She gently stroked its nose. "What indeed have you found?"

"We happened on him early this morning. He's hurt but got the better part of a tussle with a lynx. Figured we'd nurse him back to health and keep him."

Elisa looked up lovingly at her man. She needn't say a thing.

They took a last look at the little burial plot. Luke picked up the dog, and they walked to the house.

Elisa nodded. "He should be a right fine-looking pup once those wounds are healed. Let's clean him up in the kitchen."

There was a bit of excitement from the children, as Luke gently washed the dog's wounds. For his part, the dog gave out nary a peep. "Y'all be thinking of a name for this guy. He put a whipping on a lynx, so he'll need a name that suits a fighter."

Elisa figured there'd been enough excitement. "Y'all are going to bed now. We'll name the dog in the morning. Y'all sleep on a name, because it's important like naming horses."

Soon enough, the children were bedded down and Luke had the dog comfortably settled in some blankets near the fireplace. He stood beside Elisa watching the pup fall asleep.

Elisa looked up at her man and mustered a deep-throated, "Lucas?"

"The mission went well. One Arrow's gone home."

She shook her head slowly but emphatically. "No."

"What?"

She wondered how men could sometimes be clueless. "Tonight, there's a full moon. The children are bedded down. It's warm. I'm thinking we ought to go for a swim down at the creek."

Luke couldn't suppress a broad grin. Indeed, he'd found his true calling. "You know I love to swim, Lisa."

TWENTY-THREE
TRUTH

LUKE HAD HEADED OUT EARLY. He checked on the dog and gave him some water and dried beef before heading to the barn and saddling up Big Horse. He mostly wanted to relax and take in the openness of the ranch and the sense of freedom it brought to his mind. There was no escaping the harsh truths that the war embedded in his very soul. Whether secession had been right or wrong, it had been a foolhardy exercise by most any practical measure. There was no question in his mind that slavery was wrong morally and even practically, yet the war's aftermath had served to deepen long-held prejudices. Perhaps worse to Luke's thinking was that the Confederacy's flailings about states' rights had served to strengthen the hand of an ever-stronger federal government. He felt strongly that folks should fear enslavement from Washington DC every bit as much as they should abhor enslaving Black folks on plantations. It drives home what the nation's founding fathers had been thinking in limiting the powers of the federal government.

He quickly found himself a couple of miles out. Reaching into his pocket, he reread the telegram from Thorpe that Elisa had given him after their swim. It simply said that he was grateful for Luke helping break up the land fraud scheme and that he was on his way to pay a visit. It looked to be strictly a social call.

Dark clouds gathered off in the distance, and Luke figured he'd better head back home unless he intended to wait around for an impromptu shower. He'd only been gone a little more than an hour, so featured enjoying one of Elisa's fine breakfasts.

A strange sense enveloped him as he neared the ranch house. It was far too quiet for his liking. Smoke should have been pouring from Jaime's and Julia's cabin, and children should have been running around. He skirted behind the house, and the first indication of real trouble came to his ears. There were thumps and muffled words coming from the barn. The barn door was closed and the pin secured in the latch to prevent exit.

Luke scanned the yard, as he drew the Henry from its scabbard and dismounted. There were lots of footprints and hoofprints scattered about, and one of Elisa's shoes lay in the grass. He looked around before cautiously walking over to the barn door, unlatching it, and carefully pulling it back. His entire family and Jaime's were tied up and gagged. Elisa strained at her bonds and the children were beyond teary-eyed with fear. Luke looked around to be sure there was no trap before entering. He pulled out his Bowie knife, strode over to Elisa, and cut the ropes holding her.

"Thank God, you're here, Lucas!"

"What happened?" Luke cut Jaime loose, and he and Elisa continued to talk as the children were released.

"Six of them! Soldiers! All Black!"

"Soldiers? Black soldiers did this?" Luke was incredulous, but then thought back to the sullen faces on the Black soldiers at the Cogburn trial and the four deserters they'd dealt with not so long ago.

"They were Black, Luke, and well-armed. They didn't hurt

us, but made it clear that they meant business. They said something about White folks owing them."

"This is true *Señor* Dunn. They said they were under orders."

"Orders!?" Luke's cheeks began to turn a deep shade of red as anger took hold of his psyche. "Did they say what they wanted?" Then it struck Luke. Heaven's Gate had been robbed again. He turned and ran to the house. The front door hung wide open. Luke leaped up the steps and was quickly inside surveying for any damage. The place had been ransacked of most anything of value.

Jaime was right behind him, as Elisa and Julia comforted the children. "*Señor* Dunn, they took some saddles. The new ones."

Luke strode purposefully back onto the gallery and scanned the area to be certain there was no danger and everyone was all right. "They must have left just before I arrived. Get your gear, Jaime, we're going after them."

Elisa knew better than to even hint at the danger.

Luke checked the loads in his Colt revolvers and double-checked the Henry rifle before mounting up. He leaned down and gave Elisa a kiss before cantering off to follow the thieves' tracks that led southeastward from the house. Jaime wasted no time saddling up and falling in behind.

"Can't say these men are much for smarts, Jaime. They've left a trail a blind man could follow. Only problem with them not being so smart is their guns."

Jaime nodded, then pointed ahead. "*Señor* Dunn, I think I see them crossing the river."

Luke whipped out his spyglass and aimed it to where Jaime had pointed along the shores of the Nueces River. "Lookie there. They're having a heck of a time trying to swim their horses across the Nueces at that spot. Luckily, they haven't drowned the poor beasts." Luke watched as the thieves soon gave up the crossing and managed to make it back to shore. Their horses were totally exhausted, and the soldiers not much better. Luke slid the telescope back into its case. "Their weapons and gear are soaked. Likely as good a time as any to take prisoners."

Jaime was never surprised at Luke's total confidence in these sorts of matters. "Are we just going to ride in, *Señor* Dunn?"

Luke smiled. "Pretty much. I don't expect much fight in them at the moment, though we won't take any chances." Luke chambered a round in the Henry and nudged Big Horse forward toward the soldiers. He and Jaime quickly closed the ground to the thieves. They weren't but 100 yards out, when they were spotted by one of the soldiers. Luke picked up his pace. "Gentlemen, you are under arrest. Drop your weapons and raise your hands."

Two of the men stood with chests proudly puffed out and began to bring their rifles to firing position. "You can't arrest us, mistuh."

Luke saw some of his now soaking-wet belongings hanging from a couple of the saddles these men had stolen. He also saw the water dripping from the barrels of the rifles the two men were holding. He shook his head. "You want to try to shoot that sorry excuse for a rifle?" He and Jaime leveled their rifles at the soldiers. "Or would you like to give it a try and chance eating some lead?"

By now, the other four soldiers had gathered behind the apparent leader. "We is with the Texas provisional gov'mint. We is in charge." He was nothing if not insistent.

"Well how about that, soldier. Seems we're on the same side. I just did some work for the provisional government you're talking about, though I must say I heard nothing from them about robbing Texas citizens."

The lead man's brain was working overtime trying to figure Luke out.

"Shall we rush them, Claris?"

The leader looked annoyed, then a wide-eyed look of recognition spread across his face. "You be the lawman at dat trial in Corpus Christi."

Luke now realized that these men were likely AWOL from Belknap's unit. They'd surely face execution, if he arrested them and took them to Corpus. "Well, you men are in a heap of trouble."

"How dat?"

"You have some decisions to make."

The soldiers' jaws gaped a bit at Luke's boldness. "We got guns, too."

Luke smiled. "You sure you want to try them?" He gave them a hard-as-nails stare down. "Like I said, you must make decisions. You can die right here, I can arrest you and let Colonel Belknap shoot you, or you can leave your guns and horses here with all the goods you stole and swim across that river to freedom. It's pretty much up to you."

The soldiers well knew the penalty for desertion and surely had figured that Luke shouldn't be messed with. They looked one to the other.

"Something else to think on. If one of you decides to suddenly find his *cajones* and try to shoot at us, I'll have to kill him. Then all choices go away. I can't just bring in one dead deserter. I'll have to take you all to Corpus Christi along with any bodies. Any of you want to try that?" Luke could see that the leader was still weighing his chances.

Just then, they heard the sound of horse hooves. Edward Thorpe soon rode into sight. He quickly recognized Luke and apprised the situation. "Luke, what have you got here?"

"A few buffalo soldier deserters robbed Heaven's Gate, Mr. Thorpe. They're trying to make some decisions."

Thorpe looked at the soldiers, who were by now starting to dry out. "Joshua, is that you?"

One of the soldiers hung his head and ducked behind a fellow deserter.

"You know one of these men, Mr. Thorpe?"

"Joshua used to work at Magnolia. He was one of the first men I freed." He turned to the buffalo soldiers. "What do you men think you're doing?"

Joshua finally found enough confidence to move up beside Claris. "I'm sorry, Master Thorpe. I be dreadful sorry."

Thorpe had heard enough. He moved his horse up beside Luke. "What decisions have they been given, Luke?"

Luke nodded toward Claris. "Tell him, Claris."

"Yessuh." He shuffled his feet a tad and sighed deeply. "We can be shot dead right here, be taken to face justice with Colonel Belknap, or leave the guns and hosses and swim cross that there river." He was no longer so prideful or angry in his demeanor.

"If you don't mind, Luke." Thorpe dismounted and took a couple of steps toward the men. "Joshua here knows me. I'm a fair man. I gave all that stayed at Magnolia freedom and property that they can own by working it. They repaired the big house. I've got Frederick running the business. If you men make the right choice and swim across the Nueces River there, I'll let Frederick know to expect you. In any case, you sure aren't going to prove anything by seeking revenge from years of slavery. And it makes meaningless the sacrifices of those who died for your freedom."

Luke nodded approval. "Sounds like a great choice to me, men. Mr. Thorpe here is giving you a chance to build new lives." He dropped his voice. "I sure don't want to be pulling the trigger on this here rifle. It'll just continue the hate. Won't really prove anything."

"I guess I'm ready to swim, Mr. Thorpe." Joshua began to walk toward the river.

Claris hesitated. He'd had so much anger built up in his head, that it was hard to let loose of it. Just a tinge of revenge still lingered.

Luke read the man's face. "Revenge makes for a very lean

meal, Claris. It'll always leave you hungry. Go find yourself a Bible and shed that coat of anger you're carrying around. Forgiveness is tough, but it's the only way. Trust me, you'll find true freedom."

Claris's shoulders slumped and he sighed. "You be a smart man, Mistuh Dunn. And you be right. Thankee kindly, Mistuh Thorpe." He turned as though suddenly filled with new hope and sprinted toward the river with the others quickly following.

Luke, Jaime, and Thorpe didn't truly relax until the men had swum across, reached the far shore, waved, and begun heading north in the general direction of Magnolia Plantation.

Thorpe watched them run north. "Hope they make it. It's a long way to Magnolia."

Luke nodded agreement. "Sure enough. They sure as shooting won't be running all the way. What say we gather everything up and head to Heaven's Gate." He and Jaime edged forward to gather the reins of what had been the soldiers' horses. "You care for a bite to eat, Edward?"

Thorpe smiled. "Thought you'd never ask, my friend."

The three wasted no time riding up the trail to Heaven's Gate. Soon enough, a relieved Elisa appeared on the gallery. Her man was safe and had even brought welcome company.

Thorpe spent the day thanking Luke and Elisa and explaining his plans for the future. He held a bit of envy toward the King Ranch to the south. While Magnolia was large by plantation standards, it was a small fraction of the acreage of Richard King's spread. Thorpe expressed his intention to learn about the cattle business and eventually expand his business interests with a ranching venture. Luke shared his own plans for growing Heaven's Gate. The common ground was economic growth with very little discussion of the pitfalls associated with the politics of reconstruction, though they were concerned as to when Texas could fully return to determination of its own destiny. Luke's and Thorpe's concerns were that the most recent election didn't go the way the authorities wanted, so results had been nullified. Consequently, Texans were facing increased graft and alarming tax increases that tended to stifle new business endeavors. Life's truths seemed ever-harder to face. Texans could ostensibly vote provided they took an oath of loyalty to the Union. Neither Luke nor Thorpe had ever considered themselves Rebel or Yankee, so they feared facing zealots from both political extremes. These zealots tended to be embittered men resentful of the federal army, especially colored troops they believed had been sent to humiliate the defeated Confederates. Opportunists from beyond Texas borders, carpetbaggers as they were called, took over local governments and cheated residents unmercifully. Luke had pretty much resigned himself with having to deal with the overreach of the colored troops that had effectively become a police force with a big chip on its shoulder. They decided to not trouble Elisa with revisiting the incident with more deserters. They'd enjoy a scrumptious dinner with lighter conversation about the promise of the future. Thorpe departed for Corpus Christi just after dark.

It was mid-morning about a week after Thorpe's visit, when Luke pulled into Corpus Christi with a string of Army horseflesh in tow and dismounted in front of the Meaney's house.

"Gordon," he called out. "Gordon Belknap, get yourself out here."

Belknap gathered himself together, lightly kissed the sleeping Emma, and dashed to the front portico before Luke could call him out again.

"Shush, Luke." He quickly took note of the horses. "What do you have in mind with those nags, Luke?"

Belknap and his colored troop had ridden in from Brownsville. He'd spent the past couple of days making up for lost time with Emma. He'd even found time to write an article about his brief exploits along the Rio Grande with General Sheridan for "The Advertiser," an upstart newspaper in Corpus Christi.

Luke could do little at first but smile upon seeing the colonel. Belknap wore a white shirt unbuttoned at the collar, his suspenders dangled alongside his breeches, and his boots were in need of a polishing. Luke didn't have to ask what the officer had been up to. Bernice had shared with him about Belknap's return to Corpus and how the colonel and Emma hadn't been seen since he'd returned. "Been taking care of your Army property for nigh a week now, Gordon. Pretty much got them healthy again."

Belknap gazed inquisitively at Luke. "Dang. Those are my missing horses. How'd you come to be in possession of them, my friend?"

"Long story." Luke dismounted. "If you can give it a rest long enough, I'll buy you a drink at the Longhorn and tell you all about it."

Belknap looked down at himself and blushed a little as though suddenly becoming aware that he was out of uniform. "Er...let me get myself straightened out a bit, Luke. If you'd be kind enough to take those horses up to the livery and register them to me, I'll meet you shortly."

Luke remounted Big Horse and led the string toward the stables. As he ambled up the street, he thought on the future. They were heavy thoughts, as ever more harsh truths would have to be faced. What was to become of the Texas Rangers? How long would they have to endure the provisional government? Who'd be keeping law and order, delivering justice?

Luke explained his encounter with the deserters to Belknap over a couple of beers at the Longhorn. "I expect we could have brought them in, Gordon...maybe should have. But... well...it seems that some sort of healing needs to take place. Right or wrong, these men were troubled. Bringing them to you for certain execution just didn't seem right even though it violated your military code."

The colonel was understandably unhappy to lose the troops, even troublemakers. "But…"

"No but, Gordon. Call it weakness or strength, despite my being ever committed to delivering justice, I also look for redemptive potential. It's not something you'll get from a court of law or military tribunal." Luke watched the colonel's expression begin to change. Perhaps Belknap was beginning to understand. "Gordon, most of the hearty folks who settled Texas with Stephen Austin were what I like to call second chancers. Many had failed at something or were seeking better opportunity for themselves and their families. Why should it be any different for former slaves?"

"But they pledged themselves, they took an oath…"

"Did they have a choice, Gordon?" Luke leaned forward. "Edward Thorpe and I gave them a choice to live, a chance to build their futures. We gave them the opportunity that Lincoln's Emancipation Proclamation never truly did."

Belknap sighed, then smiled. "Guess you're right, Luke. I don't like it from a military point of view, but I understand what you're saying. Still, if word got out, half my men would leave. Given our law-and-order mission, that would weaken us and jeopardize many lives." Before Luke could respond, he added, "but I understand that such service should be a choice, just as you chose being a lawman and me a military officer."

Luke laughed with guarded relief. "Life is about choices. If I were a betting man, I'd wager that you'd rather be up the street in a certain hotel room than sitting here with a former Texas Ranger pontificating about life choices. Yep, there's the real truth of it, Gordon."

The colonel smiled sheepishly. "Beers are on me, Luke." He dropped a couple of coins on the table and excused himself. He paused before walking off. "Thanks kindly, my friend."

Luke rode easy-like up to the barn at Heaven's Gate. A sniffing whimpering sound followed by a wagging tail found its way along at Big Horse's hooves. El Gato, the name Luke's children had given the foundling dog, was ecstatic at Luke's return. The poor beast had been plumb tuckered out by the attention in the house and sought respite. He scratched the pup's ears and let it get in plenty of licking.

"Not bad for a dog named cat," he teased as he admired the way

Doc's sutures and plenty of family love had helped rekindle the dog's spirit. El Gato had indeed recovered right quickly from his spat with the lynx. Luke felt that he could relate to this animal that had fought tough and endured.

Belknap hadn't been exactly happy about the deserters, but had been willing to give Luke the benefit of the doubt. If they did take productive work at Magnolia, it was likely for the better and military justice would have proved nothing. For Luke's part, it had all seemed just. The Army had its horses and equipment, and a passel of potentially explosive trouble-makers had been defused.

As Luke unsaddled Big Horse, the pup continued to cavort friendly-like at his feet with tail wagging crazily.

Elisa appeared as if from nowhere. "Glad to have you back, Lucas." She chuckled. "Did Gordon appreciate the return of government property?"

Luke laughed. "Appeared so. I managed a few minutes with him at the Longhorn before he headed back to Emma. Guess he was making up for lost time."

"Can't be said for you, Mr. Dunn." Her come-hither smile coated in sarcasm wasn't lost on Luke.

Luke hung the curry brush on its hook and turned to her. "We'll just have to see about that, Mrs. Dunn." El Gato danced circles as he followed their slow arm-in-arm stroll up to the ranch house. Luke's thoughts of the future or Texas and the nation were necessarily postponed. What indeed might that future hold?

"Well, George, I don't see as we have a choice. If we reauthorize the Texas Rangers folks back in Washington are going to be super riled. I'd rather dive into a nest of rattlers than deal with their political shenanigans." General Andrew Hamilton drummed his fingers thoughtfully on the old mahogany desk and let a puff of cigar smoke spiral upward.

"Folks are expecting some sort of law and order, general." Custer eased forward in his chair. He strove to not be too aggressive despite his natural tendency to take action, to make from-the-hip decisions whether right or wrong. "That Colonel Belknap seems to have been doing right well with his colored troops. We have no shortage of coloreds with fighting experience. Why not a state police force?"

"Damn, George, that's not a bad idea. It'd sure get them nigras out of our hair and likely keep the folks back in Washington happy, too." Hamilton flicked the ash off the end of his cigar. "Kinda kill two birds with one stone."

"Think the Texans will like it, General?" The young general ran his fingers through his long hair, causing the fringe on his buckskin jacket to dance.

The general didn't exactly approve of General Custer's taste in uniforms, but wasn't up to making an issue of it. Besides, he envied that the man had such a ravishingly beautiful wife—the talk of Washington society. He looked away disdainfully. "Doesn't really matter, does it?" Hamilton ground out his cigar in the nearby ashtray.

Torches. Half a dozen horsemen pulled up in front of the Dunn's ranch house. They wore white hoods with eye holes cut out so they could see but not be seen. "Dunn! We know yer home! Git out here or we'll fire yer place with you in it!"

Luke and Elisa sat bolt upright in bed. At first, Luke thought he'd been having a bad dream.

"Don't you be hidin', Luke Dunn. Git on out here!"

The shouts were louder. Luke could see the reflections from torch flames dance through the bedroom window and across the ceiling. He sat up, drew on his pants, and pulled on the boots next to the bed. He grabbed a shirt, as he dashed out the bedroom and down the stairs. He didn't even think twice about grabbing the Henry rifle as he headed for the front door. He didn't have to check it, as it was kept loaded for just the sort of emergencies that he seemed to be dealing with at this moment. He took a deep breath, opened the door, and stepped onto the gallery.

He'd rarely seen so sinister-looking an outfit as what confronted him. Here was zealotry writ large. Three horsemen held torches, while a pair of shotguns and a rifle seemed to be the weapons of choice for the other three. Even in the torchlight, Luke quickly made out Ty Olson's horse. "Dang, but these are neighbors," he thought, as he raised the muzzle of the Henry toward the interlopers. "What y'all raising such a ruckus about, Ty?" He could see Olson flinch as though startled at being recognized despite the hood.

One of the horsemen nudged his cayuse slightly ahead of the others. "Heard you let some nigras free the other day, Dunn."

Luke nodded. "What of it? They were free anyway."

"But they was nigras breakin' man's law. They needed hangin'."

By his voice and horse, Luke had figured the apparent leader to be another neighbor, Jules Carter. "It's not your call, Jules."

"Well, you ain't the law anymore, Dunn. You don't get to decide. They was thievin' nigras an' needed hangin'."

"Seems the coloreds are free, gentlemen. We can't stuff what's been done back in the bottle." Luke laid a steely-eyed gaze on the men, as the torchlight flickered across his face. "Y'all have a problem with that?"

"You have a nice spread here, Dunn, and a growing family. It'd be a shame to see anythin' damaged in any way if'n you were to let nigras go free agin'."

Luke sensed Elisa's eyes burning into him from behind the door. She was likely even angrier than he at the not-so-veiled threat. He wasn't surprised, when she emerged and stood beside him with the heavy Sharps rifle held in the crook of her arm. Luke could just about make out the eyes of the hooded horsemen widening. "Gentlemen, I've spent the past ten years bringing justice to South Texas, protecting your farms and ranches from Comanche, bandits, and all manner of lawbreakers. I've dealt with men far tougher than you cowards hiding behind those hoods. I know a couple of you and can assure you that if something tragic were to befall my family or property at any of your hands, you would pay dearly. That's a promise." The silence that followed Luke's threat was deafening.

"There be a new law in town, Dunn. I wouldn't be castin' threats. We be settin' them Yankee do-gooders on you if'n you don't listen up."

Luke had heard rumor about the provisional government setting up a state police force instead of reconstituting the Texas Rangers. With actual law ill-defined, there was the real threat of rogue police as exacerbated by groups such as he was facing at this very moment. He'd already heard rumors of the beginnings of a vigilante-style group called the Ku Klux Klan. Any of these threats spelled trouble with a capital T. Luke shook his head ruefully. "Seems we're still fighting a war, gentlemen. No telling when things might get near normal." He looked from man to man and lowered the muzzle of the Henry. "Elisa here and me have pretty much steered clear of politics. We never cottoned to one man owning another, but didn't take sides in public one way or the other. Lincoln and his generals have had their way, and that's the way it is. What's done is done. We'd do well to not keep fighting that infernal war. I'm a peace-loving man with a family to raise and a ranch to run. I'm not looking for trouble unless it comes to my doorstep. I hope you men will think the same way and not be caught up in shenanigans that could bring you ruin. No telling what the future holds, and you might yet need my lawman expertise to save your homes and families. Now, I'm willing to let bygones be bygones and forget this evening. Y'all should be going home in peace. Let's have no more of these sorts of threats. They never end well." He sensed a begrudging acceptance of his thinking beginning to set in with the hooded horsemen.

Carter looked side to side at the men and then back at Luke and Elisa standing on the gallery with rifles in hand. "Damn it, Dunn. Leave it to you to make sense of this whole mess." He hung his head and shrugged. "Sorry about this. Let's go, men."

Luke and Elisa watched the men turn and slowly ride off. It was only then that he breathed a sigh of relief. He slipped his arm around Elisa's shoulders. "That was close. Too close...and far too easy."

"What's the world coming to, Lucas? What turns folks to acting so terribly?"

"I'm afraid the struggle is only beginning, Lisa. Broken families, lost dreams, deep-held feelings about the war. It's going to take a while for folks to get past it all. Truth can hurt. Meanwhile, we can count on some folks trying to use the chaos to their advantage. We'd best be ready."

★★

Shots exploded in the early evening air.

"Who? What the hell you want?"

"You...you crackers...you be out of here by noon tomorrow."

Bent Evans stood in the doorway of his cabin, a young'un hanging on one leg and his wife cowering behind him. He was disheveled and in only his underwear but had quickly dusted away the cobwebs from having barely fallen asleep. He held the old Enfield rifle at the ready, as he faced the heavily armed mounted men. "You ain't got no right!"

"These here papers say you ain't paid yer taxes." The leader, a Black man of considerable size, brandished a sheaf of official-looking documents. "You be off Judge Crockett's property by midday, or we'll take you off."

Evans looked from man to man. There were five of them. All looked to be former colored troops. Had it not been for his wife and young son, he might have gone down fighting to protect his humble homestead on the Nueces Strip prairie he'd striven so hard to tame. "Got nowhere to go."

"You just be gone, whitey." The leader threw the papers onto the ground in front of Evans and his family. They fired a couple of more shots into the air for effect before turning and riding off.

"Bent...wha...what are we going to do?" Evans's wife looked pleadingly, desperately into his eyes.

"There's gotta be somewhere we can go." He tried to be reassuring. He herded his family back inside the cabin. Evans looked over at the post that served to keep his wardrobe. Hidden under a tattered shirt was the butternut gray coat that had seen better days, but served as an ever-present reminder of his fighting Yankees up on the Sabine River. Now, it was naught but an albatross hung around his neck, convicting him of having fought the Union and lost more than a war. "That damned Crockett is snapping up properties all over Nueces County. I rightly don't know any law that's legitimate, Sarah."

"They can't do this, Bent." She paused tearfully. "Can they?"

Evans's mind was racing in a search for relief, for any promising solution to his dilemma. If he fought back and killed or wounded anyone, he'd wind up either dead or in jail. Either way, he'd effectively make his wife a widow and still lose his homestead.

"What about that Texas Ranger?" Sara suggested with hope for what seemed impossible.

"Ain't no Rangers no more." He despairingly bit his lip. "Ain't sure that Dunn fella could help anyhow."

"Sheriff Meaney?"

"Provisional government stripped him of his badge, too. Got them coloreds now instead."

"Maybe...maybe Dunn would help?" Her eyes pleaded.

Evans knew he'd have to ride hard most of the morning to hope to reach Luke Dunn and get back before his family was ripped from their home. He looked down at his wife...his young son. Dunn was his only hope. "I'll saddle up." He could only hope the old mare wouldn't break down on the ride to Heaven's Gate. He'd made the only choice that seemed remotely feasible, and there was no assurance Luke could or would help.

Luke had just put the finishing touches on the repair of one of the gallery posts. It had been hard work, and he'd sweated a bit. He headed to a nearby water bucket and was about to quench his thirst, when he heard the approach of a horse. From the hoofbeats, he sensed the poor beast was just about spent.

Right soon, his neighbor Bent Evans came into view. The man looked to be in a wild-eyed panic, and his clothes were in considerable disarray. Upon sighting Luke, he hollered, "Luke!

Luke! Help!" The horse could barely stand, as he was brought to a halt all lathered-up and breathing heavily. Evans half slid and half fell from the saddle.

"Bent, what's got you so fired up?"

Evans staggered toward Luke and leaned against the gallery. "Damned Nigra police tryin' to take my ranch!" Evans struggled to catch his breath. "They sayin' we ain't paid taxes an' it belongs to Judge Crockett. Said we gotta be out by tomorrow."

"That can't be, Bent." Luke delivered an incredulous look. "Simply can't be."

"We got nowhere to go, Luke." He handed the eviction papers to Luke.

Luke shook his head. "This is Sheriff Meaney's job, not police."

"There was half dozen of 'em, Luke. They meant bizness. And they done kicked Sheriff Meaney out."

"Calm down, Bent. We'll get to the bottom of this." Luke glanced at Evans's horse. He nodded to the water trough. "Be sure your horse doesn't drink too fast, Bent. Put him up in the corral and go put your tack on the gelding over yonder, and we'll go see Judge Crockett."

"Thanks, Luke…thanks. We just can't have 'em doin' these sorts of things."

"I'm still obliged to the provisional government, Bent. We'll see if that helps any." Luke poked his head in the front door of the house. "Lisa, I've got to help Bent Evans with an emergency. We're riding to Corpus. Shouldn't take long."

Elisa sighed. "Be safe, Lucas."

Luke soon had Big Horse saddled, and he and Evans headed to Corpus Christi.

★★

Luke and Evans rode up to the jail. Sheriff Meaney was nowhere to be seen. Luke dismounted and read a paper tacked onto the front door. It was a notice from Judge Crockett that Meaney had been relieved of his duties and the provisional police had taken his role. Luke shook his head incredulously. "Dang, Bent. I can't believe this."

"Told ya so. What we gonna do, Luke?"

"Let's go find this Judge Crockett. Likely at the courthouse up the street."

Luke grabbed Big Horse's reins and began the walk up the street with Evans following. As they approached the courthouse, Evans spotted the big Black man that had served the eviction notice sitting on a chair beside the front door. It was hard to miss the sign beside the door. It read in large gold letters on a mahogany board, "Judge Louis Crockett, Regional Judge, Corpus Christi District."

Luke hitched Big Horse to the post, and Evans dismounted and followed suit. Luke had just about placed his boot on the first step when the Black man arose from his seat.

"Where you think you be goin', mister?"

Luke paused. "I'm planning to see Judge Crockett. Got business with him."

"Y'all gotta have an appointment." The Black man offered up a toothless grin. "Can't let you in with no appointment."

Luke finished climbing the steps and was nearly nose-to-nose with his challenger. "I'm under orders from Governor Hamilton. You'd better let me pass."

Despite his own bulk, the man realized that Luke was just a bit bigger and obviously up to any physical challenge. He turned his gaze to Evans. "You be the damned Reb rancher from this morning. You with him?"

Luke motioned Evans to join him, and leveled just a hint of a threat at the Black man. "I figure you won't have a problem with that." Before he reached for the door, Luke paused. "You have a name?"

The man thought to return a smart retort, but figured better of it especially as he saw Luke's hand resting on the butt of a well-used Colt revolver. "James. James Thorpe."

Luke turned to the Black man. "You from Magnolia?"

Thorpe was taken by surprise. "Er…yes. I be from there."

"How come you're here and not working the land Edward Thorpe offered y'all?"

The man hung his head. Wasn't much he could say.

Luke shrugged and stepped into the courthouse. He walked straight to Crockett's office with Evans right behind. He knocked on the door but didn't wait for a response. Luke opened the door and took a stride in before freezing in his tracks.

The judge was half naked astride a local whore on top of his desk. Crockett was none too pleased. "What the? Who the hell?" He blustered and shoved himself back from the woman. He chased her out the side door while pulling up his trousers. "Who the hell do you think you are?"

Luke was grinning ear to ear. "Dunn…Luke Dunn, your honor. I'm an agent of Governor Hamilton."

"Wha…What are you looking at?"

Luke pointed to the end of the judge's shirt sticking out from his fly.

Crockett stuffed it back in. "Dunn? Should I know you?"

"My neighbor Mr. Evans here tells me that you're planning on taking his property. Something about paying taxes." Luke decided to get down to business.

"That's the law, Dunn." Crockett leaned against the desk. "Governor Hamilton, you say?"

"Whose law might you be referring to, Judge? You're not from around these parts or you'd understand Mr. Evans's situation. It sure doesn't sound like you're giving him much chance to make things right."

"It's provisional law. Evans fought with the Rebels, so he…"

"He's a human being judge. He's got a family that suffered while he was off fighting in a rebellion for a cause he believed in. President Johnson has offered amnesty to all who swear to the Constitution. Mr. Evans has done that."

"He still owes taxes."

"How much?"

Crockett snatched a file from his desk and flipped through the papers. "Twenty-five dollars."

Luke looked at Evans. He shook his head at the very idea of the rancher losing his spread for so paltry a sum. The rancher was a pitiful sight to behold. Luke sighed and reached into his pocket. He handed Crockett a twenty-dollar gold piece. "Consider this a down payment, Judge. Mr. Evans here will pay the balance after next roundup."

"You…you can't do that."

Luke stepped up close to the judge. "I walk in here and find you dallying with a common whore. I just got back from risking my life helping General Sheridan engage Apache and Mexican dragoons on the Rio Grande, Judge Crockett. You better dang well figure I can help my neighbor. Don't you agree?" The not-so-veiled threat hung heavy in the air.

"Er…yes." Crockett cowered back from Luke.

Luke had made his point. He stood back to let the judge catch his breath. "And you make sure your so-called police don't bother Mr. Evans here or any of the hard-working folks around these parts. I expect that you carrying on with the little lady need not be made public, especially to your wife. Is that understood, Judge?"

"Yes. I understand, Mr. Dunn."

Luke turned to Bent Evans and nodded toward the door. "Let's go home, Bent. Seems we're about finished here." He hustled Evans out of the judge's office.

"Bless you, Luke Dunn. I'll pay you back as soon as I'm able."

"I know you will, Bent." He strode out the front door and

found James Thorpe with three other Black policemen waiting for him.

"Stop there."

Luke stopped and rolled his eyes. "You can't be serious, Officer Thorpe. I have just come to an agreement with Judge Crockett, and you and your men are to leave us be."

The big Black man thought on that. He was obviously being silently egged on by the others.

Luke's hand caressed his Colt revolver. "I really don't see this as something anyone should be getting hurt over, Mr. Thorpe. If I were you, I'd be heading back to Magnolia and taking up Edward Thorpe's offer. It's a lot safer."

The man thought on Luke's words. He was between the proverbial rock and hard place. He took a step forward close enough to suddenly find himself staring down the muzzle of Luke's revolver. It had happened so quickly, that Thorpe's companions' mouths were agape.

"Don't come any closer."

Thorpe smiled easy-like. "I'm sorry, Mr. Dunn. I think I'll be taking your advice after all." He stepped back and offered his hand.

Luke holstered his gun and shook the big man's hand. "Good luck to you, then. The sooner we get back to work and building families, the sooner we'll have true peace."

"You be right about that, Mr. Dunn."

Luke strode over to Big Horse and mounted up with Bent Evans still following close at hand. They turned the horses back toward Heaven's Gate.

As they approached the outskirts of Corpus Christi, Luke pulled up and turned to Evans. "Well, the bluff worked, Bent." He breathed a sigh of relief. "Thank God, they didn't ask me to prove that I was working for Governor Hamilton." Luke gave a smile with just a hint of deviousness.

★★

Elisa could scarcely breathe as Luke's powerful arms pulled her tightly against his chest. "Oh my...your trip to Corpus must have gone well."

Luke stepped back from his crushing embrace. "I expect you could say that." He smiled, then turned serious. "I'm worried, Lisa."

"About those men?"

"This business they call reconstruction is not going well for Texas and likely for the rest of the country. All sorts of folks are loose with less than honorable intentions. They've recruited former colored troops to be police enforcers and brought in judges from back east who have no idea as to Texas character and values."

"What about Bent Evans?"

"I bluffed the judge into thinking I still work for Governor Hamilton. That's a ruse that's not likely to last long, and he'll be none too happy if he finds out." Luke couldn't hide a bit of a smirk.

"What?" Elisa had seen that sort of smile before.

"Let's just say that I have something on the son of a gun that his wife must not know."

"Oh, Luke, that's terrible."

"Sure 'nuf. I played the hand that was dealt me."

Elisa wrapped herself around her man. She felt his muscles reflexively tighten and accepted a long passionate kiss. She pulled back and glanced about. No children in sight. He was especially irresistible when he was stirred up from a successful mission. She felt her own fiery passions fuse with the blazing conflagration of his being.

The moth-eaten and muddied butternut gray wool tunic was long past its prime. The sergeant stripes could barely be seen in the early evening darkness. The wearer lay silently waiting.

The rifle, an Enfield to be exact, lay out before the former Rebel. Patience was not easy, but the prize he sought was worth the wait.

Hoofbeats. They were faint but approaching quickly enough.

He lifted the rifle and peered through the telescopic sight. This was a Yankee gun, but it made no never mind to him. The ancient muzzle-loader packed a wallop with its .577 caliber ball and had a range well within the distance to his intended target.

The mounted figure loomed large silhouetted as it was against the dim glow of the lights from Corpus Christi. Broad-shouldered and tall in the saddle, he sat bathed in blackness on a coal-black horse. The hoofbeats drew ever closer. The man rode at a canter. It wouldn't be long.

The hunter had found his prey. He sighted down the long barrel. The target was within range. Finger wrapped around the trigger…an easy breath…hold it…squeeze. The blast echoed in the night, though the ball plowed through its target's chest long before the victim heard it.

The dark figure fell instantly from the saddle, was dragged a few feet owing to a boot caught in a stirrup, was finally shaken loose, and then lay motionless as he bled out in the dirt of the Nueces Strip.

The hunter got up and limped over to his prey. He stood over his victim and listened to the dying man's final raspy breaths. He pulled his revolver, held it near his victim's ear, and put the man out of whatever misery he might yet be enduring. With an evil sneer he bent down and plucked the State Police badge from the dead man's vest. Every hunter took a trophy.

The man in the tattered gray looked up and down the road. No one was coming. He slipped into the shadows.

★★

Luke and Elisa had been enjoying the final majestic orange glow of the setting sun from the comfort of the new bench on the gallery, when they heard the distant rifle report from the direction of the entrance to Heaven's Gate. Luke figured it was a tad late in the day to be hunting deer.

"You hear that, Lisa?"

"Likely some hunter finally bagging his buck, love."

But soon enough, the sound of a second shot echoed through the deepening darkness. "Unusual to finish a kill with a pistol. I'm thinking it just might be worth checking, sweetheart."

Elisa sighed. Her husband's lawman brain had already engaged despite their brief romantic interlude. She looked up into his eyes, smiled resignedly, and gave him a kiss. "You know we can't relax until you go see what happened, Lucas. So do what you must do."

Luke shrugged sheepishly. "I won't be long."

Luke was soon walking up the trail to the ranch entrance. He'd strapped on his gun belt and checked the load in one of his Colt revolvers before leaving the house. He grabbed the Henry rifle, too, just to be on the safe side. With a full moon breaking the crest of the horizon, he figured to have enough light to figure out whatever had happened.

Didn't take long. Once outside his ranch, Luke hadn't walked but a couple of hundred yards when he heard the eager yapping of a couple of coyotes and caught the faint reflection of moonlight on skin alongside the road. He approached cautiously. Whoever had fired the gunshots had apparently departed. Lying face down before him on the ribbon of road along the Nueces River was a large Black man. He readily discovered the gaping hole in the middle of the man's back where a large-caliber bullet had exited. He rolled the body over. Luke's eyes grew wide with recognition. The body now had an identity. It was one of Judge Crockett's enforcers. He quickly examined the man's pockets but came up empty but for a few dollars. Luke at least figured he could eliminate robbery as a motive. He looked for any other telltale clues. Other than the bullet hole in the man's head, there wasn't anything to speak of. Perhaps as telling, Luke noted that the State Police badge was missing.

The coyotes continued to yip and whine as they stood off at a distance. Luke solved the standoff by finishing one with a well-placed shot from his Colt. With the varmints' attentions diverted, Luke headed back to Heaven's Gate to hitch up the buckboard. Come morning, he'd have to face the distasteful task of visiting Judge Crockett again. Hanging far more heavily on his mind as he trudged back to the ranch was who might the bushwhacker have been? He had a feeling that he just might be getting involved in figuring that out. The Nueces Strip never stopped giving, especially as the harsh truths of war lingered long past the end of the battles.

★★

The buckboard creaked to a stop in front of the courthouse. The Black policeman standing guard seemed none too happy with his duty.

"Judge Crockett in?" Luke said resignedly.

"You be that fella from the other day…the one with the Reb in tow. What business you got with the judge?"

Luke climbed down from the seat and motioned the man over to the side of the buckboard. "I think this is James Thorpe." He raised the blanket covering the body of the policeman. The foul odor that rose up gave no doubt as to the condition of Luke's cargo.

The guard arrogantly leaned his head over the side of the buckboard, caught the stench, and peeled back in horror. "Damn, but he be dead!"

"Somebody bushwhacked him up around Nuecestown. I found him alongside the road." Luke said matter-of-factly.

Judge Crockett, having apparently heard the conversation, suddenly appeared in the doorway. His eyes swiftly moved from the buckboard to Luke to the guard. He was just as swift to make an assumption, especially given his previous not-so-pleasant dealings with Luke. "This has got to be your doing, Dunn."

Luke stared incredulously at the judge. "Who, Judge...I only found the body. I don't..."

Crockett interrupted, "Guard, do your duty. Arrest this murderer."

"You can't be serious."

The judge snarled, "Shut your damned mouth, Dunn. Take him to the jail. I want a confession by nightfall." Crockett smiled triumphantly, then nodded toward the dead man in the buckboard. "And see to burying this fine officer of the law who gave his life in pursuit of justice."

Even the guard was taken aback, but he wasn't about to cross the judge.

Confident of his innocence, Luke put up no resistance as he was cuffed and led to the jail.

Luke found himself strapped to a chair in the jail cell in which he'd placed many a lawbreaker. The Black policeman was getting into his persuasion. He'd already raised some serious welts on Luke's face and a nasty cut over his right eye. That didn't count the gut punches that had already caused him to vomit his breakfast down the front of his shirt.

"Admit, you damn fool whitey. Admit you killed Officer Thorpe." His fist slammed across Luke's cheek.

"I...I...didn't...do it." Luke barely managed to get the words out. He felt helpless, as there was no way to get word out to any of his friends, much less Elisa back at Heaven's Gate.

Here he was being mercilessly beaten by this Black policeman. Crockett was in his very own cowardly way exacting his own form of vengeance for Luke having challenged his authority.

The policeman punched Luke in the ribs with enough force to nearly break them. Beads of sweat dotted the Black man's brow, as he had clearly warmed to his task. "Sign the paper, and I stop whitey."

The back door to the jail creaked open, and Judge Crockett stepped in. He spent a few seconds observing the goings on in the cell. "He confess yet?"

The Black policeman shot back an exasperated glance. "He be tough, boss."

Crockett nodded. "Well, you can let him go."

"Boss?" The policeman was incredulous.

"Do as I say. They found the damned bushwhacker. Hung himself...left a note admitting his crime."

Luke barely heard Crockett's words, as he sat slumped in a beating-induced stupor. Upon the ropes being untied and cuffs unlocked, he slid to the floor.

"Find his damned buckboard, throw him in it, and point it toward Nuecestown." Crockett stared ruefully at Luke's inert form on the jailhouse floor, then headed out the back door. He muttered under his breath, "I'll get you yet, Dunn, you high and mighty sonofabitch."

★ ☆

Thankfully, the horse had made this journey many times so knew its way home. The buckboard soon had pulled to a stop in front of the barn at Heaven's Gate. It sat for a full half hour before Elisa, by now getting concerned as to Luke's whereabout, happened to glance out the window. What on earth was the buckboard sitting there unattended? Where was Luke? She sighed resignedly, dried her hands on her apron, checked that all the children were accounted for, and headed out to check on what Luke could be up to.

A groan was Elisa's first clue that there was a problem. She ran the last few steps to the buckboard and peered over its side to see the bloodied hulk of her husband lying in its bed. "Lucas! Oh my! Lucas, what happened?"

Luke was just beginning to regain consciousness. Seeing Elisa's face hastened the process a bit, as he managed to get a few halting words out. "Crockett...accused...of killing the police..." His swollen lips wouldn't let him make the "m" sound.

"Oh, Lucas. Let's get you up to the house. I'll have Jaime take care of the buckboard." She proceeded to ease her Texas Ranger out of the buckboard and support most of his weight, as they headed up to the main house. She hailed Jaime along the way.

"What happened, *Señora* Dunn?"

"Lucas has been hurt. Please take care of the buckboard and fetch Doc."

As she and Luke stumbled through the front door of the house, the expressions on their children said volumes as to Luke's appearance. Elisa laid him gently on a settee in the living area and began to tend to his more obvious wounds. "What did they do, Lucas?"

"Tried to get a confession."

"But they let you go."

"Crockett had to. Found the killer. Hung himself and left a note."

"What are we to do about that judge, Lucas?"

"Just let it be, Lisa. No point pressing it. What'll be will be."

"This isn't Lucas Dunn I'm hearing."

"There will come a time, Lisa. Vengeance isn't all that satisfying." His ribs ached and it hurt to breathe. "There will come a time." With that, Luke closed his eyes and fell asleep.

Elisa wrapped her arms around Luke in a desperate

attempt to assuage her grief and fear but found herself weeping uncontrollably. What had become of Texas? What was the future to hold? The children, hesitating at first, soon gathered at her feet. The only sounds were Elisa's quiet sobs and the crackling of burning wood in the fireplace.

Luke sat on the gallery sipping coffee. His feet rested on the railing where his spurs had worn a notch. The warm morning sun bathed his still-healing facial wounds. Elisa sat beside him, her head leaning against his shoulder.

"¡Buenos *días!*" It was Jaime. He was back from running errands in Nuecestown. "I heard news in town."

Luke and Elisa looked his way. News was most often a euphemism for gossip these days. "What's your news, Jaime."

"The man that killed the Black policeman said in his suicide note that he had hoped they'd accuse you of the murder, but he changed his mind and confessed before he hung himself."

Luke shook his head slightly, as he still had a bit of an ache from the punches he'd endured. Jaime's news confirmed what he vaguely recalled Judge Crockett saying when they released him from trying to force a confession. He looked back at Jaime. "What of Judge Crockett?"

"They say he wanted to hang you."

Luke nodded. "Men like him will get their due."

"Are you forgiving him, Lucas?" Elisa was trying to hold back a look of incredulity.

"He was wrong. Yes, I forgive him, but he still has a price to pay…a punishment for his evil ways. Expect we'll be seeing what that price might be."

"Thanks for the news, Jaime." Elisa smiled. "You and Julia do come for dinner tonight."

Jaime nodded and headed back to his cabin.

Elisa looked up at Luke. "A price to pay?" she asked rather rhetorically.

Luke simply smiled. There'd be plenty of time to deal with Judge Crockett and the challenges of this post-war reconstruction business in Texas. Perhaps, they'd yet reconstitute the Texas Rangers. He stroked his mustache and allowed himself a grin as to what the future might yet bring.

A snort off to his right drew his attention. "What the heck are you doing out?" The big longhorn bull shook his massive horns and seemed to smile as he delivered a louder snort.

"Is that Bertram?" Elisa took note.

"He's all snort, Lisa." Luke rose up resigned to taking care of their prize breeder bull. He laughed. "I'll help him find his way back to the pasture. I expect a cow or two are missing his attentions."

"Why Lucas Dunn...those cows aren't the only ones missing attentions." Elisa had already figured that Luke was well along in his healing. "You hurry back here." Thoughts of Judge Crockett and worries as to the future of Texas would be placed on hold.

ACKNOWLEDGMENTS

Authoring books simply doesn't happen in a vacuum. The author provides the creative talent and crafts the stories, but there's so much more that demands acknowledgment. So, it is with the sixth Tumbleweed Saga: *Nueces Truth: Texans Face War's Realities*. I've been blessed with many friends and family who support my writings. My wife Carolyn's reviews and encouragement of my authoring has been a huge help along with very important tech support from our sons Mike and Matt.

Other supporters have included Cara Miller, Alan Bruzee, Jim May, Ernie Angell, Chris Haug, Alan Bruzee, and my dear cousins Johnny Dunn, Jim & Cindy Holmgreen, Joseph Meaney, and Eddie & Nancy Thornton. Many more friends have contributed support at some level to the creation and publication of *Nueces Truth: Texans Face War's Realities* be it encouragement, purchase, or advice.

My heart also goes out to my friend Murphy Givens, the retired "Corpus Christi Caller-Times" journalist who inspired and supported my creative efforts. Murphy passed away in late December 2020.

Naturally, I am major grateful to the wonderful folks at Wolfpack Publishing. The team they bring to publishing is first rate from promotion to editing, cover design, narration, and the myriad tasks that lead to successful book sales.

Most of my authoring has occurred in my office as decorated to channel my inner Texan, but my creative juices have often been inspired and imagination stoked in cafés and coffee houses across America. My favorites were Hester's Café & Coffee Bar in Corpus Christi, TX; Nueces Café in Robstown, TX; Java Ranch Espresso Bar & Café in Fredericksburg, TX; PAX Coffee & Goods in Kerrville, TX; Ragged Edge Coffee House and Bantam Coffee Roasters in Gettysburg, PA; 1889 Coffee House in Helena, MT; Dunn Brothers Coffee in Rapid City, SD; Postmasters Coffee & Bakery and Brio Coffeehouse in Waynesboro, PA; Birdie's Café and American Ice Co Café in Westminster, MD; Deja Brew Coffee House, New Oxford and Deja Brew at Miney Branch, Carroll Valley, PA; and Baltimore Coffee & Tea Co., Frederick Coffee Company & Café, and Dublin Roasters in Frederick, MD. I must admit to also frequenting a few Dunkin' Donuts and Starbucks around our fine nation. The décors and easy listening music in these fine establishments combined with savory cups of coffee tended to set me in the right creative frame of mind.

Last but not least, I'm especially thankful for the many folks who have read and enjoyed my books.

I do believe it's important to acknowledge how the old west represents the brave pioneering spirit of settlers that met the challenges and transcended mere survival to enable America to achieve exceptional growth. The settling of the American frontier west is replete with tales of leveraging freedom for individual achievement. I hope you'll agree that reliving our past—even through history-based fiction—often has the effect of pointing the way to an ever-brighter future. Might we be up to it? I hope that the inspiration I've drawn from my having walked the very earth my characters have trodden coupled with my extensive historical research will enable readers to fully experience the grit, adventure, and passion of my characters while sensing aromas of gunsmoke, trail dust, leather, and bluebonnets.

A LOOK AT BOOK SEVEN
NUECES LEGEND

The Nueces Strip calls him back one last time.

Two decades after stepping away from the Texas Rangers, Luke Dunn is done with war, bloodshed, and the ghosts that haunt him. But the frontier has no mercy for weary souls. When a ruthless gunman rides into Nuecestown with vengeance in his eyes, Luke has no choice but to pin the badge back on for one final mission.

The land is wilder than ever. Bandits rule the prairies, Comanche warriors fight for their fading way of life, and a shadow of pure evil stalks the frontier. As Dunn sets out to bring justice to the most dangerous outlaw he's ever faced, the battle becomes more than just a fight for law and order—it's a reckoning.

With his wife, Elisa, standing by his side and old enemies waiting in the brush, Dunn must ride into the heart of chaos. Will the legend of "Ghost-Who-Rides" end in triumph or in a final, lonely ride into the dark?

AVAILABLE APRIL 2025

ABOUT THE AUTHOR

Award-winning author Mark Greathouse's love for the Western genre draws upon his deep family roots and love of the outdoors, honed from teen years spent hiking the Appalachian Trail and family travels across America's frontier. He hopes his work reveals his passion for America's western history.

A member of Western Writers of America and the Wild West History Association, Mark also contributes articles on the history of America's west to Western-themed magazines. He was recognized as a 2024 Finalist in the Western genre by the American Literary Book Awards for his sixth Tumbleweed Saga, *Nueces Truth: Texans Face War's Realities*.

Mark began writing full time after a successful career as a business executive and later as an entrepreneurial investor and advisor. His service as president of several business and community nonprofits led to their extraordinary growth. He holds a BA in English and MBA in marketing.

Mark also donates time and books annually to support wounded military warriors. He was a Boy Scout leader (Eagle Scout) and served on a local school board earlier in life.